MAYBE NEXT YEAR

A novel
by Dave Hughes

Prickly Pair Publishing
Chandler, Arizona, USA

Visit AuthorDaveHughes.com to learn more about Dave and his books. You can subscribe to his newsletter to gain background information and insights into Dave's books and the writing process, and receive advance notice of upcoming book releases (and subscriber early-bird discounts). You will receive Dave's short story, *Cruise Virgins*, free when you subscribe to his bi-weekly newsletter.

If you would like to contact the author, please send an email to AuthorDaveHughes@gmail.com.

Cover photo: Goodboy Picture Company
Cover design: Dave Hughes

Library of Congress Control Number: 2022905211

ISBN: 978-0-9970017-6-1

This One Time at Band Camp

Monday, July 19, 2004

When Bryan Bauer arrived on the first day of band camp at his new high school, the only thing on his mind was whether he would be able to make friends and fit in. That he might meet the person he would one day fall in love with was the farthest thing from his mind.

That it would be a guy would have totally freaked him out.

The moment Chris Robertson saw the tall, slender, wholesome, yet geeky-looking new kid with the dark blond hair and the nervous forced smile, something clicked.

There were still a few minutes before the band director, Mr. Budding, would call the first rehearsal to order. The new kid was standing off to the side of the school's football field by himself, holding his trumpet and nervously fingering the valves.

Chris mustered up his courage and approached. "Hi! I'm Chris." He extended his hand, and Bryan instinctively shook it.

"Bryan."

"New in town?"

"No, I've lived here all my life. I've been going to a small, private school until now."

Prairie Village, Kansas, had one middle school and one high school, so most of the high school kids had also been classmates in middle school.

"What year are you?"

"Freshman."

"Me too."

Mr. Budding blew his whistle, signaling for rehearsal to start.

Chris said, "Welcome to Prairie Village High School. And the marching band. Hey, I'll catch up with you during break and introduce you to some of my peeps."

Chris's outgoing nature and easy, disarming smile made Bryan feel more at ease. He smiled as he watched Chris scamper off to join the other sax players, his wavy brown hair bouncing in the breeze. He looked around and spotted a few trumpet players, so he trotted over to join them.

The Last Concert
Thursday, May 17, 2007

The musicians in the Prairie Village High School Wind Ensemble and Jazz Ensemble had devoted over two months to prepare for the end-of-year concert. All for a 90-minute performance that would soon be forgotten by most of the people in the audience.

Bryan had been on stage all night. As the first-chair trumpet, he had already played through the wind ensemble portion of the concert. As he approached the end of the jazz ensemble set, his lips were nearly shot. As usual, Mr. Budding over-rehearsed the bands during their dress rehearsal and soundcheck that afternoon. As the climactic ending of the final song approached, Bryan filled his lungs with air, aimed for a high E, and prayed he had enough stamina left to reach it. He could settle for a C if he had to, but he wanted that E.

He nailed it! Mr. Budding smiled.

The audience of band parents, families, and friends of the kids in the band rose to its feet to applaud – as much because the concert was over as to show appreciation for the spirited performance. Still, a standing-O was a standing-O.

Mr. Budding rushed to the microphone stand near the right side of the stage to acknowledge the soloists.

"Chris Robertson on alto sax!"

The applause bumped up as Bryan's best friend Chris rose from his chair and smiled in acknowledgment.

"And Bryan Bauer on lead trumpet!"

Since Bryan was already standing, as is customary for the trumpet row in a big band, he smiled and waved his right hand. As the applause died down, one pair of small hands continued to clap enthusiastically, and a nine-year-old voice cried out, "YAY, BRYAN!!!"

Several people in the audience chuckled. Bryan's mother Brenda leaned over to hush his little brother and biggest fan, Brandon.

"The Prairie Village High School Jazz Ensemble!" Mr. Budding motioned for the whole band to stand up to take a bow. "Thank you for coming out this evening. Good night!"

The audience responded with one more wave of polite applause then started filing out of the auditorium.

The rush of having delivered an excellent performance subsided. The musicians gathered their instruments, music, and mutes and began wandering off the stage and into the adjacent band room. The end of the concert was both a relief and a bit bittersweet. Except for those who would play "Pomp and Circumstance" for graduation next week, they were done until marching band started up in the fall. For the seniors, this was it.

Bryan packed his trumpet in its case, returned his music folder to the folder rack, and exchanged congratulations and goodbyes with a few nearby bandmates. Then he headed out to the lobby to catch up with his mom and Brandon.

Brandon lit up when he saw Bryan approach. He ran toward Bryan with his arms spread wide. "You were awesome!"

"Thanks!" Bryan knelt, set his trumpet case down, and hugged Brandon. Bryan picked up his trumpet case, took Brandon's hand, and they headed back to their mother and then on to the car.

"You guys were great! You should put out a CD!" Brandon exclaimed.

Bryan smiled. "Well, I don't know if we're quite that good."

"I think you are! I would buy it!"

Brandon's unbridled enthusiasm and tiny worldview were adorable. The band was good for a high school band, but to him, this was the greatest band in the world. And his hero was right in the center of it.

Bryan and his mom smiled at each other. She said, "You did a very nice job, honey."

"I sure wish Dad could have heard this," said Brandon.

"I'm sure he would have enjoyed it. But he had to be at church to lead the Men's Bible Study." Brenda was always prepared to defend her husband's perpetual absence from anything related to Bryan's activities. If it wasn't the Men's Bible Study, it was a deacon's meeting, a community outreach meeting, or this, that, or the other thing. The same pattern was developing with Brandon.

They reached their car at about the same time Chris and his parents reached their car in the next row. Chris broke away from his parents long enough to run over.

"Yo, dude! You killed your solo on 'Milestones.'" He and Bryan fist-bumped.

"You too! The whole show was epic."

Chris turned to Bryan's mother. "Good evening, Mrs. Bauer."

"Good evening, Chris. You played very well tonight."

"Thanks." Chris then bent down and high-fived Brandon. "Hey, little buddy!"

"You guys sounded great!" Brandon gushed. "When I grow up, I want to play trumpet just like Bryan!"

Chris and Bryan exchanged smiles.

Chris said, "I bet you'll be great. Especially if this guy gives you lessons."

That possibility elated Brandon.

"Hey, big meet tomorrow!" Chris and Bryan were both on the school's track team. Chris turned to Bryan's mom and asked, "Are you coming?"

"I'm not sure. We'll see." That meant no.

Chris turned back to Bryan. "See you tomorrow!"

"Later." Chris and Bryan exchanged a quick bro hug and Chris hurried back to his family.

Once Brenda had pulled the family SUV out of the school parking lot and onto the street, Brandon turned to Bryan. "Will you teach me how to play the trumpet?"

Bryan replied, "Well, you might be a little young for trumpet. We should start you on the piano first. That's what I did. I took piano lessons for two years before I started on trumpet. That will help you become a better musician on any other instrument you learn later."

Brenda spoke up. "I thought you hated piano lessons. I decided not to make Brandon take lessons because you gave me such a hard time about it."

"Yeah, but now I'm glad I had them. It was way easier to learn trumpet because I already knew how to read music and count rhythms. I understand chords, so that makes it easier for me to take solos. I've always liked music."

"I think you didn't like me telling you what to do."

There was truth to that. At the time, Bryan hated it. He actually liked the music. He hated being forced to do something, especially something as un-masculine as taking piano lessons.

Bryan had been perceived as a bit of a klutz in elementary school. He had trouble throwing and catching a ball because his father never had the time nor the inclination to teach him those skills. Plus, Bryan was careful not to get dirty or tear his clothes for fear of being scolded by his mother. Practicing the piano while the other boys were out playing pick-up baseball or basketball games did nothing to help his image.

Brenda asked Brandon, "Would you like to start taking piano lessons?"

"Can Bryan teach me?"

Bryan replied, "No, I don't play the piano well enough to be a piano teacher. Besides, I'm busy with school and church stuff, and I'll have a job this summer."

Brenda said, "Think about it for a few days. If you're still interested, I'll call Mrs. Schultz and see if she has any openings for new students."

"Okay."

Bryan's father, Rev. Brad Bauer, was the head pastor at the Eternal Savior Christian Church. For Bryan and Brandon, participation in church activities was not negotiable. The best part of the services Bryan was obligated to sit through was the music. Eternal Savior had a praise band consisting of two guitars, keyboards, bass, drums, a few singers, and a five-piece horn section. The praise band played upbeat, part-gospel, part-R&B arrangements that brought the sappy lyrics and banal melodies to life. Bryan was enthralled with the horns, who added acrobatic background riffs and punchy chord blasts to liven up the tunes. If the Holy Spirit was present anywhere in the church, it was in the horn section.

Bryan's favorite was the trumpet. After taking piano lessons for two years, Bryan begged his mother and father to buy him a trumpet and switch him from piano to trumpet lessons. Since he presented this idea in the context of the praise band, Bryan's father approved. He realized Bryan showed no interest in following in his footsteps as a pastor, but if he wanted to play music in the church, that would be fine. Maybe he would decide to become a music minister. So, Brad approached the trumpet player, Arthur Budding, about giving Bryan lessons. Mr. Budding could hardly say no to his employer, and as a musician, he could always use the extra bucks a new student would bring.

Bryan was a quick study. He needed no encouragement, nor did he need to be cajoled into practicing as he had when he was a piano student.

Bryan spent Kindergarten through eighth grade at the Young Disciples Christian Academy, which was scholastically sufficient but lacking in its selection of extracurricular activities. They had a small 15-piece concert band that offered an opportunity for beginners to play easy band arrangements, but Bryan outgrew it quickly.

As ninth grade approached, Brad had every intention of transferring Bryan to the Overland Park Christian High School, but Brenda knew the public high school would be a better choice. Prairie Village High School had a good music program, and the Advanced Placement curriculum would better prepare Bryan for college. She also understood that Bryan would have a richer social experience that would prepare him for the real world better than the more sheltered, tightly-chaperoned social life at a small private Christian school.

It was the latter point upon which Brad based his strongest objection. "Who knows what he might be exposed to? Drugs, atheists, liberals! Kids dating and getting into trouble. I hear they have gangs at those schools! I want our son brought up in a good, clean, safe, Christian environment."

Brenda countered with, "Well, someday he is going to encounter those things out in the real world, and we need to prepare him to deal with them as they arise. He's not going to be living under our roof forever. Besides, it will help him get into a better college."

Brenda's opinions usually took a back seat to Brad's. He fervently believed that, as the man, he was the head of the household and he made the final decisions. But on this issue, Brenda persisted and ultimately persuaded Brad to enroll Bryan at Prairie Village.

It helped that Mr. Budding was the band director at Prairie Village. One Sunday, he pulled Rev. Bauer aside and suggested that Bryan would flourish as a musician in Prairie Village High School's bands.

As his mother predicted, Bryan was flourishing there. He was a quiet, shy, sensitive kid, but he had become part of a nice group of friends, most of whom were in the band. They were good kids. In particular, Bryan's best friend Chris seemed to bring out the best in him. They had become inseparable, and Bryan seemed happier than he had ever been.

The Track Team

Friday, May 18, 2007

After school on Friday, Bryan and Chris drove about ten miles south to the Blue Valley Invitational Track Meet, the final regular meet of the season. The state championship meet was next weekend at Wichita State University.

Bryan had never been athletic. At 6' 6", he would have been well-suited for the basketball team, but he sorely lacked ball-handling skills. The Young Disciples Christian Academy didn't have a basketball team and he had shied away from neighborhood pick-up games where his ineptitude would be on full display to the other kids.

But when the Physical Education curriculum turned to track and field during the spring of his freshman year, Bryan did surprisingly well. Mr. Ormond, the gym instructor who also coached the football team, observed that Bryan's height made him well suited for the hurdles. His long legs made him an efficient runner since he could cover more ground with each stride. Mr. Ormond passed this observation along to Mr. Riley, Bryan's history teacher who also coached the track team.

One day after class, Mr. Riley asked Bryan to stay behind for a moment. "Coach Ormond mentioned to me that you did very well during the track segment of PE this year."

"Yeah, I guess so. Thanks."

"We're always looking for good runners for our track team. Would you consider joining the team next year?"

This came out of nowhere. Bryan had never considered being on a sports team of any kind, much less taking up running as a sport.

"When do you meet?"

"Just during the spring. We have practices after school Monday through Thursday for an hour and a half. Meets are usually on Fridays."

"I'll give it some thought and check with my parents."

"Fair enough. If you decide to give it a try, I'll give you a training routine you can do on your own during the summer and fall to get in shape."

Bryan left the room and caught up with Chris, who asked, "What did Mr. Riley want?"

"He wanted to recruit me for the track team next year."

"Are you going to do it?"

"I told him I'd think about it and check with Mom and Dad. But I'm not crazy about the idea."

Chris thought about it for a second, then suggested, "What if I did it with you? We could run together all summer."

Bryan thought for a moment. Having a running partner to train with and a friend on the team would make the experience more enjoyable.

Like Bryan, Chris wasn't particularly athletic and had always been more interested in music. At 5'10", he lacked the long-leg advantage Bryan enjoyed. But this presented another opportunity to hang out with Bryan. Seeing him in the shower would be a bonus.

Bryan and Chris both made the track team their sophomore year, although the truth was anybody who could put one foot in front of the other in quick succession would have earned a spot on the team. The track team did not command the interest of the rest of the school the way the football and basketball teams did.

They performed adequately during their sophomore year, but they improved significantly during their junior year – especially Bryan. The team won most of its events during the regular season and was expecting to do very well at the state championship meet.

Bryan was thankful Chris had joined the team. Socially, they didn't fit in with the other guys on the team the way they did with the band kids. Most of their teammates weren't obnoxious or mean, but they seemed to relate to each other differently.

The de facto leader of the team was Clayton "Rocket" Crockett. Rocket earned that nickname in recognition of his prowess as the football team's star running back. He could skillfully juke right or left to avoid tackles and was capable of impressive bursts of speed to escape opponents and score touchdowns. Rocket joined the track team each spring to improve his sprints and stay in shape. Besides, the football field, and by extension, the track that encircled it, was his zone. So was the locker room, with its frequent crude banter.

None of the other track team members were football players. But they wanted to hang with the popular Rocket. So to ensure they would be tight with him, they adopted many of his behavior patterns.

Bryan, with his well-mannered, squeaky-clean persona, was an obvious mismatch with the demeanor of Rocket and his minions. He avoided locker-room discussions of the important issues of the day, such as which girls had the nicest boobs or who might go down on the second or third date.

Rocket picked up on this and took to calling Bryan 'PK' – short for Preacher's Kid. Some of the other teammates started calling him PK too, because it's what Rocket did.

Teasing Bryan became a hobby for Rocket, who poked fun at Bryan for his refusal to use crude language and his avoidance of any unwholesome subject. The teasing took on a new dimension after Rocket saw Bryan naked in the shower, prompting comments such as, "Don't knock over the hurdles with your dong" or "Dude, you could do the pole vault without a pole."

Bryan did his best to take it in stride without giving Rocket the satisfaction of seeing it bother him. He didn't find 'PK' to be inherently offensive, but he wanted to be regarded for who he was as a person rather than for his parentage or his appendage.

***

The meet went well. The 4x400 relay team of Rocket, Trevor Zimmerman, Chris, and Bryan finished first. Bryan won his two hurdles events after clearing every hurdle.

Coach Riley called the team together for a quick huddle after the meet.

"Great job today, guys. If you do this well next week, we can win the state. That would be a first for our school. You're on the verge of making history!

"As you know, the state championship is a two-day meet. Prelims are on Friday and finals are on Saturday. So, we're staying overnight at a hotel in Wichita. Nothing fancy – it's just a place to sleep for one night. You need to bring whatever you need for an overnight stay and money for lunch and dinner on Friday and a late lunch after the meet on Saturday. There's breakfast at the hotel.

"I have a sign-up sheet for the rooms. Two to a room. Don't worry, there will be two double beds. So, pair up with whoever you want to share a room with and come up and sign the sheet."

Naturally, Bryan and Chris wanted to room together, so they made their way to Coach's clipboard and wrote their names on the same line.

As they were driving home after the meet, Chris said, "It's hard to believe school's over next week. What are you doing over the summer?"

"Working – hopefully at Price Cutter, like last summer. I'm going in tomorrow morning to see if I can get hired again."

"How much will you be working?"

"No idea. The more, the better. More hours means more money. Gotta save for college, y'know."

"Yeah. I'm gonna apply to be a lifeguard again this summer. Hey, you wanna hang out tomorrow?"

"Sure – maybe after I go to Price Cutter. Sometime in the afternoon, I have to go to the church to get stuff ready for Sunday."

"Okay. Text me when you're ready."

"Should be around ten-thirty or eleven. We can grab lunch

somewhere. Plan?"

"Plan."

Chris pulled up to Bryan's house. Bryan grabbed his gym bag, fist-bumped Chris, and got out.

A Summer Job
Saturday, May 19, 2007

After breakfast Saturday morning, Bryan borrowed his mom's car and drove to the Price Cutter grocery store. He spotted a familiar face at the customer service counter. "Hey Angela, wassup?"

"Just another day in paradise. You gonna be working here again this summer?"

"I hope so. Is Mr. Rudolph around?"

"Mr. Rudolph got promoted to District Manager back in March. We have a new manager, Mr. Simonton. Nice enough guy."

"Is he here today?"

"Yeah, he's in the back. Here's an application and a pen. Go sit at one of the tables at the coffee shop and fill it out, and I'll tell him you're here."

"Great, thanks."

Bryan completed the application quickly. After about ten minutes, a forty-something man with slightly graying, well-groomed hair and a goatee appeared. "Bryan? Russ Simonton. Nice to meet you."

Bryan sprang to his feet. Mr. Simonton extended his hand and Bryan shook it firmly. "Nice to meet you too, sir."

"Have a seat. Angela tells me you worked here last summer."

"Yes, sir. I enjoyed it, and I was hoping you might have an opening this year."

"This is a grocery store. We always have an opening. What did you do last summer?"

"Well, I started out bagging groceries. But after a few weeks, Mr. Rudolph switched me to stocking shelves. I worked in produce, canned goods, and frozen food. But I'm happy to do whatever you need."

"Excellent. How many hours a week can you work, and do you have any conflicts?"

"Forty or more would be great. I can work as much as you need. The only time I need to have off is Sunday mornings. My father is the pastor at a local church and I'm kinda expected to be there. All day Sunday would be great, but at least Sunday mornings until around one."

"Fair enough. When can you start?"

We're through with classes in two weeks, so any time after that."

"Okay, how about Monday, June 4th?"

"That works."

"I'll be in touch a few days before to let you know your hours for the week."

"Sounds great! I'm looking forward to being back at Price Cutter!"

"Take care. See you in a couple of weeks." Mr. Simonton rose from his seat and headed back to his office.

Bryan smiled. That was easy. Angela must have put in a good word for him.

He pulled out his cell phone and dialed his mother.

"Hey Mom, I got the job. I start on Monday, June 4th."

"Good, honey, I'm happy to hear that."

"Do you need anything from the store?"

"I can't think of anything, but thanks for asking."

"Can I keep the car for a few hours? I'd like to hang out with Chris for a while and grab lunch."

"Okay, but please try to eat someplace responsible. And don't forget, your father's expecting you at the church."

"Yeah, I know. I'll swing by around two." Like he could forget. This had been part of his Saturday routine for almost two years.

"Okay, have fun. I love you."

"Love you too, Mom. Bye."

Bryan then texted Chris.

Ready? I have car

A few seconds later:

Ready! Let's roll

CU in 10

Moments later, Bryan pulled up to Chris' house. Chris bounded out the front door and hopped in. "Where to?"

Chris was always upbeat and happy, almost hyper. Bryan sometimes wondered if he was like that constantly or only when they were together. Maybe he was on some kind of mood meds. But whatever, Bryan didn't mind. He was used to it. Besides, being around Chris always lifted his mood, which was a good thing.

"I dunno. Maybe head out to the Great Mall?"

"Yeah, I guess."

"There are places to eat there if nothing else."

Both Bryan and Chris wished there were more interesting things to do in the Kansas suburbs of Kansas City, but resigned themselves to the fact that the Great Mall was the best they were going to do with the three available hours.

Bryan drove west, then southwest on I-35. After a few miles, he exited and turned right into the parking lot of The Great Mall of The Great Plains.

As they walked around the mall, Bryan asked, "Is it just me, or is this mall getting lamer each time we come here?"

"Yeah, totally. Five years ago, they still had a lot of great stores. Now it's a bunch of crappy discount outlets."

"There's more empty places than ever, too."

"They shouldn't be allowed to call it the Great Mall anymore."

"I know, right? They should call it the Formerly Great Mall, or the Merely Good Mall."

"Hell, it's not even good. But I guess they can't call it Discount Wasteland – Where Merchandise Goes to Die."

They both chuckled.

Bryan said, "I've got it! The Mediocre Mall."

"I like it! Truth in advertising."

"And it alliterates well."

By this time, they had arrived at the food court. Chris said, "The Mediocre Mall, with the mediocre food court. Anything here look good to you?"

' "Nah... let's head over to Slush Fun."

"Nom nom! Wholesome, nutritious cuisine at its finest."

Slush Fun was their favorite fast-food place. Of course, it was neither wholesome nor nutritious, but it was delicious and decadent. They enjoyed the fact that it was a drive-up restaurant. They could talk about whatever they wanted to in the car without being overheard by other diners. But it was the slushies, available in seemingly endless flavor combinations, that made Slush Fun their go-to choice.

When the disembodied voice on the squawk box requested their order, Bryan went first.

"I'll have the crispy chicken tender combo and a cherry-lime slushie."

Chris remarked, "Excellent choice. Cherry-lime pairs well with canola oil."

"Thank you, Mr. Food Critic. And you?"

"I'll have the bacon double cheeseburger and the chili-cheese tater tots."

Bryan replied, "Ah... the Cholesterol Classic Combo."

"Whatever, biotch."

The squawk box voice asked, "Anything to drink with that?"

Chris replied, "Hmmm... I'll have a mint chocolate-banana slushie."

"Thank you for your order."

Bryan scrunched his face into an expression he might make if he caught a whiff of an elephant fart. "That sounds disgusting!"

"Adventures in fine dining!"

"Adventures in hurling."

The Hotel Room
Friday, May 25, 2007

At 6:00 a.m. on Friday, the track team boarded a bus in the school parking lot. Most of the guys slept during the three-hour ride to Cessna Stadium at Wichita State University, the site of the Kansas State Track and Field Championship Meet.

The team did well in prelims and qualified for all their events.

After dinner, the bus transported the team to the Sleep Cheap motel, about two miles east of the stadium.

Chris pressed the key card against the card reader on the door of room 253. The little green light came on. Chris opened the door, and he and Bryan walked in.

The room was adequate, nothing more. But for a quick overnight stay costing only $31 a night, it was all they needed. At least it appeared to be clean.

The room held one queen size bed. Coach Riley told the team last Friday their rooms would have two beds. Chris didn't seem concerned. Bryan decided not to say anything about it.

They set their gym bags and backpacks down. Chris walked over to the window and pulled back the curtains, revealing a scenic view of the motel parking lot, a gas station and convenience store across the street, and the freeway interchange in the background. Nobody had promised them a resort.

"Hey, let's go over to the store across the street and get some soda and munchies," said Chris.

"Sure."

Fifteen minutes later, they were back with a 2-liter bottle of Dr Pepper, a large bag of tortilla chips, and a jar of medium-hot salsa.

Bryan grabbed the ice bucket and left the room in search of the ice machine.

When he returned with the ice, Chris had pulled the covers down halfway and propped his pillow up against the wall mounted padded headboard. He appropriated one of the hand towels for a makeshift tablecloth, which he spread out in the middle of the bed for the chips and salsa. Bryan unwrapped a couple of small plastic cups and filled them with ice and Dr Pepper. He carried them over to the bed on the little plastic tray that held the ice bucket and glasses. He placed the bottle of Dr Pepper on the nightstand.

They barely spoke. They both somehow knew what needed to be done and silently divided the tasks between them.

Chris stripped down to his underwear and a T-shirt and climbed onto his side of the bed. Bryan did the same.

Chris picked up the remote and navigated to the TV channel listings. He scrolled up and down. "Hey! Brokeback Mountain is on HBO. It just started. Wanna watch that?"

"What's it about?"

"Seriously? You haven't heard of Brokeback Mountain? It came out a year or two ago. Won some academy awards."

"Sorry… I don't get to see many movies. My parents think most movies are filled with bad language and smut and violence, so that kind of limits my movie options."

"Well, they would hate this. It's about two cowboys in the 60s who discover they're gay. But you're away from home, so why not?"

They spent the next couple of hours watching the movie in silence. The pace seemed slow, but the scenery was beautiful and they were soon drawn into the story. They took turns reaching into the bag of chips and dipping them in the salsa. Every so often, Bryan refilled their Dr Peppers. Both of them wondered how the other one was processing the storyline.

Bryan had never felt as close to someone as he felt with Chris. He and Chris could be doing something as innocuous as watching a movie and eating a snack, and it felt comfortable. He didn't feel the least bit awkward sitting on a bed in his underwear with Chris. For the first time in his life, he had a best friend.

When the movie ended, it was almost midnight. They had finished the Dr Pepper and the salsa, and only a few broken pieces and crumbs remained in the bag of chips. "I guess we'd better get some sleep," said Chris.

"Yeah, we probably shouldn't have stayed up this late. But whatever."

Chris headed into the bathroom to use the toilet and brush his teeth, while Bryan cleared the bed of the snack items. After he came out, Bryan took his turn in the bathroom. When he came out, Chris said, "Hey, why don't you leave the bathroom light on and leave the door cracked open, so if we have to go in the middle of the night, we can find it." That seemed like a good idea.

Chris had pulled the covers most of the way up to his shoulders, but Bryan could see he had removed his T-shirt. Bryan wondered whether Chris still had his underwear on, but he decided to keep his on. He turned the remaining lights out, removed his T-shirt, and climbed in.

"Did you set the alarm?" Chris asked.

"Yeah… 6:00."

"Cool. G'night."

"G'night."

And with that, they settled in to go to sleep. The air conditioner came on and made a rattling noise.

There was light shining in around the edges of the drapes. Bryan turned onto his other side to avoid it, but facing that direction he could see the slit of light from the bathroom.

Several minutes later, down the hall, two loud drunk people said a few unintelligible things to each other as they struggled to unlock their door.

Bryan couldn't remember the last time he slept in a strange bed away from home. It had been years ago since his family took their last vacation.

Bryan thought back to band camp three years ago when he first met Chris. Chris had befriended Bryan, introduced him to the other kids, and helped him get acclimated at his new school. Bryan would always be thankful to Chris for that.

Bryan glanced over at Chris, who was facing the other way. What a great friend to have! He couldn't tell whether Chris was asleep or not.

Bryan shifted positions. Being 6' 6", it was hard for him to fit into most beds. He had to sleep in the fetal position on one side or the other. At home, he could stretch out diagonally across his bed, but he couldn't do that here.

Bryan glanced at the alarm clock. 12:45. Darn. He needed to get to sleep but couldn't.

Chris rustled a little bit, shifting his position. He was still facing away from Bryan, but now his feet were brushing up against Bryan's leg. Bryan instinctively pulled away a little.

It occurred to Bryan that he had never shared a bed with someone else before, other than a few vacation trips when he shared a bed with Brandon. Brandon, being eight years younger, didn't take up much space.

Bryan started replaying scenes from the movie, especially the scene in the tent where Jack and Ennis had sex for the first time. The scene was brief, no skin was shown, and the sex seemed awkward and rough. Of course, he had nothing to compare it to. Was this what sex between two men was like?

He recalled other scenes in which they kissed and their brief dialogs. He wondered what it would be like to live for weeks at a time on a mountain, tending sheep, seeing only one other person. He thought about Jack's tragic ending. It must have been difficult for gay people in the 60s, especially in the backward areas of the west. Was this how it ended for all gay people?

Bryan rolled over onto his other side, facing Chris. As he did, he checked the alarm clock. 1:20.

A few minutes later, Chris rolled over onto his other side, facing Bryan. Their knees touched. Bryan pulled back a little. He couldn't tell whether Chris was awake or asleep, so after a few minutes, he eased his eyes open a tiny bit. Chris's eyes were closed. He was motionless, but he was breathing like he might be awake.

Bryan thought about the track meet tomorrow. He read somewhere that Olympic athletes often visualize their performance over and over in their heads. They visualize how they will move their bodies and how they will pace themselves. They visualize surging out in front of their competition. They visualize standing on the winner's podium and having their medal placed around their neck. They visualize winning.

Bryan tried visualizing how his performances tomorrow would go. He visualized surging off the starting block when the gun went off. He visualized leaping over each hurdle, and exactly how many steps he would take between each hurdle. He visualized crossing the finish line first.

He visualized the 400-meter relay, in which Chris ran third and he ran fourth. He visualized starting to run as Chris approached, reaching his hand back for the baton, feeling it, and taking it from him. He visualized breaking into a sprint and racing across the finish line first.

Bryan rolled back over onto his left side, facing away from Chris. 2:05. Crap. This visualizing might help him win his races tomorrow, but it's not helping him get to sleep. And if he can't get a good night's sleep, he won't be able to win his races.

After drinking a liter of Dr Pepper, Bryan had to pee. He quietly got up and walked tentatively through the dark room, following the narrow beam of light to the bathroom. When he returned to the bedroom and climbed back into bed, Chris shuffled a little bit.

The noisy air conditioner came on again.

After a moment, Chris whispered, "Hey… are you awake?"

"Yeah. I haven't gotten any sleep at all."

"I haven't gotten much either. What's keeping you awake?"

"Oh, all kinds of things. The caffeine from the soda. Needing to pee. Sleeping in a strange bed. Sleeping with someone else. The noisy air conditioner. Thinking about the movie. Thinking about the meet tomorrow. Trying to visualize how that will go. All kinds of things. What about you?"

"Yeah, same here."

After a few seconds of silence, Chris whispered again, "There's all that stuff. And then I wonder if, maybe, both of us are kind of waiting to see if something's going to happen."

Bryan had no idea what to say.

Chris was right. Bryan knew he had feelings for Chris, but he did everything he could to keep them pushed away. Bryan was pretty sure Chris had feelings for him too, given how he seemed to light up whenever they were together.

Bryan figured Chris is probably gay. But what if he isn't? What if he's just really friendly? If Bryan tried anything and Chris wasn't gay, that could ruin their friendship, or at least make it awkward for a while.

Besides, with Bryan's parents, being gay simply wasn't an option. He'd be disowned. So, he probably shouldn't even go there.

But he really wanted to.

He analyzed what Chris said, parsing the words to discern their true meaning. He wouldn't have said 'both of us' if he wasn't also waiting to see if something was going to happen. He wouldn't be wondering if something might happen if he didn't want it to.

Bryan had no idea if what he said next would be right or not. But the chance to be in bed with Chris away from home with nothing to stop them came rarely. He decided to go out on a limb.

"Yeah, I've been thinking about that. What about you?"

Chris replied, "I guess if something happened, that would be okay."

"I wasn't sure until now if you want something to happen. I don't want to ruin our friendship. And… I'm a little scared."

Chris reached out and put his hand on Bryan's shoulder, both to comfort him and to initiate contact. "If you're uncomfortable, maybe we shouldn't."

Bryan put his hand on Chris's shoulder. "But I want to. Let's just go slow."

Chris scooted a few inches closer and lightly kissed Bryan on the lips. He pulled back a couple of inches and gazed into Bryan's eyes, trying to gauge his reaction. He moved in again and kissed Bryan for several seconds.

Sensing no resistance, Chris placed his hand behind Bryan's head, pulled him closer, and opened his lips. Bryan opened his lips and pressed them against Chris's. Their tongues intertwined.

Bryan couldn't believe he was actually doing this, and he wanted it to continue for hours.

They shifted closer and pressed their bodies up against each other. Both of them were sporting full erections, uncomfortably restrained by their underwear.

Bryan's thoughts were racing, trying to figure out what his boundaries should be, or if he should even have any. Isn't this supposed to be wrong? But yet it felt so right. He weighed his inhibitions against his desires. Was he making this more complicated than it needed to be?

Chris felt he should check in. "How are you doing?"

"Okay. I mean, this is great. But I'm not sure if I should go any farther. I mean, I want to, but I'm kind of afraid."

"Well, then, we probably shouldn't." Chris tried his best to mask his disappointment.

"I feel like I'm letting you down."

"But if you're not sure, then we shouldn't. We can talk later."

They kissed a few more times. They both sensed that the energy between them had diminished. The moment had passed.

Chris got up and headed toward the bathroom. "I'll be back in a few minutes."

Chris was in there for at least five minutes. Bryan finally figured out why. After Chris came back to bed, Bryan spent a few minutes in the bathroom.

When Bryan returned, Chris whispered, "You okay?"

"Yeah. But now we really have to get some sleep."

They kissed each other goodnight and fell asleep, totally exhausted.

The State Championship Finals
Saturday, May 26, 2007

At 6:00 a.m., the bedside phone rang, startling Bryan out of a deep sleep. He reached out, groped for the receiver, and pulled it to his ear.

"Hello…"

An automated female voice cheerfully announced, "Good morning! This is your wake-up call! Have a great day!"

Bryan, still mostly asleep, somehow managed to place the receiver back on the hook.

Chris stirred and mumbled, "What was that?"

"Wake-up call."

"Mmmmph."

At 7:15 a.m., the bedside phone rang, startling Bryan out of a deep sleep. He reached out, groped for the receiver, and pulled it to his ear.

"Hello…"

It was Coach Riley. "Bryan? You guys need to get down here now! The bus leaves in 15 minutes."

"Almost ready. We'll be right there!"

Bryan hung up the phone. He shook Chris's shoulder.

"C'mon! Get up! We overslept! We've got to get up and get out of here now!"

Chris glanced at the clock. "Oh, shit. I thought you set the alarm."

"I thought I did too." Bryan looked at the alarm clock. He had set it for 6:00 p.m.

They sprang up out of bed. There would be no time for showers. They threw on their track shorts and tank tops, layered on their sweat pants and jackets, put on their socks and shoes, threw everything else into their gym bags and backpacks, and ran out the door.

They arrived at the front desk just as the other guys were clearing out of the breakfast room and heading for the bus. Rocket Crockett shot them a nasty glance. Several of the others gave them funny looks.

Coach Riley was waiting for them. "Here, give me your room keys. Go grab something quick to go. You've got five minutes."

Bryan and Chris headed into the breakfast room. They each shoveled a small helping of watery scrambled eggs and a couple of sausage links on their plate and devoured them in several bites. They each chugged a glass of orange juice. Then they each smeared cream cheese on a bagel, wrapped it in a napkin, grabbed a banana and a bottle of water, and ran out to the bus.

They boarded the bus and headed for the remaining seats in the back. More funny looks. Bryan wondered if somehow the other guys knew what went on last night. They couldn't possibly, but… was he projecting something?

Bryan could barely stay awake during the two-mile bus ride to the stadium.

After a half-hour for warming up and stretching, the Kansas State Track and Field Championship Finals got underway.

Bryan's first event was the 110-meter hurdles, the second event of the meet. He had already been stretching during warm-ups, but he stretched some more just to be sure. Pulling a hamstring would put him out for the rest of the day.

As the runners gathered at the starting blocks, Bryan quickly replayed his visualization of running this race. Despite being tired, Bryan was stoked for the race and he could feel a surge of adrenalin kicking in.

The runners took their marks, and a couple of seconds later, the gun fired. Bryan bolted from the starting block. He cleared the first hurdle, then the second. His foot hit the third, slowing him down slightly and knocking him off the pace.

Bear down. Push harder. You can do this!

Bryan cleared the fourth, fifth, and sixth hurdles. He hit the seventh, then cleared the eighth. He hit the ninth and tenth hurdles. He did his best to sprint across the finish line.

Fourth place. Bryan's disappointment showed on his face and in his posture as he returned to his team. What a letdown. He hadn't hit four hurdles in a meet all year. He was lucky he made it to fourth place. He still earned four points for the team, but six, eight, or ten would have been better. Several of his teammates gave him half-hearted high-fives. Chris patted him on the shoulder as he headed out to run his first event, the 4x800 meter relay.

Bryan was thirsty and in desperate need of caffeine. There was a concession stand behind the bleachers. Bryan fished his wallet out of his gym bag and headed down.

Thankfully, they had Red Bull. Bryan wasn't in the habit of drinking overly-caffeinated energy drinks, but desperate times called for desperate measures. He bought two, drank one, and brought the other one back for Chris, who would surely need it after running his half-mile segment of the relay.

Bryan returned to the stands in time to see the second half of the race. Chris held up pretty well. The team finished second.

Chris was, indeed, happy to receive the Red Bull.

Bryan figured he had about an hour to wait until his next event, the 300-meter hurdles. He found an empty stretch of bleacher bench and laid down. With the noise and energy of the meet, he wasn't able to sleep, but the rest felt good.

About 20 minutes before his next event, Bryan left the stands and chugged another Red Bull.

The rest paid off. The 300-meter hurdles went well. Despite the longer distance, there were only eight hurdles. Bryan kept up a good pace on his runs between each hurdle and sailed over each one. First place! It was a nice redemption for his previous disappointing effort.

Next, Chris ran in the 800-meter event. While Chris wasn't the fastest runner, he had good endurance for longer distances – usually. The last quarter of the race was difficult for him, and he lost steam. He finished sixth.

There was only one event between Chris's 800-meter and the 4x400 meter relay, which they both ran. Not much time for Chris to regain strength.

Rocket Crockett led off, due to his ability to surge from the starting block. Trevor Zimmerman ran the second leg, Chris ran the third, and Bryan anchored the relay. Each runner ran one lap around the track.

The gun fired. Rocket burst from the starting block and built an immediate lead. He built a three-step lead over the next closest competitor and passed the baton to Zimmerman.

Zimmerman built the lead up to five steps by the time he passed the baton to Chris.

Chris did his best. He pushed himself a little too hard during the first half of his run and started losing pace during the second half. Still, as he approached Bryan, he had a two-step lead.

Bryan knew he had a good 400 meters left in him, and he could bring this home. He started running, held his hand back, felt the baton in his hand, and turned on the jets.

He clasped his hand into an empty fist. The baton clinked as it hit the track and started rolling away.

Bryan slammed on the brakes, dodged an oncoming runner, grabbed the baton, and took off. Four other runners had passed.

Bryan sprinted like never before. The Red Bull kicked in and his adrenalin surged. With sheer willpower, Bryan ran faster than he had ever run in his life. He passed the fourth-place runner easily and set his sights on the third.

Come on. You can go faster. Just go one percent faster.

Somehow, his body found the strength to go a little faster, then a little faster.

At about 250 meters, Bryan overcame the third-place runner and aimed for the second. As they rounded the final curve into the home stretch, Bryan pulled to within a few feet. Somewhere, Bryan found a little more energy and cranked it up one more notch.

The first-place runner was too far ahead. Bryan wouldn't be able to catch him. But if he could pull a few inches ahead of this guy, he'd finish second.

Bryan was feeling light-headed from hyperventilation. He willed his legs to move even faster, but he had reached his limit. His legs simply could not move any faster, and they started to give way as Bryan and the other runner approached the finish line, neck and neck. Bryan stumbled forward and barely crossed the finish line before he collapsed to the ground. He was able to break the fall with his hands. He was vaguely aware of the left side of his face hitting the tartan before he passed out.

The next thing Bryan knew, he was lying on his back. He felt grass under his neck, arms, and legs. A light breeze blew across his face. He felt a cool, moist cloth pressing against his left cheek, and another on his forehead. He became aware of a man's voice. "Bryan? Bryan?"

He gradually opened his eyes. At first, he only perceived the brightness of the clear sky. Then faces came into focus, hovering over him from several different angles. As he continued to regain his senses, he saw Coach Riley, then Chris, then Trevor Zimmerman, then another man who appeared to be a medic or trainer of some sort. They all looked concerned.

"Bryan?" It was Coach Riley.

"Yeah…" Bryan weakly responded. "What… what's going on?"

Coach Riley answered, "You stumbled and fell just as you were crossing the finish line. You blacked out for a few minutes."

The medic asked, "Do you feel any intense pain?"

"No. My face kind of stings. So does my left knee." Bryan became aware that there was cloth pressed against his left knee.

"You scraped your knee pretty badly. You scraped your hands and face a bit too, but the bleeding's almost stopped. Do you feel like anything's broken?"

Bryan did a quick sensory assessment. "No, I don't think so. I just feel sore all over. And weak. Very weak."

"Okay, let's try to sit you up." Chris and Coach Riley moved to each side of Bryan and hoisted Bryan's torso until he was sitting upright. "Here, drink some water."

After drinking some water, Bryan felt better.

"Want to try to get up?" asked the medic.

"Yeah."

Chris and Coach Riley lifted Bryan by his armpits until he was standing. They each placed one of Bryan's arms over their shoulder, so they could support him while he stood. Some people in the stands applauded.

"Take him over to the first aid tent, and they'll bandage up his knee."

As Bryan began hobbling toward the first aid tent with Chris under his left arm and Coach Riley under his right, he sighed, "So I guess I'm out for the long jump."

"Yep – you're done for the day," replied Coach Riley.

"Did I catch him?"

"Not quite. He inched you out. So, third place."

Bryan let out a sigh and dropped his head in failure. All this for naught. It might have been worth it if he had passed the guy to finish second.

"You made a heroic effort. I've never seen you run that fast. I've never seen anyone push their limits as hard as you did." Coach Riley paused for a second. "I couldn't be more proud of you."

"But we should have had first. We would have won if I didn't drop the baton."

Chris spoke up. "It was probably my bad."

Bryan replied, "No, it was my bad. I had it in my hand."

Coach Riley raised his voice slightly. "It was nobody's fault. Don't beat yourself up. You've already done enough of that. It's sports. Stuff happens. When it does, you just have to make the best of it and move on. It's just a track meet. It's not the end of the world."

Chris wanted to say something, but he wasn't sure what the right words would be. His right hand was wrapped around Bryan's waist, providing support. He gave Bryan a few gentle pats with his hand and squeezed a little.

After a few seconds of silence, they reached the first aid tent and lowered Bryan onto a folding chair. One of the people in the first aid tent began washing Bryan's knee before wrapping it.

Coach Riley said, "Well, I've got to get back to the team. You just relax and take it easy."

Chris stayed behind until the medic was done. "I'll go get our stuff and come back and sit with you. You want anything?"

Bryan thought for a second, then replied, "A slushie would hit the spot. But I think we're out of luck on that. Just a Coke or a Dr Pepper. Anything cold."

Chris started to head off. Bryan called out, "Wait. I don't want you to miss the medal ceremony. Come back after that."

The medic said, "If you're up for it, you can go. It might help you to walk around."

Bryan raised himself off the chair. Chris started to help him up, but Bryan waved him off. "I think I can make it."

Bryan started walking slowly and tentatively, but without assistance. He gradually picked up speed.

When they reached the grandstand, he said, "I don't think I want to try climbing the steps. I'll just hang out down here."

When it came time for the medal ceremony, Bryan stood on the platform with Rocket, Trevor, and Chris. Some of the guys on the other relay teams made it a point to shake his hand and congratulate him on a hard-fought race. Rocket wouldn't look at him. He was pissed – first that Bryan had dropped the baton and robbed them of a first-place finish, then to see him get extra attention from the others.

When the meet was over, everyone headed into the locker room for showers.

Bryan didn't want to get his bandages wet in the shower, so he sponged himself off with wet paper towels and hand soap at one of the sinks. He wasn't keen on having dozens of other guys see his private parts in the crowded shower room anyway.

Chris held back and carried Bryan's gym bag as well as his own. Given Bryan's slower pace, they were the last members of the team to board the bus. They made their way down the aisle to the only remaining seats near the back.

As they passed, Rocket uttered, "What happened, PK? Too much lube on your hands?"

A couple of guys nearby snickered.

Bryan whirled around. "EAT SHIT, ASSHOLE."

The bus became eerily silent. Rocket looked stunned. He said nothing.

Bryan immediately regretted his outburst. He shuffled his way back to his seat and sat down.

Where did that come from? Bryan had never even used those words before. Profanity was strictly forbidden in the Bauer household. Of course, he had heard those words many times, but he had been raised to hold himself to a higher standard of expression.

How could this day get any worse? He had screwed up two of his events and didn't even get to compete in the last one. He had torn up his face, hands, and knee, and now he had called the most popular guy on the team an asshole. Rocket Crockett could probably beat the crap out of him if we wanted to.

And then there was last night. He had watched a movie about two gay cowboys. It held his interest in a strange way. It was tragic, but still somehow fascinating. And he had made out with his best friend. They had kissed each other – passionately. And he kind of wanted to do more.

Where are things going to go with Chris? Was he willing to go there? Last night had been exciting, but terrifying. It felt so wrong and so right at the same time.

Bryan was too tired and distraught to think about it too much, but he knew he was going to have to deal with this, and soon.

He couldn't even look at Chris. He stared plaintively out the window.

Coach Riley climbed onto the bus, having stayed behind to pick up the paperwork with the final results. He could sense the awkward silence on the bus. The bus shifted into gear and joined the traffic funneling out of the parking lot.

"Gentlemen, congratulations on a fine day and a fine season. I'm very proud of you. You represented your school admirably.

"Lots of good things happened today. Some first-place finishes. Several personal bests.

"As a team, we finished fourth. I know we were hoping for better, but fourth-best in the state is still quite respectable. This has been one of the best years for track and field in our school's history. You should all be proud of yourselves. You worked hard, improved, and excelled all season long. The most important thing isn't what place we finished, it's that each of you tried your hardest and did your best. That's all anyone can ask."

Coach Riley glanced around the bus. His pep talk hadn't brought any smiles. He sensed the tension in the bus and noticed Bryan forlornly staring out the window. He decided to continue.

"Now I want to say a word about the relay. I know Bryan and Chris feel horrible about missing the handoff. All of us are disappointed. But these things happen in sports. The placekicker misses the field goal that would have won the game. The outfielder drops the fly ball he's caught thousands of times before, and three runs score. The figure skater misses his landing and falls, and loses the gold medal. Stuff happens, often at the worst possible moments. You just have to accept it and move on.

It's all part of the game.

"But after Bryan stopped and picked up the baton, did you see what happened? Did he give up? HELL, NO! He ran faster and harder than I have ever seen him run. He gave 150 percent. He gave everything he had and then gave some more. He risked injury to try to win back that race. That took guts. That took character. That took heart.

"So, the relay finished third, not first. But that was a moment of courage and excellence I will never forget. It was inspiring! *That* is what sports are all about."

That seemed to diffuse the tension on the bus.

Bryan felt a little less hopeless. He glanced over at Chris. Chris smiled his special smile and flashed a slight, subtle wink. Bryan managed a weak smile in return.

The bus pulled into the Western Corral – one of those chain restaurants that offer cheap steaks and all-you-can-eat vegetable, salad, and dessert bars. Perfect for a team of ravenously hungry athletes.

Some team from another school was there too, ahead of them in line. Aside from them, the patrons were mostly seniors who were in for the early-bird specials.

After Bryan and Chris made their way through the line to order, Bryan nodded toward a table in the back. They placed their trays at the last four-person table. Bryan said, "let me sit facing the wall, so I don't gross people out with my scratched-up face."

As they were heading back to hit the vegetable and salad bars, Trevor Zimmerman and another teammate, Zane Gibbons, approached. Trevor asked, "may we join you?"

Chris replied, "Sure!"

Bryan would have preferred solitude, but there wasn't any reason to refuse their offer.

After they all sat down, Trevor, Zane, and Chris kept the conversation flowing. They talked about the end of the school year, what they would be doing over the summer, current movies, and the latest songs from Justin Timberlake and Avril Lavigne – but made no mention of the track meet. It occurred to Bryan how deficient his knowledge of current pop culture was, so he didn't have much to add. That was okay. A conversation about Miles Davis or Maynard Ferguson probably wouldn't have lasted long.

Trevor and Zane seemed like nice guys, and they seemed to enjoy his company, even if he wasn't contributing much to the conversation.

Bryan decided that next year, he was going to make more effort to get to know some of the guys on the team. He could do without Rocket Crockett and several of his followers, with their crude, tough-jock manner, but apparently not all the guys were like that.

Chris Comes Out

Saturday, May 26, 2007

Saturday dinner at the Robertson home was upbeat and celebratory. Chris's older brother Tyler had just returned from his junior year at UCLA, so Chris and his parents, Tom and Kathleen, were glad to have him back and hear about his school year. And, of course, Chris just arrived home from the state championship track meet.

They ordered a couple of pizzas to relieve Kathleen of cooking dinner. The three men were enjoying beers while Kathleen sipped her favorite Merlot.

After they caught up with Tyler, Tom asked, "So, how was the track meet, Chris?"

"Kinda mixed. I mean, it was a great experience just to be able to participate in a state championship meet."

Chris told them all about his races and about missing the handoff on the relay and about Bryan passing out and falling at the finish line.

Kathleen said, "Good heavens! That's some pretty serious drama. I'm glad he's alright."

"Yeah, I think the embarrassment and disappointment were more painful for him than the fall. He feels like he let the team down."

Tom said, "Well, that's sports. Stuff happens."

"Yeah, Coach Riley gave us a speech on the bus afterward and said the same thing. He said he was proud of us and we had a great year."

The family finished the pizzas and started to clear the table. Chris said, "Hey everyone, can we sit here for a few more minutes? There's something else I want to talk about."

Nobody said anything. Everyone sat back down.

"May I have another beer?" Chris asked.

"Sure," Tom said. "Get me one too."

Tyler added, "I wouldn't turn down another one."

Chris retrieved three beers from the fridge and topped off his mom's Merlot. Then he sat down and took a deep breath.

"So okay. First, I just want to say I'm lucky to be part of such a great family. I love you all and I know you love me. So, I don't think this is going to change anything, but…" Chris took another deep breath. Here goes. "I'm gay."

Nobody seemed shocked or upset, but for a few awkward seconds, they all waited to see whether someone else would say something first.

Kathleen broke the silence. "Sweetheart, thank you for telling us. We appreciate you being honest with us. That took a lot of courage. And you're right, we all love you. This doesn't change that at all."

Tom said, "I'm proud of you, son, regardless of whether you're straight or gay. We will support you no matter what."

Kathleen added, "More than anything else, we want you to be happy."

Tyler had been silent up to this point. "So… is Bryan your boyfriend?"

"Well, we haven't put a label on it yet, but yeah. I like him a lot. Well, I love him actually, but we haven't got to the point where we're ready to say the L-word yet."

Kathleen said, "He seems like a fine young man. I hope it works out for you."

Tyler asked, "So, was that it?"

Chris replied, "Wasn't that enough? What else were you expecting?"

Tyler said, "Well, I thought maybe you were going to surprise us with something."

"What? You mean you already knew? How did you know?"

Kathleen said, "Honey, it's crossed our minds. I mean, you've never dated girls and you always hang out with Bryan. And I can tell there must be something special between you by the way you talk about him and how happy you are when you're together."

"Is it that obvious?"

Tom said, "Well, I wouldn't say it's obvious, but you can see it if you look for it."

Tyler added, "Dude, you might as well be wearing a gold lamé gown, high heels, and a pink feather boa."

Chris gave him a mild smack on the side of his arm. "You're such a douche."

Tyler continued, "Hey, I'm totally cool with it. I have some gay friends at college. They're lots of fun to hang with. So yeah…"

Chris said, "Well as I said before, I'm lucky to be part of such a great family. I love you all. Thanks for being so accepting and supportive."

Kathleen asked, "Has Bryan told his family?"

"No. It's going to be rough for him. His father is the head pastor at this big church, and they're really religious and conservative. They probably won't be as accepting as you are."

"Well, he's their son and he's such a nice young man. I'm sure they'll come around."

"Maybe. But he's really scared about it."

"Why don't you invite him to our cookout on Monday?"

"Cool – I will. Thanks!"

Tyler said, "Good. I need to start getting to know my future brother-in-law."

Chris replied, "From your lips to God's ears."

***

Later in the evening, Chris was in his room watching jazz videos on YouTube. There came a knock on the door.

"Yeah?"

"Hey, can I come in?" asked Tyler.

"Sure."

Tyler entered and sat down on Chris's bed. Chris paused the video he was watching and turned around in his chair.

"Hey man. I'm proud of you for coming out. That took guts."

"Thanks. I thought it would go pretty well, but you never know, right? Mom or Dad might have freaked out."

"Nah, they're pretty cool parents. I know kids never think of their parents as being cool, but really, Mom and Dad are."

"Yeah, I know. We're lucky. Actually, I wasn't sure how you'd react."

"Seriously? You think I'd hate on you for being gay?"

"I didn't know."

Tyler feigned indignation. "I'm hurt."

"Oh, please."

Tyler smiled. "So, have you and Bryan done it yet?"

Chris dropped his jaw for dramatic effect. "That's none of your fucking business."

Tyler laughed. "That means no. If you had, you'd be telling me about it."

"Sorry to disappoint you, but I'm not telling you about my sex life."

"Awww... I was hoping to learn more about what guys do together."

"If you want to find out what guys do together, go find one and do it with him. Besides, do I ever ask you about your sex life? That is, if you have one. Do you even have a girlfriend?"

"Nah, I've had a few dates here and there, but nothing serious. But whatever. Back to you. Have you guys done anything yet?"

"Well... last night was kind of interesting. We were in the hotel room looking through what was on TV, and Brokeback Mountain was on HBO. So, we watched it."

"That's the one about the two gay cowboys, right?"

"Yeah."

"How did Bryan react to it?"

"I don't know. We haven't talked about it yet. So, we finally went to bed, and we were both lying there awake for hours. It was a strange bed and we were full of caffeine 'cause we drank a whole 2-liter bottle of Dr Pepper. But mostly, we were both kind of waiting to see if the other one was going to make a move. So finally, I said, 'I wonder if we can't sleep because we're both waiting to see if something's going to happen.'"

Tyler was listening intently.

"So yeah, that was it. We did a lot of kissing – deep kissing – and hugging. I wanted to keep going, but he wasn't quite ready to go further. So, we just kissed some more and finally fell asleep."

"So, how was it?"

"It was hot. I mean, the kissing was awesome. It's like we were really connecting. See, Bryan's pretty reserved. He doesn't show emotion easily. I felt like he was kinda letting his guard down and getting into it."

"Sooo… Does he have a nice one?"

"Why do you care? Besides, I'm not into him for his dick, I like him for the person he is. We like a lot of the same things, especially music. We get along great. We just connect, you know? I like him because he's decent and honest. He's nice. He's–"

Tyler cut in, "trustworthy, loyal, helpful, friendly, courteous, kind, obedient, cheerful, thrifty, brave, clean, and reverent."

"As a matter of fact, he is an Eagle scout."

"I'm not surprised."

Chris paused for a few seconds. "And it doesn't hurt that he's hot. I mean, he's so tall and slender. He has this perfect dark blond hair that's always tousled just right. And his smile!"

"And…"

"And, well, since we've been running so much, he's got this nice round, firm bubble-butt."

"And a big dick."

"What is it with you and big dicks? Do you need to make an announcement to the family too?"

"Nah. But just sayin'. A lot of times those tall, slender guys are packing fire hoses!"

"I can't believe we're having this conversation."

"And just think, you're going to have to try to take that thing in your ass. Unless you're going to be the top. Have you guys talked about who's going to be the top and who's going to be the bottom?"

"God, when did you become such a perv? Anyway, we aren't anywhere close to doing that yet. We kinda need to talk about what happened last night first. I'm pretty sure he wants to go further, but he's kind of scared."

"Scared of what?"

"Scared of actually admitting that he's gay. Scared his parents will find out."

"Are you sure he's really gay? Are you sure this isn't just wishful thinking on your part?"

"I'm like 99 percent sure. I mean, like Mom was saying about me earlier, he's never dated girls or expressed any interest in them. And I don't think a straight guy would have been kissing the way we were."

"Well, I can tell you're ready to get on with it, but it sounds like he needs to move slowly."

"Yeah. It will be interesting to see what he says when we talk about what happened."

"Just don't push him too hard. If he feels pressured, he might pull back."

"Yeah. Thanks. Well, I'm tired and I need to crash. I only got about three hours sleep last night."

Tyler and Chris got up and Tyler headed for the door. Then he turned around.

"Hey. When we were younger, I know I kinda picked on you a lot."

"Kinda? You used me for your human punching bag."

"Yeah, well, I'm sorry for all that. Anyway, you know how we were talking earlier about Mom and Dad being cool parents…" He paused for a second. "Well, you're actually a really cool brother. I hope we can always be close."

"Even though I'm gay?"

"Even though you're gay. Maybe *because* you're gay. One of my gay friends in college said every parent should hope they have at least one gay kid, because that's the one who will be most likely to take care of them when they get older."

"Seriously?"

"Makes sense. You probably won't have kids to deal with. So yeah, you can take care of Mom and Dad when they get older."

"Nice. First, you tell me all this gushy brotherly-love let's-be-best-friends stuff, then you shove Mom and Dad off onto me. You're such a douche."

"Aw, you know I'm kidding. C'mere." Tyler hugged Chris. Chris couldn't recall that they had ever hugged before, at least not in a meaningful way.

"G'night."

"G'night."

Exhausted
Sunday, May 27, 2007

It was all Bryan could do to stay awake during church. Fortunately, his work up in the control booth kept him occupied and awake. If he had been sitting down in the congregation, he would have fallen asleep. Not a good look for the pastor's son.

After church, Bryan wanted to crash. He needed to study for finals next week, so he tried to put some effort into that. After an hour, he went downstairs and told his mom he was going to take a nap and to wake him in time for dinner.

As soon as he got back to his room, Chris called.

Bryan decided to answer, but he would keep it short. "Hey."

"Hey. How're you doing?"

"Tired. Very tired. I was about to take a nap."

"You doing anything tomorrow?"

"Ehh. There's a family thing at the church for Memorial Day. So of course, I have to go."

"What time?"

"I think it starts at like 4:00 or something."

"We're grilling out at noon. Wanna come over? Tyler's bringing a couple of his friends."

"Yeah, I guess, as long as I leave by like 3:30."

"Cool. Hey, can I come along to your church thing?"

"Are you sure you want to? These things aren't much fun. They're going to have games and stuff for the younger kids. Not much for high school kids. I'm probably going to be looking after Brandon while Mom and Dad do their thing."

"I get it. But yeah, I'd like to see some of your world."

"You may regret it later."

"I'll take my chances."

"Don't say I didn't warn you. But hey, I need to crash. See you tomorrow."

"K, bye."

Memorial Day
Monday, May 28, 2007

On Monday, Bryan arrived at the Robertson home a few minutes past noon.

Kathleen led him through the house to the back door. A couple of other women were in the kitchen doing last-minute prep, slicing tomatoes and onions, and pouring potato salad and baked beans into serving bowls.

There were already several people in the backyard – all men, Bryan noticed. Tom was dividing his attention between obsessively tending to burger patties and chicken breasts on the grill and conversing with a couple of other men. Bryan guessed they were probably the husbands of the women in the kitchen. Chris, Tyler, and a couple of other college-age guys were standing near a cooler, drinking beers.

Upon seeing Bryan, Chris took a few steps away from the group. "Yo!" He gave Bryan a fist bump and led him back to the group.

"Hey guys, this is my best friend, Bryan." Tyler introduced Kevin and Justin, buddies of his from high school who, like Tyler, had just returned home from their junior year of college.

After a round of handshakes, Tyler reached toward the cooler. "Beer?"

"Oh, no alcohol for me. What else is there?"

Tyler fished around in the ice. "We've got Coke, Dr. Pepper, Diet Coke, bottled water…"

"Dr Pepper would be great. Thanks."

Bryan noticed Chris was drinking beer. He nodded for him to step aside. He whispered, "They let you drink beer?"

"Yeah, now and then. At home. They're cool with it."

"You can't show up at the church with beer on your breath."

"Okay, I'll just have this one. I'll brush my teeth before we go."

Bryan hoped this would be good enough. He wondered whether he should tell Chris he couldn't go, but he couldn't think of an acceptable way to do that.

The women carried the remaining food from the kitchen and arranged it on a collapsible rectangular serving table, where paper plates, plastic utensils, buns, and bottled condiments were already in place.

Everyone helped themselves to the food. The six adults sat down on a variety of patio chairs arranged around another collapsible rectangular table, while the five high school and college boys ended up at the picnic table.

Everyone dug into their food and engaged in conversation. Bryan couldn't help but notice how jovial, carefree, and happy everyone seemed. He tried to picture his father and mother here, attempting to mingle with this relaxed, free-spirited, beer-drinking crowd. He couldn't.

At one point, there was a brief lull in the conversation as Tyler got up to get more beers for himself, Kevin, and Justin. Thankfully, Chris had declined another. When he returned, Bryan asked, "So Tyler, how do you like UCLA?"

"I love it. Totally awesome school. Lots of stuff going on all the time. Just off-campus, there's a village called Westwood with all kinds of things to do. And the rest of Los Angeles is right at your doorstep. Beaches, comedy clubs, live music. And the weather! It never snows there and rarely rains. It's like perfect weather year-round."

"How hard is college, compared to high school?"

"Lots harder. You have to discipline yourself to study, especially 'cause there's so much fun stuff to do. It's challenging, but that's good. High school wasn't all that hard."

"Do you live in the dorms? What's that like?"

"I did for the first three years. But next year, I'm going to live in a house a few blocks off campus with a few of my friends. Anyway, the dorms are okay. Small rooms, communal showers, dining halls. Always someone to kick it with. Parties on the weekends. But I'm looking forward to being off-campus."

It sounded like heaven to Bryan.

***

At around 4:00, Bryan and Chris showed up at the church. Brad, Brenda, and Brandon had already arrived. A couple of dozen round tables were set up on a blocked-off section of the parking lot. Some people were spreading disposable table cloths on the tables and taping them down. A couple of large, rented food-service grills were set up off to one side. Someone was pouring charcoal into them and setting them on fire.

Nearby, a row of rectangular folding tables had been set up as a buffet line, and people were setting up the food.

In the grass nearby, a huge colorful bounce tent was being inflated. Brandon was already getting excited about that. A volleyball net had been set up. A clown was carrying in a small portable oxygen tank to make balloon animals.

As Bryan had predicted, there were very few high school kids. Maybe he and Chris would join a volleyball game if enough people wanted to play.

Chris looked around and surveyed the cluster of buildings that comprised the campus of the Eternal Savior Christian Church.

"This place is huge! All this is a *church*?"

"Yeah. We have a social hall, a bunch of Sunday School classrooms, meeting rooms, offices, stuff like that. C'mon, I'll show you around."

Bryan led Chris into the social hall. There they met Archie Kilgore, the Facilities Manager. Mr. Kilgore was probably in his late fifties. He had worked at the church for as long as Bryan could remember. He probably worked there before his father had been hired to be the pastor.

"Hi, Mr. Kilgore. This is my friend, Chris, from high school."

Mr. Kilgore shook Chris's hand. "Pleased to meet you, young man."

"You too."

Bryan continued, "Mr. Kilgore is our facilities manager. He keeps the entire place running and looking great. If anything's broken, he fixes it. He supervises the cleaning crew. Every time we have an event like this, he makes sure everything is set up. This place would grind to a standstill if it wasn't for Mr. Kilgore."

Mr. Kilgore replied, "You're too kind. I just show up and do what I can. Say, would you strong young men be willing to set up the sound system on the stage out there?"

Bryan glanced at Chris. Chris didn't seem to object. "Sure. What do you need?"

"We need a couple of pole speakers, an amp, and one microphone on a stand. Oh, and the CD player. There's a hand truck over there if you need it."

"Sure thing, Mr. Kilgore."

"Much obliged, gentlemen." Mr. Kilgore nodded at both of them, then turned his attention to several people who were hauling carts of folding chairs outside.

Bryan fetched the hand truck, retrieved the key ring from his pocket, and unlocked the large closet. He pointed out which items they needed, and he and Chris loaded up the hand truck. He grabbed a few cables and a spindle with a heavy-duty 100-foot extension cord. Then they pulled everything out to a small portable stage that had been set up at one end of the table area.

It took them about fifteen minutes to set everything up and test the sound.

Bryan was grateful to have something constructive to do so they wouldn't be standing around idly or, worse, having to mingle with others. Bryan wasn't great at small talk, and he didn't want anyone to speculate about who this new guy was. Maybe that was just paranoia, but he didn't want to take any chances.

By this time, most people had arrived and were starting to claim their spots at the tables.

Bryan found his mother and Brandon, and he and Chris joined them, leaving a spot for his father.

Rev. Bauer made his way to the stage and pulled the microphone out of its holder on the stand, like a lead singer or a stand-up comedian might do. He tapped the microphone a few times to see if it was on, which annoyed Bryan.

"Hello?" (tap, tap) "Hello?" (tap, tap) "Can you hear me out there?"

He never did this during a church service, so Bryan wasn't sure why he was doing it now.

People stopped their conversations and looked up at him, so Rev. Bauer assumed they could hear him. The parents who had kids over in the bounce tent went to retrieve them.

"Thank you all for choosing to come out and celebrate Memorial Day as part of our church family. Let us begin with prayer."

Rev. Bauer prayed for the troops in Iraq and Afghanistan who were, in his words, fighting for freedom and democracy. He prayed for God to watch over their families at home. He called upon everyone to remember all the brave men and women who had given their lives in service to our country. He thanked the Lord for America, for the food they were about to eat, and for the blessings of fellowship. Amen.

Then he called upon Mr. Wallace, the choir director, to lead everyone in the singing of God Bless America, complete with a sing-along track.

With those formalities completed, it was time for the food. People formed orderly lines leading up to the buffet tables, then passed by the grill to receive their hamburger or hot dog.

Brad joined the rest of his family and Chris at their table.

Bryan couldn't remember whether his father had met Chris or not. If he had, it had been a while ago and he might benefit from a refresher.

"Dad, I'd like you to meet my best friend, Chris Robertson. We're in band and track together. Chris, this is my father, Rev. Brad Bauer."

They shook hands. Brad said, "Yes, I think you've been to the house a few times. Welcome! Glad to have you with us."

After everyone had eaten a few bites, Brad asked Chris, "I don't recall seeing you here before. Where does your family worship?"

Bryan tensed up. Chris bought a few seconds by thoroughly chewing the food in his mouth. "Oaklawn Presbyterian Church."

"Ah… is Paul Reynolds still the pastor there?"

Bryan prayed this was not a trick question.

Chris replied, "I believe so."

Brad ate a few bites. "No, wait, I think he's at First United."

Bryan froze. Chris jumped in. "This is quite a place you have here! It's huge compared to my church."

Brad beamed. "Yes, we're now the largest congregation in Kansas."

Bryan added, "During the fifteen years Dad has been the head pastor, this church has grown from a few hundred people to over ten thousand."

"That's right. Over half of these buildings, including the main sanctuary, have been added in the last ten years."

"Wow. That's amazing!" Chris exclaimed. "And Bryan has been telling me about your band. Our band director, Mr. Budding, is in it."

"That's right. Art's been playing with us for six or eight years now. You should come and experience it for yourself."

"I'd like that!"

"And bring your family." Brad rarely missed an opportunity to invite new people to attend.

Someone approached the table and signaled Brad for his attention. "Now, if you'll excuse me for a moment."

Crisis averted. Bryan could breathe normally again.

Brad got up from the table and dealt with whatever or whoever it was that wanted his attention. He spent most of the rest of the meal up from his seat, chatting with others or tending to some detail.

For two high school kids, it was insanely boring.

As the pastor's son, Bryan's presence throughout the event was obligatory. But as soon as the gathering started to wind down and people began drifting away, Bryan and Chris slipped away and escaped in Chris's car.

***

Bryan and Chris were in desperate need of something more fun to salvage the day. Naturally, they chose Slush Fun.

Chris asked, "So what flavor of slushie goodness will it be today?"

"Cherry-lime, as usual. And what are you going to have?"

"Blue coconut."

"That sounds disgusting. There is no such thing as a blue coconut found in nature."

"Chill, biotch. It's just blue food coloring."

"I think I read somewhere that blue food coloring causes cancer."

"I think you did not."

"Yeah, well someday when your liver explodes, don't say I didn't warn you."

"Whatever. You want anything else?"

"Yeah, I'm a little hungry. Wanna split an order of mozzarella sticks?"

"Sure."

After Chris ordered, he turned to Bryan and proudly announced, "So I came out to my family on Saturday night."

"How did it go?"

"Pretty well. They said they already kind of knew, so they weren't surprised."

"So, they're okay with it?"

"Yeah, they were pretty cool about it. Mom and Dad both said they love me, they'll always support me, and they want me to be happy."

"Sweet."

"Tyler was cool with it too. He asked if you were my boyfriend."

"And you said…?"

"I said we haven't put a label on it yet. Anyway, they said they thought so. That's what kind of tipped them off. I mean, the fact that we hang out together all the time and I'm not dating girls or anything."

"Geez, are we that obvious?"

"Probably not to most people, but to observant parents, yes."

Maybe the fact that Bryan's dad was so disengaged with his kids wasn't such a bad thing after all. But what about his mother?

Bryan said, "I think maybe some of the guys on the track team have figured it out."

"So? I really don't give a rat's ass what they think."

"That's easy for you to say. I can't have it get back to my folks. Anyway, I'm glad it went well for you. How do you feel?"

"So relieved. Like a giant weight has been lifted off my shoulders. I figured they would be okay with it, but like you never know, right? They could have freaked out."

"Like my parents would."

"Don't be so negative. They might surprise you. They've probably started wondering or figuring things out. Mom said she has kinda known for most of my life. Mothers know these things."

"If my mom suspects, she's in heavy denial."

"So, are you going to tell them?"

"Not in a million years."

"Why not?"

"Okay, look. I'm glad you have liberal, open-minded parents who can accept that their son is gay. I'm happy for you. But as you just saw, my dad is the head pastor of a very large, very conservative Christian church. He constantly preaches that homosexuality is a sin. The church supported the Kansas Marriage Amendment back in 2005. So, no – I will not be coming out to my parents. Ever."

"So, then what about me? What about us?"

"You're my best friend. That's all it has to be, as far as they're concerned."

"So, I'm just your dirty little secret?"

"Don't do this to me."

"Well, what do you think you're doing to *me*?"

"I'm not doing anything to you. But I'm asking you to try to understand that my situation is different than yours. Maybe next year we can go off somewhere to college together, and then we'll have a lot more freedom. But until then, this stays quiet."

"Speaking of which, where have you thought about going?"

"Somewhere far, far away. But of course, Mom and Dad want me to go somewhere in Kansas so they can get in-state tuition."

"Oh, god. Could you imagine going to Wichita State? Wichita is even more backward and boring than Prairie Village."

"And they don't have a football team anymore, so no marching band. Of course, if Dad had his way, I'd go to Olathe Bible College so I could live at home and they wouldn't have to pay for a dorm."

"What about UK or K-State?"

"Lawrence is, what, 45 minutes away? Too close. How far is Manhattan?"

"A couple of hours. It's out in the middle of nowhere though."

"That could be tolerable. But I want to get away from Kansas. As far away as possible."

"Tyler loves UCLA. You heard him talk about it. He says California is so different – so modern, exciting, and progressive. And the weather's great too."

"How much does it cost? Especially for out-of-state?"

"It's pretty expensive, but he got a full scholarship for his tuition. So, Mom and Dad only have to pay for room and board."

"Guess we need to keep our grades up and pray for scholarships."

"He has some gay friends there, and they have no problem being out. There's even a gay student group on campus. And it's not far from WeHo."

"WeHo?"

"West Hollywood. It's like they have this whole town where lots of gay people live. Gay shops, gay restaurants, gay bars…"

Bryan started singing, "Some… where… over the rainbow…"

"Yeah, we definitely wouldn't be in Kansas anymore."

"That all sounds great."

"So, you promise? We'll both go to the same college and be together?"

"That's what I want to do, but I can't promise anything. I'm going to have to do a lot of work on my parents."

Their slushies and mozzarella sticks arrived, and they spent a few minutes digging in.

Bryan eyed Chris's blue coconut slushie and said, "Okay, my curiosity has got the best of me. Can I have a taste?"

"Sure."

"Hmmm… Surprisingly, that's pretty good."

"Never question my highly-refined culinary tastes."

Chris decided it was time to broach the next subject.

"So, moving on… what did you think of the movie?"

Bryan thought about it for a moment. "Well, it was pretty sad. I mean, they could never really live their lives together. And then Jack got killed. So, not exactly a feel-good movie."

"I guess it was hard to be gay back in the sixties and seventies, especially in rural America."

"It isn't exactly easy now."

"What about when they had sex?"

"What about it?"

"What were you thinking while it was happening? What did you feel?"

"I don't know. It didn't seem realistic. It seemed so awkward, almost rough. And it was over in, like, five seconds. I mean, is that really how guys have sex? It didn't seem intimate or romantic at all."

"Not to mention, they still had their clothes on."

"Well, they couldn't really show them naked, at least not down there."

"And they couldn't exactly show them screwing, either. I guess they just wanted to get the message across that they had sex. They couldn't really show a half-hour long passionate love scene."

"I would have enjoyed it more if they had."

"But it didn't bother you seeing two guys having sex?"

"No... I mean, the movie was about two gay guys, so you figure they're probably going to do it at some point. What did you think of it?"

"Same thing. It was too short. Kinda harsh. But the fact they even showed that in a movie was something."

They sipped their drinks and ate a couple of mozzarella sticks in silence. Chris wondered whether this was the right moment to move the conversation forward. He decided it was. Here goes.

"So… Have you thought any more about what we did the other night?"

"It's been on my mind constantly."

"And…?"

"I don't know. I mean, it was kind of exciting, but then I kept thinking I shouldn't be doing this."

"Why not?"

"Look. All my life I've been taught homosexuality is a sin. Like, that's what it says in the Bible. Dad preaches about it all the time. On the one hand, I don't really believe it, but on the other hand, what if they're right?"

"Well, according to the Bible, all kinds of things are sins. Isn't the whole point of going to church that you'll be forgiven for your sins?"

"Yeah, I guess."

"Do you wish we had done more?"

"Sort of. But I'm kinda glad we stopped when we did."

"What about sometime later?"

"I don't know."

Chris didn't want to push the issue too far or too fast.

"So let me ask you this. And you don't have to tell me if you don't want to."

"Okay."

"What do you fantasize about doing, or having done to you? What do you think about when you jerk off?"

Bryan paused. "All kinds of stuff."

"Like…"

"Hugging and kissing, like we were doing the other night. Maybe give each other massages."

"And then…?"

"Well, maybe oral."

"Okay... Anything else?"

Bryan paused. "Well, I guess I've thought about going all the way."

Chris smiled and put his hand on Bryan's thigh. "I would be okay with that."

Bryan smiled nervously. "But I'm still kind of afraid."

"Afraid of what?"

"Getting caught. Seriously, if my parents find out… well, they just can't. I don't even want to think about it."

"Okay, I get that. But it's highly unlikely we'll get caught. I mean, we wouldn't do it at your house. We can do it in my room when my parents are out."

"What if they come home and catch us?"

"Honestly, they'd probably be okay with it. They're fine with me being gay and they totally like you."

"I dunno… it would be weird to have your parents find out we were doing stuff in your room."

"I guess we could get a room at a cheap motel like the one we just stayed in. Hell, it would be worth $31 to me."

Bryan chuckled. "Is that all? Wow. Thanks."

Chris playfully slapped Bryan's arm. "C'mon, you know what I mean."

Apologies Accepted

Tuesday, May 29, 2007

Tuesday, it was back to school for finals week. Then the school year would be over.

Track was over for the year, but Bryan fervently hoped he wouldn't run into Rocket Crockett in the hallway. After his outburst on the bus, he dreaded facing him again.

As Bryan was walking to his second class, he saw Rocket coming toward him. He looked for a corner to turn or a room to duck into. No such luck. Rocket saw him. At 6' 6", it was almost impossible for Bryan to go unnoticed.

Bryan took a deep breath and decided he might as well get this over with.

"Hey, um, can I talk to you for a sec?" Bryan nodded his head to one side, and they stepped out of the traffic flow. "Hey look. I owe you a big apology. I'm really sorry about what I said to you on the bus. I was tired and sore and–"

Rocket interrupted him, "Dude, stop. I owe *you* an apology!"

Bryan looked confused. Rocket continued, "That bit about the lube? That was a total dick move."

"Well, okay, but I called you something I shouldn't have, and–"

"You called me an asshole. Yeah, well I *was* being an asshole. You called me on my shit, man. You stood up to me. I respect you for that."

"Really?"

"Yeah. And I respect how hard you tried to win the race back. You were a beast, man! And Coach was right. Shit happens. You just have to deal with whatever comes along and do your best."

"Okay, well, thanks! But still, I never use that kind of language. I don't know where that came from. I'm sorry I used it on you."

"That kind of talk doesn't bother me. But I know, you are the PK."

"So, we're good?"

"Yeah, man." Rocket reached out and patted Bryan on the side of his shoulder. "You're alright, man. I know I give you shit sometimes, but you know what? I wouldn't tease you if I didn't like you."

As they turned to go, Rocket added, "Oh, hey, Bauer."

Bauer. Not PK. Bauer.

"Yeah?"

"Hey, a bunch of us are having a party on Friday night at Zimmerman's house. Kind of an unofficial end-of-season celebration. Just some of the guys on the team hangin' out. You're invited. I wanna see you there."

Bryan smiled, happy that he was being included. "Okay, I'll try to make it."

"And if you see Robertson before I do, tell him he's invited too."

"Okay, cool. See ya."

Bryan certainly didn't see *that* coming.

***

After school on Tuesday, Bryan's mom greeted him when he arrived home.

"How was your day, honey?"

"Good. Really good, actually. Hey Mom, there's going to be a party on Friday night for the track team. Just to kind of celebrate the year. May I go?"

"Where's it going to be?"

"At Trevor Zimmerman's house."

"I assume his parents will be there."

Bryan didn't actually know, but he couldn't imagine they wouldn't be. "Yeah."

"Okay, then. And since it's the end of the school year, you may stay out until twelve."

"May I borrow the car?"

"Sure. Just be careful."

Like he wasn't always careful.

"Thanks, Mom!"

The Track Team Party

Friday, June 1, 2007

On Friday evening just before eight, Bryan picked up Chris and headed to Trevor Zimmerman's house.

"Hey, are we supposed to bring anything?" Chris asked.

"I don't know. Maybe we should bring something just in case."

They swung by Price Cutter and picked up a large bag of scoop-shaped corn chips and a jar of salsa. They also picked up a couple of 2-liter bottles of Coke.

They arrived at the Zimmermans' and rang the doorbell. Trevor answered, "Hey, glad you could make it. Come on in. Some of the other guys are already downstairs."

Trevor led them down to the finished basement. There was a big screen TV at one end, and an arc-shaped sectional sofa. Each segment was a reclining chair separated by a wedge-shaped segment with a flat surface and a cup holder, and each seat had a footrest that would pop out when the chair reclined. There was a pool table in the middle of the room and a dartboard on the wall. At the other end was a bar with four tall bar stools and a mirrored back wall with three long, shallow shelves, each holding a line of bottles. There was a refrigerator, a small sink, and some stemmed wine glasses and martini glasses hanging from the underside of the lowest shelf. Pennants, photos, and other memorabilia from the local sports teams and a lighted neon Michelob Ultra sign adorned the walls.

It was the sweetest man cave either of them had ever seen.

Trevor took the 2-liter bottles they brought and added them to a collection of soda bottles at the end of the bar. There was a stack of red plastic cups and a small cooler filled with ice. He added the chips and salsa to a card table that had been set up for munchies.

"There's beer in the fridge if you want," Trevor said. Then he bounded upstairs in search of a bowl to pour the salsa into.

Bryan and Chris greeted the others who had arrived up to that point. Bryan poured a Coke for himself.

In a few minutes, the doorbell rang, and Trevor escorted Zane Gibbons and Rocket Crockett down the stairs.

"Yo, dudes!" Rocket joyfully called out. After a round of "heys" in return, Rocket proudly held up a brown paper bag and announced, "Let's get this party started!" He pulled out a bottle of Jack Daniels.

"Dude! Where did you get that?" someone asked.

"My older brother picked it up. I figured we shouldn't be draining Zimmerman's bar. His folks might not be down with that."

Rocket set the bottle down on the bar next to the sodas. Several of the others poured some Jack Daniels into their Cokes.

Bryan was starting to feel like he might be in the wrong place, but he was determined to try to fit in. He didn't have to drink anything alcoholic.

Trevor was standing nearby, so Bryan wandered over to him and said, "Hey, thanks for having us over. Just curious – are your parents upstairs?"

"Nah... they went away for the weekend."

"So, they don't mind us being here?"

"Probably not. As long as we don't break anything or barf up anywhere, they'll be cool."

A couple more guys showed up. Rocket looked around the room and determined that everyone who was going to come had arrived. He raised his voice and easily commanded the attention of everybody in the room.

"Guys! We are here to celebrate a successful track season and the end of another school year. Everybody grab a drink. This occasion calls for a toast!"

Most of the other guys either had a beer from the fridge, including

Chris, or they had poured some Jack Daniels in their Cokes.

Rocket walked over to Bryan and clasped his shoulder. "PK! Glad you came, bro. Seriously. So, whatcha drinkin'?"

"Just Coke. I'm the preacher's kid, remember?"

"Aw, man, this is a special occasion. C'mon, try it out. Just a little bit." He picked up the bottle of Jack Daniels and was about to pour some into Bryan's glass.

Bryan acted quickly. "Here." He took the bottle from Rocket's hand, then poured a tiny amount – probably no more than a quarter of an ounce – into his glass. "There. I'm having some."

Rocket was about to goad him into pouring more, but he decided to let it go.

Rocket turned back to the rest of the guys. "Gentlemen – a toast. To an excellent track season, an excellent year, and an excellent summer!"

Everyone raised their glasses, then drank from them. Bryan hesitantly took a sip. If he showed up at home with booze on his breath, there would be hell to pay. Hopefully, it would wear off before he had to be home at midnight. He could dump the rest in the sink when nobody was looking.

To his surprise, it tasted pretty good. It was weak, but he detected the taste of the whiskey and kind of liked it.

For the next half hour, everyone stood around talking about whatever. The seniors talked about what they would be doing next, whether it was going to college, joining the military, or getting a job. Two guys at a time played pool.

Chris mingled more easily than Bryan. Bryan didn't say much, but he was having a good time. He was enjoying being one of the guys.

After a while, Rocket called for everyone's attention again. "Gentlemen! Zimmerman here has selected a few cinematic classics from his father's private video collection." Trevor held up three DVD cases, each adorned with a collage of women who were scantily clad, if at all. "Would you please introduce the nominees?"

Trevor said, "For your consideration, we have *Tawdry Teachers, Inside the Ball U Cheerleaders*, and *Horny Housewives of Hoboken*. First, *Tawdry Teachers*." Trevor held up the box so the guys could see the front while he read the description from the back. "The Tawdry Teachers of Hornitos High eagerly provide their student bodies with the real-world education they need to succeed. Whether it's one-on-one tutoring, small group instruction, or hands-on training–"

Rocket cut him off. "Aw, fuck that. Which one has the babes with the biggest boobs?"

Several guys chuckled.

Trevor looked over each box and said, "That would be *Horny Housewives of Hoboken*."

Rocket said, "All in favor?"

"BRRRAAAAAAAAAaaaaaaaAAAAAAAAAAAPPP!!!!!"
Someone's rich, resonant belch filled the room, prompting a chorus of laughs, hoots, and claps.

Rocket laughed. "Good one dude! I'll take that as a yes!"

While Trevor powered up the TV and DVD player, the other guys refilled their beverages and claimed places on the comfy sofa seats in front of the TV. When those seats were full, the other guys sat on the floor down in front. Bryan and Chris looked at each other, unsure of what they should do. Chris picked up one of the bar stools and carried it to a spot behind the arc of recliners. Bryan did likewise.

Trevor inserted the disc and pressed Play. Any hint of a plot was quickly dispensed with, and within a minute the action was underway.

Following an assortment of belches, random comments about the female performer's breasts, and some debate about whether they were real or fake, Trevor wondered aloud, "Man. Where do they find guys who are hung like that?"

Zane replied, "Jealous much?"

Rocket said, "Hey, PK! You should have that schlong of yours in porn. You'd make a fortune!"

Several other guys snickered. Bryan instantly felt embarrassed – and angry.

He resisted the urge to say the same thing to Rocket he said on the bus last weekend. He settled for, "Ummm… I'll pass."

"C'mon dude, you could get paid to get laid! It don't get any better than that."

"Yeah, but then someday you guys will be sitting around some TV screen, like you are right now, watching me have sex. No thanks!"

Bryan fervently hoped this would be the end of bantering on this topic. His wish was quickly granted.

Someone called out, "Alright, man – a lezzie scene!"

Chris gave Bryan a look that said, "Had enough yet?" Bryan nodded his head toward the stairs.

Chris said, "Hey guys, we're going to be heading out now. Thanks for having us over."

A few guys muttered, "later dudes," but most of their attention was focused on the screen.

Bryan and Chris let themselves out.

***

Once they were in the car, Chris asked the rhetorical question, "Slush Fun?"

Bryan replied, "Slush Fun! I can stay out until twelve tonight."

"By amazing coincidence, Slush Fun is open 'til twelve."

They drove in silence. Bryan thought about how the evening had devolved as it went on. He was still stewing over Rocket's remarks.

Once they had ordered their slushies and some chili-cheese tater tots, Chris said, "A tot for your thoughts."

Bryan sighed. "I guess I should be more careful what I wish for."

"What do you mean?"

"Up until now, I wished we could be more included in the group.

It's like we're always the two oddballs on the team."

"And now…?"

"Now, after seeing what they're really like, I don't even want to be part of the group."

"I guess we should stick to hanging out with the band kids. They're more like us."

"You know, earlier I was actually having a good time. Most of the guys are pretty chill. I felt like part of the team. But then Rocket decided that we all had to watch porn and it went off the rails from there."

"Yeah, that comment he made about your dick was a total fail."

"That, and he always calls me PK. I am totally over being defined as my dad's son and now for having … a big one. But what gets me is, why does he get to control everything that happens? Who put him in charge? And why does everyone else go along with it?"

"Well, part of it is he's a football star. That gets noticed. We don't get any points for being band stars."

"Or track stars."

Their slushies and tater tots arrived, so they took a few minutes to dig into them.

Then Chris picked up where they left off. "You know what? I think he's viewed as the leader because he has assumed the role."

"What do you mean?"

"When he walks into the room, he takes charge. He asserts himself. He acts like he's the cool one."

"Which is funny, because he's like the least cool."

"I know, right? And I'll bet some of the others think so too."

"But they follow him and act like him and do what he says anyway. Why?"

"Because everyone wants to fit in. Everyone wants to be liked. So, everyone does what they think they need to do to be tight with the leader. It's like, if he's cool and you're with him, that makes you cool too."

Bryan paused to let that sink in. It hadn't occurred to him until now that any of the others might be concerned about fitting in.

Bryan said, "You know what? While we were sitting there, I was looking at those guys wondering how many of them really wanted to be sitting there watching that movie and how many of them were just going along with it because it's what Rocket wanted to do."

"I think most of them were just going along. And yet, we were the only ones who were strong enough to get up and leave."

"Yeah. Of course, we have less interest in that subject matter than the other guys."

"Most of them, anyway. I wouldn't be surprised if a few of the others are gay. Or at least wondering if they're gay."

"Really? Like who?"

"Could be anybody. But I wonder about Trevor Zimmerman."

"But it was Trevor who brought out those movies."

"Because Rocket wanted him to. Besides, if he's gay, wouldn't that be a great way to keep anyone from suspecting? I mean, if he's interested in watching straight porn, he can't possibly be gay, right? And what about Rocket?"

"Seriously? Rocket?" This possibility had never occurred to him. "Maybe that's why he acts so tough and so crude – to throw people off."

"And why he's so interested in your schlong, as he called it."

Bryan chuckled. Then he said, "I wonder who gave him the nickname Rocket."

"He probably gave it to himself."

"Yeah, probably."

"It's pretty good marketing if you think about it. Especially if he wants to be noticed by college football recruiters."

"Maybe he's smarter than I give him credit for."

"Maybe, but he's still a douche."

"Yeah. After all, he's the one who gave me the nickname PK. I mean, yes, I am a preacher's kid. But he says it like an insult. It's like he's picking on me every time he calls me that."

"And why do you think he does that?"

"I have no clue. What have I ever done to him?"

"Wanna hear my theory?"

"Sure."

"He envies you."

"WHAT???"

"Seriously. You're smarter and more talented. You're better looking. You've got a bigger dick, which seems to be important to him. And you're a better person. He's probably afraid that if the other guys get to know you better, you'll be more popular than him."

"So, he puts me down to keep me from being better liked than him."

"Bingo."

Bryan took a moment to let all that settle in.

"Hmmm… That kinda makes sense. Did I tell you what he said to me at school on Tuesday? I was walking down the hall hoping I wouldn't see him, because of what I said to him on the bus."

"Which totally rocked, by the way."

"Not really. But I was tired and angry and it just spilled out. Anyway, I saw him coming down the hall, so I went up and apologized. And then he said, 'No! I owe you an apology for what I said!' You know, about the lube. And then he said he admired me for how hard I ran to try to win back the race."

"Rocket said that???"

"I know, right? Anyway, then what he said next totally blew me away. He said he respected me for standing up to him and calling him on his … stuff. And then he said he only teases me because he likes me."

"That's a funny way to get someone to like you."

"Ya think? But I guess some people are like that. Like it was his way of trying to get noticed by me."

"I guess what he really craves is attention."

"Yeah, that explains a lot, doesn't it? And think about this. If he respects me because I stood up to him, maybe he doesn't respect all the other guys who suck up to him."

"Who knows? But they serve his purpose by treating him like some kind of hero."

"Still, it blows me away that he actually likes me and respects me, but then he picks on me."

"Pretty messed up, isn't it?"

"Now that I understand all that, I feel kind of sorry for him."

Bryan's mood improved. The giant had been slain. Then he said, "Well, they're about to close and I need to hurry up and get home."

Chris collected their trash, stepped out of the car to throw it away, and got back in. Bryan pulled out of the restaurant and started driving toward Chris's house.

"You know, my whole life, I've been the preacher's kid. It's like I'm not Bryan, I'm Rev. Bauer's son. When I went to that Christian school, all the kids knew I was Rev. Bauer's son. When I'm at church, I'm his son. That's why it's so annoying when Rocket calls me PK. It's just more of the same."

"Well, maybe you need to start letting people know who Bryan is."

"What do you mean?"

"You're always so quiet. You keep to yourself. It's like you're afraid to let people know you. So, people use the only information they have – that you're Rev. Bauer's son."

"You think so?"

"Rocket puts himself out there. People know who he is, or at least what he wants them to think he is. He may be a douchebag to us, but he projects confidence. At least people notice him."

"Well, I don't want to be like him."

"I'm not saying that. But open up a little. Let people get to know you. Hell, it's taken me almost three years. But you're a good person. People will like you."

Of course, the main reason Bryan didn't share much about himself was that there was one thing he didn't want anyone to see.

Bryan pulled into Chris's driveway.

Chris asked, "Hey, you doing anything tomorrow?"

"Not really. But it's my last weekend before I start working, so I want to do something besides go to the mall."

"Okay. Let's go into KC and hit some used record stores."

"That would be awesome."

"We can grab lunch in town."

"Cool. Can you drive? I think Mom needs the car tomorrow."

"Yeah, probably. Pick you up at ten?"

"Sounds good."

Gay Pride Day
Saturday, June 2, 2007

On Saturday morning, Chris pulled into Bryan's driveway at 10:00 sharp.

Bryan kissed his mom goodbye. "We'll grab lunch out somewhere."

She replied, "Please try to eat sensibly. And be back in plenty of time for dinner. Have fun."

Bryan hurried out and got in the car.

Chris pulled out of the driveway and headed east toward the Missouri state line.

Three of their favorite used record stores were located within a few blocks of each other in downtown Kansas City, so Chris found a convenient parking spot and they hit them all. They were in music nirvana as they thumbed through the endless bins of new and used records and CDs. They completely lost track of time.

They emerged from the third store at around 12:30. Bryan asked, "What do you want to do for lunch? I am starving."

"How about Bateman's Barbecue? There's one down on Main Street, near Linwood."

"Let's do it."

As they drove south on Main Street, they passed the World War I Museum and Park. There was some sort of event going on, with brightly colored balloons tied together to form large arches.

Bryan said, "Hmmm… I wonder what's going on."

Chris replied, "Judging from all those rainbow-colored balloons, it's probably some sort of gay festival."

They continued to Bateman's Barbecue, where they feasted on pulled pork sandwiches slathered with Kansas City's famous barbecue sauce, onion rings, and barbecue beans. They talked non-stop about everything they had found in the record stores and what they'd like to listen to first.

As they were walking back out to the car, Chris said, "Hey. We have time. Let's go check out the festival."

Bryan wasn't that interested, but he could tell Chris wanted to. "Okay. For a little while."

Chris drove back up Main Street and parked the car a couple of blocks from the festival. Other people were walking toward the festival, making a wide range of fashion statements.

Bryan glanced over at Chris. "You planned this, didn't you?"

"It was merely a coincidence that this was right on our way."

As they approached the entrance, they heard someone yelling into a PA system. They saw a cluster of people, mostly men, standing behind a crowd-control barricade and holding signs. They weren't close enough to be able to read them.

As they got closer, they were able to make out what the speaker was saying more clearly. He was ranting about how God hates homosexuals, using extremely vulgar and obnoxious language.

Bryan froze. Chris took his hand and tried to lead him on. "C'mon, just ignore them."

"We have to go back." Bryan broke free of Chris's hand and turned away.

"Oh, come on. They're just haters. Ignore them."

"Some of them might be from my church."

A couple of men were passing by at that moment. One of them said to Bryan, "Unless your church is in Lincoln, Nebraska, it's highly unlikely."

The other one said, "They're from the Eastlawn Baptist Church in Lincoln. They're here every year. Next weekend they'll be at a Gay Pride Day somewhere else. They do this all over the country, all year long."

"But why?" Chris asked.

"Because they're homophobic assholes who don't have anything better to do with their lives. Can't you feel the love of God flowing out of them?"

The first one said, "Honey, just walk right past them. Don't give them a reaction. That's what they want. Just totally ignore them. And whatever you do, do not make eye contact."

And with that, the two men resumed walking to the festival.

Chris turned to Bryan, "Okay now, come on. Ignore them. Just walk right on past. Don't let them get to you."

Bryan hesitantly walked with Chris past the protesters. He glanced in their direction. The man with the microphone saw that and pounced. He proceeded to spew invectives aimed directly at Bryan and Chris. Chris grabbed Bryan's hand and pulled him on.

Once they were inside the festival and out of earshot of the protesters, Bryan asked, "Can we sit down somewhere?"

They found a tree and sat down on the ground in the shade. Chris put his arm around Bryan. "Put it behind you. As that guy said, they're trying to get a reaction from you. Don't give it to them. They just want to make you miserable. Don't give them the satisfaction."

"But… what if they're right? What if being gay really is wrong?"

Chris debated what to say next. He hadn't been to church in years, so he was at a distinct disadvantage. "Think about how Jesus spoke to his followers. Do you think he talked to them that way?"

"Well, no."

"Was that the type of message he preached?"

"No."

"Besides, who made them the official messengers of God, anyway?"

Bryan had no answer for that.

"Right. Nobody. So, there's no reason you should listen to them or believe them. They are … what are they called? … oh, yeah … false prophets. Forget about it."

Bryan remained silent a few moments longer. Then he said, "Yeah. You're right." He stood up. "Okay, I'm doing better now. Thanks."

Chris stood up and hugged Bryan. "Okay, let's take a look around."

Bryan and Chris walked around among the booths of various organizations and businesses. There were booths for LGBT employee organizations at some of the area's corporate employers, booths for gay realtors, insurance agents, sports teams, and social clubs. They were amazed that there were so many LGBT organizations and businesses in Kansas City.

They stopped at a T-shirt vendor and Chris began looking through their merchandise. There were rainbow-colored designs and messages of all sorts. He spotted one shirt he liked and held it up to show Bryan. It read, 'I'm not gay but my boyfriend is' above an arrow pointing to the left. Other shirts with the same message had an arrow pointing to the right. "Check this out! We could each wear one of these with the arrow pointing at the other one!"

"No," Bryan replied firmly.

"Oh, come on. I'll pay for them."

"No. Where would we wear them, anyway?"

"I dunno. Maybe at the mall or something."

"Not under any circumstances."

"Maybe next year at college." Chris picked out two larges, one with a left arrow and one with a right arrow.

"There is no way I am bringing that into my house."

"I'll hang on to it until next year."

Bryan gave up. Whatever – it was his money.

Chris picked out a couple of other rainbow T-shirts for himself.

Bryan said, "You can't wear any of those when you come to my house. Ever."

"Okay, okay. Take a chill pill. Geez."

Chris paid for the shirts and they moved on.

Next, they stopped at the booth for the Kansas City LGBT

Community Center. Chris turned to Bryan and said, "Look! They have an LGBT youth group called Pathways. They meet every week. We should go check it out." Chris picked up a couple of flyers and signed himself up for their email list. Bryan didn't want to dampen Chris's enthusiasm, so he said nothing. Chris could go by himself if he wanted to.

They passed a booth for the KC Leather Lords, staffed by a few tough-looking men wearing various types of leather harnesses, vests, and chaps.

They stopped at a booth for the Kansas City Equality Alliance, or KC-EQ for short. Chris signed up for their email list too.

Next, they passed a booth for an LGBT band. Chris lit up. "Look! They even have a gay band we could join!"

Bryan replied, "When? We'll be busy with everything going on at school. Then after that, we'll be going someplace else to college."

"We could at least go to their concerts." Chris approached the booth and started chatting with one of the band members. "I can't believe you have a gay band here. What do you do?"

"We rehearse every Thursday night and we perform three or four concerts per year."

"Sweet!" Chris signed up for their email list.

Another band member joined the conversation. "And then sometimes we travel to other cities where they have LGBT bands and play with them, like St. Louis."

Chris got more excited, if that was possible. "You mean there's an LGBT band in every city?"

"There's like fifteen or twenty scattered around the country."

"That's awesome! Thanks!"

As they turned to walk away, Chris said to Bryan, "See? There might be a gay band wherever we end up."

They wandered over to the food truck area. Someone was selling cherry lemonades. Bryan bought two larges and gave one to Chris.

They could hear music coming from somewhere, so they headed in the direction it was coming from. On a portable stage, a 20-something lesbian with an acoustic guitar and a mullet was passionately singing what was probably an original song – something about sisterhood, freedom, and world peace. When she finished, she received an enthusiastic round of applause from her devoted followers. Then a drag queen came onstage to make announcements and tell jokes while the next act was setting up.

Bryan glanced at his watch. "We should probably get going pretty soon."

Chris was having a great time and probably would have stayed until the festival closed. "Maybe another half hour?"

"Okay."

They wandered down another row of booths. Chris pulled Bryan over to one of them. "Bryan – there's a gay church!"

This was a revelation to Bryan. A church for gay people? That would be heresy to his dad. Chris picked up a brochure. "We should check it out sometime."

"You forget that I have to work at my church every Sunday morning."

"Couldn't you get a week off?"

"What would be the point? I couldn't start going regularly. And you don't even go to church."

Chris decided he should change the subject. "So, what do you do at your church anyway?"

"Well, for the past two years, I've been the webmaster. Remember a couple of summers ago I took that course in website design at the community college? After that, I rebuilt the church's website. Now I keep it up-to-date with upcoming events, special services, announcements, that sort of thing. Then each Saturday I put together the PowerPoint we show during the services on Sunday morning. Then during the services, I run it."

Chris looked puzzled. "You show PowerPoint slides at church?" It had been years since his family attended church, but he couldn't imagine why they would need PowerPoint at church.

"Yeah. And I usually run the sound. Another guy records the service on video, then I post it on the website afterward."

"Would you show me sometime? I'd like to see what it is you do."

"Sure. How about tonight?"

"Okay. My parents are going out tonight, so they won't care. Hey, maybe after we do that, you could come over and we could listen to some of the stuff we bought today."

"Cool. I'll have to ask, but I probably can."

Then they passed the booth for the Parents Support Network, a group for parents of LGBT kids. Chris walked up to it and Bryan followed.

Chris said, "This group could be useful when you come out to your parents."

"Which would be never."

"Well, what if they find out anyway?" Chris picked up a brochure and shoved it in Bryan's hand. "Here, take this. Just have it in case you ever need it."

"I won't need it if I'm dead."

"Oh, please."

A gentle, friendly-looking older lady approached Bryan and Chris. "Hi, I'm Ruth Ann. Are you enjoying the festival?"

Chris replied, "Totally! This is our first time. I never knew there was so much stuff."

"Yes, Kansas City has a much more vibrant community than you might think."

"So, what does your group do?"

"We meet twice a month at a local church. Mostly, we just talk. We provide support to parents who are still coming to terms with having a lesbian, gay, bisexual, transgender, or questioning child. We share our stories of how we dealt with hearing the news and how we grew into acceptance and support for our children. Usually, the parents take comfort in knowing they're not alone and other parents have gone through what they are experiencing. We try to provide a welcoming space for them to ask questions and express their feelings and emotions."

Chris replied, "Sweet!"

Ruth Ann asked, "Do your parents know about you?"

Chris replied, "I came out to my folks last weekend. They were pretty cool with it. They had kind of figured it out anyway."

"Well, that's wonderful. You're very fortunate."

Bryan spoke up. "I'm not so fortunate. My dad's the pastor at a very conservative Christian church. There's no way I can come out to them. He'd either kick me out or kill me."

Ruth Ann's face showed a genuine look of concern. "What about your mother?"

"She might not be quite as bad, but there's no way she would go against my father."

"Dear, your mother probably already knows. Or at least it has occurred to her. My son came out to me when he was twenty-seven. I knew when he was five."

Bryan furrowed his brow. Not *his* mother.

Ruth Ann continued, "Your mother carried you inside her for nine months. She knows you more deeply than you realize. She observes you and thinks about you constantly. Mothers have intuition about these sorts of things."

"Maybe so. But if she suspects I'm gay, I'm sure she prays for God to take it away every single day."

"We've had a lot of parents who reacted badly at first, but then they came around. I have witnessed some amazing transformations."

Bryan tried to smile. "It would take a miracle."

Ruth Ann smiled back. "Well, keep us in mind if your parents find out. And good luck, sweetheart."

Chris sensed that Bryan was ready to leave. "Thank you, Ruth Ann!"

"You're welcome, dear."

They headed back toward the entrance of the festival. Bryan was dreading another encounter with the protesters. Thankfully, they had packed up and left.

***

Bryan was silent during their walk back to the car. Chris was yammering on about all the things they had discovered and experienced. A whole new gay world had opened up for Chris, and he was eager to become a part of it.

As they began the drive home, Chris turned to Bryan. "So, what did you think?"

Bryan took a moment to compose his thoughts and select the words he wanted to use.

"It was okay. It's great that they have all these groups and everything, but it all seems out of reach for me."

"How come?"

"Well, they have a gay church, but I can't go to it. They have a gay youth group, but I can't go to it. They have a gay band, but I can't play in it. I mean, where would I tell Mom I'm going each week? They have a parents' support group, but my folks would never go. It's like being in a big candy store and being told you can't have any candy."

"I thought you would enjoy being around people like you."

"But that's just it. Those people aren't like me. I didn't feel like I belonged there at all. I don't want to be a drag queen. I have no desire to wear leather stuff. I don't want to swish around and call other guys 'honey' and 'gurrl.' I don't need to wear rainbow clothes or have other people know about my private life."

Chris said nothing. Bringing Bryan to the gay pride festival had been a terrible idea.

Bryan continued, "And besides, why do I need to attach a label to myself? Why do I need to join some community? You keep talking about me coming out to my parents. I don't see why I need to come out to anybody. I don't see why I need to identify myself one way or another. Why can't I just be me?"

"So, you're not even willing to say you're gay?"

"And if you'll notice, I haven't."

"Well, then what about us? What are we? What am I to you?"

"You're my best friend."

"Best friends don't usually kiss the way we kiss or do some of the other things we've talked about doing."

"I don't know what other people do in private. And other people don't need to know what we do when we're alone."

"Whatever. But doesn't it seem like we're becoming a bit more than just friends?"

"Well, yeah, there's some attraction between us. We can do stuff if we want, but that's between you and me. And that's my point. We can have our special friendship. I don't see why we have to tell everyone else about it by labeling ourselves, joining a community, and wearing rainbow clothes."

Chris realized further debate was pointless. It would probably make things worse.

They rode in silence. When they were a few blocks from Bryan's house, he said, "I'm sorry. I know you had a good time today. I guess I rained all over your parade."

"Let's just say it didn't turn out the way I had hoped."

"I'm still glad you took me there. And I had lots of fun going to the record stores and eating barbecue."

"Well, good."

"You still want to come with me to the church after dinner?"

"Yeah, sure. Text me when you're ready."

"And we can go to your place and listen to music after that."

Chris pulled into Bryan's driveway. Bryan said, "I'll try not to be such a downer next time."

Chris smiled weakly. "Good."

The Control Booth

Saturday, June 2, 2007

Brad arrived home after the Saturday afternoon service at around 5:30, as usual. Brenda made the final preparations for dinner and had it on the table at 5:45.

After the family said grace and began eating, Brad said, "I have some great news to share! I just heard back from my agent, and I have been offered a book deal for three books over the next three years, from the same company that publishes Billy Graham's books!"

Brenda said, "Oh, honey! That's wonderful!"

Bryan said, "I didn't know you were a writer. I mean, I know you write your sermons, but writing books is kind of different."

Brad replied, "Oh, they'll be written by a ghostwriter. That's how all the big guys do it. I'll give the guy an outline with the points I want to cover, he'll do the actual writing, then I'll look it over before it goes to press."

Brenda said, "I'm very happy for you, dear."

Brad continued, "I've been working toward this for years! Now I can reach an audience far beyond our area. There will be book tours, and that will pave the way for speaking gigs. And then maybe a TV show!"

Nobody said anything else as they continued eating. After a moment passed, Brenda turned to Bryan and asked, "Did you have fun today with Chris?"

"Yeah. We visited several used record stores and went through all of their jazz. We each bought a few CDs."

"That's nice. Where did you eat lunch?"

"Bateman's Barbecue."

"What did you have?"

"Pulled pork sandwiches, baked beans, and onion rings."

"I guess that's not too bad. Only one of those things was deep-fried."

Bryan turned to his father. "Dad, do you have your sermon notes for tomorrow? I'm going to go in after dinner and finish the PowerPoint."

"Yes, I sent it to you in an email."

"Okay, thanks. Mom, may I take the car?"

"Yes, honey."

"And may I go over to Chris's afterward? We want to listen to some of the stuff we bought today."

"Didn't you just spend all day together? You certainly spend a lot of time with him."

"He's my best friend. And we like the same music. Besides, this is my last free weekend before I start my job."

"Well, then I suppose it's okay. Don't stay out too late. And try to stay away from that slushie place. That stuff is diabetes in a cup."

"I will, Mom. Thanks!"

After dinner, at around 6:15, Bryan texted Chris.

> *Ready? I have Mom's car.*

> *Ready!*

Bryan picked Chris up and they headed to the Eternal Savior Christian Church.

Bryan unlocked the door, then re-locked it after they were both inside. "Okay, first let me show you the offices."

Bryan led Chris down a couple of hallways, then he unlocked the door to the office suite. He picked up a copy of the church bulletin from one of the boxes in the outer office. Then he unlocked the door to his father's office. "This is where Dad works."

One wall was lined with beautiful mahogany bookshelves filled with books – presumably theology books and other topics of interest to pastors. There was a large, expensive desk, a plush high-backed chair, and a credenza behind it with a few framed photos of the family and other miscellaneous stuff. At the other end of the room, there was a sitting area with a small couch, a couple of individual chairs, and a coffee table in the middle for small meetings and consultations.

Chris said, "Wow. Pretty swank."

"Yeah, nothing is too good for Rev. Brad Bauer, pastor of Kansas's largest church. By the way, he just got a book deal for three books."

"Books about what?"

"I don't know – being faithful, being a good Christian, whatever. He's hoping there will be book tours and speaking gigs, and a TV show someday. Like he wants to be some famous televangelist."

"Wow. That's pretty awesome."

"Not really. He's not writing them himself. He's using a ghostwriter. And this just means he'll have even less time for Brandon and me than he does now."

They left the office, headed out the door to the courtyard, and walked under a covered walkway to the main sanctuary.

"See that smaller building over there? That's where they used to have services. They built the big sanctuary about five years ago. Now they use that other building as a chapel for smaller services, funerals, weddings, that sort of thing. They have the Saturday afternoon service there."

Bryan and Chris entered the new sanctuary building. Bryan led Chris down a hallway around to one side, then through a door to the backstage area. He stopped and flipped on some light switches. Then he led Chris onto the stage.

"My god!!! This is huge!!!" Chris's eyes were open wide with disbelief as he looked out across the expansive seating area.

The sanctuary resembled a performance venue more than a traditional church. Instead of rows of long wooden pews, there were rows of padded seats like those in a movie theater or a concert hall. The curved rows formed a semi-circle around the room and slanted upward as they went back. There were eight more rows of seats in a balcony that extended over the last few rows of the main floor. In the middle of the balcony, the rows were interrupted by a control booth with two sliding glass windows. There were theatre lights mounted from the ceiling at various points around the room.

Chris turned around to take in the stage. It was huge, too. There was a gigantic pulpit on one side and a smaller lectern on the other. Behind the lectern, a band was set up. There was a drum set behind plexiglass panels, a few guitar amps, microphone stands, and five music stands and mic stands for a horn section. In front of all the instruments, there was another row of mic stands for vocalists. On the other side, there were several rows of choir seats and several microphones hanging from the ceiling.

Chris was amazed. "Good lord! Is this a church or a concert hall?"

"Kinda both. Sometimes they have concerts by Christian bands or speaker events with evangelists who are on tour."

"Could you imagine our band having concerts here?"

"Yeah, that would be epic."

Chris was still taking it all in. "I've never seen anything like this. Back when I went to church, they had a small choir and a pipe organ."

"Yeah, that's pretty traditional. And I bet your church had a bunch of old people in it, right?"

"Yeah, I guess so. I don't remember. We haven't gone in like seven or eight years."

"Churches like that are slowly dying out. Nowadays, if you want to reach younger people and their families, you have to have modern music and a more modern-looking building. Newer churches have praise bands." Bryan waved his hand in the direction of the band set-up.

"What's it like?"

"The music's actually pretty good. The horn section, at least. The songs themselves are kinda hokey, but some of them have great horn charts. Kind of like Earth, Wind, and Fire meets Tower of Power. Mr. Budding plays trumpet in it."

"Really? He goes here?"

"Well, he's in the band. It's a gig. They get paid. Anyway, that's what got me interested in playing the trumpet. I asked Mom and Dad if I could have a trumpet and take lessons, and they got me private lessons with Mr. Budding."

"I didn't know that."

"Yeah. That was back when I was still going to Young Disciples Christian Academy in seventh and eighth grade. It's part of the reason I got to go to Prairie Village for high school. They had this lame little band there and I wanted to play in a better music program. Mom and Mr. Budding convinced Dad to let me do it. Anyway, c'mon. Let me take you upstairs."

Bryan led Chris up a set of stairs and into the control booth perched above all the seats on the sanctuary floor. There was a soundboard, a light board, some recording equipment, and a couple of computers. From this vantage point, Chris could see two giant screens mounted high on the wall to the left and right of the stage. There were also banks of speakers mounted on the walls and hanging from the ceiling.

Chris was awestruck. "Man!!! This is wicked! All this for a church?" Maybe wicked wasn't the right word to use in a church, but whatever.

"Yeah. We mix all the sound from the band and the singers here. There are four video cameras mounted around the room, and you see the one that hangs out over the stage on a boom? We control it remotely from up here. We record the 11:00 service each week. Afterward, one of the other guys does a little post-production and loads it onto YouTube. Then I put a link to it on the church's website."

"What are those big screens for?"

"That's where the PowerPoint I put together every week gets shown. It has things like the prayers people say together, the words to the hymns, stuff like that. It shows announcements before and after the service. At other times, we show images like crosses, pictures of Jesus, candles, nice scenery, stuff like that. After Dad writes his sermon, he sends it to me. Sometimes he has quotes or phrases he wants to emphasize, so I put those onto slides so they can be displayed when he says them. Then during the service, one of us, usually me, advances the slides at the right times as the service goes on."

"And you get paid for doing this?"

"Yeah. It started a couple of years ago when I wanted to buy a new trumpet – the one I have now. Dad paid for it, then he set me up in this job so I could earn the money and pay him back. I've finished paying him back, so now I have some spending money. But I'm saving most of it for college. I get paid for being the webmaster, too."

"Sweet. So, who do I have to blow to get a job here?" Chris asked.

"Dad. And I'm pretty sure that's not part of his hiring process."

"I was hoping you could put in a good word for me."

"Ah-ha. Well, I don't think we need anybody right now. And maybe you should see what the services are like before you sign up for this."

"I'd like to attend a service just to hear the band and see all of this in action."

"How about next week?"

"I'll check with my parents."

"Anyway, I have to get to work on the PowerPoint. It will take me about 20 or 30 minutes. I brought one of the CDs I bought today. Let me play it for you through the sound system."

Bryan opened the sliding glass windows separating the control booth from the sanctuary, then flipped on the sound system and started the CD. Thunderous sound filled the room.

"Wow! This is amazing!"

"Okay, well enjoy. I've got to get to work."

Bryan launched PowerPoint on the laptop in the control booth. He checked his church email account and found the information he needed from his father.

Twenty minutes later, Bryan finished his work. He shut everything down and they left the church and headed to Chris's house.

Games Grown-ups Play

Saturday, June 2, 2007

When they arrived at Chris's house at around 7:45, it was empty. They headed to the family room, where the good stereo was.

Bryan asked, "Where are your folks?"

"They're hangin' with a few of their friends. Remember those other people from the cook-out? Mom and Dad hang out with them a lot. Most weekends, they'll get together at someone's house. Sometimes they have people over here. They'll have a few drinks and play games or something. Sometimes they watch a movie."

Bryan couldn't imagine his parents doing this. Definitely not the drinking part. They rarely invited anyone over to their home, even though his mom kept the place immaculate. Their social life consisted entirely of organized activities at the church. "How late do they stay out?"

"Usually 'til 10:30 or 11:00. Sometimes a little later."

"What about Tyler?"

"He's seeing a movie with some of his buds. They'll probably go bar-hopping afterward. He'll be out until at least midnight. So, we have the place to ourselves for like three hours. We can play tunes as loud as we want."

"Well, until the neighbors call the police."

Bryan thought some more about Chris's parents and their friends. "So, what kind of games do they play?"

"Oh, sometimes card games, sometimes board games. They have this card game called Hand and Foot they've been playing a lot lately. And this new game called The Big Black Deck."

"What's that?"

"Here, let me show you." Chris walked over to a closet on the far wall of the room. He searched through their stack of games and retrieved a long, slender all-black box labeled The Big Black Deck. He carried it over to the table in front of the couch and removed the lid. There were hundreds of cards inside, nothing else.

Chris explained, "Okay, so there are question cards, which are black, and answer cards, which are white." He pulled out about a third of the cards and put the white cards in one stack and the black cards in another. "You start by taking six answer cards." Chris picked six cards from the top of the stack, then Bryan took six.

Bryan asked, "Do I show them to you?"

"No, keep them to yourself. Next, one person draws a black card and reads what's on it. Then everyone else picks which card they think has the best response. They place their answer cards face down on the table. Then they swirl them around so you can't tell whose card was whose. Then the person who asked the question will read each of the answer cards out loud. Then he or she will pick the answer they like best. If that was your card, you get a point."

Bryan looked at his six answer cards.

> The Zombie Apocalypse
>
> A sensual hot oil massage
>
> Richard Nixon
>
> Lying naked on a bear-skin rug
>
> A blowjob in a taxi cab
>
> Heroin chic

What a bunch of weird answers. Bryan wasn't sure he wanted to hear the questions.

Chris continued, "Okay, so we can't play the game like you're supposed to, because you need at least four people. But we can take turns asking questions and picking answers like we would do if we were playing the game for real."

"Okay…"

"At least you'll get a taste of what the game is like. I'll ask the first question." Chris drew a black card from the stack.

"Last Christmas, I gave my grandmother … blank." Chris put the card down on the table. "So now we each pick one of our cards with our favorite answer."

Bryan looked over his cards. Only the second one and the fifth one made any sense in this context. He figured the second one would be the less offensive option.

Chris said, "Okay, now read the question and insert your answer."

"Last Christmas, I gave my grandmother a sensual hot oil massage."

"Ewww….!" said Chris. They both chuckled. Then Chris read his.

"Last Christmas, I gave my grandmother a case of herpes."

They both laughed.

"Okay, so now you pick one new answer card to replace the one you just used."

Bryan picked a card that read:

A moldy tuna salad sandwich

Bryan said, "I wish I had this one for the last question."

Chris said, "Yeah, sometimes it works that way. But oh well. Okay, now you read a question."

Bryan picked up the top card from the Questions stack and read, "There should be a national holiday to commemorate … blank."

After a few seconds, Chris asked, "Ready?" Bryan nodded. Chris said, "There should be a national holiday to commemorate losing your virginity in a back seat." He paused. "… to your cousin."

"Nooo…! Does it really say that?"

"Well, I added the part about the cousin."

"You're a perv. Anyway, here's mine: There should be a national holiday to commemorate the Zombie Apocalypse."

They each drew a new answer card. Bryan drew:

The aura surrounding Uranus

Chris read the next question. "I'd rather have blank than blank any day of the week. Okay, this is a two-parter. You select two cards – one for the first blank and one for the second."

Bryan picked two of his cards and said, "I'd rather have oral sex in a taxi cab than a moldy tuna salad sandwich any day of the week."

"Good choice!"

Bryan said, "I can't believe your parents play this game. Especially with other people."

"Oh, yeah. They have a blast. A couple of weeks ago when they played it here, people were laughing all night long."

"I can't imagine my parents playing this game – ever. Not in a million years. Okay, now read yours."

"I'd rather have the soccer team all at once than Mom's new boyfriend any day of the week."

"I've heard that about you."

"Whatever. Now you draw two answer cards."

Bryan drew:

> Toenail fungus that won't go away
> A huge hard cock

His face reddened. "Who thinks this stuff up?"

"I heard the game was invented by a group of guys who went to high school together. They're making a ton of money now."

"Can you imagine a bunch of our friends sitting around creating a game like this?"

"Actually, I can. Anyway, read the next question."

Bryan picked up a Question card and read it aloud. "The most unusual thing I've ever had in my mouth is … blank. Now I wish I still had that card for the moldy tuna salad sandwich."

"Oh well."

Bryan looked over his answer cards. The cards he now held in his hand were:

Richard Nixon

Lying naked on a bear-skin rug

Heroin chic

The aura surrounding Uranus

Toenail fungus that won't go away

A huge hard cock

There was only one choice that made any sense.

Chris read his answer. "The most unusual thing I've ever had in my mouth is the ghost of Adolf Hitler. I know, that's lame. I just wanted to get rid of that card. What about you?"

Bryan showed Chris the card that said 'A huge hard cock.' "That one."

"You have to read it out loud."

"Why?"

"Because the game is more fun that way."

"Not for me."

"Oh, come on. It's just you and me. Read the damn thing."

Bryan realized he was being a spoil-sport, so he read it. "The most unusual thing I've ever had in my mouth is a huge hard penis."

"That's not what it says!"

"Same thing."

"Oh, come on. You can't even say cock?"

"I was raised not to use that kind of language. When it's necessary to refer to male genitalia, you should use the proper terminology."

"Really? You'll say penis, but you won't say cock or dick? They all mean the same thing."

"Yes, but one is the proper biological term and the other two are crude slang words."

"So, if there's a guy named Richard and he prefers to be called Dick, you wouldn't call him that? What would you call him – Penis?"

"Don't be silly. Of course, I'd call him Dick. When used in the context of a nickname, it's a perfectly acceptable word."

"And what about cock? Cock is in the Bible. Jesus said to Peter, 'Before the cock crows, you will deny me three times.'"

"Pretty good for a guy who hasn't attended church in ten years."

"More like seven."

"Whatever. But again, it's the context. In this case, it's another word for rooster, not penis."

"Well, anyway, enough of this." Chris gathered up the cards and put them back in the box. "After all this talk about huge hard cocks in mouths and blowjobs in taxi cabs, I know something more fun we can do. Oh, and by the way, I know that card said 'blowjob in a taxi cab,' not 'oral sex.' But I'll let it slide."

Before Bryan could reply, Chris leaned over and started kissing him. After about a minute, Chris's wandering hands ventured below Bryan's waist.

Bryan pulled himself away from Chris's mouth. "Ummm, should we be doing this here? What if your parents or Tyler come home early?"

"Okay, well then let's go up to my room."

***

An hour later, they were lying side by side, Chris's head nestled comfortably on Bryan's shoulder.

After a few minutes of blissful silence, Chris whispered, "That was wonderful."

"Yeah, it was." Bryan squeezed Chris lightly.

Chris asked, "Are you doin' okay?"

After a couple of seconds, Bryan replied, "Yeah."

"Good."

"Thanks for asking."

They cuddled and kissed for another ten or fifteen minutes.

Bryan glanced at Chris's alarm clock. "Well, I hate to eat and run, but…"

"Yeah, I know. You have to go."

They got dressed. Then Chris hugged Bryan tight and whispered in his ear, "Thanks." There was so much more he wanted to say, but… baby steps.

Bryan smiled. "Maybe next time, we'll actually listen to music."

Chris winked at Bryan. "Maybe."

Chris Goes to Church

Sunday, June 10, 2007

Chris arrived in the lobby at the Eternal Savior Christian Church at 10:55. He didn't expect the parking lot to be packed. It took him ten minutes to find a parking space in the farthest corner of the lot and five minutes to walk to the sanctuary. He texted Bryan.

Arrived. Coming to control room door.

Bryan left his post long enough to scamper down the stairs and let Chris in. "About time. Glad you're here."

Bryan introduced Chris to Mr. Elliot, the other man in the control room. Bryan had set up a folding chair next to him for Chris. He whispered to Chris, "Okay, remember the sliding windows are open. No jokes or commentary during the service."

Chris feigned indignation. "Moi?"

Promptly at 11:00, the service began. Mr. Elliot started the video recording, and Bryan halted the looping slide show with announcements and launched the file with the slides that would be shown during the service.

The opening hymn was a joyful, raucous number. The horn section was in fine form, and the band stoked up the crowd. Bryan advanced the slides in time with the song lyrics. He occasionally leaned over to the mixing board and adjusted the level of one instrument or another. Chris was impressed.

Soon, they got to the announcements. After a few mundane announcements, Rev. Bauer gave special emphasis to an all-day event coming up next month.

"On Saturday, July 14, Eternal Savior is proud to host Rescued Through Love. This will be an all-day conference dedicated to helping the parents and families of those who are struggling with same-sex attraction. It will show us how, through the divine power of God's love, we can help them and support them as they strive to find freedom from the homosexual lifestyle.

"The conference will feature several nationally-known speakers and recognized experts in the field of spiritual restoration, from organizations such as Family-Focused Ministries and the National Association to Prevent Homosexuality.

"People from all over the Kansas City area, as well as other parts of Kansas and Missouri have already signed up. If you, someone in your family, or someone you know are struggling with same-sex attraction, please help spread the word about this important event. You can register online on our church's website, Eternal Savior dot org. Let's fill this place up and save some souls!"

The conclusion of the announcement was greeted with a smattering of amens and scattered applause.

Bryan glanced over at Chris. He looked horrified. Thankfully, he remained silent.

The service proceeded as usual, with scripture readings, group prayers recited in unison from the PowerPoint slides, more singing, and the offering collection. Then Rev. Bauer launched into his sermon, titled 'Be Ever Vigilant.' The gist of the sermon was there is evil and temptation all around us, even in the most unexpected places, and we must be ever vigilant to spot it and avoid it.

Among the examples, Rev. Bauer cited a recent occurrence at the bookstore at the Great Mall.

"Just the other day, at the Book Galaxy store in the Great Mall, not too far from where we sit right now, they had filthy, pornographic magazines on display on the lower shelf of their magazine rack, where they could be easily viewed or even skimmed by any child who was unfortunate enough to pass by. Now, I suppose those sorts of publications somehow qualify as free speech under the First

Amendment, so we cannot legally stop them from selling them. But they are supposed to keep that kind of smut up on the top shelf, behind a solid covering that allows only the title to be visible, out of reach and out of sight of our impressionable young children.

"Now, it makes me sick to my stomach to imagine that my precious, innocent, seven-year-old son Brandon could visit that store and see that sort of filth as he makes his way back to the children's section, which of course is in the back of the store."

Chris whispered to Bryan, "I thought he was nine."

"Shhh!!!"

"So, I call upon all of you to take a stand for the Lord. Call Book Galaxy and demand that they stop exposing our children to this filth! Write to the company headquarters – we will provide the address on the blog on our website, Eternal Savior dot org. Tell them Book Galaxy will get no more of your business until they stop selling child pornography!"

Chris's eyes bugged out. Bryan shot him a glance that clearly communicated that he should not say a word.

The service ended without any more eye-popping incidents. As Bryan and Mr. Elliot were shutting everything down in the control booth, Bryan leaned toward Chris and whispered, "We can talk later."

Progressive Book Promoters
Thursday, June 14, 2007

It was Thursday, Bryan's day off. He and Chris were roaming around the Mediocre Mall, bored. They had already played five rounds of Race Car Driver at Game Universe and didn't want to spend any more time or money on that.

As they passed Book Galaxy, Chris lit up. "Hey, let's go into Book Galaxy and see if they're still selling child pornography!"

Bryan rolled his eyes, but why not stop in the book store for a few minutes?

They approached the magazine racks, beyond the cash registers on the left wall. Chris stopped at the first section, made a show of scanning each shelf left to right. Then he took a few sideways steps to the next section and repeated the process. "It must be here somewhere!" he said just loud enough so only Bryan would hear. Bryan stood back and hoped nobody else was watching.

After Chris finished scanning all the magazine shelves, he turned to Bryan and breathed a fake sign of disappointment. "Darn! Nothing. Those good, decent Christians from your church must have already been here and cleaned them out."

"C'mon. Let's move on."

When they reached the front of the store, they stopped to look at the tables where the latest releases were on display. The books were stacked in piles of varying heights, each topped with a wire stand that held a copy of the book upright, cover facing forward.

As they glanced at the various titles, Bryan said, "I wonder how they decide which books they're going to display here and which ones just get stuck in the shelves farther back."

He didn't expect an answer from Chris and didn't get one.

Suddenly, Chris perked up. "Wait! I know a game we can play. Wait a second. Stay here."

Chris walked to the front of the store and picked up a handbasket from the stack at the entrance. He returned to Bryan and shoved the handbasket in his direction. "Here, hold this. Follow me."

Chris led Bryan farther back into the store. Bryan asked, "So what is this game?" although he wasn't sure he wanted to know.

"Hmmm… Let's call it 'Progressive Book Promoters.'"

Chris stopped when he reached the Women's Studies section. He scanned the bookshelves for a few seconds, then selected three books and dropped them into the basket Bryan was holding.

Then he led Bryan over to the Gay & Lesbian Studies section. He surveyed the offerings and pulled one out. "Oh, wow. I can't believe they're still selling this!"

Chris showed Bryan a copy of *Gay Sex 101*. Bryan gasped and said, "Put that back!"

Chris placed it in the basket. "I used to come in here and skim through that book every time I came to the mall." He turned around and faced the opposite shelf, where there were books on subjects like auto maintenance and do-it-yourself home projects. "I'd stand here like this, like I was looking for a book about how to build an addition onto my house or something. Then, when no one was watching, I'd turn around, pull out this book, and flip through a few pages for just like ten or fifteen seconds. If someone started coming down the aisle toward me, I put it back and turned around again. I think I've seen every picture in the book at least twice."

"It has pictures?"

"Actually, they're just drawings. But good ones."

"Drawings of what?"

"Everything – dicks, butts, every position and activity you can imagine." Then he added, "and probably some you can't. Here, take a look."

"No! Geez, put that away!"

Chris returned it to the basket, then selected a couple of other titles and added them to the basket.

"Okay. So now the fun begins."

Chris led Bryan back to the display tables at the front of the store.

"Here… stand on this side, so you're standing between me and the cashier." Bryan did as he was told. "Let's see… There's Barack Obama's new book. It's already a bestseller. He doesn't need any more promotion."

Chris took the display copy of Obama's memoir out of the wire stand, picked up the stand, added the book to the stack, then placed the stand back on top of the stack. Then he reached into the basket and pulled out one of the books from the Women's Studies section. He placed it on the display stand and took a step back to admire his work.

Bryan read the title and immediately wished he could disappear. *Validating Your Vagina: How to Reclaim and Celebrate Your Feminine Sexual Energy.*

Next, Chris selected the latest Stephen King novel. He took the display copy off the stand and added it to the stack. Then he retrieved another title from the handbasket and placed it upright on the stand: *The Tao of the Female Orgasm.*

Bryan whispered to Chris, "You can't put that out there where everyone who passes by can see it!"

Chris replied, "Why not? Who are we to deprive females of good orgasms?"

Bryan knew further protest was useless. Chris pulled out the next book: *The Gay Man's Guide to Anal Health.*

Bryan whispered, "I can't believe you're doing this."

Chris replied, "Why not? A healthy anus is a happy anus!"

"Said no one, ever."

"Then you can attribute that quote to me!" Chris picked up the book and glanced at the back cover. "I wonder if it includes a daily workout routine."

It was all Bryan could do to not bust out laughing. "C'mon. We've got to get out of here. We're attracting attention."

Chris finished swapping out the last few titles. They both headed for the entrance, and Bryan dropped the empty handbasket back onto the stack on his way out.

They hurried through the mall. When they arrived at the food court, they sat down at one of the high-top tables in the middle.

They looked at each other and laughed. Bryan was still mortified by what they had done, but at the same time, it was funny. "Validate your vagina? What does that even mean, anyway?"

Chris feigned an announcer's voice. "Ladies and gentlemen, before you leave the parking garage, please stop by the manager's office and have your vagina validated."

"That doesn't even make sense. How could a gentleman get his vagina validated?"

"You might be overthinking this."

"No, I'm not. Anyway, I can't believe you did that."

"Oh c'mon, what's the harm? We didn't steal anything. We didn't damage anything. One of the clerks will notice it and take the books back to where they came from. There's no one in the mall today. They're bored. It will give them something to do. They'll have a good laugh."

"Yeah, well, remember how Dad got all worked up because someone accidentally left a copy of some adult magazine on the lower shelf? Think what will happen if anyone from his church sees that. Next Sunday, he'll be calling for a boycott of Book Galaxy. Within two weeks, word will have spread to churches all over the country, and the whole chain will get boycotted. They'll lose business and be forced to close. And then all these people, who rely on their jobs at Book Galaxy for their income, will be unemployed. All because you wanted to validate vaginas and promote healthier anuses as a prank."

"Again, you're overthinking this. Besides, what if this brings widespread attention to those books? They'll become bestsellers and those struggling authors will become rich and famous. Not to mention all the validated vaginas and healthy anuses. The world will be a better place, all thanks to us."

"Whatever. Anyway, I'm hungry. Does anything here look good to you?"

"Of course not. So, what do you suggest? Let me guess..."

"Actually, I'm going to surprise you. Let's go to Maggini's for pizza."

"Mmmm... Pizza! Approved!"

Values and Beliefs
Thursday, June 14, 2007

Maggini's Italian Ristorante was a locally-based chain with several locations scattered around the Kansas City metro area. There were a few other Italian dishes on the menu, but everyone went there for the pizza. It was a fun, unpretentious, somewhat noisy place. The tables were covered with red checkered table cloths, the flooring consisted of small white hexagonal tiles with an occasional black one mixed in, and whimsical knick-knacks were mounted on the walls. It was usually pretty busy, so there was frenetic energy about the place that added to the fun vibe.

Bryan and Chris ordered the Kitchen Sink pan pizza. They opted for the whole wheat crust as a nod to nutritional responsibility. Their Dr Peppers came in tall plastic glasses with free refills, ensuring that Maggini's would be lucky to break even on their table.

After they had ordered, Bryan introduced a topic that had been on his mind since Sunday. "So, what did you think of the church service?"

Chris knew this question would come sooner or later, and he'd been thinking about how he would answer. Truthfully, he found it appalling. It was the most cult-like thing he had ever seen, but he knew he could never say that. He chose his words carefully.

"There were some cool things about it. As you said, the band was great. Those were some tight horn parts, and those guys were awesome. The music wasn't what I would choose to listen to, but they played it well."

"Yeah, me neither. But it appeals to the masses."

"And then I was amazed at the whole production. I mean, you showed me all the stuff in the control booth before, but it was interesting to see it in action during the service."

"Yeah, it's pretty high-tech, especially for a church."

"But then there was that bit about the porn magazine in Book Galaxy. How did that go from 'kids could see a dirty magazine' to 'Book Galaxy sells child pornography?'"

"I know, that kind of went off the rails. Anything to stoke up the crowd, I guess."

"But the biggest thing was that Rescued Through Love conference. It's so hateful and anti-gay, but your dad was talking like it's the most righteous thing, like they're doing something wonderful for people. How can you put up with that?"

"I don't have any choice. I mean, what can I say? I'm just a teenager, so what do I know?"

"But if you don't question him on it, he'll never change his mind. He'll assume you and everyone else agree with him."

"And I'm telling you there's no point. Once he's committed to something he's not going to change his mind. He's been preaching against homosexuality for years. It's right up there with abortion, pornography, filth in TV shows and movies, alcohol, drugs, gambling, infidelity, sex ed in schools, and who knows what else. All the evils of the world, basically."

The waitress delivered the pizza to their table, and they eagerly dug in. After a few bites, Chris asked, "You don't actually believe that stuff, do you?"

"Of course not."

"So why do you keep going?"

"Because I have to. I don't have a choice. As long as I'm a minor and living under his roof and eating his food, I have to do what he expects of me. I'm used to it; I've lived with it all my life. I can ride it out for another year or so. And doing the stuff in the control booth provides some diversion. Up there, it seems like I'm not a part of it as much as I would be if I was sitting in the seats. Plus, I get paid."

"I see. So then, how much of the whole religion thing do you believe?"

Bryan took a moment to compose his answer.

"Well, I believe there probably was a man named Jesus of Nazareth who walked around the Middle East two thousand years ago, teaching things like how to be a better person and do the right things and treat other people well.

"Now as to whether he actually performed miracles, like raising people from the dead, or walking on the water, or feeding a whole crowd with five loaves of bread and two fish, I don't know about that. That's kind of hard to believe, not to mention the whole bit about him raising himself from the dead."

Chris asked, "So what about the idea that if you accept Jesus Christ as your Lord and savior you'll spend eternity in heaven, and if you don't, you'll spend eternity in hell?"

Bryan replied, "Yeah, that doesn't make sense if you think about it. I believe our souls live many lives over time. We reincarnate, as the Hindus and Buddhists believe. So, it's not like you only get one life, then you spend eternity in heaven or hell."

"Do you even believe there's a hell?"

"No, I don't. I believe when we die, our physical bodies remain, but our souls leave our bodies and return up into the universe somewhere. That's what heaven really is. It's where our souls go between lives."

"So basically, you don't believe most of what your dad preaches in church every week."

"Not really."

The waitress came and checked in on them. They ordered refills on their Dr Peppers.

Bryan asked, "Okay, so I've told you what I believe. What do you believe?"

"My family used to go to this Presbyterian church, but we quit going when I was around nine or ten. We weren't getting anything out of it. It was much simpler than the services at your church, but basically, it was the same. Each week you had a pre-scripted worship service that was always about the same. It's like everybody would gather together in this room with stained glass windows, go through the same motions, then leave an hour later and go on with their lives. It seemed pretty meaningless, so after a while, we just stopped going."

Bryan asked, "Do you believe in God, or are you an atheist?"

"I believe there's a higher power of some sort. I mean, somehow all of this got created. I know some of what we have now was discovered and built by man, and we probably evolved from lower life forms, but so much of our world is still miraculous, you know? Like how a plant grows, how our brains work, and everything that goes on in our bodies. And all the different plants and animals of every kind. And everything in the universe. There has to be some higher power that designed and created it all.

"I think if there is a god, as religions define it, he just wants us to be good to each other and take care of the planet, which we're doing a pretty shitty job of. He doesn't care if a bunch of people gather in a big fancy room for an hour every week and worship him by singing songs or reciting prayers somebody else wrote. And I really don't think he cares whether two men or two women fall in love with each other and do stuff together."

"Yeah, that's pretty much what I believe too."

Chris took a couple of bites of pizza, then asked, "So, do you think what we're doing is wrong?"

"What, eating pizza? Well, my mom would prefer that I was eating something healthier. And smaller."

"No, silly. Doing sexual stuff."

Bryan glanced around the room to see if anyone at the nearby tables heard what Chris just said. Nobody seemed to be paying any attention. He ate a couple of bites of pizza before he answered in a softer voice, "I don't know. I've been wrestling with that a lot over the past couple of weeks. As you said, the idea that two guys like each other doesn't seem wrong. I mean, it makes both of us happy and it isn't hurting anyone, so what's the harm? It just feels right, you know?"

"Hey, is that last piece yours or mine?"

"I think it's yours. Anyway, you may have it."

Chris transferred the last slice of pizza from the pan to his plate. "Yeah, but what about doing stuff together?"

"I don't know. I mean, just the fact that I'm doing anything at all feels kind of weird. I was raised to believe you don't have sex with someone until you're married. So, I never thought I'd be doing anything until I was older. Certainly not in high school."

"Yeah, but two guys can't get married in most places. So, what does that mean for us?"

"That's part of what I struggle with."

"Well, it seems like the rules are different for gays and lesbians than they are for straight people if they're not going to let us get married. Besides, nobody waits until they get married anymore, anyway."

"Some people do."

"Not very many. But never mind straight people. Back to us. When we talked a couple of weeks ago about what we might do together, you said you'd be willing to go all the way. Is that still the case, or are you having second thoughts?"

The waitress came and the conversation halted. She took the empty pan and their plates and left the check.

Bryan asked, "Can we finish this conversation out in the car?"

They figured out how much to leave for a tip and divided the bill.

Once they were in the car, Chris restarted the conversation. "So, we were talking about doing stuff together and going all the way. Are you having second thoughts?"

"Oh, I've been having second thoughts, and third thoughts, and tenth thoughts, and fiftieth thoughts. I mean, the Bible says it's wrong and Dad certainly thinks it's wrong, but as I said earlier, I don't believe most of that stuff. But here's the thing. Before we started kissing or doing anything else, I didn't have to deal with this whole gay thing. You and I were just close friends. But if we're doing stuff like oral, or even anal, then I'm doing things I have to hide from my parents. From everyone, for that matter. It's like if I'm not doing anything gay, I don't have to say I'm gay, and they can't find out I'm gay. But if we're doing this stuff, then that means I'm gay, and now there's something they could find out about."

Chris took a moment to process all of that.

Bryan continued. "This is like walking a tightrope for me. You heard my dad at church. You know what he believes. It would be horrible if he found out. But I feel like I'm holding back on you. I want to be able to give you everything you want. We can pretend that if we're careful enough we'll never get caught and they'll never find out, but there's always the chance they will. It just seems like there's no good answer – at least not until next year."

"Yeah, I get it. But let me ask you this. Let's say, in a hypothetical situation, your parents weren't a factor. Either they were okay with you being gay, or they died, or maybe it's next year and we're living someplace else. In other words, there are no consequences if other people find out we're gay and we're having sex. In that case, would you have any issues with being in love with another guy and having sex with him?"

Bryan thought for a second. "No, I guess not. Especially if it was you."

"Awww…" Chris put his hand on Bryan's thigh. Bryan put his hand on top of Chris's. They smiled at each other.

A big grin lit up Chris's face. "You know what I was thinking about during the sermon?"

"Do I want to know?"

Chris snickered. "I was thinking, what if we did it right out there in the middle of the stage?"

"You're insane. And perverted."

"No, seriously. What would be a bigger 'fuck you' to all their homophobia than that?"

"Oh, I don't know… maybe doing it in Dad's office? Right there on his desk."

"Ooh, kinky! Now I have something else to look forward to."

"Ummm, no. That will never actually happen."

Bryan pulled into Chris's driveway.

Chris said, "What's your weekend look like?"

"Friday, I work seven to three. Saturday, three to eleven."

"Wanna chill here tomorrow night?"

"Sure."

"Bring a couple of your new CDs." Chris started to pull at the door handle but stopped.

"Thank you for the talk. I know this stuff is kind of hard for you."

"You're welcome."

Chris leaned over and kissed Bryan on the cheek before getting out of the car.

A Night to Remember

Friday, June 15, 2007

After dinner on Friday night, Bryan asked his mom, "May I go over to Chris's? We still have some new CDs we haven't listened to yet."

"Yes, dear."

Bryan rode to Chris's house on his bike. When he arrived, Chris got a couple of sodas from the refrigerator and led Bryan up to his room.

"Where are your folks tonight? Playing crude games with their friends again?"

"Nah, they're going to have a few people over tomorrow night for that. Tonight, they're having a date night. What do you want to listen to?"

"You ever heard of Rob McConnell and the Boss Brass? They're from Canada."

"No…"

"Check it out. You'll love it."

Chris put the CD in his player and started it. It was fantastic big band music. As Bryan predicted, Chris loved it.

Chris didn't have any chairs in his room other than the chair at his desk, so Bryan kicked his shoes off, propped one of the pillows on the bed upright against the headboard, and sat down on one side of the bed, leaning back against the pillow. Chris was already in his socks; he joined Bryan on the other half of the bed.

Bryan asked, "What do your folks do on a date night?"

"Usually just dinner and a movie. Maybe a concert or a play if there's something they want to see."

"That's really sweet. I can't remember the last time my parents went out together for an evening. Probably last year on their anniversary."

"Yeah, it keeps the spark in their romance. Sometimes when they get home, they head for the bedroom a little early, if you know what I mean. They're coming up on twenty-five years, and they're still totally in love with each other."

"I'm sure my parents still love each other too, but I don't think there's much of a spark left. At least they don't let on in front of me and Brandon. I mean, they get along well and they don't fight or anything, but I don't know how often anything happens in the bedroom." Bryan paused for a moment. "I try not to think about my parents in the bedroom anyway. It's just kind of ick, you know?"

"Well, it's not like I fantasize about my parents screwing, but I'm glad they do, for their sake."

"What about Tyler?"

"I don't fantasize about him screwing, either."

"No, stupid. I mean where is he this evening?"

Chris laughed. "Who knows? Hangin' out with his bros somewhere."

They listened to the CD some more. The opener, an exciting, up-tempo tune filled with intricate brass parts, finished with a screaming trumpet climax. Next, a slightly less energetic, medium-tempo tune began.

"Your parents certainly leave you home alone a lot."

"Well, I'm seventeen. I'm not a little kid anymore."

They listened some more. They remained quiet during a beautiful alto sax solo.

Chris said, "But isn't it convenient?"

"What?"

"That they leave me home alone." Chris turned slightly toward Bryan.

"Maybe they think you won't get into any mischief."

"Maybe they think I will."

Chris leaned into Bryan and planted a gentle kiss on his lips. Bryan smiled, turned more toward Chris, and kissed him back. After a few minutes of increasingly passionate kissing, their bulges were straining their shorts.

Chris whispered, "It's awfully warm in here." He took off his shirt and unbuckled his belt.

Bryan did likewise and replied, "We might be a little overdressed for the occasion."

Chris got off the bed momentarily to discard his remaining clothes. He left his desk lamp on but turned the ceiling light off. He removed the big band CD and replaced it with a mellow, romantic Paul Desmond CD. He got back in bed and they resumed kissing.

Bryan's mind raced with streams of competing thoughts while they deep-kissed. *Is this really about to happen? Do I want it to happen? Yes, but... What if I'm wrong and Dad's right? No... that can't be. It's one thing to talk about doing it, but to actually do it? That's entirely different. Are we really about to do this? We will unless I stop it. But I can't. I won't. I don't want to stop it. I don't want to disappoint Chris. Is Satan going to rise out of the mattress and claim my soul? No, of course not, I don't believe that, but... Do I really love him? Yes, I do. Then shouldn't it be alright?*

To Bryan, it felt like that moment when a skydiver is about to step out of the airplane.

***

At some point, the CD ended. Neither of them noticed when it happened.

Chris snuggled up against Bryan, with his head resting in the crook of Bryan's shoulder. They laid there for several minutes without speaking, blissfully exhausted.

Bryan replayed what he had just experienced several times. He never imagined how wonderful intimacy with another human being would be – both physically and emotionally.

He had no regrets, whatsoever. Satan had not risen up and claimed his soul. He was at peace with what he had just done. He no longer had any questions swirling in his mind – especially about one thing. He was gay. Completely, unquestionably, unapologetically gay. And he was fine with it. And he loved Chris, and he wanted to spend the rest of his life with him. And he couldn't give a shit what his mom and dad thought about it.

Bryan was about to whisper "I love you," but thought better of it. It seemed too soon. It seemed like an even bigger step than the one he had just taken.

Then they heard the garage door open. Chris bolted out of bed and started the CD again. Bryan got out of bed and they hurriedly put their clothes back on.

They shared another long embrace. Chris whispered in Bryan's ear, "I will never forget this night."

"Me neither."

Chris led Bryan downstairs to the door. Mr. and Mrs. Robertson were nowhere to be seen. They were already in their bedroom, continuing their date night.

Chris and Bryan kissed again and said goodnight.

Kisses in the Moonlight
Friday, June 22, 2007

Bryan worked during the day on Friday, so on Friday evening he and Chris predictably ended up at Slush Fun.

As they were enjoying their slushies and nibbling on chili cheese fries, Chris asked, "How's your job going? It's been, what, three weeks now?"

"Yeah, it'll be three weeks on Monday. It's pretty good. My manager, Mr. Simonton, is pretty chill. Did I tell you he's gay?"

"No! How did you find out?"

"When I went into his office on the first day to fill out some paperwork, I saw that he had a little rainbow sticker stuck on one corner of his bulletin board. And he had a picture of him and another guy on his desk. So, I mentioned that I had been at the festival the previous weekend, and–"

"See? Aren't you glad I took you there?"

"Yeah, I guess. Anyway, so it turns out the other guy is his husband. They moved here from LA a few months ago to be closer to his husband's parents. They're getting older, so they want to be available to care for them."

"Cool. Hey, you know what? After I came out to my folks, Tyler and I were talking. He said one of his gay friends at college said every parent should hope they have at least one gay kid, because that is the one who will be most likely to take care of them when they get old."

"Well, that seems to be true in this case." Bryan filed that bit of information away in case, heaven forbid, his dad ever finds out.

"So, what do they have you doing?"

"Mostly restocking. Sometimes when it's busy I'll bag groceries. A couple of days ago, they had me working at the meat counter. You know, weighing and wrapping stuff people order from the butcher case."

"It's a good thing you're experienced with handling meat. Would you like some more practice?"

"Ha, ha. Anyway, get this. The guy who's the manager of the meat department? His name is Mr. Weiner."

"Nooo… You're kidding!"

"I kid you not."

"Is his first name Richard? And if so, does he go by Dick?"

"Dick Weiner. Very funny. Now I won't be able to keep a straight face whenever I see him. Thank you very much."

"My pleasure. But… What if his first name was Oscar?" Chris adopted a fake voice. "Good afternoon, ma'am, I'm your butcher, Oscar M. Weiner."

Bryan laughed. "And one of the bag boys is named Phil Baggs."

"Are you shittin' me?"

"Yeah. I just made that up."

"That was pretty clever. But wouldn't it be great if people's names matched their occupations? Like a dentist named Dr. Payne."

Bryan thought for a moment. "Or the wedding officiant, Mary Peeples."

"The female evangelist, Penny Costal."

"Funny, except there is no such thing as a female evangelist."

"Why not?"

"In conservative churches, they don't let women be ministers."

"Well, I guess if they're homophobic, I shouldn't be surprised that they're sexist, too."

Bryan let that one go. "So anyway, hmmm… how about the horticulturist, Pete Moss?"

"The Russian lawyer, Sue Yurazoff."

Bryan chucked, then said, "The optometrist, Anita Seymour."

Chris countered with, "The proctologist, Seymour Butz." They both laughed.

Bryan said, "The undertaker, Doug Graves."

"Good one." Chris took a few seconds to think of his next name, then he started laughing hysterically. His face turned red. He was laughing so hard he couldn't speak. After a moment, he took a couple of deep breaths to calm himself down. "The gy…" He broke down into another fit of uncontrollable laughter.

Bryan couldn't imagine what could be so funny. "This had better be worth it."

Chris finally pulled himself together long enough to blurt out, "The gynecologist, Harry Beaver."

Bryan almost choked on his cherry-lime slushie, which drove Chris to laugh even more. They laughed hysterically for at least half a minute. Bryan glanced over at the car to their right. "Those people are staring at us like we're nuts."

"Who cares? Are they having as much fun as we are?"

"Probably not." Bryan admired Chris for not caring about what others think. He needed to work on that.

Finally, their laughter subsided. Bryan hadn't laughed so hard in, well, probably his entire life. Hanging out with Chris was such a refreshing change from his usual droll environment of propriety, wholesomeness, and clean living. He turned to Chris and smiled at him affectionately. "You are sooo crude!"

Chris glanced back at Bryan with a sparkle in his eye. "And you wouldn't want me any other way."

No, probably not, Bryan thought.

For a few seconds, they gazed into each other's eyes in silence.

Then Chris leaned over to kiss Bryan. Bryan wanted it, but he put his hand up and gently pushed back on Chris. "Not here."

Chris sighed. Bryan reached out his hand and placed it on top of Chris's. Chris turned his hand over and they interlocked their fingers.

"I'm sorry. I'm just not comfortable with kissing out where other people can see us."

They finished their slushies in silence.

Then Chris asked, "Well, okay, do you want to go someplace else?"

"Like where? Can we go back to your place?"

"Not tonight. My parents are having some of their friends over. But I have an idea." Chris started the car. "Throw this away?"

Bryan gathered their trash, carried it to the nearest trash can, then got back in the car. Chris backed out, pulled out of Slush Fun, then turned right onto the next street. The street led into a light industrial area of warehouses and construction companies, with small offices and high fences which surrounded construction equipment and supplies. Since it was 9:30 at night, the area was deserted.

Chris pulled the car into a parking lot and drove around behind one of the buildings. He turned the car around and parked it, facing out. "How about this?"

"Are you sure this is okay?"

"Why not? Nobody will see us back here. We're not hurting anything."

Bryan figured Chris was probably right. But still, what if? He had never done anything like this before.

They unfastened their seat belts and leaned into each other. They placed their hands behind each other's shoulders and pulled close. Their lips met, their mouths opened, and within seconds they were kissing passionately, eyes closed.

Quickly, the rest of the world melted away. They became completely immersed in the bliss of the present moment. Their hands glided up and down each other's backs as they pulled closer. Chris moved one of his hands down to Bryan's thigh and slid it slowly up toward his crotch. Both boys' throbbing erections were straining at their shorts.

Bryan focused his entire being on all the wonderful sensations that were washing over him. The stimulating touch of Chris's hands as they caressed Bryan's back, thigh, and crotch. The silkiness of Chris's wavy dark brown hair as Bryan ran his fingers through it. The feel of his moist lips, and the lingering cool taste of blue coconut slushie on his tongue. The warmth of Chris's breath as he gently exhaled from his nostrils onto Bryan's cheek. With his eyes closed, it seemed as if a white light from heaven was bathing him in peaceful, loving serenity.

A loud knock on the driver's side window shattered their reverie. Bryan opened his eyes into the blinding white beam of a policeman's flashlight. They suddenly sat upright, facing forward.

"Shit," Chris uttered under his breath. Bryan was too petrified to say anything.

The cop yelled sternly, "Roll down your window."

Chris turned the key in the ignition far enough to turn the electrical system on, then rolled down the window.

"Driver's licenses, please."

Both boys fished out their wallets as their tented shorts quickly deflated. They removed their driver's licenses and handed them over.

The cop returned to his car for a moment.

Bryan stared straight ahead and tried not to contemplate the worst that could happen, but he couldn't avoid it. He muttered, "Just shoot me now."

Chris whispered, "Come on, it probably won't be that bad."

Yes, it probably would.

The cop returned and shined his bright flashlight around the interior of the car, then back onto their faces.

"Have you boys been drinking?"

"No, sir," they said in unison. The cop sized them up for reddened eyes or any hint of the smell of alcohol or pot in the car.

Chris asked, "Officer, have we violated any laws?"

Bryan bristled. *Please shut up. Don't make it worse.*

The officer lowered his face slightly and scowled at them over the top of his glasses.

"Only the laws of nature."

Thankfully, Chris said nothing else. Bryan wanted a hole to open up under him and swallow him forever.

The police officer continued. "There is no law against kissing. If I had caught you with your pants down, I would have booked you for indecent sexual exposure." The cop diverted his flashlight onto the driver's licenses he was holding, then back to Bryan's face. "We wouldn't want that, would we..." He paused for emphasis. "...Mr. Bauer?"

Bryan's heart sank.

"This is private property. I could book you for trespassing, but since you have clean records and you're not drinking or doing drugs, I'm going to let you go. But the next time you fairies feel like queering it up..." he paused and glared at them with disdain. "Get a god damn room."

He handed their driver's licenses back to Chris. "Now get out of here."

The cop got into his car and drove away. Chris and Bryan sat for a moment in stunned silence.

Bryan muttered, "My life is over."

Chris turned the key in the ignition, started the car, and began the journey to Bryan's house. "C'mon, lighten up. We didn't get a ticket. Nothing's going to happen."

"You don't get it, do you?" Bryan snapped. "He recognized my last name. He knows who my dad is. He probably goes to our church."

"And...?"

"He was such a prick, he'll probably tell my dad."

They barely said a word as Chris drove Bryan home. Chris thought having Bryan's parents find out he's gay might be for the best in the long run. It will be rough at first, but after the initial shock wears off, they'll come around. Maybe his parents could go talk to them. The future in-laws will need to meet each other sooner or later anyway.

Maybe Bryan's parents will join that parents' support group.

As they approached Bryan's house, Chris placed his hand on Bryan's thigh. "No sense in worrying about something that might not happen. And if something happens, it will happen whether you worry about it or not."

"That's easy for you to say."

Chris removed his hand as he pulled into the driveway. "Good night."

"Later."

Bryan headed straight for his room. Good thing neither of his parents saw him, so they wouldn't see the panic on his face.

The Truth Comes Out
Sunday, June 24, 2007

After church on Sunday, the Bauer family headed out to a local restaurant, as was their custom. They typically went to a cafeteria, a buffet, or perhaps a family-friendly sit-down restaurant, but never a fast-food chain. Today it was Brenda's turn to choose, so she chose Haney's. Of all their usual choices, Haney's had the healthiest offerings. There was nothing deep-fried to be found.

Brad was not in a good mood. Most weeks, he was physically drained but still riding an emotional high. Usually, the uplifting music, the energy of the crowds, and the fulfillment that came from doing what he loved most would carry him through the rest of the day. When he was on stage in his huge church, passionately orating on that week's sermon topic and doing the Lord's work, he was truly in his zone.

Today he seemed stern and preoccupied. At a couple of points during his sermon, he forgot his place and improvised until he got back on track.

Brenda and Brandon sensed his bad mood but had no idea what might have triggered it. Bryan was pretty sure he knew.

There wasn't much conversation. Everyone instinctively knew they shouldn't ask Brad how he thought the service went.

As they got up to leave, Brad opened his wallet and fished out two dollars for the tip. As was his custom, he placed the money inside a dollar bill-sized folding card that read on the outside, 'Here's a tip you can really use.' On the inside, it read, 'You can save money, but only Jesus can save your soul. Let Jesus Christ become the Lord of your life today.' This was followed by John 3:16 and the name, address, and website of the Eternal Savior Christian Church.

As was his custom, Bryan lingered behind his family as they left the table, then surreptitiously left a five-dollar bill on the table.

Brad's mood didn't improve for the rest of the day. Normally, Sunday was family day. Bryan and Brandon knew not to make other plans so they could be available if Mom or Dad wanted to go somewhere or do something together, as a family. Today, they did nothing. The mood in the house was subdued and somewhat awkward. Bryan asked Brandon if he wanted to throw a Frisbee in the park, which Brandon happily agreed to. While they were outside, Brad invited Brenda into his office to chat for a little while.

***

On Monday, Bryan worked 7:00 a.m. to 3:00 p.m. Monday was Brad's day off, although he usually worked on church stuff from his home office anyway.

When Bryan returned home after his shift, Brenda didn't greet him with her usual kiss or ask how his day had gone. She seemed preoccupied with doing something in the kitchen. Bryan went upstairs and played with Brandon for a little while until it was time for dinner.

Dinner was quiet. Usually, Brad would have something to say about things happening at the church. Brandon was usually talkative about whatever he had been doing that day, but even he sensed something was off. Brenda seemed distant and worried about something.

After dinner, Bryan returned to his room and checked his phone for text messages. He got his trumpet out and stuffed his practice mute in the bell to minimize the volume. He pulled out one of his jazz play-along books and inserted the accompanying disc in his CD player. Just as he was about to put his headphones on and start playing along with the rhythm tracks on the CD, there came a knock at the door.

"Yes?"

It was his mom. "Your father would like to speak with you in his office."

Bryan sighed. He gently set his trumpet down in its case and reluctantly stood up.

Bryan and his mother entered his father's office, and she closed the door behind them. They sat down on the sofa across from Brad's desk. It was actually a hide-a-bed for those rare occasions when they had guests. It was firm and not particularly comfortable. Brad stopped what he was doing on his computer, stood up from his chair, and walked around to the front of his desk to face his wife and son.

"Son, I understand you recently had the opportunity to meet Officer Rudowski of the Overland Park police force."

Bryan replied, "The name doesn't ring a bell."

"I believe this meeting took place on Friday evening. And your name certainly rang a bell with him."

Bryan said nothing.

"Son, there is never a good time to lie to your father, but this would be a particularly bad time."

"Well, Chris and I were in his car when a policeman approached us. It was after dark and he was shining a bright flashlight in our eyes. He didn't tell us his name, and I couldn't see his name badge."

"Fair enough. In any case, Officer Rudowski attends our church. After the service yesterday, he mentioned that he encountered you and your friend parked in a deserted parking lot behind some buildings. Would you please tell us what you were doing there?"

"Well, we were at Slush Fun, and we had finished our food and drinks. The place was busy, so we figured we should leave and let another customer have our space. We wanted to hang out some more, so we drove down a side street next to Slush Fun, and we ended up at this construction supply place down the road. There was no one there, so we figured we wouldn't be bothering anyone, and it wouldn't hurt anything if we parked there for a while."

"Okay, let's get right to the point. Officer Rudowski informed me that when he approached the car, he saw you and your friend kissing. According to him, you two were going at it pretty hot and heavy. Would you please explain what that was all about?"

Bryan scrambled for an answer that might somehow explain their make-out session in a less-incriminating way. Maybe he and Chris were practicing for when they would be kissing girls? No, Dad wouldn't buy it. There was no use in trying to bluff. Might as well tell the truth and get it over with.

"Well, Chris is my best friend. He's the best friend I've ever had. We always have a great time whenever we're together. We have so much in common – music, track, school, you know. So, we're real close. Anyway, Friday night we were just talking and cracking jokes and stuff, and I guess we got kind of silly and–"

"Yeah, well I've had best friends too, but we didn't make out in parked cars." Brad paused and glared at Bryan. "It sure sounds to me like this boy is recruiting you into becoming a homosexual. Is that it? Is he leading you into the homosexual lifestyle?"

"No, sir, it's not like that at all. That's not how it works."

Brad's voice became more forceful. "Well then, how does it work? We didn't raise you to be a homosexual. So, if you're out there kissing some boy, he must have somehow enticed you to do that."

Bryan almost couldn't believe the nonsense and misinformation that was coming out of his father. But then, yes, he could. It's the same stuff he preached from the pulpit. Bryan was already defensive; he was now starting to get angry.

"Nobody raises their kid to be gay. People aren't out there recruiting people to be gay. Some people just turn out that way–"

"Oh, cut the crap! Stop with the liberal nonsense! So tell me, if homosexuals don't recruit, then how do they find other people to become homosexuals? Homosexuals can't reproduce, so they have to recruit. And most of the time they go for impressionable children. God did not create mankind so that two men or two women can reproduce.

No! It's God's divine plan that a man and a woman fall in love, get married, and bear children. That's the only path. Two men kissing each other and doing heaven knows what else is an abomination in God's eyes. It's disgusting. It's a terrible sin. It says so in the Bible. You know that. We did not raise you to be that way, and no son of ours is going to be a homosexual. Is that clear???"

"Yes, sir." Bryan knew it would be pointless to say anything else. Changing his father's mind was hopeless.

"I regret that I ever agreed to let you go to that public school." Brad cast an angry glance toward Brenda. "I knew you'd get exposed to all sorts of bad information and bad influences and bad people. We should have sent you to Overland Park Christian High School three years ago, and that's where you'll be going in the fall."

"Dad, no! I love it at Prairie Village! They have a great jazz ensemble and concert band, and I'm one of the best runners on the track team. I have all my friends! I'm really happy there! Please???"

"They have a band at Overland Park Christian High School. You'll make friends there. And they have good teachers. You'll get a good, faith-based education there. It's not up for debate."

Bryan turned to his mother in a last-ditch grasp for help. "Mommm….???"

She shrugged and said, "I'm sorry, dear. I'm with your father on this. I don't want you to be a homosexual, either."

This was going even worse than he had imagined. Bryan thought about saying that he would be the same person regardless of which school he attended, but he knew it would do no good.

Brad said, "Alright. Starting now, you are grounded until further notice. You are to leave home only to go to church or your job. No more car privileges. And under no circumstances are you to have any further contact with that Robinson boy."

"Robertson."

"Whatever. Have I made myself clear?"

"Yes, sir."

"Your phone, please."

Bryan reached in his pocket and surrendered his phone.

"And no using the computer except to do your work for the church. Now, I have arranged for you to see a counselor. Very fine man. We went to college together. He specializes in leading people out of the homosexual lifestyle and back into righteousness with the Lord. The three of us will go in for your initial session on Wednesday at 4:00. You will continue to see him weekly after that."

"I have to work on Wednesday from three to eleven."

"Change it. Tell them to adjust your schedule or give you a couple of hours off. Your salvation is far more important than some summer job."

Bryan sighed. After a moment of tense silence, Bryan asked, "Is that all?"

Brad replied, "That is all. You may be excused."

Bryan got up from the sofa and turned toward the door.

Brandon scurried back into his bedroom and closed the door as quietly as he could.

Bryan shuffled back to his bedroom. He closed the door, didn't bother to turn on a light, and threw himself face-down onto his bed.

The Morning After
Tuesday, June 26, 2007

The next morning, Bryan couldn't muster the will to get out of bed. There would be no phone, no computer, no contact with friends, and no place to go until work at 3:00. There was no reason to even get up. And he certainly didn't want to see his dad. He wasn't too crazy about seeing his mom, either. She was in complete agreement with his dad on this.

Finally, Brenda came upstairs and knocked on the door. "Bryan, it's 9:00. Time to get up. You can't stay in bed all day."

A few minutes later, he grudgingly pulled himself out of bed, threw on his robe, and walked to the bathroom to take a shower. He finally showed up in the kitchen at around 9:45. His plate was still at the table. Thankfully, his dad was gone.

He dropped a couple slices of bread in the toaster and poured himself some milk and orange juice. When the toast was ready, he sat down at the table to eat.

Brenda walked in and sat down across from him. Bryan barely acknowledged her presence and gazed downward at his food or occasionally to one side or the other.

After about half a minute, she asked, "Is there anything you would like to talk about?"

"No."

After another ten seconds or so, she got up and walked away.

Later, Bryan asked, "I know I'm grounded, but may I go out for a run?"

"Yes, dear, you may."

Bryan ran over to the high school and spent the next two hours alternating between running laps around the track and sitting in the bleachers to rest. Over and over, he contemplated his situation and what his options might be. He came up with nothing.

Why even bother running? The Overland Park Christian High School had no track team. At least he was someplace outdoors and not trapped in the house.

Finally, he returned home, took a shower, changed into his work clothes, then took off on his bike for Price Cutter.

***

After Bryan left for work, Brenda pulled the Prairie Village phone book off the shelf in the pantry and opened it on the kitchen counter. Within moments, she located 'Robertson, Thomas & Kathleen' on 80th Street, just a few blocks away. She picked up the phone and nervously dialed the number.

Kathleen answered, "Hello?"

"Hello, is this Kathleen Robertson?"

"Yes."

"This is Brenda Bauer calling."

"Oh, you must be Bryan's mother. How are you today?"

"Fine, I guess. Umm… So, Brad – that's Bryan's father – and I would like to invite you and Tom over to our house for a little chat. We were wondering if you might be available this evening. Say around 7:30?"

"Let me check the calendar… Yes, this evening would be good. What's your address?"

"546 Sycamore Terrace."

Kathleen jotted it down. "Okay! We're looking forward to getting to know you. See you at 7:30."

***

Bryan arrived about 15 minutes early. He found Mr. Simonton and asked if he could speak to him in his office.

When Mr. Simonton and Bryan were seated with the door closed, Mr. Simonton asked, "So, what's bothering you?" It was that obvious.

"Mom and Dad found out I'm gay. Dad went postal. Now I'm grounded, except for work and church. They took away my phone. I can't use the computer. They're going to take me out of Prairie Village High School and send me to this stupid little Christian school in the fall. And worst of all, they said I can't ever have any contact with Chris again. So basically, my life is ruined. Seriously, I just want to die."

Mr. Simonton put his hand on Bryan's knee. "I'm really, really sorry. How did they find out?"

"Some cop caught us kissing in the car on Friday night. As it turns out, he goes to my dad's church, and on Sunday, he told Dad. And of course, Dad's all like 'no son of mine is going to be a homosexual' and now he's taken away everything that matters in my life."

"Wow, that's harsh."

"Oh, and now I have to start seeing some therapist who is supposed to 'lead me out of the homosexual lifestyle.' And Dad made an appointment with this guy for 4:00 tomorrow, like it doesn't even occur to him that I might have to be at work then."

"Oh, no. These ex-gay counselors are horrible. Be careful – they can seriously mess you up."

"Wonderful."

"But anyway, you can take a couple of hours off tomorrow. Just clock out when you need to, then come back after you're done and finish your shift. That is, if you feel like it. You might not."

"At this point, I just want to be out of the house as much as possible. I don't even want to look at Mom and Dad. I can't believe they're doing this to me. I mean, Chris came out to his parents, and they're totally cool with it."

"Well, some parents react badly at first, then they come around and start to accept it a little better."

"It will be a miracle if that happens with my folks. They're pretty hard-core."

"Well, I'm really sorry this is happening to you. You're a good kid. Your parents should be proud of you. Anyway, I am always here if you need someone to talk to."

"Thanks. May I use your phone for a minute? I need to call Chris."

"Sure." Mr. Simonton got up and left Bryan alone in the office.

***

Chris's phone rang. Price Cutter showed up on the caller ID. He figured it was probably Bryan.

"Well, hello, Price Cutter! Do you deliver?"

"Hey, Chris."

"I only accept deliveries in the rear. I'd like to order a two-pound kielbasa, a squirt bottle of Mayonnaise, and–"

"Very funny. Listen, this is serious."

"Okay, what?"

"I go on dinner break at 7:00 tonight. Can you come see me at the store? It's really important."

"Yeah, I guess so. Hey, I sent you several texts. Did you see them?"

"No, that's part of what I need to tell you tonight. Anyway, I gotta start my shift. Just meet me at the booths in front, okay? Bye."

"Bye."

When Parents Collide

Tuesday, June 26, 2007

Price Cutter had a small area off to the side of the front entrance with four booths that looked like they had been acquired from a fast-food restaurant that had closed. Whoever decided to put them there apparently thought people would come in, visit the salad bar or order something from the deli counter, and sit there to eat. No customers ever did. The only time those booths got used was by employees on their break.

Bryan had just put a frozen dinner in the microwave. He was sitting in one of the booths with a cup of Dr Pepper from the deli's soda fountain.

Chris arrived a few minutes after seven. "Wassup?"

Bryan stood up and gave Chris a quick hug. "Thanks for coming. Sit down."

Bryan told Chris everything his father had done to him.

"Oh my god…"

"The worst part is, I'm not allowed to have any more contact with you."

"Whaaat???"

"Yeah. Like Dad is so unhinged, he thinks you recruited me into being gay."

"Are you shittin' me???"

"I would never kid you about something like this. This is serious. I mean, my life is literally over. They might as well put me in a monastery up on some mountaintop."

Chris sat silently for a moment as he let everything settle in. "So, what are we going to do?"

"Well, unless something changes, I guess the only time we can see each other is if you come to the store during my break like we're doing now. Oh, and Mom let me go out for a run earlier today. I suppose you could meet me and we could run together."

Chris frowned.

"Yeah, I know, it's not much. But it's all I can think of. I'm only supposed to use the computer when I'm doing church stuff, but you can send me emails and I'll check for them whenever I can."

"This sucks."

"Big time."

"Remember that lady at the pride festival booth? She said sometimes parents react badly at first, but then they get better."

"Yeah, Mr. Simonton said the same thing. But I don't know, Dad was pretty freaked. I can't see him letting up."

"What about your mom?"

"She just sat there and didn't say a word for most of it. But she's on board with everything. Of course, she just does whatever Dad says anyway. Now we really have to go someplace far away for college."

"Yeah, but the next year is going to totally suck."

"It totally sucks now."

Bryan finished his dinner. "Well, I've got to get back to work."

They stood up and hugged each other again.

***

As Tom and Kathleen drove the few blocks to the Bauers' home, Tom said, "I'm looking forward to meeting Bryan's parents. After all, if things work out for him and Chris, they could be our in-laws someday."

Kathleen replied, "I've got a feeling something's up. His mother seemed nervous on the phone when she was inviting us."

"Maybe she's just shy about meeting new people."

"Well, Bryan is sort of quiet and shy. Maybe he gets it from her."

"I guess it's true that opposites attract."

"I know! Could you imagine two Chrises together? Nobody else would get a word in edgewise!" They both chuckled.

They arrived, walked up to the house, and pressed the doorbell. Brenda opened the door and ushered them in.

Bryan's father began introductions. "Rev. Brad Bauer. This is my wife, Brenda."

"Tom Robertson. Pleased to meet you!"

"I'm Kathleen. Thank you for inviting us over."

After a round of handshakes, Brenda waved toward the living room sofa. "Please have a seat. May I get you anything to drink? Coffee? Water?"

The Robertsons noticed the Bauers had no drinks next to their chairs, so they declined and made their way to the sofa.

Brandon came bounding down the stairs, smiling and brimming with energy. "Hi! My name's Brandon!"

Brenda was grateful for the diversion. "Brandon, you know Bryan's friend Chris? These are his parents, Mr. and Mrs. Robertson."

"I know! We saw them after the concert, remember?"

"Oh, that's right," Brenda said.

Tom extended a hand to Brandon, which he shook enthusiastically.

"Wasn't that a great concert?" Brandon exclaimed.

"Why, yes it was," Kathleen replied. "Your brother is very talented."

"So is Chris! And you know what? When he comes over and they practice together, they let me listen!"

Brad was becoming visibly impatient, so Brenda turned to Brandon and said, "Honey, would you please go up to your room for a little while? We want to have some grown-up time."

"Okay. Bye! Come back and see us again!"

And with that, he ran back upstairs to his room.

Kathleen said, "He's adorable!"

Brad replied, "Yes, well, he can be a real handful sometimes."

Tom said, "So, Rev. Bauer. Which church do you pastor?"

"The Eternal Savior Christian Church, over on 79th."

"Ah yes. I've driven past it many times. That's quite a large place."

"Yes, thank you. Over the past fifteen years, we have grown to become the largest congregation in Kansas. We'd love to have you visit sometime. Visitors are always welcome."

Tom and Kathleen glanced at each other, hoping the Bauers had not invited them over to recruit them to join their church.

Brad continued. "But let's get down to business. One of the members of my congregation is a police officer with the Overland Park police force. He informed me that while he was on duty this past Friday night, he encountered your son and our son in a parked car in some dark, hidden parking lot. KISSING."

Tom replied, "Well, okay. I mean, is that all? I don't think there's a law against kissing."

"According to the police officer, they were going at it pretty hot and heavy."

Tom tried to diffuse the tension with a slight chuckle. "Well, teenagers have been kissing in cars ever since cars were invented."

Brad's face reddened and his voice got louder. "Kissing in cars is not the point. The point is, it was your son and our son. Boys and girls kiss in cars. Boys and boys do not."

"Well, apparently our boys do."

"Are you telling me this sort of behavior is acceptable to you? Being a homosexual is not an option for our son."

Kathleen said, "Rev. Bauer, we completely accept the fact that our son is gay. We love him for exactly who he is and we support him completely."

"So, it's fine and dandy with you that your son has chosen this degenerate lifestyle and he is destined to spend eternity in hell???"

Tom replied, "Those are not our beliefs. You're entitled to your beliefs and we're entitled to ours."

Kathleen said, "Our son is a fine young man and we're proud of him. We want him to be able to live his life authentically and be happy. Your son is a very nice young man too. You should be proud of him."

"Well, if you want your son to have an authentic and happy life, you need to rescue him from the homosexual lifestyle before it's too late. There's a counselor I can recommend – Dr. Ronald Babcock. Very fine man. I've known him since we went to college together at Oral Roberts. He has built a ministry around helping people leave the homosexual lifestyle. Our son is going to start seeing him tomorrow. Here, let me give you his card."

Kathleen shook her head. "That won't be necessary."

"And on Saturday, July 14th, my church is hosting the Rescued Through Love conference. It's for parents and families of people who are struggling with same-sex attraction. It will show you how to help your son recover, with love."

"We're not interested," Kathleen said.

"Well, you do what you want with your son, but he is to have no further contact with our son from this point forward. He's already been a bad enough influence."

Tom sprung to his feet. "Rev. Bauer, are you implying that our son is somehow responsible for your son being gay?"

"That seems pretty obvious. Where else could he have picked it up? We certainly did not raise our son to be this way."

Kathleen shot back, "Children do not choose to be gay. Some of them just turn out that way. It's who they are."

Brad sneered dismissively. "That's a bunch of liberal nonsense. Oh, and by the way, in our church we don't call them gay, we call them homosexuals. I've never met a happy homosexual. Every homosexual I've ever met was miserable."

"And how many homosexuals have you met?"

"Very few, thank God. And I don't know why they call it a lifestyle

– it's really a deathstyle."

Tom turned to Kathleen. "Dear, it's time for us to leave." They walked briskly to the door and opened it themselves. Kathleen turned and glanced at Brenda. Brenda averted her eyes downward. Tom and Kathleen left without saying another word.

They remained silent as they got into their car and drove away, rattled by everything that had just taken place.

Finally, Tom said, "I'm going to need a shower when we get home, just to wash the stench off."

"I know. And that poor boy. I feel so sorry for him."

"And they're sending him to a shrink? To try to make him straight?" Tom shook his head.

"I've read about that. I think they call it reparative therapy. It's very harmful."

"And Rev. Bauer. What a piece of work! For a man of God, he didn't seem very loving."

"And did you notice Brenda didn't say anything the whole time? I wonder what was going on inside her head."

"Who knows? Their church probably tells women that they must remain subservient to their husbands. Just stay home, keep house, and raise the kids."

Kathleen placed her hand on Tom's leg, thankful that he treated her as his equal.

"You know, if this attempt at therapy doesn't work out–"

"And it won't," Tom interjected.

"–do you think they might kick him out?"

Tom thought for a moment. "I hope not. I mean, how could any parent kick their own child out of the house?"

"Well, unfortunately, it happens."

"That guy is such a stubborn hothead, I wouldn't put it past him."

"But what if they do? Would we take him in?"

"I guess so. I mean, we couldn't stand by and do nothing while he's living on the street, homeless."

"I suppose he could sleep in Tyler's room once he goes back to college."

"Well, if it ever comes to that, we'll work it out somehow."

They arrived home and walked into the kitchen. Tom asked, "Wine?"

"Definitely."

Tom poured a glass for each of them and they sat down at the kitchen table, sad and emotionally exhausted.

Chris was up in his room. When he heard his parents downstairs, he came down to talk with them.

Tom said, "Good evening, son. Have a seat."

Kathleen said, "We just got home from visiting with Bryan's parents. It wasn't a pleasant visit."

"Not at all." Tom took a sip of his wine. "First, they told us that on Friday night, some cop found you and Bryan kissing in the car."

Uh-oh. Chris wondered what kind of trouble he was about to be in. "Yes, sir, we were."

"That, in and of itself, isn't a problem. We know he's your boyfriend and, well, people kiss. No big deal. There's no law against kissing. But kissing in a car in a dark spot often leads to other things, and if that cop had caught you doing other things, then you would have been in real trouble."

"Yes, sir."

Kathleen took over. "Sweetheart, we're happy you and Bryan have found each other. Now that you have come out to us, you don't have to hide the fact that you're seeing him. You can kiss him in your room."

Tom continued, "We know you two will probably want to, you know, experiment with other things sooner or later. And that's okay. We're all human. We have urges and desires. We were teenagers once too, you know."

Kathleen and Tom glanced at each other and smiled. They had been high school sweethearts.

Kathleen said, "We'd rather have you do whatever you're going to do in the privacy of your room where you'll be safe, and you won't get in trouble like you would if you did it in a parked car."

Chris said, "Thanks. It's cool of you to say that and everything. But it doesn't matter now."

"What do you mean?" Kathleen asked.

"I just came back from seeing Bryan at the store. He said his parents grounded him. They're taking him out of Prairie Village and sending him to some small Christian high school. And worst of all, they have forbidden him from ever seeing me again."

"Oh honey, I'm so sorry," Kathleen said. "Actually, his father told us he didn't want Bryan to see you anymore. He also said they were going to send him to some kind of religious counselor who was going to attempt to turn him straight."

Tom added, "I'm sorry too, son. Hopefully, this will work itself out somehow."

Chris replied, "Yeah, but it seems pretty hopeless at this point." Chris got up from the table and started to head back upstairs.

Kathleen called after him. "Oh, Chris? We hope it never comes to this, but if his parents ever kick him out of the house, tell him he can come to stay here with us."

Chris smiled a little and replied, "Thanks."

Brandon Knows

Wednesday, June 27, 2007

Wednesday morning, Bryan got up at a more normal time. After breakfast, he decided to play his trumpet for a while. He hoped playing music would bring some joy to his heavily restricted world.

After he had been playing for about 20 minutes, he heard a knock at the door – Brandon's knock.

"Come in."

Brandon let himself in and closed the door.

"Hey, Bryan." Brandon wasn't quite his usual jovial self, but he was trying.

"Hey, kiddo."

"Can I ask you a few things?"

"Of course."

It was a rhetorical question. Brandon knew he could always go to Bryan whenever he had something he wanted to talk about.

"Are you doing okay?"

"Not really. Mom and Dad aren't very happy with me right now."

"I didn't think so. I heard some of what Dad was saying when he had you in his office on Monday night."

"I'm sorry you had to hear any of that."

"He kept using this word when he was yelling at you. He was using it again when he was talking to Chris's mom and dad last night. It sounded like 'home special,' or something like that."

"Wait a minute. He was talking to Chris's mom and dad last night?"

"Yeah. They came over for a visit while you were at work. Anyway, I couldn't understand everything they were talking about, but Dad kept saying that word that sounded like 'home special.' Chris's parents were saying stuff about being gay, but nobody sounded very happy. What's going on?"

"Okay, I'll try my best to explain. But listen… This needs to be our little secret, okay? I'll be in even bigger trouble if Mom and Dad find out I told you what I'm about to tell you. But you need to know. So… our little secret, okay?"

"Okay!"

"Good. That's really important. So, here goes. You know how, when people grow up, sometimes a man and a woman will fall in love. And then they get married, right? Like Mom and Dad."

"Yeah…"

"But in some cases, a man and a man might fall in love, or a woman and a woman–"

"Like you and Chris!"

That caught Bryan off-guard. "Why do you say that?"

"Because of the way you two act when you're around each other. The way you look at each other, talk to each other, and laugh with each other. You're always hanging out together. I can tell you guys are really happy together."

"You're very perceptive. But yeah, Chris and I like each other a lot. And yeah, I'm really happy whenever I'm around him. I guess you could say that we love each other. Anyway, when two men love each other, we say they're gay."

"So that means you two are gay?"

"Yes, I guess it does. Anyway, that word you kept hearing is 'homosexual.' It's just a big word that's kind of scientific, but it means the same thing as gay."

"Okay, so what's the problem?"

"Well, there are some people who believe that being gay is wrong. They believe the only right thing is for a man and a woman to love each other, not two men or two women. And that's what Mom and Dad think and it's what they teach at Dad's church. So, they are upset with me because they found out about me and Chris."

"So? You two love each other. What's wrong with that?"

"I don't think there's anything wrong with it, but Mom and Dad do. And if they have a problem with it, that makes it a really big problem for me."

"What about Chris's parents? Are they mad at him? They got pretty mad last night."

"No, Chris is lucky. His parents don't have any problem with him being gay."

Brandon thought for a minute.

"So… are you in trouble?"

"Yeah. I'm in big trouble. I'm grounded. And they say I can't ever see Chris again."

"Why???"

"Because they're mad at me for being gay. They think I can just decide to stop being gay, but it doesn't work that way."

"So, what are you going to do?"

"I have no idea."

Brandon sat and thought about all this. Finally, he said, "Well, it's fine with me if you're gay. And I hope you and Chris can spend the rest of your lives being happy together."

"Aw, thanks, kiddo."

Brandon gave Bryan a big hug. "I love you. You're the best big brother in the world!"

"That means a lot to me, especially right now. I love you too. And you're the best little brother in the world."

After a few seconds, Brandon asked, "So, if we love each other, does that mean we're gay?"

Bryan laughed. "No, two brothers loving each other is different. It's family love, like the way we love Mom and Dad and Grandma. Romantic love is kinda the same, but kinda different."

Brandon looked puzzled.

"Someday you'll fall in love with someone special and you'll understand. Anyway, remember, you can't say anything to Mom and Dad about this conversation."

"Okay, but… why not?"

"They'll get even madder at me if they find out I was talking to you about being gay. And then I'll be in really big trouble. They probably think you're not old enough to understand this yet. So, remember – it's our little secret."

Bryan and Brandon did their secret pinky-shake.

"Okay, now I'd like to play my trumpet some more."

"Can I stay and listen?"

"Not today, okay? I kinda want to be alone right now."

Brandon understood.

Dr. Ronald Babcock – First Visit

Wednesday, June 27, 2007

Bryan's parents drove to Price Cutter to pick Bryan up. Then they drove about five miles to a generic one-story brick office building labeled PARAGON in bold block letters. Bryan had no idea what this building could be a paragon of.

They entered a tiny waiting room where a bored girl sat at an inexpensive, plain desk that had probably been purchased as a kit from an office supply store and assembled on the spot. She looked to be a year or so out of high school and probably had this job because she couldn't find anything else. She looked up but didn't smile or speak.

"We are the Bauers. We're here to see Dr. Babcock," Brad said.

"I'll let him know you're here."

The girl got up from her desk and disappeared down a hallway. She couldn't have been any less interested, but ushering in new visitors was probably the most exciting thing she did all day.

A moment later, she returned. "Right this way, please."

She led them down a short corridor with closed office doors on both sides. Most doors had nameplates slid into brass-plated holders that announced their occupants. A tax accountant. A financial planner. A Reiki healer. A marriage counselor. They passed a couple of doors with nameplates that said, 'available.' Apparently, Paragon was a place where you could rent a small office at an inexpensive rate and get the benefit of an address, a receptionist, a kitchenette, and restrooms. Bryan expected a little more from someone who was supposed to be so highly regarded in his field, but whatever.

They reached an office whose nameplate contained two lines:

Closer Walk Ministries
Ronald Babcock, PhD

The office was sufficiently appointed with a desk, two guest chairs, and a few plastic potted plants. Dr. Babcock was standing as they entered and greeted Bryan's parents warmly.

"Hey, Brad, great to see you!" Dr. Babcock pumped Brad's hand warmly.

"Likewise, Ron. Thank you for making time for us. You remember my wife, Brenda?"

They had obviously met before – probably at some church function. Dr. Babcock shook Brenda's hand more gently and formally. "Of course. How could I ever forget such a pretty face?"

Ick. Bryan was not liking this guy already.

Brenda said, "Always a pleasure, Dr. Babcock."

"Ron. Please call me Ron."

Brad turned to Bryan. "And this is our son, Bryan."

Bryan dutifully stepped up and shook Dr. Babcock's hand. He squeezed a bit too hard and shook a little too enthusiastically.

"Nice to meet you, Bryan. My goodness, you look so much like your father looked when I first met him at Oral Roberts. A few inches taller, but otherwise, a dead ringer." Dr. Babcock glanced at Brad, then back to Bryan. "Goodness, how the years have flown."

Two comfortable guest chairs were positioned in front of Dr. Babcock's desk. He had added a folding chair that at least had a padded seat, and positioned it next to the two larger chairs. Naturally, that chair was for Bryan.

"Please sit down. Make yourselves comfortable. Would anyone care for water?"

Brad and Brenda shook their heads.

"Yes, please," Bryan said. "Water would be good."

Dr. Babcock reached into a small refrigerator next to the credenza behind his desk and produced a puny bottle of water.

"Thanks," Bryan said. He unscrewed the cap, took a swig, and screwed it back on.

Brad glared at Bryan, as if the only proper response would have been to decline. *Screw that*, Bryan thought. *If this guy doesn't want them to have water, he shouldn't offer it. He's stocking it in his refrigerator, after all.*

Bryan noticed a family picture on the credenza. In the picture along with Dr. Babcock was a plain, although not unattractive, woman and three girls of varying ages. Bryan guessed they were around six, nine, and twelve. In many ways, this picture resembled a picture that hung on the wall in their bedroom hallway, except that instead of three girls theirs had two boys. The picture looked staged – because it was. The participants wore forced smiles, just like in the picture at home.

Dr. Babcock produced a pad of lined yellow paper and asked, "How may I be of service today?" He knew why they were there, but it was as good an opening line as any.

Brad said, "Well, we discovered a few days ago that our son is struggling with same-sex attraction. He is being recruited into the homosexual lifestyle by another boy at school. They were caught by an officer of the law, kissing in a parked car. I have grounded Bryan and ordered him not to have contact with this boy again."

Dr. Babcock wrote a few words on his pad, then spoke. "I see. Before we progress further, let's begin with prayer, shall we?"

Brenda reached for Bryan's and Brad's hands. Brad, in turn, reached across the desk and clasped Dr. Babcock's hand. Fortunately for Bryan, he was a little too far from Dr. Babcock to comfortably reach his hand. Everyone bowed their heads.

"Our heavenly Father, we give thanks that you have gathered us here in your presence. We open our hearts to your love and divine guidance. We pray for your wisdom to lead us down the path of righteousness. We confess that we have sinned and fallen short of your glory. We give praise and thanks that, through your grace, we know we are forgiven. In Jesus' name, we pray. Amen."

Everyone muttered the obligatory "Amen."

Brenda asked, "So, Dr. Babcock, what is your process? How does this work?"

Dr. Babcock smiled. "After our initial consultation, Bryan and I will continue to meet weekly. We will explore what happened to him at some point in his life that may have caused him to have these desires. Depending on what we find, we will implement techniques to guide him back to the path of righteousness. We will seek to replace his unhealthy feelings toward men with healthy desires for women. And of course, we will be guided by prayer throughout the entire process."

Brad said, "So in other words, you can reprogram him to be attracted to women rather than men."

"Sounds like brainwashing," Bryan said.

Dr. Babcock replied, "I prefer to think of it as positive visualization and affirmation."

Bryan glanced up at the framed diploma, prominently mounted on the wall above Dr. Babcock's head. The regal gold lettering conferred upon him a Doctor of Theology degree from Bob Jones University. Not Psychology, not Psychiatry – Theology.

Bryan said, "I see your degree is in Theology. How does that qualify you to do this?"

This question visibly annoyed Brad, but he remained silent.

"You are correct. I do not practice psychological counseling or psychiatry. I can't prescribe medications. I provide pastoral counseling. I guide people through spiritual healing. I firmly believe that through the power of prayer, guidance from scripture, and the Lord's saving grace, all things are possible. And that includes replacing homosexual urges with a desire for the opposite sex."

Brenda asked, "What kind of success have you had? Can you guarantee that you can make Bryan straight? And how long will it take?"

Dr. Babcock let out a small sigh and said, "No, there are no guarantees. Some of my clients have successfully left the homosexual lifestyle. They have found wonderful Christian women to marry and are now raising a family. Others remain celibate and refrain from giving in to temptation. We have support groups that meet on an ongoing basis to help everyone remain on their path. And unfortunately, some are already so firmly entrenched in that lifestyle that leaving it proves to be too great a challenge.

"As for how long it takes, it's different with each person. A lot depends on how long they have been living that lifestyle and how committed they are to Jesus and their recovery." He turned his glance toward Bryan. "In your case, since you come from good Christian parents, you have been raised in the Church, and you have only recently begun to experiment with homosexuality, that bodes well for your success.

"It's important that we clear up a common misconception. There is no such thing as a homosexual. The person we may think is a homosexual is actually a heterosexual who has a homosexual problem, that is, the problem of attraction to the same sex. God created us all in His image according to His divine plan – that is, as heterosexuals.

"Our goal with these sessions is to try to identify what events or factors may have occurred at some point during Bryan's life that have led him to seek or be receptive to the affection of other men. Then we can determine the best methods to address and correct those factors.

"You see, heterosexuality is complementary, while homosexuality is compensatory. A man and a woman complement each other naturally, both physically and spiritually. Usually, men with homosexual urges are attempting to seek in other men the masculinity or wholeness they think they lack in themselves. In other words, homosexual impulses result from an inner sense of emptiness, and men seek to fill that emptiness with other men."

Brad and Brenda nodded.

Dr. Babcock asked, "Are there any questions at this point?"

Everyone glanced at each other, then shook their heads.

"Alright, then. Brad and Brenda, may I ask you to wait in the lobby for a few minutes while I chat privately with Bryan? Then I will excuse Bryan and invite you back in for a few moments."

After Brad and Brenda left the room Dr. Babcock asked, "Bryan, I want to hear your side of the story. Your father claimed that you were caught kissing another young man in a parked car. Is that what happened?"

"Yes, sir."

"Is that the first time you and he kissed?"

"No, there were a couple of times before that."

"How long have you and this boy – what's his name?"

"Chris."

He jotted that down on his yellow pad.

"How long have you felt attracted to Chris?"

"I don't know. It sort of developed gradually over two or three years."

"How long have you known him?"

"Almost three years. I met him when I started ninth grade at Prairie Village High School. He and I were both in the band. I was new to the school and didn't know anybody. He came up and introduced himself. He introduced me to all his friends and now they're my friends too."

"So, he helped you get integrated into your new school and make friends."

"Yeah."

Dr. Babcock jotted more notes on his yellow pad.

"That was very kind of him. So, can you recall when you first started feeling some sort of attraction to him, like wanting to kiss him or do other things with him?"

"No, not really. As I said, it happened slowly over time. He's the best friend I've ever had. We laugh together and joke around a lot. We like hanging out together. We're both in the band, so sometimes he comes over to my house or I go over to his house and we practice together. We're both on the track team, so sometimes we go running together. We can tease each other and we know we don't really mean it. It's like we can talk about anything and it's okay."

"It sounds like you feel a sense of intimacy with him."

"Yeah, I guess. I've never thought of it that way."

"And have you ever felt that sort of intimacy with anyone else?"

"No."

"Have you and Chris talked about doing physical things with each other? I mean, beyond kissing."

Bryan was starting to feel uncomfortable about where this line of questioning was heading. Any moment now, Dr. Babcock was going to start probing into what they have done with each other. And that's none of his damn business.

"Not much. But before we go on, I need to ask you something. Why do you need to know all these details? How is this going to help?"

Dr. Babcock paused, like he was trying to come up with a plausible explanation. Then he said, "Okay. Here's an analogy. Suppose you know where you want to go, but you don't know the directions for how to get there. For me to give you directions, I have to know where you are now. In other words, for me to be able to help get you from Point A to Point B, I have to know where your Point A is."

Dr. Babcock glanced at the clock on his desk. "We're almost out of time. But I would like to ask you to do something every day for the next week. Each morning, when you first awaken, say this prayer. 'Dear Lord, I can't make it through this day without You. Today, I will choose not to think impure thoughts. Today, I will choose not to act on those impulses in any way. I choose to submit my will to the direction You have for my life. I choose to follow You. I choose to allow Your Holy Spirit to walk before me, to guide me, to speak for me.'"

"Can you write that down? I probably won't remember it."

"The exact words aren't so important. But what matters is that each morning, you are praying that for just this day, you will reject any homosexual thoughts or desires you may have. You are asking for God's help to get you through this day. You are asking for His strength, which will help you overcome your struggle."

"Okay."

"One last thing. Let's set up a time to meet next week. What days and times are you available during the day?"

"I work at Price Cutter. Tuesday or Wednesday mornings are good, or any time on Thursday. At least, that's my schedule now. It could change."

"Hmmm… let me see if I have anything available during those times." Dr. Babcock studied the calendar on his computer. Bryan couldn't see the screen, but he suspected that his calendar was mostly open. "I could do Tuesday morning at 10:00. How does that sound?"

"Okay." One time was as bad as another.

"Well, then, it was nice meeting you, Bryan, and I look forward to seeing you Tuesday morning at 10:00. Would you please send your parents back in for a few minutes?"

"Sure."

A moment later, Brad and Brenda returned to the office. Brad asked, "How did it go?"

"Pretty well. We've only scratched the surface, but I'm confident we will be able to make more progress in the coming weeks. Do you have any questions for me?"

Brenda asked, "Is it possible we did something wrong? Is there any way we might have caused this?"

Brad replied, "I don't see how this could be our fault. We have raised him according to the Bible. The church has always been part of his life. We sent him to a Christian school up through eighth grade. But Ron, I have to be honest with you. I wasn't keen on the idea of sending him to the public school starting in ninth grade. Brenda felt it would be better for him academically, plus he's so interested in music and they have a good band program there. But I worried that he would run into other kids who weren't raised in the faith and they would be bad influences on him. Now it looks like that has happened. I think this all started when we let him go to the public school. What do you think?"

Dr. Babcock replied, "Actually, that's probably not the case. Research shows that most aspects of a child's personality are formed during the first few years of his life. Usually, the seeds of same-sex attraction are planted during that time."

Brenda gasped, then asked, "Oh, my. What could we have done? How could we not have noticed?"

Brad added, "We don't know if it was us. It could have been somebody else."

"But who?"

Dr. Babcock jumped in, "It's too soon to know. There's no point in speculating now or beating yourselves up over anything. Let's see what is revealed over the next few weeks. And by the way, we have scheduled his next appointment for 10:00 on Tuesday morning."

Brenda asked, "Do we need to be here?"

"No, just him until further notice. I don't expect you'll need to come in again until we have a corrective action plan in place."

Brad replied, "But will you keep us informed of his progress?"

"Of course."

The More You Know
Friday, June 29, 2007

After Bryan arrived at work on Friday, Mr. Simonton caught up with him and said, "Hey, when you finish stocking these shelves, come into my office for a few minutes. I want to hear about what happened on Wednesday."

A few minutes later, Bryan was seated in the chair next to Mr. Simonton's cluttered desk.

"Okay, so we went to this office building in a business park. It's got a lot of little one-room offices for all kinds of random things. So, this guy has his diploma on the wall and it says he has a doctorate in theology. Not psychology or psychiatry or anything like that – theology. And it turns out this guy is someone Dad knew when he was in college at Oral Roberts. Now he's gone into business to try to lead people out of the homosexual lifestyle, as he put it, and back to the Lord – and heterosexuality."

"Oh, great, he's one of those 'pray the gay away' guys."

"Yeah."

"What's his name?"

"Dr. Ronald Babcock."

Mr. Simonton turned to his computer and searched for this name. "Oh, Lord. This guy is bad news. He's affiliated with several right-wing, anti-gay organizations, like Family-Focused Ministries and the National Association for the Prevention of Homosexuality. He goes around and speaks at these conferences called Rescued Through Love where they try to tell parents how to convert their children into being straight."

"Yeah, well get this. They're having one of those conferences at my dad's church in a couple of weeks."

"Oh, no. So, what happened during the meeting?"

"It was mostly introductory stuff, like what kinds of stuff he's going to try and how long it might take. He thinks something must have happened back when I was a small child that made me turn gay, so he's going to try to find out what that is."

"Wait, let me guess. It's having an absent or weak father and a dominant, overbearing mother that causes boys to turn out gay."

"He didn't say that, but he said we seek out other men to fill some kind of emptiness. And get this. He said there's no such thing as homosexuals, only heterosexuals who have a problem with same-sex attraction."

"Well, of course. To them, nobody was born this way."

"Then he started asking questions about when I first started feeling attracted to Chris. And I thought he was going to try to get me to tell him what kinds of things Chris and I have been doing, but then we ran out of time."

"Something to look forward to for next week, I guess."

"Yeah, I can't believe I'm being subjected to this. And if I can't somehow convince them I'm straight, how long will I have to keep going? I mean, where is this going to lead?"

"I don't know, but hang in there. Don't let them get to you. Try to look at it as some sort of perverse entertainment. Maybe you can write a book about it someday."

"I'm not into horror stories, but who knows?"

Dr. Ronald Babcock – Second Visit
Tuesday, July 3, 2007

Bryan borrowed his mother's car and drove to the Paragon office building for his second appointment with Dr. Ronald Babcock.

"Good morning, Bryan."

"Good morning, Dr. Babcock."

"How was your week?"

"Well, I'm grounded indefinitely. My parents took away my phone. I can't use the computer except for church stuff. I can't go anywhere except work, church, or here. I can't see any of my friends. And I can't have any further contact with Chris. So basically, I'm stuck at home by myself with nothing to do. Other than that, my week has been great."

Dr. Babcock couldn't think of an appropriate response, so instead, he suggested, "Let's begin with prayer, shall we?"

Dr. Babcock extended both hands across his desk, so Bryan had no choice but to hold them. Dr. Babcock gave Bryan's hands an odd little squeeze, almost like he was massaging them.

"Our heavenly Father, we give thanks for the opportunity to learn and become better people so we can live our lives according to your plan. We open our hearts and minds to receive your divine guidance. We pray for strength to overcome temptation. We confess that we have sinned and fallen short of your glory. We give praise and thanks that, through your grace, we are forgiven. In Jesus' name, we pray. Amen."

"Amen."

"Speaking of prayers, did you remember to say the prayer I gave you every morning?"

"Yes, most days." He hadn't, but he knew he couldn't say that.

"Good. Okay, then, let's pick up where we left off. How old are you?"

"Seventeen."

"Okay, so by age seventeen most boys have been having sexual thoughts or fantasies of one type or another for several years. What sorts of private thoughts have you had?"

"Private ones."

Dr. Babcock was a bit taken aback at how abruptly Bryan stonewalled that question. He shifted course.

"Okay, then. How old were you when you first realized you felt attracted to other males?"

"I don't know." Bryan thought for a moment. "I had a friend in first and second grade who I liked a lot. Sometimes I felt like I wanted to kiss him. I never did, though."

"Why not?"

"He never seemed interested. And I guessed he wouldn't like it if I tried to kiss him, so I didn't."

"Is there some reason you stopped being friends?"

"His family moved away after second grade. We wrote a couple of letters back and forth, but we lost touch pretty quickly after that. I have no idea where he is now."

"After he moved away, were there other times you felt attracted to other males – either men or boys?"

"Hmm… Well, sometimes when I was lying in bed at night waiting to fall asleep, I would imagine I had one of my friends in bed with me."

"And how old were you then?"

"Third and fourth grade, maybe fifth."

"What did you imagine would happen?"

"I would imagine we were lying in bed close to each other, maybe holding each other. And maybe we'd be kissing."

"Anything else?"

"Well, like maybe if we were both laying on our side, and we were up against each other, then it might go in."

"So, you would imagine you and the other boy were having anal intercourse?"

"Yeah. But mostly kind of just pressed up against each other."

"And that was around third or fourth grade?"

"Yes."

Dr. Babcock scribbled a few words on his pad of paper.

"Did you ever actually have friends over to spend the night?"

"Not very often."

"So, on those occasions when you did have sleepovers, did anything ever happen?"

"No."

"You're sure? Did any of the boys ever suggest or attempt anything with you?"

"No."

Bryan noticed Dr. Babcock was holding his pen in his right hand, which was resting on the yellow pad. But he had surreptitiously slipped his left hand down below the surface of the desk.

"Interesting. Up to that point, had anyone ever tried to have oral sex or anal intercourse with you?"

"No."

"Had anyone ever showed you a picture of men having oral sex or anal intercourse or described it to you?"

"No."

"Even pictures of naked men, or anything like that?"

"No."

Dr. Babcock's left hand was still somewhere below the surface of the desk. He seemed a little too interested in fishing out these details.

"That's curious. Then how do you suppose you got the idea to imagine this sort of thing and think about it happening with you and another boy?"

"I don't know. I guess it just occurred to me naturally."

"Well, I wouldn't expect the idea of an unnatural act to occur to you naturally."

Bryan frowned.

"Now, do you remember whether either of your parents had explained the birds and the bees to you at this point in your life?"

"What do you mean?"

"Where babies come from. What a man and a woman do together when they're married."

"Only in general terms. Not in any kind of detail."

"I see. And was it your father or your mother who had that conversation with you?"

"My mom."

"Okay, well let's shift gears a bit. Tell me about your relationship with your father while you were growing up."

"What do you mean?"

"Well, for example, did you look up to him? Did you spend a lot of time together? Were you close?"

Bryan took a moment to think about what would be safe to say, and how he should say it.

"Well, he provides for us very well. We have a nice home. There's always food on the table. We've never had to go without anything. I admire how he has been able to build his church into the huge church it is today. He's very passionate about what he believes in."

"So, you admire him a lot. So do I – I think very highly of him. He has accomplished many great things. But would you say you and he are close?"

"Not really."

"Were you closer when you were younger, like say, five years old?"

"No, not really. The church has always taken up a lot of his time. He works very hard. Even when he's not officially working, he's thinking about it."

"Are you close with your mother?"

"More than my dad, yes."

"Has your father been affectionate with you?"

"Like in what ways?"

"Does he ever hug you or put his arm on your shoulder?"

"No."

"When you were little, do you remember if he ever held you or carried you? Like maybe picked you up and put you on his shoulders?"

"Not that I can recall. Maybe when I was little, but I don't remember."

"Does he ever tell you he loves you or he's proud of you? Anything like that?"

Bryan was starting to feel like he was out on a limb. How much should he tell this guy? Will it get back to Dad? Why is he asking all these questions? Maybe some of this stuff needs to come out. Maybe this is an opportunity for things to get better. Maybe some good can come from this.

"No, I can't recall he ever has. I mean, I know he loves me and my brother. He's never hit us or abused us or anything. And like I said, he provides well for us. But I guess our family has never been touchy-feely."

"Do you feel like your father is interested in you?"

Bryan decided this was a chance to get some things off his chest – things he had been holding inside for a long time. Isn't this what counseling is for? For identifying and working through issues? Maybe this guy, who Dad has known since college and respects, can reach Dad. Maybe Dad will listen to him since he's a fellow minister and a counselor.

"Honestly? Not really. I mean, I've been going to Prairie Village High School for three years now, and he has never come to a band concert or a track meet. Not once. There's always something going on at the church that's more important. Back when I was in Scouts, he didn't get involved like some of the other kids' dads did. The only time he would come to a Court of Honor was if I had reached a higher rank, and even then, Mom had to twist his arm to go. I think he feels like it's his job to go out and earn the money and it's Mom's job to keep the house and raise the kids."

Bryan stopped talking. He had said plenty – maybe too much. Dr. Babcock was taking a lot of notes on his yellow pad.

Finally, he spoke. "Thank you for sharing all that. It sounds like you had a few things building up inside you that you wanted to get off your chest."

"Yeah, kinda."

"Well, good. That can be therapeutic, even cathartic. I'd like to go back to something you said at one point in the middle of all that. You said your father has never abused you. Now, I know this is going to be a difficult question, but just do your best. Has anyone ever abused you?"

"No. You mean, like, sexually?"

"That's what I was getting at. It could be something sexual, but also anything you thought was inappropriate or made you feel uncomfortable."

"No, nothing. I guess I've been lucky that way."

"You mentioned you were in Scouts. How about then, like on camping trips or something. Did the scoutmaster or any other adults ever do anything inappropriate?"

"Oh, no. No."

"How about any of the other scouts?"

"No."

"Were you also in Cub Scouts?"

"Yes."

"Anybody there?"

"No."

"A babysitter, maybe? Female or male."

"No. Why are you asking me all these questions?"

"Sorry, I know it's uncomfortable. But a colleague of mine has done a lot of studying into the causes of homosexual attraction and behavior in adults. She has found in her research that virtually every time someone exhibits a tendency toward homosexuality as an adult, they were sexually abused as a child."

"Well, that's not the case here."

"I'm thankful to hear that. I wouldn't wish that on anyone."

"May I ask you a question on a different topic?"

"Of course."

"That prayer you gave me, that you want me to say every morning. It basically asks for God's help to get through that day. Does this mean I'm going to have to say that prayer every day for the rest of my life?"

"Maybe. That sort of depends on you, and on what we uncover during these sessions about why you are struggling with same-sex attraction. Some people have a breakthrough – a moment when they completely resolve and wash away whatever it was that was causing them to feel attracted to men. They never have the desire for someone of the same sex again. They are completely freed.

"But other people are never able to completely break free. Some level of same-sex attraction will always be there, lurking beneath the surface. For them, the best approach is to take it one day at a time, like they do in Alcoholics Anonymous. For those people, it may seem like too big a challenge to be able to say they will never have a homosexual thought for the rest of their lives. That's too much to commit to. But it's easy to say that you can make it through one day without having a homosexual temptation or acting on it. So, they just set a goal for that day."

"So, it's like an alcoholic will always be an alcoholic, but he just promises to not take a drink that day."

"Yes."

"And a homosexual will always be a homosexual, but he promises not to act on it that day."

"Not quite. Remember what I said last week. There is no such thing as a homosexual, only a heterosexual who struggles with same-sex attraction. We are all, at our core, heterosexuals."

"Well, either way, what you're saying is that some people will have same-sex attraction for the rest of their lives. They won't ever be completely cured."

"That's right."

"So, what does that mean for me? If I don't experience one of those miraculous breakthroughs and I feel some level of same-sex attraction for the rest of my life, I'll never be un-grounded? Will I have to keep going to therapy for the rest of my life?"

"I don't know. It's too soon to jump to conclusions about how much you are going to benefit from these sessions."

"But how can we tell? What is going to convince Mom and Dad that I'm cured, or whatever you want to call it, so that I can get at least some of my life back?"

"I suppose that's between you and your parents."

What little hope Bryan had that something good might come from this experience vanished. It all seemed pointless.

Post-Analysis Analysis
Tuesday, July 3, 2007

Later that day at work, Bryan had a chance to talk privately with Mr. Simonton.

"So, how did it go?"

"It was really weird."

"Are you straight yet?"

Bryan rolled his eyes.

"Sorry, this probably isn't the best occasion for snark."

"That's okay. I knew you were joking."

"So, what happened? At least, what do you feel like sharing?"

"Okay, so first he asked me all these questions about what I fantasize about. And when I first started feeling attracted to guys. And it's like he's hanging on every little detail. Like he's getting off on it. In fact, at one point I noticed that his left hand, the one he wasn't writing with, had disappeared down below the desk."

Mr. Simonton's eyes bugged out.

"It's like he was playing with himself while I was telling him all this stuff."

"Maybe his name should be Dr. Grabcock."

Bryan chuckled. "Okay, *that* was funny! But anyway, he also kept asking me if I was ever molested by anybody. And I wasn't. But then he said one of his colleagues says she has never met a gay or lesbian person who wasn't molested at some point in their life."

"I can't believe anyone still buys into that crap. If that's true, then what about all the people who were molested by priests and ended up being straight? Anyway, go on."

"But he kept at it. He kept asking me if it might have been a scoutmaster, a babysitter, or some uncle. He wouldn't let it go."

"It almost sounds like he's trying to bait you or implant memories that don't actually exist."

"Yeah. He said he's trying to pinpoint whatever it was that made me gay, so then he can try to fix it."

Mr. Simonton shook his head.

"Then we got onto me and Dad. He was asking questions like did Dad ever hug me? Did he pay much attention to me? Does he ever tell me he loves me or he's proud of me? That sort of thing."

"Ah, the old absent father, dominant mother theory. That one's been around for decades."

"Yeah, well, in my case it's true. It's like to my dad, raising the kids is the mother's job. He spends all his time doing church stuff. And when he's not doing it, he's thinking about it. I mean, I don't think that made me gay, but that's what it's like in our house. And the whole time, I'm sitting there wondering whether I should be telling him this stuff. I mean, what if it gets back to Dad?"

"Well, one of two things will happen. Either he'll start paying more attention to you or he'll be angry that you told Dr. Grabcock all this stuff."

"Yeah, he'll probably get angry. He'll say I don't appreciate everything he's done for me. But whatever. It felt kind of good to get it off my chest."

"If it jolts him into thinking he needs to spend more time with his kids, then maybe your brother will benefit too."

"And here's the most depressing thing. He said not everyone will be cured. A lot of people will have to pray at the beginning of every day to not act on being gay just for that day. And they have to do that every day for the rest of their lives."

"Sounds like Alcoholics Anonymous."

"Yeah, he used that analogy. And then I said, so how will we know if I'm cured? How do we measure that? How will we know when I can stop going to therapy? Or will I have to do this for the rest of my life? When can I be un-grounded and get at least some of my life back? And he couldn't answer that. He said that was up to Mom and Dad."

"And, of course, the answer is you'll never be cured, because there's nothing you need to be cured of. This so-called reparative therapy is a bunch of crap."

"Yeah. So basically, it's hopeless. And I'm screwed."

Bryan and Mr. Simonton looked at each other for a moment. There was nothing else Mr. Simonton could say, but Bryan could tell at least he empathized. Bryan was glad he had Mr. Simonton to talk to. Otherwise, he'd be completely alone – and even more screwed.

Dr. Ronald Babcock – Third Visit
Tuesday, July 10, 2007

Bryan arrived for his third visit with Dr. Babcock. After the opening pleasantries and prayer, Bryan asked a question that had been on his mind since he first met Dr. Babcock two weeks ago.

"Dr. Babcock, why did you decide to pursue reparative therapy? What training or qualifications do you have that qualify you to do this?"

"Well, as you observed during our first meeting, I have earned a Doctorate in Theology. Part of my study for that degree included training on counseling techniques and applying spiritual and biblical reference points to the counseling I offer. On top of that, I have done a significant amount of research into what causes same-sex attraction. Through my work with organizations such as Family-Focused Ministries, I have developed a network of colleagues who have done similar research and are also experienced in these practices.

"Besides all that, I can bring first-hand experience to this subject. I don't often share this with people, but I feel it's appropriate in this case. You see, I used to be a practicing homosexual. I believed it was just an alternative path that some people take. I believed that whole business about how you should follow your feelings, not follow the Lord, and that was okay.

"After I graduated from Oral Roberts, where I knew your father, I decided that my same-sex attraction and my choice to live openly as a homosexual was incompatible with pursuing a career in ministry. So, I took a secular job.

"I was quite promiscuous back in those days. At the time, I thought that was freedom. But looking back on it now, I can see it was actually enslavement. I met a man who I fell in love with, or at least I thought it was love. We were together for five years.

"That was back in the early years of the AIDS epidemic. Friends of ours started catching that terrible disease. I came to understand this was God's way of showing us this lifestyle was wrong and this was not how he intended us to live. It's God's design for men to be with women and women to be with men. It's what brings forth children. Homosexual activity does not bring about life, and now with AIDS, it brings about death.

"One day, after learning that yet another friend had contracted AIDS, I wandered into the nearest church. I fell on my knees and prayed. I begged for God's forgiveness and mercy. I pleaded to be delivered from this deadly lifestyle. I cried, and I prayed some more. Right then and there, I committed my life to the Lord. I went home and told my partner I had committed my life to the Lord, and I couldn't continue living with him in this lifestyle. I offered to lead him to the Lord too, but he refused. So, I left. I gathered up some of my belongings, loaded up my car, and left everything else behind. I didn't want it anymore – not any of it.

"I enrolled at Bob Jones University in South Carolina and pursued a Master's Degree and a Doctorate. And while I was living there, I met a wonderful young lady named Rachel. she is now my wife and the mother of our three beautiful daughters." He gestured toward the photo.

"So, you see, I have lived through this experience myself. And I realized that I was powerless to cure myself. I can only escape homosexual attraction through daily prayer and the grace of our Lord Jesus Christ."

"Wow. That's quite a story. So, do you still say that prayer every morning? And has it helped you?"

"Yes, I do. Although every time I kiss my wife and tell her I love her, and every time I look at my three daughters, I think about how richly I am blessed. I know in my heart that I am on the right path. That's all I need to keep my thoughts focused where they should be. But enough about me. I'd like to ask you a few questions to follow up on what we discussed last week."

"May I ask you one other question first?"

Dr. Babcock almost sighed out loud. Who's running this session anyway? But it's important to listen. So, he replied, "Okay."

"Last week, you talked about how some people have some sort of breakthrough, and after that, they never feel any same-sex attraction again. How does that happen? What kind of things lead to a breakthrough like that?"

"That's a good question. It varies from person to person, just like what happened early in a person's life that resulted in same-sex attraction varies from person to person. But generally, if we can identify that cause and find some way to resolve it or overcome it, then such a transformation could occur. That's why I have been asking you so many questions. Now, for a moment, I'd like to ask you about your younger brother. What's his name?"

"Brandon."

"And how old is he?"

"He's nine."

"Do you feel that your father is treating Brandon the same way he has treated you during your lifetime?"

"I guess so. What do you mean?"

"Try to think back to when you were nine years old. Was your relationship with your father at that point similar to Brandon's relationship with him now?"

"Yeah, probably. Although Brandon also has me. We're real close. I mean, we both know I'm his big brother and Dad is the head of the household and the authority figure, but I think I fill in some of the gaps in terms of male influence in his life."

"Tell me more."

"Well, I try to play with him several times a week. Sometimes I drive him to Cub Scouts or church when he has something going on there. He likes to listen to me when I'm practicing my trumpet. Sometimes Chris comes over and we practice together. We have these CDs that have piano, bass, and drums on them, and we play along with them. It's kind of like an at-home concert. Brandon loves it, and we don't mind having him there."

"That's very nice of you. So, when you play with him, what do you do?"

"You know, board games like Monopoly or Risk or Life. Sometimes I take him out to a park near our house and throw a ball or a frisbee."

"Nice. And do you talk a lot?"

"Oh yeah. Like I said, we're real close. He's at that age where he's full of questions, and sometimes he feels more comfortable asking me than asking Mom or Dad."

"What sorts of questions?"

"You know, like what's happening in the country or the world, what big words mean, why things are the way they are, what's it's like to be grown up, that kind of stuff."

"Does he ask you about private matters, like sex?"

Uh-oh. Bryan realized he may have said too much and he'd better be careful here.

"Not really. I mean, he's only nine. He's not thinking about that kind of stuff yet."

"But if he does, how do you answer him?"

"I answer in the most age-appropriate way I can. I mean, I'm going to be honest with him. You can't bluff kids or tell them to wait until they're older. They can tell when you're not being truthful with them, and when that happens, you lose their trust. If they're asking now, they want to know now. But you can answer their questions in a way that's appropriate for their age."

"That's very mature of you. When you were younger and you asked your mother or father questions, did you get the impression they were bluffing you or not being truthful with you?"

"Well, I don't think they ever actually lied, but I found out that a lot of stuff was off-limits or made them uncomfortable. So, I learned not to ask them questions about certain things."

"Like what?"

"Anything that wasn't G-rated."

"When you were younger, did you feel like you could ask your dad non-G-rated questions?"

"Not really."

"Have you told Brandon anything about homosexuality, or about you and Chris?"

Red flags were going up everywhere.

"I've never volunteered any information. He has asked me a couple of questions. He figured a lot of it out himself. He's a smart kid."

Dr. Babcock paused and wrote a few things down. Then he moved to a different topic.

"So, last week we established that you and your father haven't been particularly close. You mentioned your father doesn't show much affection. He doesn't tend to verbalize things like praise or that he loves you. And you mentioned he doesn't seem too interested in your activities. Do you wish he had hugged you more? Do you wish he had been more expressive of his love for you?"

"Yeah, I guess so. I mean, it's always been the way it is, so I've just accepted that. It's hard for me to imagine what it would have been like if it was different."

"Well, research has shown that in many cases, homosexuality results when a boy lacks a significant connection with his father, or perhaps some other male authority figure like a grandfather, an uncle, or a big brother. Based on everything you have told me, you fit that profile."

Bryan couldn't argue.

"That could manifest itself as same-sex attraction later when the boy grows up. He seeks affection and affirmation from another man to make up for what he didn't receive from his father. You see, same-sex attraction isn't actually about the sex itself, it's about wanting to feel valued by another man.

"Now, in some cases, that lack of connection can be compensated for or repaired. One technique for that is called Hug Therapy. I would like to give it a try."

Bryan didn't like the sound of this at all, but as with everything else, he didn't feel like he had any choice.

"Well… okay. How does it work?"

"Please stand up." Bryan stood up, and Dr. Babcock rose and walked around his desk to Bryan. "In its most basic form, all you have to do is receive a hug. Ideally, it would be from your father. Maybe this could make up some lost ground with your father."

Dr. Babcock stepped closer to Bryan, wrapped his arms around him, and gave him a lengthy, tight hug.

After a long, uncomfortable twenty seconds or so, Bryan took a step backward. Dr. Babcock took the hint and released him.

"How did that feel?"

"Really awkward, to be honest."

"Do you think you would feel more comfortable if it was your father?"

"Maybe. But I don't get it. How come, if I hug you or my father, that's good, and it will help me overcome same-sex attraction. But if I hug Chris the same way, it's bad?"

"When you hug your father, you are receiving love and affection that would be appropriate coming from your father. When you hug Chris, that's done in a sexual context. In that scenario, it's about physical attraction and lust."

Bryan didn't buy it, but whatever.

"Well, it might have been nice if Dad had hugged me when I was little. And if he had, and that was normal for us, it would probably feel normal now. But if he started hugging me now, it would seem kind of awkward. Like, this isn't normal for us."

"Then let me show you another way we can employ Hug Therapy.

Come over here." Dr. Babcock led Bryan to the couch on the opposite side of his office. He sat down at one end. "You sit here. Now swivel around so you're lying on the couch with your head in my lap."

Bryan apprehensively did as he was asked. Dr. Babcock placed his right arm under Bryan's head and shoulders and lifted Bryan's head toward his chest, like he might cradle a small baby. He laid his other arm across Bryan's chest. He rocked, ever so gently.

"Now, try to imagine you are still a baby. In this position, we're recreating what it might have been like if your father had held you and cuddled you back then. Do you remember your father ever holding you like this?

"No, but I don't remember anything from when I was a baby."

"Does this feel comforting?"

"No, it feels really uncomfortable. Are you suggesting that I should go home and ask my father to do this with me?"

"It's worth a try."

Bryan sat up. "No. I'm sorry, I am not comfortable with this." He got up off the couch and headed toward the door.

"Well, okay, we'll discuss other options next week."

"There won't be a next week. I've had enough. These sessions aren't helping and they're making me extremely uncomfortable."

Bryan walked out the door.

Enough is Enough

Tuesday, July 10, 2007

When Bryan returned home after his third appointment with Dr. Babcock, his mom greeted him as he came in.

"How did your appointment go today?"

"Terrible."

"Why? What happened?"

"He wanted to try out this thing he called Hug Therapy. First, he gave me this long, tight hug. I mean, not the real quick kind people do when they say hello or goodbye. This was like how you and Dad might hug. It went on for like twenty seconds or so, and finally, I had to step away because it was so weird."

"Why would he do that?"

"He thinks maybe Dad didn't hug me enough or pay enough attention to me growing up. So, he thinks maybe getting a lot of hugs now will make up for that."

"Well, it's probably true that your father didn't give you as much attention or affection as he might have."

"Yeah, but I don't think that made me gay. And getting a bunch of hugs now isn't going to make me un-gay. But wait, it gets worse. So, he sat down on the couch. Then he had me lie down on the couch with my head and shoulders on his lap, and he cradled me in his arms like I was still a baby."

His mom looked bewildered.

"Mom, it was the creepiest thing ever. I got up and walked out. And I'm never going back."

"Well, honey, that all sounds rather curious. But he's supposed to be an expert on this. He must know what he's doing."

"Mom, he's a perv! Last week, he was trying to get me to tell him all about my fantasies, and it's like he was getting off on it."

"Well, I don't think your father is going to approve of you stopping therapy after only three weeks."

"You know what? I don't care. Really – I don't. He isn't going to be happy with anything I do. Going to see this guy isn't going to make the gay go away."

"Well, you haven't given it much time. This might take several months."

"Yeah, and that's another thing. He says a lot of people are never really cured of being gay. They have to pray every day just to get through that day without giving in to temptation. So, they'll always have their same-sex attraction, they just never act on it."

"Well, that's better than acting on it."

"But it makes for a miserable life. Anyway, I'm not going back, and that's that."

Bryan retreated to his room until it was time to go to work.

Exceptions to Every Rule
Friday, July 13, 2007

On Friday, Bryan worked an early shift at Price Cutter, so he was home in time for dinner at 5:00.

Brad seemed more upbeat than usual. He mentioned that over 500 people had registered for the Rescued Through Love conference, and he expected more people to sign up at the door. He seemed excited and pleased about that.

Brenda said, "Speaking of the conference tomorrow, we have to be there at 8:00 a.m. I will have breakfast on the table at 7:15. Brandon has a hike with his Cub Scout pack, and they're meeting at 9:00 at the school. Bryan, I need you to drive him there by 9:00 and pick him up at noon. Then when you get home, you can make lunch for the two of you. Would you do that for me?"

"I thought I wasn't allowed to drive while I'm grounded."

Brad said, "Do what your mother tells you. Minus the attitude."

Brenda continued. "Now I know you have to be at work at 3:00. So, I've made arrangements for Brandon to go to the Kleinschmidts' for playtime with Carter and dinner. Can you drop him off on your way to work?"

"Yes, ma'am."

"Good. Brandon, we'll pick you up from the Kleinschmidts' at around 7:30 or 8:00. Okay?"

"Okay," Brandon answered.

Funny how Bryan was grounded and had no car privileges except for work, church, and therapy appointments, but there could be exceptions made when it served his parents' interests. He was just glad they hadn't forced him to attend the conference.

Rescued Through Love
Saturday, July 14, 2007

Saturday morning went according to plan. Bryan drove Brandon to Young Disciples Christian Academy, the same school he had attended through eighth grade. The school sponsored Brandon's Cub Scout pack, the same one Bryan belonged to until he turned eleven and joined the Boy Scouts.

Bryan was back home by 9:10. He had almost three hours at home by himself! He rarely had the whole house to himself, especially since he had started working. Either Mom or Brandon or both were always there. For the next three hours, he could play his trumpet or blast his Maynard Ferguson CDs as loud as he wanted.

But wait! This was a rare opportunity to spend some quality time with Chris. Bryan's mood improved just thinking about it. He raced to the kitchen phone and dialed Chris's cell phone. After a couple of rings, Chris picked up.

"Hello?" It seemed noisy in the background, like Chris was in a crowd.

"Hey, it's me. Got a couple of hours? Brandon's off on a Cub Scout hike and Mom and Dad are at the Rescued Through Love conference all day. You could come over and maybe we could–"

"Sorry man. I'm at the conference too."

"Huh? What are you doing there?"

"Protesting!"

"WHAT???"

"Yeah! About fifty of us from EQ-KC are across the street from the church protesting the conference. Here, listen!"

Chris turned his phone toward the crowd. It was chanting, "Hey hey!

Ho ho! Homophobia has got to go!"

Bryan exploded. "ARE YOU OUT OF YOUR FUCKING MIND??? What if they see you?"

"Of course, they're going to see us. That's the whole point!"

"Not them, YOU. What if they see YOU?"

"What if they do? They know I'm gay. Duh."

"But if they see you there, they're never going to let me see you again."

"You think they're ever going to let you see me again anyway?"

"Oh, fuck it. Never mind. Bye." Bryan slammed the receiver back onto the phone.

Bryan was fuming. He flipped on the stereo in the family room and loaded his Maynard Ferguson *Live at Jimmy's* CD into the tray. He cranked the volume loud enough that he might as well have been sitting in the club when the recording was being made, right in front of the band.

Bryan sat down on the couch and let the music blast at him. It didn't help. After about three songs, he turned it off. He climbed the stairs to his room and plopped down on his bed.

Chris was right. When would his parents ever let him see Chris again? He probably wouldn't be un-grounded unless he could convince his parents he had magically turned straight. Even if he was un-grounded, they wouldn't allow him to see Chris. He'd have to find ways to sneak out to see him. And since his parents had already enrolled him at the Overland Park Christian High School for next year, he wouldn't even see Chris at school.

Even if his parents came around to accepting that Bryan was gay… forget it, that's not going to happen. At that very moment, they were attending the Rescued Through Love conference, sponsored by his dad's church. They were filling their heads with who-knows-what and reinforcing the notion that people can change their orientation if they would only pray long enough and try hard enough.

Bryan lay in his bed staring at the ceiling for at least half an hour. He searched for options, for ideas, for answers. He came up empty.

***

Meanwhile, in the main sanctuary of the Eternal Savior Christian Church, Dr. Stephen Michalowski was delivering his opening keynote speech to almost 600 people. Most of them were the parents of gays and lesbians, or as they were more commonly known in those circles, 'people suffering from same-sex attraction.'

Dr. Michalowski presented some supposedly immutable facts about the serious spiritual affliction of homosexuality.

"Number one: Homosexuality is a developmental problem. It is not a sexual problem, it's a gender identity problem. Gender identity is defined as one's sense of oneself as male or female. And this sense of self is the culmination of a person's relationships, his past hurts, his childhood wounds, his low self-esteem, his deeply-held shame, and his inability to form healthy and meaningful relationships.

"Number two: Homosexuality is not about sex. Those who promote homosexuality and claim it is a natural alternative lifestyle will try to convince you it is only about sex. But that is false. Homosexuality is not about sex. It is an outward expression of an inner sense of emptiness.

"Number three: There is no homosexual gene. Many homosexuals and many of those who promote homosexuality will tell you that they can't help it; they were born that way. My friends, this is completely, unequivocally false. There is no genetic basis for homosexuality. As I said a moment ago, it is a developmental problem."

Dr. Michalowski held everyone's rapt attention. Some people were studiously jotting down notes every time he said something they perceived to be profound or important.

"To understand this, we have to look back at the first few years of a pre-homosexual child's life. During the first eighteen months, he is in the Androgynous Phase. That is, he does not perceive gender in himself or the people around him. During this phase, he bonds with his mother, which is natural.

"But it is the next eighteen months, from about one and a half to three years old, that is crucial. This is what scientists call the Gender Identity Phase. The child develops a greater awareness of the world around him, including the differences between males and females. At this crucial time, the child, who has already bonded with his mother, should recognize his father as being different from his mother. He should begin to understand that he is a male, his father is a male, and he is going to grow up to be like his father. In other words, his father should become his masculine role model.

"Now if the father is absent or weak or emotionally detached, or if the mother is overprotective or domineering or is perceived by the child to be competing with the father, that boy may remain bonded to his mother and reject his father as a role model.

"And that, my friends, is why we so often see Narcissism as a common characteristic of a male homosexual. Narcissism is a preoccupation with oneself. It is being overly sensitive to criticism, rejection, or being disliked by others. It is a defensive posture. It is a shame posture.

"So, if a little boy grows up feeling shame, he is going to feel cautious, fearful, easily hurt, overly sensitive, unlikeable, inferior. All because he did not bond properly with his father.

"What a homosexual is searching for in another man is the sense of masculinity he does not find within himself.

"So, I say to all the fathers in the room – and if you only remember one thing from this talk, I want you to remember this – IF YOU DO NOT HUG YOUR SON, SOME OTHER MAN WILL."

A visceral sense of horror filled the room. Many people in the audience were stunned. Some gasped. Mothers and fathers looked at each other and wondered what either or both of them might have done years ago to cause a Gender Identity Deficit in their child.

For Brenda, what she had suspected for many years had now been confirmed. Brad had always acted as though raising the children was her responsibility. He never once changed a diaper. He never went to Bryan's concerts or track meets. There was always something more important at the church.

Brad was confused. He had refrained from hugging his son because he thought that if he showed him physical affection and he liked it, it would turn him gay. But Dr. Michalowski just said, 'If you don't hug your son, another man will.' So, if he hugs his son, he won't turn out gay, but if another man hugs him, he will? That didn't make any sense.

And besides, his father never hugged him.

***

At around 11:45, Bryan pulled himself together and left to pick up Brandon. Brandon saw him coming, waved goodbye to his fellow Cub Scouts, ran to the car, and climbed in.

"Hey, kiddo, how was your hike?"

"Great!" Brandon was about to launch into his typical monologue, in which he would describe everything that happened in complete detail. But he sensed that this time, maybe he shouldn't.

"Cool. Hey! I know Mom said I should make lunch for us, but how would you like to go out somewhere?"

Brandon lit up. "Sure!"

"Okay. So, let's go home, you can change out of your uniform, then we'll go. You can pick."

Brandon contemplated his options for about two seconds, then replied, "I know... Slush Fun!"

Brandon knew Slush Fun was Bryan's favorite place, so surely this would cheer him up. Besides, he liked Slush Fun too.

Bryan immediately regretted letting Brandon choose. Anywhere but

Slush Fun. He was already bummed out about Chris. Going to the place where he and Chris hung out all the time would only rub it in more. But what could he say? Bryan was at a complete loss for any kind of excuse to go someplace else instead. He forced himself to smile. "Okay! Slush Fun it is!"

Brandon was giddy with excitement. "Mom will be so mad at us if she finds out!"

"But she won't find out, will she?"

"I won't tell!"

"Well, then, it will be our little secret." Bryan reached his hand over, and they did their secret pinky-shake.

Once they arrived at Slush Fun and ordered, Bryan was starting to feel better. He truly loved Brandon and enjoyed spending time with him. He hadn't spent as much time with him over the past couple of months since he had been working and hanging out more with Chris. Brandon's glee over getting to spend time with his big brother, along with subverting their mother's wishes for them to eat healthier food, was infectious.

Just as the food was arriving, another car pulled into a space farther down the row on the opposite side. It was Chris, with three other young people Bryan didn't recognize. He guessed they were probably kids from Pathways who had been at the protest. A new wave of sadness washed over Bryan, completely erasing any improvement in his mood over the past half-hour.

Bryan turned to Brandon. "Hey, I have an idea. Let's take our food over to Hanson Park and eat at one of the picnic tables. If either one of us spills food in Mom's car she will be so upset, and she'll know we came here."

"I'll be careful."

"No, I think this is a better idea. And we can stop by the house and get the frisbee and throw it afterward."

That sealed the deal. Brandon was in. Bryan pulled the car out and drove away. Chris didn't seem to notice.

***

After the lunch break at the Rescued Through Love conference, where presenters and attendees had mingled over catered box lunches, Dr. Ronald Babcock was addressing the audience at the afternoon keynote.

"Many of you are here today because you have two questions for which you seek answers. One, why is my child homosexual? And two, what can I do about it?

"My colleague and friend Dr. Michalowski spoke this morning about the root causes of homosexuality early in a child's life. This afternoon I am going to share with you the pathways to recovery. Or, in other words, what you can do about it.

"First, we need to be clear on one thing. There is no such thing as a homosexual. There is only a heterosexual who has a homosexual problem. There is only a heterosexual who struggles with same-sex attraction.

"Individuals don't have to be homosexual. Homosexual identity is something that can be overcome. When a patient, with the guidance of a therapist, can identify what was missing from his life early on, then we can examine ways to fill those needs today in a healthy way.

"When a gay man's sense of masculinity is restored, when he no longer looks to other men for the parts of his masculinity that he feels is missing in himself, then his same-sex attraction disappears. There is no more mystique and no more eroticization.

"One of my recent patients experienced a complete and total recovery. The boy and his father made an emotional breakthrough during a therapy session. When this connection between the father and the son was restored, the son's homosexuality disappeared.

"Now, I have to be clear that complete eradication of homosexual attraction may not be possible in every case. For some people, their unwanted same-sex attraction will be something they struggle with for the rest of their lives."

Dr. Babcock walked to the front edge of the stage as if to be closer to the audience. He lowered his voice, although he still had his microphone to ensure that he would be easily heard. "My friends, I hesitate to share this story. It is deeply personal. But I feel called to do so today. I feel the love and the warmth of the Holy Spirit in this room. So, I would like to share this story with you now.

"You see, I used to be a practicing homosexual. I believed it was just an alternative path that some people take. I believed that whole business about how you should follow your feelings, not follow the Lord, and that was okay.

"After I graduated from Oral Roberts, where I knew your father, I decided that my same-sex attraction and my choice to live openly as a homosexual was incompatible with pursuing a career in ministry. So, I took a secular job.

"I was quite promiscuous back in those days. At the time, I thought that was freedom. But looking back on it now, I can see it was actually enslavement. I met a man who I fell in love with, or at least I thought it was love. We were together for five years.

"That was back in the early years of the AIDS epidemic. Friends of ours started catching that terrible disease. I came to understand this was God's way of showing us this lifestyle was wrong and this was not how he intended us to live. It's God's design for men to be with women and women to be with men. It's what brings forth children. Homosexual activity does not bring about life, and now with AIDS, it brings about death.

No one in the room stirred. All eyes were riveted on Dr. Babcock.

"One day, after learning that yet another friend had contracted AIDS, I wandered into the nearest church. I fell on my knees and prayed. I begged for God's forgiveness and mercy. I pleaded to be delivered from this deadly lifestyle. I cried, and I prayed some more. Right then and there, I committed my life to the Lord. I went home and told my partner I had committed my life to the Lord, and I couldn't continue living with him in this lifestyle. I offered to lead him to the Lord too, but he refused. So, I left. I gathered up some of my belongings, loaded up my car, and left everything else behind. I didn't want it anymore – not any of it.

"I enrolled at Bob Jones University in South Carolina and pursued a Master's Degree and a Doctorate. And while I was living there, I met a wonderful young lady named Rachel. she is now my wife and the mother of our three beautiful daughters." He gestured toward Rachel, who was sitting in the front row.

"So, you see, I have lived through this experience myself. And I realized that I was powerless to cure myself. I can only escape homosexual attraction through daily prayer and the grace of our Lord Jesus Christ."

A chorus of amens arose from the audience.

"My friends, I now know that the opposite of homosexuality is not heterosexuality. Remember, we are all, at our core, heterosexuals. No, my friends. The opposite of homosexuality is holiness. It is through God's grace and the power of prayer that those who are afflicted with same-sex attraction can live a righteous life."

More amens.

"And so, every single morning when I wake up, I pray, 'Dear Lord, I can't make it through this day without You. Today, I will choose not to think impure thoughts. Today, I will choose not to act on those impulses in any way. I choose to submit my will to the direction You have for my life. I choose to follow You. I choose to allow Your Holy Spirit to walk before me, to guide me, to speak for me.'"

Everyone leaped to their feet and showered Dr. Babcock with thunderous applause to thank him for baring his soul before them and to congratulate him on his triumph over homosexuality.

The conference closed with a presentation by Dr. Jennifer Moreland, who claimed she had performed extensive research on sexual abuse and the devastating impact it had on children and families. She claimed to be a recovered lesbian.

The most memorable moment of her speech came when she made this unequivocal statement:

"Mothers, fathers, and family members. What I am about to say will not be easy for you to hear. I have been ministering to people who struggle with same-sex attraction for over fifteen years. And during all those years, I have never met a woman who was struggling with lesbianism, who had not been sexually violated or sexually threatened at some point in her life. Not one woman. And I have never met a man who was struggling with homosexuality, who had not been sexually violated or sexually seduced at some point in his life. Not one man."

Gasps filled the auditorium. Many parents, including Brad and Brenda, began scrolling back through their children's lives, wondering who it might have been that abused their child. The scoutmaster? The choir director? An uncle or cousin? The father or older brother of a playmate?

So many people would be needlessly accused.

***

After the conference ended and people were filing out, Brad and Brenda invited Ron and Rachel to have dinner with them at a nice restaurant.

Brad wanted to discuss with Ron what steps they would take next with Bryan, who had declared that he would no longer be attending counseling.

No Way Forward

Saturday, July 14, 2007

That evening, at a few minutes before seven, Chris entered Price Cutter. He walked across the store, right to left, looking up and down each aisle for Bryan.

He found him in the canned fruits and vegetables aisle, straightening up the shelves. He was filling gaps by moving cans to the front of the shelves and making sure every product was in its proper place.

"Hey."

"Hey." Bryan continued to straighten up cans.

"Are you going on your break at seven?"

Bryan glanced at this watch. He hadn't been paying attention to the time. He needed to keep himself busy. "Yeah, I guess. I'll meet you in one of the booths up front in a few minutes."

Bryan walked to the frozen food aisle, selected a Hungry Hombré entrée from the freezer, and headed toward the deli counter. He grabbed a plastic-wrapped fork and a handful of napkins from the end of the salad bar. He yanked a Styrofoam cup from the dispenser on the side of the soda fountain and filled the cup with ice and Dr Pepper. He entered the booth area, placed the entrée in the microwave, and set the timer for five minutes. He would save the cup and the entrée box and pay for them later.

He turned to Chris. "You want anything?"

"Nah… I've already eaten."

Bryan sat down across from Chris. "Hey, look. I'm sorry I yelled at you this morning. I'm sorry I dropped an F-bomb on you."

"Never mind that. Did you get my email?"

"No. I haven't checked my email all day. I was playing with

Brandon until I came here."

"Okay, well, we need to talk. I don't care about you yelling at me or saying fuck. But I can't believe you were angry with me for being there to protest that fucking conference. I mean, the whole reason I was there was for you."

"Why? Did you really think it would do any good? They spent thousands of dollars to hold that conference. Hundreds of people showed up for it. Did you really think they would walk out on stage and say, 'The conference is canceled. Those protesters across the street are right! We've been totally wrong about this. Gay people are wonderful! Go home and hug your gay kids.'"

"Probably not. But if we do nothing, how is anything going to change?"

"I don't know. But holding protests is not going to change them. You're never going to change anyone's mind by annoying them."

"Well, EQ-KC has been at this a lot longer than you or I have. They must think protesting has some benefit or they wouldn't be doing it. And we got some news coverage. Besides, remember those people from the Eastlawn Baptist Church who were protesting at the Pride Festival? They got to you a little bit, didn't they?"

"Did you like seeing them there? Do you think they convinced anybody not to be gay anymore?"

"Probably not."

"Okay, then. You were just as annoying to the people who went to the conference this morning as the people from Eastlawn Baptist Church were to us. And no more effective."

"God. It almost sounds like you're standing up for them."

"I'm not. But back to us. If my parents saw you there, there's no way they'll ever let me hang around with you again."

"And under what conditions are they going to let you see me again anyway? Remember, I'm the evil queer boy who recruited you into the gay lifestyle."

Bing! The microwave signaled that Bryan's entrée was ready. He got up, carried his dinner from the microwave to the table, helped himself to a soda refill, and sat down.

Bryan said, "Maybe in a couple of months they'll come around and realize that me being gay isn't so bad after all." He didn't really believe that, but you never know.

"Yeah, right. After that conference, they're probably more homophobic than ever."

Bryan took a couple of bites from his dinner. Chris was right, but he still didn't like to hear him talking about his parents that way.

Chris continued, "So what's it going to take for them to un-ground you?"

"I don't know. I'll probably be grounded until I can somehow convince them I'm straight."

"Right. And part of convincing them you're straight is not hanging around with gay people like me. And didn't you say your folks are going to send you to some Christian school next year?"

Bryan nodded.

"So, I won't ever get to see you. I won't see you in band or classes or at lunch or on the track team. So, the only way I'll get to see you is if I come to the store on your break."

"And I'm only working here for the summer."

"Right. And we can't talk on the phone 'cause they took your phone away. So where does that leave us?"

Bryan sighed. "Nowhere, I guess. At least, not for now. Maybe next year we can still try to go to college together."

"Maybe. But that's a year away."

"So, what are you saying?"

"I'm saying I just don't see a way forward for us. Look, Bryan, you're the most wonderful guy I've ever met. The moment I laid eyes on you when you showed up at band camp three years ago, I knew you were special. You're everything I want in a partner, except for being so closeted. And I've tried to be patient with that. It's been really hard to pull you along, but I've tried. And sometimes it felt like you were pushing back, like you wanted to stay in your closet and keep everything the same."

Bryan stared down at his food and poked at the last few bites of his dinner.

"I can't go on like this. I can't go on not being able to see you or even talk with you on the phone. And I don't see how anything is going to change with your folks. Yeah, maybe next year we'll go to college together. But I've got my whole senior year ahead of me. I'm meeting a lot of new kids at Pathways. There are other gay kids at school too. I'm not going to stay home by myself, wishing I could see you when I can't."

Bryan sat motionlessly.

Chris got up from his side of the table and walked over to Bryan. He placed his hand on Bryan's shoulder. "I love you, Bryan Bauer. I always have and I always will. Maybe someday things will be different and we can make it work."

And with that, he leaned down and kissed Bryan on the cheek. Then he turned and walked out.

The Showdown
Sunday, July 15, 2007

On Sunday, the day after the Rescued Through Love conference, Bryan just went through the motions at church. With being dumped by Chris added to everything else that had happened over the past three weeks, Bryan felt more depressed and hopeless than he had ever felt in his life.

The family's weekly post-church lunch out had been weird. Nobody said anything of substance. Brandon picked up on Bryan's low mood and was not being his usual happy, exuberant self. His parents – especially his dad – seemed strangely upbeat. That concerned Bryan. What kind of half-baked quackery had they heard at the conference? What new things were they going to try in their quest to cure him of being gay?

Not long after they returned home, Brenda drove Brandon to the local pool, where some friends in his Cub Scout troop were going swimming. For all Bryan knew, Chris was going to be one of the lifeguards on duty.

While they were gone, Brad called Bryan into his office. He pointed to a stack of handouts and notes from the conference on the corner of his desk. "Son, would you please scan all these handouts from yesterday? Then I would like you to create a new section on the website. Call it 'Resources for Parents and Families of People Struggling with Same-sex Attraction' or something. I know that's kind of long, so see if you can come up with something shorter. Anyway, upload all this stuff and create a Resources page. There's also some URLs they can link to."

Wonderful, Bryan thought. Won't this be fun.

"Oh, and Bryan?" Brad took a step closer to Bryan. "I probably don't tell you this often enough, but I appreciate the great job you do on the church's website and the PowerPoints each week."

Well, that was unexpected, especially after all the conflict of the past three weeks. Bryan smiled. "Thanks, Dad."

Brad took another couple of steps forward and hugged Bryan. After a few seconds, he released the hug and took a couple of steps back again. He acted like he had just checked an item off his to-do list.

For a few seconds, neither of them said anything. Bryan fished for something to say to move them beyond this strange moment. "When do you need it done by?"

"There's no hard deadline, but sooner rather than later. Maybe within the next two or three days? I want to be able to send an email out to everyone who attended the conference to let them know it's there."

"Okay."

Bryan gathered up the documents, left the office, and returned to his room.

***

A short time later, Brenda returned from taking Brandon to the pool. She climbed the stairs to Bryan's room, knocked on the door, and said, "Bryan, would you please come to your father's office for a few minutes?"

Bryan had no idea what to expect. The last time he was summoned to his father's office in this manner, he was busted for being gay. But a few minutes ago, it was all hugs and appreciation. If there was something else, why didn't he tell him then?

Brad began. "Son, according to your mother, you have decided that you won't be continuing your counseling sessions with Dr. Babcock. Is that true?"

"Yes, sir."

"At what point were you planning to tell me?"

"I don't know. I guess I was just waiting for a good time, and that hasn't come yet."

"Be that as it may, why do you think you don't need to continue on your path to recovery?"

"It wasn't doing any good. And it was making me extremely uncomfortable."

"Change, especially change of this nature, is usually uncomfortable. Often, the right path is not the easiest. Sometimes, it's the most difficult."

"It's not about being easy or difficult. It was creepy!"

"Oh really? And why is that?"

"He kept asking me if I was ever molested, or if anyone had ever touched me inappropriately, stuff like that. I kept telling him no, but he wouldn't let it go."

"Well, this is a common thread among people who feel homosexual attraction."

"Then he kept asking me to tell him what kind of things I fantasize about, or what Chris and I do together, that kind of stuff."

"And…"

Bryan started to get agitated. "And the whole time he had his hand down below the desk like he was playing with himself! It's like he was getting off on hearing me talk about this kind of stuff!"

"Now, surely, you didn't see him doing anything like that."

"Well, no, I couldn't see what his hand was doing. But I could tell he was getting some kind of cheap thrills from hearing me talk about that stuff."

"I think you're imagining something that wasn't actually there."

"And then, he started talking about how maybe I wasn't hugged enough while I was growing up. And he wanted to try this thing he called 'Hug Therapy.' So, he made me stand up and he gave me this long, really awkward hug."

"And what's wrong with a hug? I hugged you a little while ago. Was there something wrong with that?"

"He was getting a boner!!!"

Brenda let out a little gasp.

"And then, he sat down on the couch and had me lie across the couch. Then he held my head and shoulders in his arms and started cuddling me like I was a baby or something. I'm telling you, it was the weirdest thing I've ever experienced. It was totally creepy. I felt … violated! Anyway, I can't see how doing this kind of stuff is going to stop me from being gay. I mean, think about it. If I'm attracted to men, wouldn't I enjoy holding and being held by another man?"

Brad said, "But it doesn't sound like you enjoyed it."

"It grossed me out. Oh… wait… so is that it? Is he trying to cure me by making me feel disgusted when I'm held by another man?"

"It seems to have had that effect."

"Well, okay, then – I'm cured! I can stop going! Success! I must be straight now. Mission accomplished!"

"Not so fast. After only three weeks? Nobody gets cleansed of their homosexual tendencies that quickly."

"Maybe I'm a fast learner. But you know what else he told me? He said most people never actually get over their same-sex attraction. They just push it down. They try to ignore it. They have to pray to get through each day without acting on the homosexual thoughts they still have. Like he said the first week, some people just remain celibate and pray they don't give in to temptation."

"Prayer is a powerful thing. That's why it works."

"Yeah, well it means those people are never actually cured. So, what then? Do I have to see him every week for the rest of my life?"

Brad didn't have an answer for that.

"That works out well for Dr. Babcock, doesn't it? Seventy-five dollars a week! Ka-ching!"

"Well, I don't think he's in this for the money."

"Oh, please. Would you keep preaching at the church if you had to do it for free? And let me tell you something else about Dr. Babcock. He told me he used to be a homosexual. Had a partner and everything. But then he had this Road to Damascus moment, found some woman to marry, and now he has three kids. Like that proves he's straight now. Brad replied, "Yes, I am aware of his background. That's why I believe he can help you. He's been down that road himself. He knows what it takes to leave the homosexual lifestyle."

"Yeah, well, he isn't really cured. He says he still has to pray every day to keep those homosexual impulses away. And based on what I've just experienced, he's not being too successful."

Brad became defensive. "What are you saying?"

"I'm saying he still has plenty of homosexual thoughts – including for me. It's totally obvious. I can tell by how he holds my hands when we pray – he gives them these odd little squeezes, like he's massaging my hands. He's getting off on hearing what I fantasize about. And the hugging. And the boner. And the way he looks at me. And you know what else? He keeps talking about how much I look like you when you were in college. He used to be openly gay. He probably had this big crush on you when you were in college together. Now he sees me, and I remind him of you."

Brad was silent. Brenda looked like some pieces were starting to come together.

Bryan said, "He seemed awfully happy to see you a couple of weeks ago."

Brad finally spoke. "Well, even if that's the case, which I can't believe it is, the fact remains that despite what urges he may still have, he is not living the homosexual lifestyle anymore. He has a wife and three daughters. He is living as God intended."

"He is living a lie."

"No, the Bible makes it perfectly clear." Brad reached for the ornate Bible on his desk and opened it near the beginning. He thumbed through several pages until he reached Leviticus. "Here it is. Leviticus chapter

18, verse 22. 'You shall not lie with a male as with a woman; it is an abomination.'"

Bryan replied, "Well, there you have it. All neatly summed up in one short little verse." Bryan turned to Brenda. "So, Mom, that means God is commanding you to be a lesbian."

Brenda recoiled. "What???"

"Yes, that's exactly what it says. It says you shall not lie with a man as you would with a woman. It is an abomination."

Brad replied, "Obviously, it's talking about men."

"It doesn't say that. It just says 'you.' Or maybe women don't even count in the Bible. Oh, that's right. They're just property. Back then, a man could have as many wives as he wanted. Jacob had two, right? And some handmaidens. And Solomon had like 700 wives and 300 concubines. Man, that dude must have been quite a stud."

"Well, that was the way it was back then, but–"

"Oh, okay. So, we can leave the multiple wives thing back in the old days. But that one about gays – that still applies today."

Brad said nothing.

"Oh, and while we're in Leviticus… Do you mind?" Bryan stepped forward and took the Bible from Brad's hands. "Let's see… Ah, yes. There's Leviticus chapter 11, verse 7. 'And the swine, because it parts the hoof and is cloven-footed but does not chew the cud, is unclean to you.' But that doesn't stop us from eating ham and pork and bacon. And how about verse 12? 'Everything in the waters that has not fins and scales is an abomination to you.' So, eating fish is okay, but not shrimp or crab or lobster or anything like that. Yet we eat those things. So, where do you draw the line?

"And one more. Let's look to Leviticus chapter 15, shall we? 'If a woman conceives, and bears a male child, then she shall be unclean seven days; as at the time of her menstruation, she shall be unclean. … Then she shall continue for thirty-three days in the blood of her purifying; she shall not touch any hallowed thing, nor come into the sanctuary, until the days of her purifying are completed.'

"So, really Mom? Did you stay home from church for 40 days after Brandon and I were born because you were unclean?"

Brenda said nothing.

Brad said, "Well, aren't you quite the biblical scholar?"

Bryan replied, "I thought maybe you'd be proud of me for that. I guess not. But wait, there's more in chapter 12. 'And when the days of her purifying are completed, whether for a son or a daughter, she shall bring to the priest at the door of the tent of meeting a lamb a year old for a burnt offering, and a young pigeon or a turtledove for a sin offering, and he shall offer it before the Lord, and make atonement for her; then she shall be clean from the flow of her blood.' So, did you bring a lamb for a burnt offering after we were born? And did you offer a bird to atone for some kind of sin?"

His parents were speechless.

"Okay, so none of that stuff applies anymore. But the one line about sleeping with a man? That one's still in full force. Right? That's what you believe? You think you can pick and choose which verses apply to you and which don't?"

Bryan clapped the Bible shut and slammed it down onto the desk. "Well, that's BULLSHIT! I am your son. I'm a good kid. I don't smoke or drink or use drugs. I've never gotten in trouble. I get A's in school. I'm the first-chair trumpet and a star of the track team. I go to church every week, I maintain your website, and I do tech stuff for your services every week. So, I've found someone I really like. No – someone I LOVE. That's right, I LOVE someone. And he happens to be a man instead of a woman. So what? It's still love. And he makes me happy – happier than I've ever been in my life.

"I don't deserve this abuse you've put me through these past three weeks. And that's just what it is – ABUSE. I deserve to be loved – for exactly who I am. So, no. I am not going to see Dr. Babcock again, nor will I tolerate any other kind of gay conversion therapy BULLSHIT you might think of. IS THAT CLEAR???"

His parents sat there shocked.

Bryan turned and stormed out of the room.

After a moment, Brad said, "Where did THAT come from?"

Brenda replied, "Looks like the apple didn't fall far from the tree."

Nothing Is Normal

Saturday, July 21, 2007

During the week following the blow-up, everything seemed strangely normal – like nothing had ever happened. Except that Bryan was still grounded and still couldn't use his phone. Neither of his parents said anything about him going to see Dr. Babcock on Tuesday. Something had to be up, but Bryan couldn't put his finger on anything.

On Saturday, Bryan, Brandon, and Brenda sat down for lunch. Brad was already at the church, finishing his sermon and preparing for the upcoming services.

Brenda seemed preoccupied, like something heavy was on her mind. No one said much as they ate.

Finally, she asked Bryan, "What does your day look like, dear?"

"I'm heading down to the church to get the PowerPoint slides ready for tomorrow. I'll be back at around 2:30 to change into my work shirt, then I work from three to eleven."

"Sounds like a full day."

Bryan finished his chicken salad sandwich and baked beans and put his dirty plate in the dishwasher. "Okay, bye."

Brenda stood up. "Goodbye, sweetheart." Bryan usually gave her a quick little kiss on the cheek, but this time she took a step toward him and opened her arms. She gave him a warm hug that lasted at least five seconds and then kissed him on the cheek as she released him from the hug. "I love you."

"I love you too, Mom."

Bryan took a couple of steps back toward the table and fist-bumped Brandon. "Later, kiddo."

"Later!"

And with that, Bryan headed to the garage. He donned his helmet, pulled his bike out, closed the garage door with the keypad, and rode off toward the church.

After Brenda and Brandon finished lunch, Brenda walked out to the garage. She returned with two small rolling suitcases, Brandon's and hers. She said, "Guess what, honey? We're going to visit Grandma for a few days!"

That seemed sudden, but whatever. Brandon loved going to see Grandma.

"You'll need to pack about three days' worth of clothes. Don't forget your toothbrush and your comb. And you can take a couple of your games and two or three books to read."

Brandon grabbed his suitcase and ran up to his room, excited about their sudden trip.

Brenda returned to the garage and retrieved Bryan's suitcase – the larger one you'd check on an airplane. She carried it and her suitcase to her room.

***

When Bryan arrived at the church office, his dad's door was closed. He could hear him talking on the phone. He thought better of interrupting him, so he hung around in the outer office.

He found the bulletin for this week's services. That would give him most of what he needed for the PowerPoint – the hymn selections, the group prayers, and other announcements. All he needed was his dad's sermon notes.

His dad was still talking. Bryan didn't intend to eavesdrop, but he couldn't help hearing bits and pieces of what his dad was saying.

"There are no direct flights to Montgomery. We're going to have to connect in Atlanta. It's only an hour and 20 minutes, though."

"2:55. That means we need to leave here at around one."

"Okay, it's booked. I'll forward the flight info to your email."

"Nah, Brenda is taking him to Tulsa to see his grandmother, so he'll be out of the way."

"Did you line up a couple of other guys? Great. Hey, thanks for all your help with getting this organized."

"Okay. We roll at one! … Bye."

How odd. Bryan couldn't recall any talk about anyone traveling to Montgomery or Tulsa.

Bryan waited about ten seconds, then knocked on the door.

"Yes? Come in."

"Hey, Dad, what's up? I'm going to work on the PowerPoint for tomorrow. Do you have your sermon ready yet?"

"No, not yet. I'm running behind. I've had a bunch of other stuff to deal with today. I'm just getting started. Can I email it to you later?"

"I have to work from three to eleven today."

"Well, go ahead and take the laptop home. You can get the other stuff done this afternoon, then add my stuff in after you get home tonight. Maybe they'll let you off early."

"Okay."

Bryan turned and left. His dad was always doing this to him. Like everything revolves around his schedule and he couldn't care less about what Bryan might have going on.

Bryan walked up to the control booth. He stuffed the laptop, the power cord, and the wireless mouse into the carrying case and headed out. He could work on this at home until it was time to leave for work. He returned to his bike, slung the laptop case over his shoulder, and pedaled home.

***

When Bryan turned into their driveway, he saw that his mother had opened the garage door and was loading a couple of suitcases into the trunk. When she turned and saw Bryan, she seemed startled. But he had returned home sooner than he said he would.

She closed the trunk and called out to Brandon, "Get in the car, honey."

Bryan rode up. "What's going on?"

Brandon said, "We're going to see Grandma! Hurry up and pack!"

Brenda replied to Brandon, "No, it's just you and me going this time. Bryan has a job and he has to work, remember?"

"Awwwww..."

"Please get in the car. Time to go!"

Brenda quickly got into the car and shifted it into reverse. Bryan, still straddling his bicycle, moved to the side to avoid being hit. She backed out quickly. She turned around to guide the car down the driveway. She didn't look back at him.

Bryan watched as the car backed down the driveway. From the passenger seat, Brandon was staring at him in disbelief, unable to understand what was going on. He had never gone to Grandma's without Bryan. It had always been him and Bryan and Mom, and sometimes Dad depending on his schedule.

Brenda backed the car into the street. Bryan and Brandon waved at each other until the car was out of sight.

***

Bryan entered the house. Something was not right. Too many fishy things were happening. His dad was talking about going to Montgomery – but when? He mentioned Mom and Brandon going to Tulsa – but today? Why hadn't Mom said anything about this at lunch? Why had Mom given him a bigger hug than usual, then avoided looking at him just now?

Bryan bounded up the stairs to his room, carrying the laptop. He pulled it out of the case and started it up.

He logged onto the church's web hosting provider, as he had done many times before when working on the church's website. He navigated to the email hosting section and opened his dad's email folder. He scrolled up and down his dad's inbox, looking for anything that might give him a clue about what was going on.

When he scrolled back to the top, a new email appeared. It was from Ronald Babcock, Ph.D. titled, "Re: Montgomery itinerary." He clicked on it. The reply only said, "Got it. Thanks!" Bryan scrolled down to read the original message his dad had sent to him.

A half-hour earlier, his dad had forwarded to Dr. Babcock a travel confirmation with flight numbers and times, a car rental for a Cadillac, and a hotel reservation for a deluxe suite at the Helton Grande. Nice. On the infrequent occasions when the family traveled, they stayed in budget hotels. Maybe there's some kind of religious conference going on there.

He took a closer look. The outbound flight was tomorrow – Sunday – at 2:55 p.m. The return flight was the next day. There was a connection in Atlanta.

Then he looked at the passenger listing. There were three passengers listed on the flight to Montgomery – his dad, Dr. Babcock … and HIM.

Only two passengers were returning on Monday – his dad and Dr. Babcock. WHAT THE ACTUAL FUCK???

Bryan returned to the list of emails in the inbox and clicked the 'Sent by' column to sort the emails by sender. His dad and Dr. Babcock had exchanged a lot of emails over the past few weeks.

He scrolled down a bit, and selected one from about four weeks ago with the subject, 'Progress Update.' He opened it.

> Dear Brad,
> The first session went okay.
> He is hesitant to tell me what he thinks about. Until he does, it will be hard for me to help him redirect his thoughts. Hopefully, we can build more trust in the coming weeks.

We prayed. I gave him a prayer to say every day during the coming week.

In Christ's love,

Ron

Bryan was incensed. Dr. Babcock had been reporting back to his dad on everything they had talked about! So much for doctor-patient confidentiality.

He scrolled up to the next 'Progress Update' email from the following week's appointment.

Dear Brad,

This week didn't go so well. I tried to get him to share more about what sort of thoughts he has, but he wouldn't give details.

I asked if anyone had ever molested him or touched him inappropriately. He said no, but this is a pretty universal theme among those who struggle with SSA.

One thing he mentioned is he thinks you haven't been involved enough in his life. I asked if you ever hug him, and he said no. I suspect this might be an issue. Boys need strong male role models in their lives. If he doesn't feel he's getting enough love or attention from you, he will try to find it from other men.

Maybe try showing a little more interest in him. Compliment him now and then. Tell him you love him.

He asked many questions about the journey ahead. Asked if he would always feel SSA or if it would go away.

In Christ's love,

Ron

Bryan was livid. It's a good thing he wasn't going to see Dr.

Babcock ever again because if he did, he would probably punch him out.

He scrolled up to 'Progress Update: Week 3.'

Dear Brad,

Your son is a nice young man, but he's a tough nut to crack. And he asks a lot of questions. He asked about my training and qualifications to do this work. I shared the relevant portions of my past with him.

He asked about how those who can completely break free of their SSA were able to do it. So at least he's thinking along those lines.

We talked about his relationship with Brandon. They seem to be very close. I suspect Bryan is giving him too much information. Brandon is asking him questions he should be asking you. It appears that Bryan is overstepping his role as a brother and trying to take over some of your role as the father. Brandon appears to idolize Bryan. It seems unhealthy, in my opinion.

We talked more about his relationship with you.

As a colleague of mine likes to say, "if you don't hug your son, another man will." So, try to spend more time with your son. Talk to him. Keep it positive. Tell him you love him. Hug him.

I introduced him to hug therapy. That's where I sit on the couch, he lays down with his head on my chest like he might have done with you when he was a little boy. I hugged him. It's supposed to bring him comfort and make him feel validated. It didn't go well. After a moment, he got up. Said he was very uncomfortable. It might go better if you try it with him.

Then he announced that he didn't want to participate in any more sessions and left. I will leave that for you and him to work out. I'll keep the appointments on my calendar unless you advise otherwise.

In Christ's love,
Ron

Bryan felt betrayed. He felt like he had been violated. And he was furious over the part about Brandon.

He closed the message and scrolled up to 'Re: Re: Progress Update: Week 3.'

Dear Brad,

Okay, I will cancel future appointments. I'll find the link to the place Michalowski was talking about at RTL and send it to you.

In Christ's love,
Ron

Bryan scrolled farther down the email to read the message his dad had sent to Dr. Babcock.

Dear Ron,

I talked to him. No go. He simply refuses to participate in his own recovery. Now he is exhibiting rebellious behavior. He yelled and cursed at Brenda and me. Highly disrespectful and inappropriate.

Go ahead and cancel future appointments. Let us know how much we owe you.

I'm afraid we'll have to move on to Plan B.

I was hoping it would not come to this, but – whatever it takes, I guess.

B.

Babcock sent another email five minutes later. The subject read

'Youth Restoration Project.' Bryan clicked to open it. It contained the URL www.YouthRestorationProject.org.

This looked ominous. Bryan right-clicked and opened the link in a new tab.

Bryan looked around the website. It was filled with phrases such as 'leaving the homosexual lifestyle,' 'unwanted same-sex attraction,' 'leading them back to God's light,' 'God's plan for their lives,' 'healing broken souls,' 'restoring their faith in the Lord,' and on and on. There were a few pictures that showed plain, almost austere surroundings. One picture showed a small dining hall. One showed a small yard with a few shrubs. One showed an adult speaking to a small cluster of sad, homely teens.

It was a gay conversion facility.

Bryan found the address, copied it, and pasted it into Google Maps. It was thirty miles or so outside of Montgomery, Alabama. He jotted down the URL and stuffed the piece of paper in his pocket.

He scanned the subject lines of the emails from the past week. He spotted an email from Youth Restoration Project with the subject 'Receipt and Confirmation,' dated last Tuesday. He opened it.

> Dear Rev. Bauer,
>
> We have received your payment of $2,400.00. This covers the pro-rated fee of $600 ($60 per night) for the remainder of July and $1,800 for August. Thereafter, payment of $1,800.00 will be due on the first day of each month.
>
> We have Bryan's room ready and we look forward to his arrival on Sunday, July 22 at approximately 8:00 p.m.
>
> Thank you for choosing Youth Restoration Project for your son's healing. We look forward to serving him.
>
> In Christ's love,
> Jeanine Lawrence, Administrator

Bryan couldn't believe his eyes.

He closed the lid on the laptop, changed into his Price Cutter uniform shirt, and raced downstairs to his bicycle.

The Only Viable Option
Saturday, July 21, 2007

Bryan reached Price Cutter in record time. After chaining his bike to the bike rack, he hurried in. Hopefully, Mr. Simonton would be there.

As Bryan passed by the meat counter, he saw Mr. Simonton in the butcher shop talking to Mr. Weiner. Mr. Simonton immediately noticed the distressed look on Bryan's face and held up one finger, signaling 'just a minute.'

Mr. Simonton finished his conversation with Mr. Weiner and emerged from the back. "What's up?"

"Can we talk? In your office?" Bryan was on the verge of panic.

"Sure."

As soon as they were both inside and Mr. Simonton had shut the door, Bryan let loose. "Okay. So, I went down to the church after lunch to work on stuff for the services tomorrow and Dad's in his office with the door closed and I can hear him talking to some guy – I think it was Dr. Babcock but I don't know for sure – and they were talking about flying to Montgomery and then he said something about Mom taking Brandon to Tulsa to see our Grandma and like no one had said anything about any of this before and I could tell something funny is going on but like none of this makes any sense and so–"

"Whoa! Whoa!" Mr. Simonton interrupted. "None of this makes any sense to me either. Here, sit down. Breathe. Take a few deep breaths. Try to relax."

Bryan took a few deep breaths but worried that he might hyperventilate.

"Now, back up. Why is your father going to Montgomery a problem?"

"Okay. So, remember how I told them I wasn't going to see Dr. Babcock anymore? And I thought they were going to try to force me to go, or find someone else, or do something – I don't know what – but anyway, nothing happened. And I'm thinking there's no way they're just going to let this go."

"And…" Mr. Simonton wished Bryan would just get to the point, but he tried his best to just listen and let Bryan decompress and spill it all out.

"So anyway, I could tell something weird was happening, so I logged onto the web hosting account – I know how to do that because I'm the webmaster for the church's website – and I went into the email accounts and I looked at Dad's emails. And there's a whole bunch of emails between him and Dr. Babcock. And first of all, Dr. Babcock was telling him about everything we talked about in our sessions! I mean, I thought it was supposed to be confidential, but I guess not. Anyway, after I said I wasn't going to see Dr. Babcock anymore, he sent Dad a link to this place in Alabama they're going to send me to. I mean, it looks like a concentration camp or something. Here, take a look at it."

Bryan handed Mr. Simonton the paper with the URL on it. Mr. Simonton started typing the URL on his computer.

"And then when I came home from the church, Mom and Brandon were out at the car and Mom was putting suitcases in the trunk. She was taking Brandon to Tulsa to see our grandma! We had just been eating lunch together an hour before that and she didn't say anything about them going to Tulsa!"

Mr. Simonton was looking around on the website. "Oh, no…", he muttered.

"And so, we're out at the garage and Brandon's all like what's going on here and why can't I come and all that. And she gets in the car and she's backing down the driveway, and she couldn't even look at me!"

Mr. Simonton was reading more of the website. "No… No… No…"

"And so, then I read Dad's emails and I discovered all this and now it all makes sense. Now here's the worst part. Remember how they were talking about flying to Montgomery? That's tomorrow! Tomorrow at 2:55! Dad bought three tickets for him and Dr. Babcock and me to fly there tomorrow, but only two tickets for him and Dr. Babcock to fly back on Monday. They're going to leave me there!!!"

Mr. Simonton did a Google search on Youth Restoration Project. "Oh, HELL NO."

He turned away from the computer and faced Bryan. He took a deep breath. "Okay, so… This is as bad as it looks – or worse. I've read stories about places like this. I think they had something about this on 60 Minutes a while back. Basically, they lock kids away in these places and try to convert them to be straight. It's called gay conversion therapy. It's really brutal. It's almost torture. Well, it *is* psychological torture."

"Does it work?"

"Of course not. These places have a very low success rate. There may be a few people who come out and convince themselves to marry someone of the opposite sex, but they're still gay. Most people come out of there more fucked up than they were when they went in. Not that you're fucked up. I didn't mean for it to come out that way. But yeah, it's very psychologically and emotionally damaging."

"Sounds kind of like rehab, where they send people for alcoholism or drug addiction."

"Yeah, except most rehab places are beautiful, peaceful, comforting places, run by legitimate professionals, and the people choose to go there voluntarily."

"This place looks more like Guantanamo Bay. But how can they keep people there against their will?"

"When you're a minor, your parents have control over you."

"Well, okay, so they're going to kidnap me and take me there tomorrow. What am I going to do?" The panic was starting to return.

Mr. Simonton took a moment to think. "Well, as I see it, you have two choices. Either go and just try to play along with their game and not let them break you–"

"Nope. Going there is not an option. What's the other choice?"

"Disappear."

"Disappear? Like, hide out somewhere?"

"They can't take you if they can't find you."

"Yeah, but I could only hide for so long. When they find me, they'll be even madder because I screwed up their plans, and they'll send me there anyway."

"I mean disappear for good."

"You mean like run away from home? Forever?"

"Yep."

"But that means I'll never see Brandon or Chris or any of my friends again. Where would I go? Where would I stay? How will I support myself?"

"Well, Bryan, you're almost an adult. You graduate from high school next year. Lots of kids have to start supporting themselves when they get out of high school – it's part of becoming an adult."

Bryan knew Mr. Simonton was right. There was probably no other choice if he didn't want to be sent to the Youth Restoration Project prison camp.

Mr. Simonton continued. "As to where you go, somewhere far away. The farther away, the better. A big city would be easier to disappear into. Is there any place you've ever thought you might want to live?"

"Chris and I have been talking about going to UCLA together. His older brother goes there now. He really likes Los Angeles."

"Well, Frank and I lived in LA before we moved here. That would probably be a good choice. You could finish your last year of high school there, then you'd qualify for in-state tuition."

"But how would I get there? I don't have a car."

"Even if you did, they'd be able to track you down using the description of your car and your license plate. The highway patrol in every state would be looking for you."

"I could hitchhike."

"Yeah, but that's not safe. You can't fly, because once they start looking for you, they can find out where you went from the airlines. Probably the same for Amtrak."

"They can do that?"

"Yes. Once your parents file a missing person report with the police, then if you don't turn up in a day or two, they open a case with the FBI. They have a whole system in place to try to locate missing children. The FBI can get a warrant to authorize the airlines or Amtrak or anyone else to give them information."

"Then how can I travel anywhere without them being able to track me?"

"Hmmm… Wait, I have an idea." Mr. Simonton turned to his computer and started typing. After a moment, he continued. "Okay, this just might work. You can get there by bus."

"But can't they track bus tickets just like airplane or train tickets?"

"Yes, but check this out. They have an Explore America pass where you get two weeks of unlimited bus rides for one price. You can get on and off buses anywhere and anytime you want. They would be able to find out that you bought the ticket at the bus terminal in Kansas City, but they wouldn't know where you got off or got on again or where you ended up."

"Hmmm… So, you're saying I'm just going to crisscross the country on a bus for a couple of weeks until I finally get to LA?"

"No, you can just ride directly to LA. But they will have no way of knowing what you did. You don't need to specify a destination when you buy the ticket. They probably assume most people who buy these passes are traveling for vacation and they'll return home."

Bryan thought for a moment. "You know, I think that might work."

"I think it's your best option. Maybe your only option."

"Okay, so we know how I'm going to get there. Then what? Where do I go? Where would I stay?"

"I'm still in touch with some of my friends there. I'm sure a few of them would be willing to put you up temporarily. I don't know if anyone is going to be willing to house you permanently, but I can try to find out. At least you'll have someplace to stay while you figure out what you're going to do."

Things were starting to seem a little less hopeless to Bryan. But questions and details and what-ifs were swimming around in his head.

Mr. Simonton continued, "Now, this is none of my business, but how much money do you have?"

"About three thousand dollars."

"What bank do you use?"

"MaxxBank. I opened my account at the branch right here in the store."

"Okay, good. Do you have your debit card with you?"

"Yes."

"Then the first thing you need to do is go to the teller window and close your account. Take it all in cash. Hide most of the money in your suitcase. Just keep enough for the trip on you."

"But then I can't use my debit card."

"Until you get settled in LA and open a bank account there, you'll need to pay for everything with cash. Otherwise, they could probably get access to your bank account and see where you've used your card."

"My parents can do that?"

"They can if their name is on the account too. Even if it's not, the FBI can get a warrant for that. It will take a few days."

"Wow. Big Brother really is watching."

"That's right. And it's gotten much worse since 9/11. Anyway, so your mother and your brother are on their way to Tulsa for a few days. What about your father?"

"He'll be at the church until after the 4:00 service. He's usually home around 5:15 or 5:30."

"You have church services on Saturday?"

"Yep, and three on Sunday morning."

"Okay, so it's 2:45 now. You have, at most, two and a half hours to go home and pack whatever you are going to take. Do you have a suitcase?"

"Yeah, a large one and a small one."

"Then you're probably going to have to make do with whatever you can fit into those. Focus on the stuff that means the most to you, stuff that can't be replaced. You only need clothes for about a week. Don't bother with anything you can easily buy after you get there. Oh, and do you have a backpack you can carry on?"

"Yes."

"Use it for things you'll need during the trip, like music, something to read, maybe a couple of bottles of water and snacks. Here's my number. Call me when you're ready and I'll pick you up and take you to the bus station. And don't cut it too close with your dad."

"Mr. Simonton, I can't believe you're doing all this for me. Thank you, thank you, thank you! You are literally saving my life."

"I can't believe your parents are doing this to you. Well, I guess I can. But I'm happy to do whatever I can to keep you from being sent to that place."

"Okay! I'll call you in an hour or two."

"Don't forget to close your account."

"Okay, thanks!"

What Really Matters
Saturday, July 21, 2007

Bryan rode his bicycle home and stored it in the garage. It occurred to him this would be the last time he would ever ride that bike. He wondered how would he get around in LA.

Bryan looked for his suitcases. The larger one was missing. Shit! Where could it possibly be? He wasn't sure, but he thought he saw it there earlier this week.

He grabbed the smaller carry-on suitcase with wheels and carried it into the house. What if that's all the stuff he can take? No wait... he could take one of his parents' suitcases if he had to.

Bryan raced around the house. Maybe his suitcase was in some closet.

When he got to his parents' bedroom, there it was, standing upright near the door. He picked it up. It was full.

He carried it back to his room and opened it. Apparently, between the time he left for the church and when he came back home, his mother had packed his suitcase. But why? Of course – so they could take it with them when they abducted him tomorrow and shipped him off to gay conversion hell. This was obviously a well-orchestrated scheme, all planned out behind his back. No wonder they weren't saying anything after he said he wasn't going to see Dr. Babcock anymore.

Bryan opened the suitcase and dumped everything out. It was almost all clothes, plus some toiletries.

Okay, now, what to take? Bryan looked around the room, and at everything in his desk and closet. What goes and what stays? He couldn't decide on anything.

Mr. Simonton's words echoed in his head. "Focus on the stuff that means the most to you, stuff that can't be replaced. You only need clothes for about a week. Don't bother with anything you can easily buy after you get there."

What meant the most? Easy. Music! His music collection would bring him happiness and comfort wherever he ended up. With his music to keep him company and cheer him up, he wouldn't feel quite so alone in the world. Bryan gathered up his thirty or so CDs and lined them up along one of the long sides of his suitcase. Wait – the cases might get damaged. He selected several of his favorite T-shirts and wrapped them around the CDs for padding.

Next, his music books. Not the elementary ones he had started trumpet lessons with, just the more advanced ones and the jazz play-along books he was using now. And of course, his trumpet. He placed his trumpet case on his bed next to the suitcases.

He looked up at the framed cork board on the wall, where his track ribbons and medals were mounted. Nah. While he was proud of his track accomplishments, those things wouldn't be useful in his new day-to-day life.

Bryan picked a few of his favorite books and videos. His larger suitcase was now half-full and getting pretty heavy. He picked a few pairs of shoes and threw them in. He grabbed a bunch of his socks and filled in the gaps. He added a few more shirts and some underwear, and the suitcase was almost full.

Bryan opened the smaller suitcase. He realized he hadn't packed any pants yet, so he grabbed three pairs of jeans, a pair of nice slacks, three pairs of shorts, and his running shorts. The suitcase was now three-fourths full. He filled the remaining space with some of the toiletries he would need every day.

What about a coat? Hmmm… Did it ever get cold in LA? Tyler said it was pretty warm year-round. He threw in a light jacket. If he needed anything else, he could buy it there.

Bryan pulled open each of his desk drawers. Paper, pencils, pens, scissors, notebooks… Nope. He opened the drawer with his small collection of electronics – his camera, his iPod, his portable CD player, his headphones. Yes to all. These went in his backpack.

Finally, Bryan was satisfied with his choices. What time is it? He had totally lost track of time. He glanced at the small alarm clock next to his bed. 4:30. Oh yeah, better take the alarm clock.

Then he saw the church's laptop. He would need a computer for school and for looking for a job and a place to live and all kinds of other things once he got to LA.

Did he dare?

Yes. Fuck it. If he got caught, he would be in a lot more trouble than just for stealing the church's computer. Bryan stuffed the laptop in the smaller suitcase under a couple of layers of clothing. He pulled the charging cable and the wireless mouse out of the carrying case and stuffed them in around the edges.

He checked his closet one last time. There, on the upper shelf, was his first trumpet. It was an inexpensive student model he played for the first three years before he bought the good trumpet he played now.

Bryan flashed back to the ride home after his last band concert, when Brandon said he wanted to learn how to play the trumpet. Bryan wasn't sure if he was serious or if he was just saying that in the excitement of the moment. In any case, Bryan hadn't played this trumpet for over two years and he had no further need for it. Brandon could have it, either way.

Bryan sat down at his desk and pulled out a piece of notebook paper and a pen.

> Dear Brandon,
>
> By the time you read this, I'll be gone. I didn't want to go, but I had to. Dad and Mom are having a real hard time dealing with me being gay, and it was about to get worse. They were going to send me away to someplace very bad. I had no choice

but to leave. Try not to worry about me. I'll be okay.

I want you to have my trumpet. I hope you learn to play it someday after you take piano lessons, and I hope you enjoy it as much as I did. And I hope this will help you remember me.

I'm going to be gone for a very long time, probably many years. Someday, when you are grown up, I will find you, and we can be brothers and best friends again. I will explain everything to you then.

I will miss you very, very much. I will think about you all the time. You're the best brother ever. I love you more than you will ever know. Someday, we will be together again.

One more thing. Don't say anything about this letter to Mom and Dad. Hide it away someplace where they will never find it. This will be our little secret. Okay?

I love you. Never forget that.

Bryan

Tears were streaming down Bryan's face. He folded the letter and placed it inside the trumpet case. Then he carried the trumpet case and the elementary method books into Brandon's room and put them in his closet. He would find them soon enough.

He carried his larger suitcase and backpack down the stairs and placed them next to the front door. He went back upstairs for his smaller suitcase and his trumpet. If he took nothing else, he was taking his trumpet, his most prized possession in the world.

He walked over to the phone in the kitchen and dialed Mr. Simonton's number.

"Russ Simonton."

"It's Bryan. I'm ready!"

"Okay, I'm on my way. Oh, and Bryan?"

"Yes?"

"Do you know where your birth certificate and your Social Security card are?"

"I think so."

"If you can find them, take them. Also, your passport if you have one. You're going to need them."

"Okay, thanks."

"See you in about ten minutes."

Bryan raced upstairs to his father's office. There was a safe in the closet. They were probably in there.

Bryan had seen his mother open the safe before. The combination was taped to the bottom of the canister on the desk that held pencils and pens. Bryan lifted the canister. Yep, still there.

Bryan opened the safe. There were about a dozen manila office folders, labeled for things like insurance, car titles, investments, and such. There was a folder with his name, one with Brandon's name, and one each for Mom and Dad. He pulled out the folder with his name.

Bingo! There was his Social Security card, his birth certificate, his final grades from each year of school, a couple of vaccination cards, and a few other things. He grabbed the whole folder. As he was about to shut the safe door, he spotted his confiscated cell phone on the upper shelf. He grabbed that too.

Bryan walked down the short upstairs hallway back to the stairs. Suddenly it hit him. This would probably be the last time he would ever be inside this house, this place where he had lived all his life. Anger and grief hit him simultaneously.

He glanced at the pictures on the hallway wall. The largest picture, in the center of the arrangement, was a family photo that was taken at a local portrait studio a couple of years ago. His dad sat in a chair in the middle. Behind the chair to the left, his mom stood with her hand lovingly placed on his dad's shoulder. To the right of his dad's chair stood Brandon with his big, cute, infectious smile. Bryan knelt on one knee beside Brandon, with his right arm draped over Brandon's shoulder.

Just one big happy typical middle-American suburban family, perfectly posed against a non-descript grayish-pastel backdrop. Yeah, right. As if. It looked so artificial, so contrived, so inauthentic.

No. That's not how it is in real life. Some real families have gay kids. Some real families have asshole fathers who would send those kids to prison camps. All real families are screwed up in one way or another. This family was being ripped apart by hatred, non-acceptance, and allegiance to some imaginary higher power that supposedly had one plan, and only one plan, for all people's lives. Bryan's family, especially his beloved little brother, was being ripped away from him. So was everything else in his life.

Bryan pulled the picture down off the wall and laid it face down on the floor. He twisted the little prongs that were holding everything in place and pulled the cardboard backing out. He took the picture and carefully ripped it from top to bottom, separating himself from the rest of the family. He put the rest of the family back in the frame, replaced the cardboard backing, and twisted the prongs back in place. He re-hung the picture, bare cardboard showing where he had been moments before.

There was an individual picture of Brandon to the left and one of Bryan to the right. He pulled both of them down. Mom and Dad could go to hell, but he had to have a picture to remember Brandon. They could order another one. And there was no reason for a picture of him to remain there if he was no longer part of the family.

Mr. Simonton was waiting in the driveway. Bryan stuffed the folder, the remnant of the family portrait, and the framed pictures of him and Brandon into the large suitcase, which was now bulging at the seams.

Mr. Simonton popped the trunk, and Bryan hoisted his worldly possessions into the trunk and shut the lid. What if any neighbors saw this? Oh well, nothing he can do about that. He climbed into the passenger seat and Mr. Simonton backed out.

Role Models

Saturday, July 21, 2007

Mr. Simonton headed north toward Shawnee Mission Parkway. Bryan watched the neighborhood where he had spent his entire life pass by for the last time. He vowed to never set foot in Kansas again.

They remained silent for a few minutes. Finally, Mr. Simonton asked, "So, how are you holding up?"

Bryan sighed. "Okay." He wasn't okay, and Mr. Simonton could tell.

"What are you feeling right now?"

"All sorts of things. Tired. Sad. Angry. Confused. Betrayed. Overwhelmed. Scared. Hungry."

"All valid emotions. After all, your entire life just got completely uprooted in the last four hours. Let's take care of the last one first. Where do you want to eat?"

"I don't know. You pick. I've made enough decisions for a while."

"Okay. There's a place in KC called Burger Betty's. Ever been there?"

"No, but Chris and I drove past it a few weeks ago, the day we went to Gay Pride."

"It's a fun, upbeat place. Lots of good food – comfort food. And let's just say we won't be the only gay people there."

"That'll work."

"Oh, and dinner is on me."

"Mr. Simonton, no. Really, you don't have to…"

"I insist. You've had a horrible day. At least let me send you off well. Oh, and from now on, call me Russ. I'm not your boss anymore."

Bryan let it go. Considering everything Russ was doing for him, he should be paying. But whatever.

"It's Frank's favorite place. He'll be pissed that I'm eating there without him."

"Bring him along! I mean, why not? I'd like to meet him."

Russ pulled into a parking lot and called Frank. "Hi, Honey. I just picked up Bryan. We're heading to Burger Betty's for dinner. Wanna join us? … Okay, I'll swing by and pick you up."

Russ hung up, then turned back onto the street. "It's on the way."

"Cool." Bryan didn't care. They could drive clear across town if they had to.

Russ said, "I've put together a bunch of information for you. We can go over it after dinner. But for now… The next westbound bus doesn't leave the station until 11:20, so we have lots of time. It will arrive in Los Angeles at around 9:15 Monday morning."

"So, it runs all day and all night?"

"Yep. At some of the stops, the bus stays for half an hour, so you'll have time to go to the restroom or get something to eat or drink. But I expect you'll be doing a lot of sleeping."

Bryan wondered what kind of sleep he'd be able to get on a bus, especially if some stranger was sitting right next to him. He calculated the duration of the trip. 34 hours. But wait, he would be crossing two time zones. 36 hours. Whatever. It all seemed pretty grim. His mood was sinking by the minute.

Of course, spending a day and a half on a bus with a bunch of strangers was still better than spending several months trapped at the Youth Restoration Project prison camp. There's that.

They picked up Frank, then drove to Burger Betty's. They were early for dinner on a Saturday night, so they got a table easily. Nothing about the place was fancy. It was kitschy and whimsical. The predominant color was purple. There was a long bar against one wall, and a small stage with a glittery backdrop at the other end. There were movie posters, posters for drag shows, and other kinds of campy décor.

Bryan's father would be horrified. But he didn't matter anymore. Bryan decided he liked it.

The waitress brought the menu. It listed all kinds of burgers – no surprise, given the name of the place – along with chicken and pulled pork sandwiches, fries, and all sorts of other greasy sides. His mother would be horrified. But she didn't matter anymore. Bryan wished he could try one of everything.

Bryan glanced over the colorful, festive concoctions on the drink menu. He wished he could try one of everything on it, too. He was suddenly being forced to become an adult; he should be able to drink like one.

Russ said, "Order whatever you want. Seriously. You've got a long trip ahead of you. Enjoy yourself for the next hour or two."

For the next couple of hours, they talked about all kinds of stuff. How Russ and Frank went to Canada to get legally married before it was legal anywhere in the US. What they liked and didn't like about LA. How Bryan had gone to a Christian school through eighth grade and then public high school starting in ninth grade. How he met Chris and how their friendship had developed. Playing trumpet in marching band and jazz band. The track team, including the disaster at the state track meet.

Tacitly, they all agreed the topic of Bryan's parents and the fate he had narrowly escaped would be off-limits.

Bryan enjoyed watching how Russ and Frank interacted. After 25 years, they had practically become one. He tried to imagine what they might have looked like as college kids, meeting each other, wondering if the other was gay, even wondering if they were gay. He tried to imagine them getting to know each other, dating, and falling in love. They were probably not too much different from him and Chris, although he hoped neither of them had religious baggage. That was, what, the early 80s? It was probably a lot harder to be openly gay then.

He decided to ask. "So, tell me a little more about your story. How did you guys meet? What was it like being gay at college in the 80s?"

They spent the next twenty minutes or so recounting their story. They practically alternated sentences. It was adorable. Russ and Frank were somewhere in their mid-forties, nearly thirty years older than Bryan, but he was thoroughly enjoying spending time with them and getting to know them.

Bryan wondered what he and Chris would be like in their mid-forties. Would they turn into Russ and Frank? That seemed like a desirable future outcome. He thought of his father and Chris's father. Mr. Robertson was a pretty decent-looking man. And his dad, for all his faults, was undeniably handsome. He was still slender, kept his hair impeccably groomed, and wore perfectly-fitting suits. He was quite the dashing, telegenic figure on the stage at the Eternal Savior Christian Church. Bryan was thankful that at least he benefitted from a good gene pool.

Maybe he and Chris could still go to college together. Maybe they would end up spending their lives together. Maybe they would be as happy as Russ and Frank.

Bryan looked around the restaurant, which was now mostly full. There were pairs and small groups of men, women, and mixed groups of men and women. There were people of all sorts, black and white, younger and middle-aged. Everyone was talking, laughing, eating, drinking, and having a good time. The noise level and the energy in the room were high, and the merriment was infectious.

Bryan asked, "So, is everyone in here gay?"

Frank scanned the room. "No, probably not. Lots of straight people come here too, either with their gay friends or just because they like the atmosphere."

Russ added, "They certainly don't come for the 5-star cuisine."

Frank continued. "No one really knows who's gay and who's straight. And no one really cares, which is how it should be."

After a couple of hours, Frank looked around and said, "We should probably give up our table. There's a line outside now."

Russ paid the bill and they left. Bryan was in a much better mood.

"Guys, thank you very much for dinner and all the good talk. I really needed it."

"You're welcome. The pleasure was ours."

"That was a fun place. It figures I would wait until my last night in town to go there."

"Well, you're in luck. There's a Burger Betty's in West Hollywood and a couple of others around LA. I think there's one in Long Beach. There are several other locations scattered around the country."

Frank glanced at his watch. "It's only 7:45. We still have a couple of hours until you need to be at the bus station. Would you like to come back to our house and chill for a while?"

Bryan looked at Russ. Russ seemed to be in favor.

"Well, okay. I mean, I don't want to impose any more than I already have."

Frank replied, "It's not imposing at all. We'd be sitting at home by ourselves anyway. Just an old suburban married couple living it up on Saturday night."

It took only a few minutes to get to Russ and Frank's house. It was a charming, one-story home on a lovely tree-lined street. It was a little smaller and ten or twenty years older than Bryan's now-former home. They entered through the kitchen door and were enthusiastically greeted by two excited Labradoodles, who started barking at the sight of someone new.

Frank said, "Bryan, meet Ralph and Herbie. Ralph and Herbie, meet Bryan. Don't worry, they're friendly. Probably too friendly."

Bryan knelt to pet them and was immediately slobbered with kisses.

Russ asked, "Something to drink?"

Bryan replied, "Coke? Dr Pepper? Whatever you have is fine."

"We have Coke." He paused. "Would you like something a little stronger?"

Bryan paused for a second. Should he? His conservative upbringing clashed with his desire to be more like all the happy, laughing people at Burger Betty's. Why the hell not? He did not answer to his parents anymore. He was his own man now. It was almost an act of defiance. And it might calm him down.

"Sure. Why not?"

"How does Captain Morgan sound?"

Bryan had no idea who or what Captain Morgan was or what it would taste like. No time like the present to find out. "Good. Not too strong."

Russ asked Frank, "And for you?"

"I'll have the same."

Frank led Bryan into the living room. "Have a seat." Ralph and Herbie followed. Bryan sat down and petted them some more.

Russ came in with three Captain and Cokes. Bryan took a sip.

They already had plenty of conversation, so Russ suggested, "How about a movie?"

Frank and Bryan nodded. Russ walked over to a bookcase full of DVDs and scanned their collection. "Hmmm… what would be a good choice for embarking on a bus trip?"

Bryan had no idea what to suggest. His family rarely watched movies, since Hollywood was one of his father's frequent immorality targets.

Frank lit up. "I know! Priscilla, Queen of the Desert!"

Russ said, "Perfect! Have you ever seen it?"

"No." Bryan had never heard of it.

For the next 103 minutes, Bryan became completely absorbed in the movie. The Australian outback, the flamboyant characters, the challenges they faced, and the secrets they revealed all transported him away from his life. The scene with the ping-pong balls made him think of Chris. Chris would have laughed hysterically.

There was plenty of stuff in the movie for Bryan to process later, but when the movie ended, he asked, "So I have a question. What's the deal with drag queens? I mean, I saw some at the Pride Festival, I saw posters for drag shows at the restaurant, and now the movie. I don't get the appeal. I mean, if I was attracted to someone who looked like a woman, I'd be straight. If I felt like dressing up like a woman and acting like one, I'd be transgender."

Russ and Frank shot each other a nervous glance, like they were trying to decide which one of them was going to try to answer this. Bryan wondered if he had said something horribly offensive.

Russ took a stab at it. "Well, drag queens go back a long time, and they have played a significant role in our history. For whatever reason, gay men have always loved female singers, from Judy Garland, Ella Fitzgerald, and Billie Holiday back in the forties and fifties to Cher, Madonna, and Whitney Houston now."

Bryan had heard some Ella recordings and loved them. He wasn't so much into Cher, Madonna, or Whitney. Would he have to learn to like them to fit in?

"Anyway, back then, gay people didn't have anywhere to go except bars. They tended to be small hole-in-the-wall places. Most actual entertainers couldn't be seen performing there. So, I guess some guys decided to dress up like them and lip-sync to their songs. If they had a good voice, they might actually sing. So basically, they were providing entertainment for themselves, since nobody else would."

Frank asked Bryan, "Have you ever heard of Stonewall?"

"Not really."

"Back in the sixties, the police would raid gay bars, just to harass the patrons. They'd round them up, take them down to the station, and make them pay a fine or maybe spend the night in jail. Anyway, one night in 1969, near the end of June, the police raided a gay bar in New York City called the Stonewall Inn. But on this night, the drag queens had had enough, so they fought back. It took the police completely by surprise. It turned into a riot that lasted all weekend."

Bryan was trying to imagine a bunch of men dressed up like women fighting police officers.

Frank continued, "And that night is now regarded as the birth of the modern gay rights movement. All because a bunch of drag queens decided they weren't going to take any more shit and fought back."

Russ took over. "Today, sometimes they just perform for fun, but sometimes they perform as part of fundraisers for good causes, like the gay community center."

Bryan said, "Oh wow, I had no idea." He realized there was probably a lot he didn't know about the gay community yet. It was kind of like the more you know, the more you realize you don't know. "That was a great movie. Thanks!"

Russ removed the disc from the DVD player and noticed the time on the display. "It's about ten o'clock. It's almost time to take you to the station. So, let's sit down and go over a few things." Russ led Bryan to the kitchen table. He gave Bryan a couple of sheets of paper filled with information.

"Okay. So, this afternoon I called a couple of our friends, Robert and Trevor. They are willing to have you stay with them for a week or two. I don't think they're going to want to have you live there permanently, but at least you'll have a place to land.

"Here's the address of the Los Angeles LGBT Youth Project. It's a great place. They offer a lot of services to LGBT youth, and they have some resources to help kids who have been kicked out of their homes. I'm pretty sure they have some volunteer attorneys who offer pro-bono legal services to kids who need it."

"Pro-bono?" Bryan asked.

"Free. Now, are you 18 yet?"

"No, I don't turn 18 until October."

"Okay, then the first thing you should do is get yourself emancipated."

Bryan knew Lincoln had emancipated the slaves, but he didn't see the connection. "What does that mean?"

"The court can declare that you are, legally, an adult. Then your parents no longer have control over you. If they were to find you, they wouldn't have the legal ability to take you back home – or do anything else, for that matter. Essentially, you turn 18 early. You should also have your name changed. They can probably do both at the same time. So, on your bus ride, think about what you would like your new name to be."

"Okay."

"Now, were you able to find your birth certificate and your Social Security card?"

"Yes."

"Good. So once your name is legally changed, you can get a new driver's license and a new Social Security card. Do you have a passport?"

"No."

"Okay, then no need to worry about that. Now after you get that done, you'll be able to do things like open a new bank account, get a job, get a new cell phone plan, and so on."

"Can't I do that as soon as I get there?"

"Well, you could, but they might be able to find you because you're using your current name. Besides, you'd have to go through a bunch of additional hassle changing your name in all those places."

"Yeah, I guess that makes sense. How long will it take to get emancipated and change my name?"

"I don't know, but I don't think it should take too long. Maybe two to four weeks."

That seemed like a long time.

"So anyway, the bus station in Los Angeles is in the middle of downtown. It will be Monday morning, and Robert and Trevor both have to work, so take a taxi to the LGBT Youth Project and talk with someone there to get things started. You can hang out there for the rest of the day, and Trevor will pick you up after work. Any questions so far?"

"What about school?"

"Yeah. I guess that depends on where you end up living. But you should probably wait to enroll until you have your new name and you're emancipated. Otherwise, they'll expect your parents to come in and enroll you."

"When I was getting my birth certificate and my Social Security card out of the safe, I also got my final report cards from each year."

"That's great. You'll need that stuff to apply for college."

"But they all have my current name."

"Well, you'll need to explain that you've changed your name to a few people and provide a copy of the court order. There's probably no way around that."

Russ glanced at his watch. "10:15. We should get going. Anything else?"

Bryan's head was already swimming with all the new information. "I guess not."

"Don't worry, I've written down everything I can think of. If you have any questions, please ask. You can call me using Robert or Trevor's phone. You can set up a new email address with your new name. But remember, no more calls on your cell phone. Oh, that's another thing. You can get a new SIM card and put it in your current phone when you set up your new account."

Bryan nodded. He wanted to get one of those new iPhones that had just come out, but this could be a Plan B.

"Okay, let's go."

Russ and Bryan stood up. Frank came in and said, "It was a pleasure to meet you. It sucks that you have to go through all this. But trust me, you'll be better off in the long run."

They started to shake hands, but they both decided a hug was in order.

"Good luck!"

"Thanks. I'll need it. And thank you for being so kind."

Bryan petted Ralph and Herbie one last time before heading out the door with Russ.

Me Time

Saturday, July 21, 2007

After the Saturday afternoon church service, Rev. Brad Bauer treated himself to an extravagant steak dinner. Since Brenda had taken Brandon to visit her mother, there was no one home to cook and no one to eat with. Bryan would be at work until eleven, so why not?

After dinner, he came home, removed his clothing, and carefully hung up his suit, shirt, and tie. He strolled into his office wearing only his boxers. He reached behind the safe in the closet and pulled out a half-full bottle of Woodland Premiere, his favorite fine bourbon, and carried it over to his desk.

He thought about calling Ron and asking if he wanted to come over. A couple of drinks was the least he could do to thank Ron for all he had done over the past few days to help set this up. But then, Ron still had the wife and kids at home. Besides, there would be tomorrow night at the Helton Grande in Montgomery for a 'boys night' with Ron.

He made a quick trip to the kitchen for a glass with ice and carried it back to his office. He plopped down onto his comfortable office chair, poured himself a glass, and turned the computer on.

The last few weeks had been rough. This evening was 'me time.'

Into the Darkness

Saturday, July 21, 2007

For the first five minutes of their ride to the bus station, Russ and Bryan remained silent. Bryan was trying not to cry.

Russ broke the silence. "So, what's on your mind?"

"Chris." Bryan paused, then continued. "You and Frank seem like a great couple. You seem so happy together."

"Yes, we are. I'm extremely fortunate."

"Several times this evening, I thought about Chris and me. I imagined him and me being in our forties, like you and Frank, living in a nice home somewhere with a couple of dogs. That's all I want. That's all I would need to be happy." Bryan sniffled a couple of times. "And now, I don't know if I'll ever see him again. I mean, maybe we'll go to college together. Maybe I'll see him again. But maybe not. And I didn't even get to say goodbye! He doesn't even know this is happening! He'll find out I'm gone, and he won't know where I've gone or why or what happened."

Russ couldn't think of anything to say that would help. The best he could do was, "Yeah, that really sucks."

"Do you think I could call him from the bus station? Maybe they still have payphones there."

Russ thought about it for a moment. "Well, it's up to you, but I wouldn't. What if he says something to his parents or any of the other kids at school? At some point, the police are going to come and question him. If he knows nothing, he can't tell them anything."

"Yeah, I guess you're right. But what if they come and question you?"

"I'll say you came in on Saturday before your shift and resigned.

Simple enough. Nobody will suspect I had any involvement with this. Don't worry, I can handle any questions that come my way. Oh, that reminds me. Do you have your paycheck automatically deposited, or do you get a paper check?"

"It gets automatically deposited."

"Okay, I'll switch it so that your final check gets sent to the store. When you get settled in, tell me your new address and I'll mail it to you."

"Thanks."

Bryan still couldn't stop thinking about Chris. "When do you think it would be safe for me to contact Chris?"

"I don't know. I guess it depends on how long the police and the FBI continue to investigate your disappearance. And there's no way to know that."

"At least until I turn 18."

"Right. Once you become an adult, you're free."

Bryan was startled by the realization that the police and the FBI would be trying to find him, like he was some sort of criminal. He hadn't committed any crime but he was still a fugitive.

They arrived at the Kansas City bus terminal. Russ parked the car, then accompanied Bryan into the terminal, carrying one of his suitcases.

Bryan approached the ticket window, purchased one Explore America pass, and checked his two suitcases. He would carry his backpack and trumpet onto the bus with him.

Bryan returned. "Well, I guess this is it. Wish me luck."

"You'll be fine. You're a smart, honest, decent, hard-working, and very nice young man. Things will turn out fine for you in the long run. There will be plenty of challenges and rough spots, but if anyone can handle them, you can."

"Thanks. I hope so."

"Please stay in touch. Call me after you get your new phone number, or from Robert and Trevor's phone. Email me after you set up a new email address. I put all my contact information on that paper I gave you. Please check in every so often and let me know what's going on. And if you're ever back in the area, I hope you'll stop by."

Bryan had no intention of ever setting foot in Kansas again, but he knew better than to say that right now.

"I will. Mr. Simon–, I mean Russ, I can't thank you enough. You have literally saved my life. May I have a hug?"

The two men hugged each other for the first and last time.

"Goodbye, Bryan."

"Bye, Russ."

It was 10:50. There was only one bus at the station; it had been sitting there when Russ and Bryan arrived. The destination sign read 'Los Angeles.' The door was open. The driver was milling around outside, smoking a cigarette. He noticed Bryan approaching and examined his ticket. Bryan carried his trumpet and his backpack onto the bus. Fortunately, it was only about half full. He found an unoccupied pair of seats about two-thirds of the way back.

The bus remained in its diagonal parking lane with the engine idling for another half-hour. Bryan replayed all the events of the day and the evening. He tried to process everything he had experienced and all the new information he had absorbed. Exhaustion was setting in. He could deal with this later. Russ said he had written everything down. Bryan hoped he hadn't forgotten anything.

11:00 passed. It occurred to Bryan that if tonight had gone as usual, he'd be clocking out at Price Cutter and riding his bike home. He would be finishing the PowerPoint for tomorrow's services with the information Dad had emailed him. Dad would probably already be in bed since he had to get up at 6:00 a.m.

The laptop was now in his suitcase. Not only would the church not have their PowerPoint for tomorrow, but they also wouldn't have the laptop it runs on. His dad would be livid. Bryan couldn't give a shit.

Soon, he would have been getting into bed – his familiar,

comfortable bed. The one he would not be sleeping in tonight or ever again. When he got up this morning, he could never have imagined that he would never sleep in that bed again.

He might never see his parents again. That was kind of the point of this wild scheme he and Russ hatched. Maybe someday far in the future, when they had no power over him whatsoever, he'd see them. But maybe not. He wasn't sure how he felt about that. On the one hand, they were his parents. They brought him into this world. They put a roof over his head and fed him and clothed him and took care of him. Yeah, they were all religious and strait-laced and strict, but he had always taken that in stride. He knew they loved him, although the way they expressed it always seemed more like a formality than a genuine emotional expression. Like 'we are your parents and you are our son so we're supposed to love you.'

But on the other hand, what kind of parents would send their supposedly beloved child off to some gay conversion torture camp? Bryan realized that in their own strange, warped way, they thought they were doing it because they loved him and wanted his life to turn out right. But more accurately, they wanted his life to turn out the way they wanted it to. Is that something you do to someone you love? What about what he wants? It's his life.

It really wasn't about his life at all. It wasn't really about his salvation. It was about what other people would think. The exalted Rev. Brad Bauer has a gay son? After all these years of preaching hatred toward homosexuals from the pulpit? After hosting that damn Rescued Through Love conference? Having a gay son was completely incompatible with his dad's dream of becoming a famous, nationally-known evangelist, with books and TV shows and rallies in huge arenas. All that was more important than Bryan's happiness.

Yeah, running away was the best thing to do.

But what about Brandon? Poor little Brandon was losing his big brother, his hero. His brother was being ripped away from him, due to no fault of his own. He couldn't imagine what a traumatic experience this would be for Brandon. Hopefully, when Brandon was grown up and out of the house, they could reconnect. But that would be at least nine years away. What would Brandon be like in nine years? What would he be like? Would Brandon hate him for abandoning him? What would his parents tell Brandon about why he left? Would they turn Brandon against him?

Bryan almost wanted to get off the bus. Maybe this was an awful idea after all.

Precisely at 11:20, the driver stepped into the terminal and called out, "All aboard!" A couple of passengers hurried out and boarded the bus. The driver climbed into his seat, shut the door, and backed the bus out. A minute later, the bus was climbing the entrance ramp onto I-70 West.

Too late to turn back now.

In about a mile, the bus crossed from Kansas City, Missouri into Kansas City, Kansas. There wasn't much to see out the window, especially at night. Trees lined both sides of the highway, hiding whatever was behind them. Occasionally, the bus would pass a few lighted businesses at an interchange, or an apartment building, or a cheap motel. The lights became fewer and farther apart as the bus barreled past the suburbs that were all he had ever known.

Bryan leaned against the window. The seatback was not nearly high enough to support his head. Another curse of being 6' 6". He undid the Velcro tie that was keeping the window curtain contained in a fan-folded bunch. He pulled the dark blue curtain across the window so he wouldn't have to rest his head directly against the glass.

He glanced around the bus. Most other people looked like they were already asleep. Good. They wouldn't see the tears streaming down his cheeks.

The bus surged fearlessly into the darkness, full speed ahead. It was an apt metaphor for this moment in Bryan Bauer's life.

Exploring America, Part 1
Sunday, July 22, 2007

Bryan slowly awakened after six fitful hours of trying to sleep on the bus. He noticed the bus wasn't moving. As he eased his eyes open, he saw flashing, spinning red and blue lights reflected across the inside of the bus, like it was some kind of mobile disco.

Oh, god, no. Police. Bryan's heart sank as dread overtook him. He saw that the guy sitting across the aisle from him was awake, so he leaned over and asked, "Where are we?"

"Goodland, Kansas."

Shit. He didn't even make it out of Kansas before they caught up with him.

He glanced at his watch. 6:15. The sun was just starting to come up.

As he continued to wake up and gain clarity, he realized that if the police were there for him, they would have boarded the bus by now. He started to relax a bit. Besides, his father would just now be getting up. He wouldn't have had time to notice that Bryan wasn't there.

He shuffled up the aisle to the front of the bus. The bus was parked between a couple of fast-food chain restaurants. There was a gas station and convenience store just beyond that. Across the street, there was a diner and a cheap motel. There wasn't much else.

The driver was standing just outside the bus, smoking a cigarette. Bryan stepped down from the bus. He could see a car pulled over, with two police cruisers behind it. "What's going on?"

"I dunno… probably a speeder or a drunk driver."

Bryan breathed a sigh of relief.

"How much longer will we be here?"

The driver glanced at his watch. "Ten minutes. If you want to get something to go or use the restroom, make it quick."

Bryan thought about it but decided to stay on the bus. He didn't want to risk being stranded in Goodland, Kansas if the bus took off with all his possessions but without him. Too bad – breakfast would have been nice.

***

At 9:45, the bus pulled into the bus station in Denver, Colorado for a two-hour stop.

Even though he would continue on this bus, Bryan got off to walk around a bit and get some fresh air.

He watched as the driver unloaded suitcases from the cargo hold for the passengers who were disembarking. He wanted to be sure that his suitcases weren't unloaded, or worse, taken. Bryan shuddered to think they could have been removed and taken at a previous stop while he was asleep. Thankfully, he saw his suitcases in the cargo hold.

He asked the driver, "Is it safe to leave my stuff on the bus while I go walk around a bit?"

"Probably. I can't guarantee anything, but I don't let people on without a ticket."

"Do you know if there's somewhere to eat nearby?"

"Yeah, there's a pancake place down that way. Two blocks, then make a left."

"Thanks."

Denver seemed nice. It looked modern, neat, and tidy. The tall, glassy office buildings were attractive, although a bit generic and impersonal.

Bryan found the restaurant and enjoyed a nice stack of pancakes with scrambled eggs and sausage. He figured he should load up here. No telling what options he might have at the stops on the rest of the trip. He glanced at his watch. 10:30. Twelve hours down, twenty-four to go.

Sunday Without Bryan

Sunday, July 22, 2007

Meanwhile, at the Eternal Savior Christian Church, Brad was livid. The 9:30 service would begin in minutes, and he had just been informed that not only was Bryan not up in the control booth above the sanctuary, but the laptop computer used to run the PowerPoint slide show during the service was gone.

Brad pulled out his cell phone and found Bryan's phone on his contact list. He pressed the Call icon, then realized that he had confiscated Bryan's phone when he grounded him and it was in the safe at home. He called the landline phone at the house, but no one answered.

Christ. Where could he be? Brad wondered if, instead of coming straight home from work last night, he spent the night with that Robinson kid – the one who was recruiting Bryan into becoming a homosexual. The one he had forbidden Bryan from ever seeing again. Bryan had become rebellious over the past week, so this was certainly plausible.

Oh well. Nothing he could do about it at this moment. Brad slid the little switch on his wireless mic box on, forced himself to smile, and swaggered out onto the stage of his massive, nearly full sanctuary. The show must go on!

"Brothers and sisters in Christ, welcome! Thank you for coming to worship the Lord on this beautiful morning! Due to technical difficulties, we will not be showing the usual slides during the service. Please refer to your bulletins for the order of worship, the prayers, and the hymns. Now, let us lift our voices and sing praises to the Lord!"

The praise band launched into the opening hymn, and the service got underway.

***

At 10:30, after the service, Brad tried calling home again. Still no answer.

He texted Mr. Elliot, who worked up in the booth. Still no Bryan. Still no laptop.

Brad was angry about Bryan's inexplicable absence and the disruption to the service caused by the missing PowerPoint slides. But what if Bryan couldn't be located by 1:00, when Dr. Babcock and two other men would arrive at his home to force Bryan to travel with them to the airport?

He and Dr. Babcock had all this meticulously planned out. He had shelled out a lot of money for the airplane flights, a rental Cadillac, a night in a suite at the Helton Grande in Montgomery, and forty days of accommodations and treatment at the camp. He saw all this evaporating before his eyes, and he was furious.

Brad soldiered his way through the 11:00 service. After fifteen years as the head pastor, he had honed his ebullient, charismatic persona and his professional stage presence to perfection. Today, he needed every bit of his skill to deliver an inspiring performance, since his mind was swirling with anger and unanswered questions.

Any other week, he would spend twenty to thirty minutes after the service shaking hands, greeting congregants, and mingling with his flock during the social hour. Today, he rushed out the side door to his car and made a beeline for his house.

Exploring America, Part 2
Sunday, July 22, 2007

At 11:40 a.m., following the two-hour break in Denver, the bus carrying Bryan resumed its journey westward. The cityscape along the Sixth Avenue Freeway wasn't much to look at, but after the bus merged back onto I-70 at the west end of Denver and began climbing into the Rocky Mountain foothills, the scenery improved. Bryan watched as the bare, brown hills were gradually replaced by evergreens as the bus climbed to higher elevations. The mountainous terrain was a welcome relief from the plains of eastern Colorado and Kansas.

Within an hour, the bus was high in the mountains. Bryan was awestruck by the splendor of the towering peaks and the massive forests. He was amazed that there could be snow on the mountaintops even in July. There was a huge, fascinating world out there beyond the Kansas City suburbs. Bryan decided that once he completed college and began his career, he wanted to spend his vacations exploring it.

Bryan began feeling more optimistic about the adventure he had so suddenly embarked upon and more hopeful for his future. While being forced out on his own on such short notice was scary in many ways, he took encouragement from knowing that his future was completely in his hands. He could make his life into whatever he wanted, free from the expectations and limitations that had been forced upon him up to this point. He could live freely as the openly gay person he was meant to be.

Bryan thought about what he wanted his new name to be. On the one hand, it didn't matter too much, as long as it was something different. On the other hand, it labeled his identity. And like his future, he now had the opportunity to define himself any way he wanted.

He liked Bryan – perhaps only because he was accustomed to it. It occurred to him that if he chose something completely different, it would take him a while to learn to respond to it as instinctively as he responded to Bryan. He decided on Ryan. That sounded almost the same, yet it was different enough that someone doing an internet search for Bryan probably wouldn't find him.

Next, Bryan brainstormed possibilities for his new surname. He thought of people he had known whose last names sounded cool and other names he liked. He briefly considered Ferguson, in honor of his trumpet-playing idol, Maynard Ferguson, who passed away the previous year. For a while, Ferguson remained his leading candidate. Ryan Ferguson. Not bad.

Then he thought of Chris. While he was still hurting from being dumped a week ago, he realized he couldn't blame him. If he had stayed and attended the Christian high school, they would be so close yet so far away. It wasn't fair to expect Chris to waste his senior year by remaining committed to a boyfriend he couldn't see. When Chris broke up with him, it wasn't because he was mad at him. Chris said he still loved him. He left open the possibility that they could still go to college together, which could easily lead to spending their lives together and maybe, someday, getting married.

What if he changed his last name to Robertson? Then, if they got married, they would already have the same last name. Even if they never reunited, Robertson would be a tribute or homage to Chris – the first person Bryan seriously loved, the person who so patiently challenged Bryan to become the person he truly is, and the first person he made love to. No matter what would or would not happen in the future, Chris made an indelible impact on Bryan's life.

Ryan Robertson. Bryan liked the sound of that. And it alliterated, like his current name. Ryan and Chris Robertson. Chris and Ryan Robertson. Yeah.

Now for a middle name. This was the least consequential of the three, but still, why not make it count for something? Bryan thought for a few minutes. Then it occurred to him that if he had chosen his last name to honor and remember someone, why not do the same for his new middle name?

Ryan Brandon Robertson. Yeah, that would work. He had time to roll it around in his head. He could revisit it and change his mind if he was inspired by something else. But if nothing better came to him, he would be happy with this.

The Best Laid Plans

Sunday, July 22, 2007

When Brad entered the house, he headed straight for Bryan's bedroom. Bryan wasn't there and, oddly, there was an assortment of folded clothes scattered on his bed.

Brad searched through the rest of the house. No Bryan.

He pulled out his cell phone and called Brenda in Tulsa.

Brenda answered the call. "Hello, dear. How are you?"

Brad had no time for pleasantries. "Bryan's missing."

"What???"

"Bryan's missing. He didn't show up for church this morning, and he's not here at the house."

"Well, I don't know where he is. He's not here with us."

"Where do you think he might be?"

"How should I know? Have you tried calling the Robertsons?"

After the contentious visit with the Robertsons a few weeks ago, he didn't relish the idea of speaking to them again.

"No, I haven't. Would you mind calling them?"

"No! *You* call them. This whole thing was your idea. You deal with it."

"Oh, alright. What's their number?"

"I don't know. Look it up in the phone book."

"Where is it?"

"In the kitchen pantry, left side."

"Alright. Talk to you later."

Damn. Of all the times for her to throw a hissy, why now? Shouldn't she be more concerned that her son is missing?

Brad found the phone book, then found the Robertsons' number. He paced the floor for a couple of minutes, then finally called.

Kathleen answered, "Hello?"

"Hello, Kathleen? This is Rev. Brad Bauer calling. By chance, is Bryan there?"

"No, he hasn't been here in over a month. If I'm not mistaken, you have forbidden Chris from ever seeing him again. He's heartbroken, by the way."

"Yes, well… Is Chris there?"

"No, he's at work today."

"Would you be so kind as to call him and ask if he's seen or heard from Bryan?"

"I'll ask him when he gets home."

"It's quite urgent. He seems to have disappeared and we need him here by 1:00."

"I'll ask him *when he gets home.*"

"Okay, fine." Brad hung up.

Brad called Brenda again.

"He's not at the Robertsons'. What other friends does he have?"

"None that he's been hanging out with, especially since you grounded him and took his phone away. Have you called the store?"

"No. What's the name of that place?"

"Price Cutter. Really, dear, you should be more involved with your sons' lives. Maybe we wouldn't be dealing with this."

"Whatever. Bye." The last thing he needed right now was a lecture from his wife on how he should raise his kids. He found the number for Price Cutter and called.

"Thank you for calling Price Cutter. Angela speaking. How may I help you today?"

"Hello. Is Bryan Bauer there?"

"No, sir. Today is his day off."

"Would you double-check, please?"

"Just a moment, please." Angela put Brad on hold. A minute later, she returned. "I checked the schedule, and he no longer works here."

"What the…? How did that happen?"

"I'm sorry, sir, we don't discuss personnel matters over the phone."

"But I'm his father!"

"I'm sorry, company policy. You'll need to come into the store and talk to the manager in person. He'll be back in the store tomorrow morning."

Brad hung up.

The doorbell rang. It was Ron Babcock. Brad let him in.

"He's gone, Ron. He wasn't at church this morning. I can't find him anywhere. If we can't track him down in the next half hour, everything will be all fucked up."

"Calm down. If we have to, we can rebook the plane flights."

"Yeah, but there will be change fees. Christ, I've spent a fortune on this already."

"So, what have you tried? Have you called his friends?"

"Only the Robertsons, and they were no help. I don't know any of his other friends."

"Didn't you say you took his cell phone? Start calling his contacts."

"That's a brilliant idea! It's up in my safe. Hold on."

Brad ran upstairs and unlocked the safe. The phone was gone. "SHIT! GODDAMMIT!"

Ron heard that from the living room. Brad stomped back down the stairs.

"The little bastard took the phone! How did he know it was in the safe? How the hell did he get in there???"

"Have you called the police?"

Brad took a couple of deep breaths and tried to calm down. "No. I guess that's next."

He dialed 911. When the operator answered, he said, "I'd like to report a missing person."

"Okay, what is your name?"

"Rev. Brad Bauer, pastor of the Eternal Savior Christian Church. The missing person is my son, Bryan."

"How long has he been missing?"

"Since earlier this morning."

"Are you sure he's not visiting friends or something?"

"Not that I'm aware. I've called around to a couple of places."

"Do you have reason to believe he is in imminent danger?"

"I have no idea."

"What is your address? I'll send an officer over to take a report."

"546 Sycamore Terrace."

"Okay, we will send an officer. He or she should arrive within the next hour."

"Thank you."

During the call, the other two men who were going to help with abducting Bryan and escorting him to the airport arrived.

Brad said, "Guys, Bryan is missing. I have no clue where he is."

One of the other guys, Stan, asked, "Did he take one of your cars?"

"No, I have one of the cars, and Brenda drove the other car to Tulsa."

Arnie, the other one, asked, "Does he have a bike?"

Brad hadn't thought of that. "Let me go check!"

He returned a moment later. "Nope. The bike's still there. Someone must have come and picked him up."

Stan said, "Or he took a taxi or a bus."

Ron asked, "Do you suppose he found out about this?"

Brad replied, "That would explain why he disappeared so suddenly. But how could he have found out?"

"Who else knew?"

"Just Brenda."

They all exchanged glances. No wonder Brenda seemed so standoffish with Brad earlier. He thought back to their call, when she said, 'This whole thing was your idea. You deal with it.'

"That bitch. I can't believe she would tell him."

Arnie said, "But that still doesn't explain how he got away or where he is. If she has the car in Tulsa, she didn't take him."

Brad said, "Wait a minute. We don't know that for sure. He was at the church yesterday at around 1:00. But then he left to go back home. He was supposed to work from 3:00 to 11:00 yesterday. I wouldn't have seen him when he got home, because I was in bed before 11:00. But then when I called the store just now, they said he doesn't work there anymore. So yeah, he might have gone to Tulsa with them! Who's up for a road trip to Tulsa?"

Stan said, "We don't know for sure they're in Tulsa. If she's in on this, they could be anywhere."

Arnie said, "Stan's got a point. When you talk to someone on their cell phone, you don't know where they are."

Ron turned to Brad and said, "Okay, let's calm down. You're coming unglued. Let's take a step back and review everything we know. Then we can identify our options."

Brad's head was spinning. "Well, whatever we do, we've got to do it quick. We should be on the way to the airport now."

Ron replied, "Unless he walks through the door in the next five minutes, that's not going to happen. I think we need to give up on the idea that we'll be taking him to Alabama today."

Brad plopped down into a chair, buried his head in his hands, and heaved a sigh of resignation.

Ron said, "Okay, so the first question is, is Bryan with Brenda and Brandon? If so, the second question is, are they in Tulsa or somewhere else? How can we find those answers?"

Arnie asked, "She's visiting her mother, right? Do you have her mother's number?"

Brad said, "I could probably find it."

"So, call her mother. Ask her if Brenda, Bryan, and Brandon are there. She'll either say they're all there, only Brenda and Brandon are there, or none of them are there."

Brad said, "It's worth a try. I'll have to go up to the computer in my office to find her number."

Ron said, "Okay, we'll wait here and brainstorm other possibilities."

Brad went upstairs to his office and fired up his computer. After a few minutes, he found Brenda's mother's address and phone number on the internet. He called.

Fortunately, her mother was there and answered. "Hello?"

"Hello, Doris. It's Brad. I was–"

"Oh, hello, Brad! It's nice to hear from you. I'm so sorry you and Bryan couldn't make it here this time. How are you?"

"Not so good. I–" Wait a minute. She had just answered his question. "No, actually, fine. Is Brenda nearby?"

"Yes. Shall I put her on?"

"Uh… no. That won't be necessary. Never mind. Thank you. Bye!"

"Bye." Doris shook her head and hung up. That was odd.

Brad returned to his friends downstairs.

"Well, scratch that. Brenda and Brandon are at her mother's, but not Bryan."

Stan said, "Well, we still don't know whether she told him what was going to happen."

Ron replied, "Even if she did, that doesn't change anything at this point. He's gone, and we have to try to figure out where he is."

Brad said, "Do you suppose he called some homosexual group and had them come pick him up? Don't they have organizations that recruit kids and help them run away from home?"

Ron said, "I wouldn't be surprised. But how would we know what they are or how to find them?"

Arnie said, "The police should know."

Brad said, "Yeah. Or I guess I could try searching on the internet."

Ron said, "I can try contacting my colleagues at Family-Focused Ministries and the National Association to Prevent Homosexuality. They probably know."

Arnie and Stan looked at each other, then at Brad and Ron. Arnie said, "Well, it looks like there's not much more we can do today."

Brad replied, "Yeah, I guess not. So, you guys can go if you want to."

Stan said, "I mean, if there's anything we can do, we'll stay, but–"

"No, that's okay. Thanks for your time, guys."

Arnie said, "Keep us posted. You'll be in our thoughts and prayers."

After handshakes, Arnie and Stan left. Ron stayed. He walked up to Brad and put his hand on his shoulder. "I'm really sorry."

"Thanks."

A few minutes later, a handsome 30ish police officer arrived at the door.

"Good afternoon, sir. Did you report a missing person?"

"Yes, I did. Please come in."

"I'm very sorry. I'm sure you are under a lot of stress right now. I'm Officer Timothy Garlow." Officer Garlow handed Brad a business card.

"I'm Rev. Brad Bauer, pastor of the Eternal Savior Christian Church. This is my friend, Dr. Ronald Babcock." Everyone shook hands.

Officer Garlow produced a notepad and jotted down their names. Then he said, "Okay, let's start with some basic information. What is the name of the missing person?"

"That would be my son, Bryan."

"Full name?"

"Bryan Bauer. That's spelled with a Y."

"Middle name?"

"Ronald."

"Date of birth?"

Brad looked flustered. "Uh… I'll have to find that for you."

"How old is he now?"

"Sixteen, I think."

Ron interjected, "Actually, I believe he's seventeen. That's what he told me a couple of weeks ago."

"Okay, seventeen."

"Height?"

"He's a few inches taller than I am, so I'd say 6'6"."

"Weight?"

"I don't know. He's pretty slender. I'd say maybe 180? 190?"

"Hair color and eye color?"

"Blond hair, blue eyes."

"What was he wearing when you last saw him?"

"I don't know, probably just a T-shirt and shorts. I only saw him for a minute yesterday."

"When did you last see him?"

"Yesterday at around 1:00 in the afternoon, at my church."

"Do you know if anyone else has seen him more recently?"

"Well, that's where it gets iffy. My wife may or may not have seen him after that. He left the church to come back home. I don't know if he saw my wife or not."

"Where is she now?"

"In Tulsa, Oklahoma, visiting her mother. Our younger son is with her."

Officer Garlow seemed puzzled. How could Bryan have seen his mother if she is in Tulsa?

"Do you suppose he might be with them?"

"I thought about that, so I called, and he's not."

"Is there anyone else who might have seen him, or any place he might have gone?"

"Well, he was supposed to go to his job at the Price Cutter grocery store yesterday at 3:00. But I called a few minutes ago and they said he no longer works there."

Officer Garlow scribbled some notes on his pad.

"So, when did you first become aware that he was missing?"

"When he didn't show up for church at 9:30 this morning."

"So, all last night and earlier this morning, you were not aware that he wasn't here?"

Brad started becoming uncomfortable. "No. He was supposed to be at work until 11:00 last night, and I was in bed before that. I get up at 6:00, since I have to be at the church by 7:30, so I figured he was still asleep."

"Have you called any of his friends to ask if he is with them or if they have heard from him?"

"Just one, so far. His … uh … best friend. I didn't get to speak with him, he was at work. His mother hasn't seen or heard from him. My son, I mean."

"What is the friend's name?"

"Chris Robinson. No, wait. Robertson. Chris Robertson. One or the other."

"How about his other friends?"

"Well, I don't know any of his other friends. My wife might know that. He hangs out with Chris most of the time. But here's something. I went to get his phone out of the safe so I could start calling his contacts, and the phone was gone."

"If it's his phone, what was it doing in a safe?"

"Uh, well… he was grounded, so I took it from him."

"Does he have a car?"

"No."

"Did he take one of yours?"

"No, I have one and my wife has the other one in Tulsa. His bike is still here."

"So, you don't know what method of transportation he used to leave."

"I think he was kidnapped. Or at least someone came and took him away."

Officer Garlow was momentarily taken aback. Why hadn't he said Bryan was kidnapped until now?

"Is there any sign of forced entry or a struggle?"

"No."

"Um… If he was kidnapped or otherwise taken, have you received a ransom note or call, or a message of any sort?"

"No. I don't mean that he was kidnapped by someone who is holding him for ransom. I suspect that homosexuals have come and taken him away."

Officer Garlow paused. He gave Brad a suspicious, disbelieving look. Then he glanced at Ron, who was smiling at him.

"Um… Why do you suspect that homosexuals have taken him away?"

"It's my understanding that they have organizations that help kids run away from home. It's one of the ways they recruit children into their lifestyle. I'm sure the police must know about these organizations."

Officer Garlow paused another moment to contemplate how he should proceed. He looked at Brad and Ron again, trying to discern whether they were serious. He sensed that Brad might be a few bricks short of a full load. He sensed that Ron was ogling him.

He decided to wrap up his questioning as quickly as possible. This would be a case one of the detectives could take over.

"Okay, do you have a picture of him? Preferably electronic."

Brad tried to recall if there were any pictures of Bryan on his computer upstairs. "I don't know. My wife usually handles that stuff. Can I get back to you on that?"

"Sure. You can send it to the email address on my card. If you find a print of him, do you have a scanner?"

"We have one at my church, yes."

"Okay, then I'll take the information I have so far, write up a report, and upload this information to the National Center for Missing and Exploited Children. We will also engage with the Kansas Bureau of Investigation. Both of those organizations have processes and resources in place to spread the word and try to track down missing people. I'll have a detective visit you tomorrow. In the meantime, if he shows up or if any new information surfaces, please call the police department immediately. The number is on my card."

"Thank you, officer."

"Oh, and the number you used to place the 911 call – is that your home number or cell phone number?"

"That was our home number."

"Do you have a cell phone number?"

Brad gave it to him.

"You mentioned that your wife is in Tulsa. May I have her name and number?"

"Brenda." He looked through his phone contacts again and gave him her number.

"When will she be back?"

"On Tuesday, I think."

Officer Garlow seemed surprised by that answer.

"And, Dr. Babcock, may I have your number?"

"Certainly!" Ron smiled and gave the police officer his card.

"Okay, then, we'll be in touch. I hope your son turns up soon."

Brad opened the front door for Officer Garlow and he quickly left.

Brad and Ron stood silently for a moment, processing everything that had just happened.

Then Ron said, "Well! He was certainly an arresting officer, wasn't he?"

Brad replied, "I can't believe you were actually cruising him at a time like this. And since when do you have a uniform fetish?"

"I'm developing one right now."

Brad shook his head. "Well, I guess that's all we can do for the time being. Man, I am exhausted. Can I offer you a bourbon? I could really use it right now."

"That would hit the spot."

Brad retrieved the secret bottle of bourbon he kept stashed behind the safe in his office closet. Then he walked to the kitchen for glasses and ice. He poured two glasses, then he and Ron sat down at the kitchen table.

Brad said, "It's nice to be back in touch again after all these years, despite the circumstances."

"Yes, it sure is. It's been what? Twenty years?"

"Yeah, that's about right. We graduated in 1987."

"Well, the years have certainly been kind to you."

"Thanks. I think we've both done pretty well." The years hadn't been so kind to Ron. He was forty or fifty pounds heavier with gray overtaking his remaining thinning hair. But Brad wasn't about to say that.

Ron said, "I was so looking forward to *reconnecting* with you at the hotel in Montgomery this evening."

The double-entendre was not lost on Brad. He perked up. "We could still go. It's already paid for. If we dash to the airport, we could still make the flight. Or there's probably a later one."

Ron briefly entertained the idea, then said, "That would be sweet, but we shouldn't. When Rachel finds out Bryan is missing and we couldn't take him to the Youth Restoration Project camp, that will raise all kinds of questions about why we went anyway."

"Yeah, you're probably right. Besides, I need to stay close by in case the police call with something."

They took a few more sips and finished their drinks, then looked into each other's eyes.

Brad said, "But we have now."

***

Four hours later, Brenda and Brandon arrived back home. When she opened the garage door with her remote, she saw Brad's car in its usual spot. When they entered the house, Brad was nowhere to be found. It was shortly after 5:00, so maybe he had gone someplace for dinner. But why was his car still in the garage? There were no restaurants within walking distance.

Brenda and Brandon each went to their bedroom to unpack.

Brenda noticed that the bedspread and sheets were in complete disarray. It didn't surprise her that Brad didn't make the bed that morning. But unless he tossed and turned all night long, the bed shouldn't look like *this*. As she made the bed, she noticed a few stains that weren't there yesterday.

She unpacked her clothes, then took her toiletries into the bathroom to return them to their places. The shower had been recently used, and there were two damp towels on the rack.

When Brandon finished unpacking, he came into his mom's room. "Do you know where Bryan is, or when he's coming home?"

"No dear, we haven't been home very long. I don't know anything yet."

"Where's Dad?"

"I don't know, dear. He's probably eating dinner someplace."

"When are we going to eat?"

"I'll start fixing dinner in a few minutes. Why don't you go read a book in your room until I call you for dinner?"

Brandon could tell his mom was upset, so he figured staying out of her way was a good idea.

Brenda pulled out her phone and contemplated calling Brad, but decided to wait until he arrived home. She needed some time to process things. She noticed that a voicemail had come in while she was on the road. She pushed a couple of buttons and held the phone to her ear.

"Hello, I'm trying to reach Mrs. Brenda Bauer. I hope I have the right number. This is Officer Timothy Garlow with the Prairie Village Police Department. I just spoke with your husband about your son's disappearance. First of all, I'm very sorry this has happened. Let me assure you that we will do everything in our power to see that he gets home safely. Please return this call at your earliest convenience. I have a few questions. Also, please let me know when you plan to return to your home. I would like to bring a detective to your house, but it would be best if you were there, too. You may call me back at this number, 913-555-5827. I'm on duty until 6:00 this evening, but please leave a message if you don't reach me in person. Thank you. Goodbye."

Brenda glanced at the clock. 5:50. She pressed reply. After a few rings, Officer Garlow answered. "Garlow speaking. How may I help you?"

"Good evening, Officer Garlow, this is Brenda Bauer returning your call. I received your voicemail message."

"Thank you for calling, ma'am. I'm very sorry about your son. May I ask you a couple of questions?"

"By all means."

"First, when do you plan to return home?"

"I'm here now."

"Good. As I mentioned in my message, I would like to bring a detective to your home tomorrow to ask a few more questions and maybe look around a bit. Is there a good time?"

"The sooner the better."

"Okay, well I'll check with her as soon as she gets in tomorrow morning. We'll shoot for mid to late morning. I'll call first."

"That will be fine."

"Now, what is your son's birthday?"

"October 14, 1989." Brenda shook her head. Brad didn't know that? On second thought, no big surprise.

"When was the last time you saw him in person?"

"At around 1:30 yesterday. He came home just as Brandon – that's our younger son – and I were leaving to go visit my mother in Tulsa."

"Do you remember what he was wearing?"

"He was wearing a V-neck T-shirt. It was light blue around the shoulders, with several stripes across the chest, and dark blue below that. And tan cargo shorts."

"Excellent. And do you have a recent picture of him? Electronic is preferable, but a printed picture would work. Your husband mentioned that he has a scanner at his church."

"No, I don't think we have an electronic picture. We just have prints. We're not very modern, I guess. I'll find something and give it to my husband."

"Okay, thank you. Do you have any idea where your son might have gone?"

"No, none at all."

"Do you have any questions for me?"

"Yes. Aside from a detective visiting us tomorrow, what can you do? What happens next?"

"Right now, I am uploading some information to the National Center for Missing and Exploited Children. They, in turn, will send the information out across their nationwide network. The picture will help a lot. Our department has sent out a missing person alert, so all our officers are keeping their eyes open. Your description of what he is wearing will help. Immediately following our visit tomorrow, we will engage with the Kansas Bureau of Investigation. They can pull in the FBI if needed. In the meantime, it will help if you can contact more of his friends and any groups he belongs to. Your husband said he contacted the Robertsons, but he didn't know of anyone else."

"Okay, thank you very much, Officer. I appreciate everything you're doing."

"We'll do everything we can to bring your son back safe and sound. I'll be in touch in the morning. If anything happens in the meantime, please call the department number and someone will help you."

"Okay. Good night."

"Good night."

Devastation

Sunday, July 22, 2007

Shortly after 5:00, Chris returned home from working his shift as a lifeguard at the community pool. Kathleen greeted him. "Hello, sweetheart. How was your day?"

"Hi, Mom. It was fine. Kind of hot, but it's July in Kansas."

"By chance, have you heard from Bryan today?"

"No, I haven't heard from him since we broke up. Why?"

"That's what I thought. But I received a call from his father at around 12:30. They don't know where he is. They needed him there at 1:00 for some reason."

"Huh. That's strange."

"Well, I told him I would ask you. So, you've been asked. Anyway, dinner should be ready at around 6:00."

As Chris headed up to his room, thoughts began spinning in his head.

It's Sunday – why wasn't he at church? Where would he have gone? And why? Did he take one of their cars? Did he run away? There was that conference last weekend. Did his parents do something crazy after that? What did they need him at 1:00 for?

Chris entered his room and sat down on the side of the bed. He couldn't imagine what the answer to any of these questions might be. Suddenly, another possibility occurred to him.

Did he kill himself? Did things get so bad and hopeless for him that he decided to end it? I broke up with him last weekend, on the same day as the conference. Did that push him over the edge? Is this my fault? At least partly? Maybe I shouldn't have tried so hard to pull him out of the closet. Maybe I shouldn't have led him into doing some of the stuff we did together. I did all that, then I broke up with him. Oh my god... he killed himself and I'm part of the reason.

Chris buried his head in his hands and started sobbing. Several memories from the past couple of months popped into his head.

That time at the Gay Pride Festival when we were at the Parents Support Network booth and Bryan said, "There's no way I can come out to them. He'd either kick me out or kill me." And right before that, when I tried to give him that pamphlet. "Here, take this. Just have it in case you ever need it," and Bryan said, "I won't need it if I'm dead."

Then there was that time we were kissing in the car and the cop showed up, which led to Bryan being outed to his parents and all this happening. Bryan said, "Just shoot me now." And later, after the cop left, he said, "My life is over."

Oh my god... how could I not have seen it? How could I not have paid attention? I'm so fucking selfish and insensitive. Even if he's not dead, he's missing. Did he run away from home? If he did, at least he's alive, but now he's out in the world all alone. Does he have any relatives besides his grandmother? He's never talked about them. In any case, he's gone. I may never see him again. And I'm partly to blame for all this. Oh god... I'm a terrible person.

Chris stretched out on his bed and cried for a good fifteen minutes.

Then Tyler knocked on the door and called out, "Hey man, time for dinner!"

Chris tried to pull himself together. He walked to the bathroom, moistened his washcloth, and wiped off his face. His eyes were still red. He looked miserable – because he was. He walked down the stairs and over to the kitchen table. Kathleen, Tom, and Tyler were already sitting down. They were all taken aback as soon as they saw Chris's face.

Kathleen stood up. "Oh, honey, what's the matter?"

Chris tried to hold back more tears as he said, "It's Bryan. He's missing. I don't know where he is or what's happened to him. But I'm worried. Either he's run away or…" He couldn't hold back the tears any longer. "… or he killed himself."

Kathleen hugged him. "Honey, I see why you're so upset. But we don't know. That was over five hours ago. He may have turned up by now. It was probably nothing serious."

"But what if it is? And if it is, it's partly my fault!"

Tom said, "Why do you think it's your fault?"

"Because I broke up with him. I tried to get him to come out more. He kept telling me his parents would freak if they found out, but I kept pushing him. Then they found out, and they freaked. Oh god, I'm a horrible person."

Kathleen said, "Well, even if you made a few mistakes and did things you regret now, you didn't do it on purpose. You didn't do it to hurt him. You're not a horrible person."

Chris tried to stop crying and sniffled a few times. "Yeah, thanks, but… May I call them? I'm sorry, I know I'm holding up dinner."

"Yes, dear. It would be good to know for sure. If they found him and he's safe, then you can stop worrying about it. If not, at least you'll know more about what's going on."

Chris picked up the phone and started dialing.

Kathleen said, "And remember, dear… if he's still missing, they are going through hell, too. Remember to offer your support."

The phone rang four times. Just as Chris thought the answering machine would kick in, someone picked up. A woman's voice answered, "Hello?"

"Hello, Mrs. Bauer. It's Chris Robertson, Bryan's friend. I was just calling to ask if Bryan is back, or is he still missing?"

Chris could hear Brenda sigh. "No, he's still missing. We haven't a clue as to where he might be. Have you heard anything from him?"

"No, ma'am. I'll let you know the moment I do."

"We would appreciate that. Thank you."

"And would you please let me know if you – I mean *when* you find out anything? I'm really concerned too. I mean, I know I'm not supposed to have any more contact with him, but–"

"I know, he's important to you. Yes, I'll keep you posted."

"Thank you, Mrs. Bauer. I know this must be difficult for you and your family. I'll keep you in my prayers."

"Thank you, dear. I appreciate your concern. And thank you for being his friend. I'm sorry about what's happened recently."

"That's okay. The important thing now is that we find him."

"Okay, well, we'll be in touch. Goodbye."

"Bye, Mrs. Bauer."

Chris hung up the phone and sat down at the table.

Tom said, "So I take it they haven't heard anything."

"Nope."

Tyler reached over and put his hand on Chris's arm. "I'm really sorry, man."

After dinner, Chris texted all their friends in the band and the guys on the track team he had numbers for, to ask them if they've seen or heard from Bryan, and to let him know if they do.

Two minutes later, he received a text reply from Rocket Crockett.

Hey, man, I'm really sorry. I'll keep my eyes open and spread the word. Keep me posted.

Confrontation

Sunday, July 22, 2007

After Brenda and Brandon finished dinner, she sent Brandon back up to his room. He looked puzzled, but she assured him he wasn't being punished for anything.

At around 6:30, Ron Babcock turned his car into Brad's driveway and parked in front of the garage door. He and Brad got out, and Brad let them in through the kitchen door. Brad was carrying a brown paper bag with his hand wrapped around the neck of the bottle within.

Brenda was waiting for them at the kitchen table, drinking a cup of coffee and reading a magazine. Brad was startled to see her sitting there. She closed her magazine and set it down on the table. Ron looked embarrassed and quickly figured out that he had walked into a very awkward, uncomfortable situation. Brad nonchalantly placed the brown paper bag on the kitchen counter, hoping that it would somehow go unnoticed.

Brad spoke first. "Well, hello, dear! I wasn't expecting you home until Tuesday." He approached Brenda to kiss her, as if nothing was wrong.

Brenda wasn't having it. She rose to her feet. "Our son is missing, you nitwit. Did you think I would just stay away for another two days and do nothing?"

Brad said nothing.

"Apparently, you were hoping I would." Her words dripped with accusation.

Ron took a few steps backward toward the door. "Well, I should probably be on my way…"

"Not so fast. You stay right here." Brenda gestured toward the kitchen table. "Why don't we sit down?"

Brad and Ron glanced at each other with dread in their eyes, then sat down.

"Coffee anyone? Looks like you might need it."

Brad and Ron nodded. Brenda had obviously figured out that they had been drinking. She poured and served their coffee, topped off her own, then sat down.

"Okay, first things first. What happened? How did your grand scheme to send our child off to the secret gay conversion therapy camp fall apart?"

Brad decided he needed to take charge. He was the man, damn it. The head of the household. He was not about to be emasculated by his wife, especially not in front of his old college roommate and newly re-acquainted buddy. "Why don't *you* tell me how he found out about it?" he demanded.

"What are you talking about? How should I know?"

"You must have told him. How else would he have found out? Nobody else knew."

"I can assure you I didn't say a word. And besides, Rachel knew, since you were going to be gone overnight," she said, turning to Ron. "The wives of the other two guys you enlisted in this plot to kidnap our son probably knew."

Brad replied, "Even if they knew and wanted to tip him off, which I doubt, I don't think any of them would know how to contact him, especially since he didn't have his cell phone and he was supposed to be at work from 3:00 to 11:00. And they would have no way of knowing where he works."

"Well, none of that really matters. In any case, he found out, and now he's gone. So, what have you done? What do you know?"

"I called the Robertsons. They said they haven't seen or heard from him, but I don't know if I believe them. Kathleen was pretty standoffish with me."

"Can you blame her, after the way you treated them a few weeks ago?"

Brad glared at her. He stopped himself from saying what he really wanted to say because Ron was there. "Anyway, then I called the store. They said he no longer works there, like he had gone in and resigned. So obviously he found out ahead of time – probably sometime yesterday."

"Have you heard any more from the police?"

"Well, an officer came out to the house and took some information. He said a detective would be visiting tomorrow."

"Have you tried calling anyone else?"

"Oh, that's the other thing." Brad straightened up and regained his combative demeanor. "I went to get his cell phone out of the safe to start calling people on his contact list, and the phone is gone! How the hell did he get his phone out of the safe? YOU are the only other person who knows the combination."

"I have no idea. But I was already on my way to Tulsa with Brandon, remember?"

"Unless you gave it to him earlier and told him what was going on."

"I most certainly did not!" she snarled. She had had enough of being falsely accused, especially in light of what else had happened. "So now let's talk about the other issue at hand. Even though our son is missing, we have no leads, and nothing else is being done, it looks like you two have had a fun day together. Would you care to tell me about it?"

"Well, I certainly wouldn't call it a fun day. I've been tearing my hair out all afternoon. I'm incredibly angry and frustrated about all this. None of this is what I wanted to happen. Ron, here, has been good about suggesting ideas and offering support."

"I see. Yes, I can tell he's been supportive in *sooo* many ways. Anything to alleviate all that anger and frustration that your plan to send our son away fell apart, I suppose. And where have you been for the past couple of hours?"

"After the day I've had, I needed to get out of the house for a little while. So, we went out to eat. And yes, we had a couple of cocktails. I needed it."

Brenda glanced over to the bag on the counter. "Looks like you were just getting started."

Brad had no response. He was still trying to figure out how much to read into what she had just said.

Brenda continued, "Or maybe you were just replenishing your stash."

Ron wanted to be anywhere else in the world but here. He sensed an opening. "Do you need me to be here tomorrow morning when the detective visits?"

Brad was about to answer, but Brenda beat him to it. "No, that won't be necessary. You've done quite enough already." Brenda glared at him.

Ron got up from his chair and started heading for the back door. "Well, do keep me informed of any updates and let me know if I may be of assistance."

Brenda replied, "Good night. Tell Rachel I said hi."

Ron exited as quickly as he could.

As soon as he was gone, Brenda glared at Brad. Then she spun around, stormed up the stairs, entered the master bedroom, and slammed the door.

Brad lifted the bourbon out of the bag and threw the bag away. He added a few ice cubes to a glass, then carried the bottle and the glass to his office. He figured he could check his email and do some church stuff for a while to give her time to cool off. When he walked in the door, he noticed the hide-a-bed was open and outfitted with the stained sheets that had been on their bed earlier that afternoon. He walked over to the master bedroom door and turned the knob. It was locked.

The Detective Visits
Monday, July 23, 2007

At 10:30 a.m. Monday, Officer Timothy Garlow arrived at the Bauer home, accompanied by Detective Sue Wagner.

After introductions, Detective Wagner asked, "May we have a look around, please?"

Brenda replied, "Sure, be my guest."

Officer Garlow and Detective Wagner walked through the kitchen to the back door. They looked at the door inside and out. There was no sign of forced entry. They walked around the house and looked at all the windows.

They came back inside and Detective Wagner asked, "May we see his room?"

Brenda and Brad escorted them upstairs. They noticed the folded clothes on the bed but didn't ask about them.

Detective Wagner asked, "Can you tell if anything is missing?"

Brad looked around. "I can't think of anything at first glance."

"Can you tell if some of his clothes are gone?"

Brenda looked through the drawers, then looked at the laundry basket in the closet. She tried to remember what she had packed into his suitcase on Saturday. The clothes on the bed were among the clothes she had packed.

"I think some of his clothing may be gone."

"Does he have a suitcase? Is it still in the house?"

Brenda said, "Just a moment, please." She walked over to the master bedroom and looked around the room. No suitcase. Either Bryan took it or Brad moved it. She returned to Bryan's bedroom and asked Brad, "Did you see Bryan's suitcase in our room?"

"No, I don't recall it being there."

"Would you go check and see if it's in the garage? And look for his smaller suitcase, the carry-on with the wheels."

"What do they look like?"

Brenda sighed. "Never mind, I'll go look."

A moment later, she returned. "It looks like both of his suitcases are gone."

Detective Wagner asked, "Is there anything that looks different? Anything you can think of that might be missing?"

Brenda walked over to Bryan's closet. "I can tell several of his shoes are gone." Then she noticed an empty spot on the shelf. "And his trumpet." She looked around the room. "Both of them. And his CDs – they're usually on that shelf."

The officers finished looking around Bryan's room and everyone went back downstairs. Detective Wagner said, "There are no signs of struggle or forced entry, no ransom note or similar communication, and his suitcases and some of his possessions are missing. Therefore, it's unlikely that he has been kidnapped or otherwise abducted against his will."

She paused to see if Brad would say anything.

Brad said, "Are you sure? My understanding is that there are homosexual organizations that take children from their homes."

Detective Wagner and Officer Garlow exchanged wary glances.

Detective Wagner replied, "With all due respect, sir, I seriously doubt such organizations exist. We have never encountered anything like that before."

Brad wanted to argue the point but decided against it.

She continued, "At this point, the most likely scenario is that he chose to leave. Can you think of any reason why he might have wanted to leave?"

Brad knew exactly why, but he didn't want to tell them. "Um… I guess maybe he was upset with being grounded."

"How long has he been grounded?"

"Oh, about three weeks."

"What was he grounded for?"

Uh oh. Brad thought about how much information he should volunteer. The last thing he wanted was for anyone to find out that his son was a homosexual, or more accurately, struggling with same-sex attraction. What if that got back to his congregation? What if that got out into the community? "Uh, well… let's just say he had been misbehaving."

Detective Wagner asked, "Mrs. Bauer, we know you were visiting your mother yesterday. Are there any other relatives on either side of the family where he might have gone?"

Brenda replied, "I have a sister in Connecticut. We're in touch, but we're not that close. Bryan hasn't been there in years."

"Have you checked with her?"

"No, I haven't, but I'll call her."

"What about any relatives on your side, Rev. Bauer?"

Brad replied, "Well, I'm not really in touch with them. Let's just say they don't have the same beliefs we do."

"Any other friends besides Chris Robertson?"

Brenda replied, "That's who he spent most of his time with. I can ask Chris if he can give me the names and numbers of some of their other friends. I spoke to him on the phone yesterday. He said he's willing to help."

"Okay, good."

Officer Garlow asked, "Were you able to find a picture and have it scanned?"

Brad replied, "Oh, no, I totally forgot." He turned to Brenda. "Do we have any electronic pictures of Bryan?"

"No, I don't think so." She thought for a moment. "There's the picture of him from the last time we had our family portrait done. It's hanging in the hallway upstairs. Let me go get it."

She climbed the stairs, turned down the hallway, then let out a shriek. "OH MY GOD!!!"

The other three raced up the stairs. Brenda was in a panic, tears gushing from her eyes. She pointed to the family portrait hanging on the wall. The picture had been ripped from top to bottom, with the right side of the picture – where Bryan had been kneeling next to Brandon – torn away, revealing the cardboard backing.

Everyone was speechless.

Then Brenda said, "And two pictures are missing. There were individual pictures of Bryan and Brandon here and here." She pointed at the empty spaces on each side of the family photo.

Detective Wagner put her arm around the sobbing Brenda to comfort her.

Officer Garlow looked back through his notes from yesterday, then said to Brad, "You mentioned yesterday that his phone had been taken from a safe. Where is that safe located?"

"It's here in my office." Brad led Officer Garlow and Detective Wagner into his office. They stepped around the open, unmade hide-a-bed to reach the closet. "It's in there."

Officer Garlow asked Detective Wagner, "Should I dust it for fingerprints?"

"Yep."

"Maybe we should also check that photo frame."

"Good idea."

While Officer Garlow was dusting for fingerprints, Detective Wagner asked a few more questions.

"What is his cell phone number?"

Brad pulled his phone out of his pocket and read them Bryan's number from his contact list.

"Is his number connected to your account, like a family plan?"

"Yes."

"Good. Would you please log onto your account and pull up his call log?"

Brad sat down at his computer and powered it up. While the computer was booting up, Detective Wagner asked, "Does he have a credit card?"

Brenda said, "No, he doesn't. But he has a debit card for his checking account."

"Which bank is the account with?"

Brenda answered, "MaxxBank."

"Do you know the account number?"

"It might be in the safe."

"Okay, well after Officer Garlow is through, perhaps you can open it."

Brad asked, "Why do you need his bank account number?"

"So we can look at any transactions that come through on his debit card. That could tell us where he's been and where he is."

"Of course!"

"It takes a few days, though. The KBI has to get a warrant before the bank will release that information. Do you know his Social Security number?"

"It's in the safe too. By the way, I don't see anything on his call log since we grounded him."

A few minutes later, Officer Garlow finished his fingerprint work. Brad lifted the canister on his desk that held pencils and pens and glanced at the combination that was taped to the bottom. Then he opened the safe.

"SON OF A BITCH."

Brenda asked, "What is it?"

"His folder is gone. That's where we kept his Social Security card, his birth certificate, his grades, everything. GONE."

Detective Wagner closed her notepad. She glanced at Officer Garlow, who subtly nodded. "I think we have everything we need for now. Please remember to find a picture, scan it, and send it to the email address on my card." She handed a business card to Brad.

Brenda asked, "May I have one too, please?" She handed her a card. Officer Garlow gave her his card too.

Detective Wagner said, "And remember to check his cell phone log once or twice a day. If you see any activity, please contact me."

Everyone walked down the stairs and to the front door.

Detective Wagner turned to Brad and Brenda and said, "Please contact us if anything happens. Anything at all. We will be in touch if we have any further questions or if we get any new information."

Brenda replied, "Thank you for all you're doing to find our son."

Officer Garlow said, "We'll do everything we can. Good day."

***

As Officer Garlow and Detective Wagner were driving back to police headquarters, Garlow asked, "Well, what do you make of all that?"

"Something's fishy. There's something that guy knows but isn't telling us. Unless they're terribly strict, you don't ground a kid for three weeks just for misbehaving. Did you notice how he hesitated before he said that? And that bit about homosexuals kidnapping his son – that's pretty far out in left field."

"Yeah, when he said that, it made me think of the guy who was there yesterday. I didn't tell you this. I didn't think it was relevant until now. But when I was there yesterday to take the report, there was another guy there named Dr. Ronald Babcock. As it turns out, he's not a medical doctor, he's a Ph.D. – in theology. He gave me his card, and he runs this organization called Closer Walk Ministries. I visited his website, and he provides counseling to try to convert gay kids to become straight."

"Oh, really! And what's the church Rev. Bauer's at?"

Garlow flipped through his notes. "Eternal Savior Christian

Church."

"That's one of those Evangelical churches, isn't it? They're pretty right-wing, from what I hear."

"Yeah, I checked out their website, too. They have a whole section on there with resources for parents who think their kid is LGBT."

"It's clear that Bryan ran away from home. That ripped photo was a rather startling indication that he doesn't want to be part of the family anymore. Based on what we have learned, I surmise they found out he's gay and they're trying to convert him into being straight."

"Makes sense. It doesn't change anything, but it provides a motive. But we still have no idea where he is."

"I think we should pay a visit to that kid who was his best friend. What was his name?"

Garlow looked back through his notes. "Chris Robertson – or Robinson. Rev. Bauer couldn't remember which."

Detective Wagner got out her phone and called the Bauers. Brenda answered and gave Detective Wagner the Robertsons' address and phone number. Officer Garlow turned the car around and drove to the Robertsons' home.

They knocked on the door, and Kathleen answered.

Officer Garlow said, "Good morning. Is this the Robertson residence?"

"Yes, it is."

"Is Chris home? He's in no trouble, by the way. We are investigating the disappearance of one of his friends."

"Yes, please come in. I'll call for him to come down."

Kathleen held the door open for Garlow and Wagner to enter, and offered them seats in the living room. Then she went upstairs and returned with Chris.

"Good afternoon, Chris. I'm Detective Wagner from the Prairie Village Police Department. This is Officer Garlow. May we ask you a few questions?"

"Yes, of course."

"Your friend, Bryan Bauer, has been missing since sometime Saturday afternoon or evening, or possibly as late as Sunday morning."

"Yes, I know."

"Do you have any idea where he might be?"

"No, ma'am."

"When was the last time you saw him or talked to him?"

"A week ago, Saturday night. That would have been, um… July 14th. At around 7:00 in the evening. I went to see him at the store where he works, Price Cutter."

"And you haven't seen or heard from him since then?"

"No, ma'am. His father grounded him and took his phone, so the only way I could see him was to go to the store."

"Did he ever say anything about leaving or running away?"

"No, ma'am."

"Can you think of any reason why he might run away? Maybe trouble at home?"

Chris looked at Kathleen, who nodded.

"Yes, well… his parents found out he's gay. And they're really religious and conservative, so that didn't go over too well with them."

"Is that why they grounded him?"

"Yes."

"Did he say anything about them taking any other actions with regard to him being gay?"

Kathleen said, "I can answer that. This all started when a police officer found Bryan and my son kissing in a car in some dark parking lot. Rev. and Mrs. Bauer invited us over to their house to tell us about it. Of course, we already knew that Chris is gay and they were boyfriends, so that didn't bother us. But they did say they were sending Bryan to some kind of therapist. They tried to tell us we should send Chris to him, too."

"Do you recall his name?"

"I think it was Babble or Braddock or something like that."

Officer Garlow said, "Babcock?"

"Yes, that was it. Babcock."

Detective Wagner said, "Thanks. Chris, are there any of your other friends who might have had contact with Bryan more recently? Can you think of anyone who might know where he is?"

"I doubt it, since he was grounded and they took his phone. But I sent a text to all our friends at school saying that Bryan is missing, and no one's said anything yet."

"Okay, good. Thank you for doing that. That was very helpful. Here's my card. Please let me know if you hear from him or if any of your friends do."

"Can I tell you something else?"

"Of course."

"I'm afraid that maybe he's killed himself."

"Why do you say that?"

"Because there were a few times when he'd say things. Like, when we got caught by the policeman, he said, 'just shoot me now,' and, 'my life is over.' And a couple of other times he'd say stuff like that. I mean, I just thought he was being dramatic. I didn't think he was really serious. And then…" Chris paused and sniffled a few times. "The last time I saw him, on Saturday night a week ago? I went there to break up with him. So, between that and being grounded and having his parents trying to convert him to be straight, I'm worried he may have killed himself."

Detective Wagner said, "Well, we just did an investigation at his home, and every indication is that he left on purpose. He took a couple of suitcases with clothes and his CDs, and his trumpet. He somehow got into their safe and got his phone and his personal records. He wouldn't have taken those things with him if he was planning to kill himself."

"Yeah, I guess not."

"Do you have any other questions for us?"

"No, I don't think so."

"Well, you have my card. Please don't hesitate to call me if you hear from him or you hear anything from your friends. Thank you very much for your help."

Detective Wagner and Officer Garlow got up to leave. Kathleen ushered them out the door.

Back in the car, Garlow asked Wagner, "So, what next?"

"Back to the station, I guess. I'll contact the KBI and ask them to get warrants so they can access his bank account and check with the airlines, trains, and buses."

Welcome to Los Angeles
Monday, July 23, 2007

Bryan woke up at around 5:30 a.m., as the bus pulled into the station in Barstow, California. He was starving. He managed to grab a small dinner at the Green River, Utah, stop at 7:00 p.m. yesterday. The bus had stopped for an hour in Las Vegas at 2:00 a.m., but he slept through that. The bus would stay in Barstow for half an hour and there was a restaurant nearby, so he was able to eat a quick breakfast and use the restroom.

The sun had just started to rise as the bus pulled away and returned to I-15 for the rest of the trip into Los Angeles. The Rocky Mountains he had admired during the drive from Colorado into Utah on Sunday afternoon were now replaced by stark desert wasteland, mostly flat with occasional small mountain peaks in the distance. Not much to look at.

He tried to catch a couple more hours of sleep, but with the daylight streaming into the bus and the anticipation of finally being close to LA, the best he could manage was a couple of brief dozes.

At 7:25 a.m., after a brief stop in San Bernardino, the bus turned onto I-10 for the final sixty miles of its journey to Los Angeles – just in time for Monday morning rush hour traffic. As the bus lurched along in the stop-and-go traffic, Bryan gazed out the window at mile after mile of bland suburbia. The endless nondescript office buildings, shopping centers, fast-food restaurants, billboards, apartments, and houses soon blurred together into an uninspiring suburban mosaic. The occasional graffiti along the freeway walls was not quite the 'Welcome to Los Angeles' sign he might have hoped for.

Finally, as the bus approached the I-5 interchange, the bold skyline of downtown LA came into view. It was a stark contrast to the endless tableau of one- and two-story buildings he had seen up to this point.

The bus exited the freeway and turned onto a dirty street in a stark, rough-looking industrial neighborhood. There was scarcely a surface that had not been tagged with gang-themed graffiti. The mostly anonymous businesses were enclosed behind solid blocks walls. The few doors and windows that were visible were protected by heavy iron bars. Sleeping homeless people and trash were everywhere.

The LA he was being introduced to couldn't have been farther from the sunny picture painted by Chris's older brother Tyler and Bryan's former boss Russ Simonton. He thought, *Could this be the same city that also contains Beverly Hills, Hollywood, beaches, and Disneyland? In what parallel universe do those exist?* He was expecting a sunny land of milk and honey with endless entertainment and unlimited possibility. What he was seeing was a gritty, dystopian hellscape.

The bus stations Bryan had experienced up to this point were plain, utilitarian places located in the less-traveled, lower-rent back streets of most cities. But at least they were safe. The Los Angeles bus station was surrounded by high fences with security guards at the entrances. Tents lined the sidewalks. It looked like the middle of a combat zone.

Bryan's heart sank. *I traveled 36 hours for this? This is my future?*

He decided to spring for a taxi rather than stand on the street to wait for a bus, then attempt to navigate transfers encumbered by his two suitcases, backpack, and trumpet.

As the taxi headed north on Alameda, the scenery gradually improved. Islands of trees, grass, and shrubs replaced the solid block walls and barbed wire-topped fences. Office buildings with windows replaced the stark warehouse buildings. Graffiti, while still present, was less ubiquitous.

The cab turned onto the 101 freeway. Several miles later, it exited onto Hollywood Boulevard. After several blocks, it turned left onto a side street and dropped Bryan off in front of the building housing the Los Angeles LGBT Youth Project. He gathered his belongings and hauled them through the door.

The receptionist looked up from her computer and smiled at Bryan and his luggage. "Good morning! New in town?"

"Yes, ma'am. I arrived by bus this morning."

"Where are you from?"

Bryan wondered whether he should divulge any information about where he came from, for fear that the receptionist might report him to police as a missing person. But he felt that this was probably a safe place. "Kansas."

"Welcome to LA. How may we help you?"

"I was told you might have services available for LGBT youth."

"Yes, we do. You've come to the right place. Why don't you have a seat over there and I'll see who's available to talk with you."

"Do you have a restroom?"

"Yes, down the hallway on your left."

"And would you please keep an eye on my stuff?"

"Sure. Why don't you move it over here behind my desk?"

Bryan carried his suitcases, backpack, and trumpet to the spot the receptionist indicated, then found the restroom. When he returned to the lobby, the receptionist led him to a small office staffed by an intake specialist.

"Hi, I'm Cynthia." She offered her hand, which Bryan shook.

"I'm Bryan. Nice to meet you."

"Have a seat." She motioned toward the guest chair facing her desk and Bryan sat down.

"Melanie mentioned that you just arrived from Kansas."

"Yes, I got in this morning. I've been on a bus for 36 hours."

"Goodness. You must be tired. So, what brings you to LA?"

"Well, basically, I needed to leave home. My parents recently found out I'm gay, and they're not cool with it at all. See, my dad's a pastor at a large church, so they're really religious and conservative. Anyway, I found out they were going to send me to this camp in Alabama where they try to convert gay kids to be straight, and I really didn't want to go."

Cynthia frowned, but in a caring, empathetic way. "Oh, no. I've heard about those places. I'm sorry you're in this predicament. Do you have a place to stay tonight?"

"Yes. My manager at my last job used to live here, so he contacted a couple of his friends and they're going to let me stay with them, at least for the first week or so."

"Okay, good. So many kids who arrive here have no place to go. We have some beds here, but often there aren't enough and kids end up sleeping on the street."

Bryan was shocked. "Do you have a lot of kids that show up here?"

"All the time. From all over the country. It's tragic how many parents kick their kids out and how many kids come here to escape bad living situations. We have a lot of resources to help homeless kids, but it never seems to be quite enough. What do you need? Food? Clothing? Any medications?"

"Well, I'm starving right now, but I'll be fine after I get something for lunch. Are there restaurants nearby?"

"Yeah, there are all sorts of places. We also have food here, if you can't afford anything."

"Thanks, but I have some money. I closed my bank account back home. I'll be opening a new one here pretty soon. And I brought two suitcases full of clothes and stuff."

"Sounds like you're better off than 99 percent of the other kids who show up here. So how may we help you?"

"My manager suggested that I should change my name and get legally emancipated. He said you might have attorneys who volunteer their services."

"Yes, we do. How old are you?"

"Seventeen."

Cynthia turned to her computer and typed a few things. Then she picked up her phone and dialed a number.

"Hello, Hal? It's Cynthia from the LGBT Youth Project. How are you today?" Pause. "I'm fine, thank you. Anyway, I have a young man here who just arrived in town and wants to see about changing his name and getting emancipated. Can you help?" Pause. "He's here right now. Let me ask."

Cynthia turned to Bryan. "Are you available at 3:00 this afternoon?"

Bryan replied, "Yeah, I don't have anything else to do."

Cynthia turned back to the phone. "Yes, he'll be here at 3:00. His name is Bryan. Thanks so much, Hal. You're an angel." Pause. "Okay, see you this afternoon. Bye!"

Cynthia jotted down a name and phone number on a notepad, then tore off the sheet and gave it to Bryan.

"The attorney's name is Hal Morris. He'll get you all taken care of. How does that sound?"

"That sounds fantastic. I wasn't expecting this to happen so fast."

"Sometimes things work out well."

"Is it okay if I go get something to eat, then hang out here for the afternoon? One of the guys I'm staying with is going to pick me up here at around 5:30, so can I stay here until then?"

"Yes. We created this center so it would be a safe place for young people to hang out. There's some food and bottled water in the kitchen area. There's a library with some books and a few computers if you need them. So, make yourself at home."

"Thank you very much, Cynthia. I appreciate your help."

"My pleasure. I hope things work out well for you. Remember, we're always here if you need anything."

Bryan walked back up the street to Hollywood Boulevard and turned right. He discovered that he was walking on the Hollywood Walk of Fame, with all the stars of famous actors and actresses embedded in the sidewalk. After several blocks, he turned around and walked in the other direction. After walking past more stars, he reached the Guinness World Records Museum and the Ripley's Believe It or Not Museum. The

Hollywood Wax Museum was across the street. After the long bus ride through hundreds of miles of desolate landscape and the gritty area surrounding the bus station, he was amazed that he was now standing in the middle of world-famous Hollywood! There was so much for him to discover.

He passed plenty of restaurants of all types, but considering his tired and unshowered condition, he opted for the familiar surroundings of a fast-food hamburger joint. There would be plenty of other occasions to explore all the wondrous new things around him.

After lunch, Bryan walked around Hollywood some more. He returned to the LGBT Youth Project office at 2:30 and waited in the lobby for Hal Morris to arrive.

At a few minutes past 3:00, a 40ish, somewhat short and compact man with wire-rimmed glasses and curly, thinning hair rushed into the lobby. He was smartly dressed in a jacket, open collar white shirt, stylish jeans, and expensive-looking loafers. He greeted the receptionist, who then pointed in Bryan's direction. Bryan stood up as Mr. Morris approached.

"Bryan? Hal Morris." Hal quickly scanned Bryan, smiled, and shook his hand vigorously. "How are you today?"

"I'm good, thanks. I appreciate you meeting with me on such short notice."

"My pleasure." He turned back to the receptionist. "Is there a room we can use?"

"The small meeting room down the hall on the right should be open."

"Thanks."

Hal led Bryan down the hall to a room with a rectangular table and six chairs. Hal sat down in a chair at one end, and Bryan sat in the chair to his right.

"Welcome to Los Angeles. Why did you decide to come here?"

Bryan gave Hal a brief explanation of how his parents found out he was gay, grounded him, forced him to go to counseling, and how he discovered they were about to send him to a gay conversion therapy camp. He told him about Mr. Simonton and how he had suggested LA and helped Bryan plan his escape.

As Bryan's story progressed, Hal's demeanor shifted from upbeat to concerned and empathetic.

When Bryan finished, Hal asked, "So, how may I help you?"

Bryan replied, "My manager suggested that I should get legally emancipated so I can do things on my own without my parents' involvement. That way, if they find me, they can't force me to go back home. I also want to change my name so it makes it harder for them to find me."

"How old are you now?"

"Seventeen."

"And when's your birthday?"

"October 14th."

"Hmm. Well, your boss was correct that becoming emancipated would prevent your parents from being able to force you to come back home. Unfortunately, this process typically takes four to six months. And except in a few rare circumstances, it requires the parents' consent for you to be emancipated. Since you turn eighteen in less than three months, there isn't enough time for the process to work."

"So, what do I do?"

"You'll just have to wait it out."

"And what about changing my name?"

"Unfortunately, while you're still a minor, that requires your parents' consent."

Bryan let out an exasperated sigh and buried his head in his hands. Then he said, "So, I was counting on doing all these other things like opening a bank account, getting a job, getting a cell phone, and enrolling in school using my new name. If I do all of that stuff with my current name, won't that make it easier for them to find me?"

"Not necessarily. For example, the bank account. A bank's customers aren't searchable on the internet. Same thing with a company's list of employees or the list of kids enrolled at a school. In fact, they go to great lengths to keep that private."

"But can't the police get that information?"

"Yeah, but that's like looking for a needle in a haystack. If they don't even know what city you're in, they're not going to get a warrant for every bank, every employer, and every school in the country. And if you opt for an unlisted number, it will be very difficult for them to find your number or your address."

"So, if I wait until I turn eighteen to change my name, then I'll have to change it in all those places."

"Oh, well. It will be a hassle, but it can be done. And I'll be happy to help you with the name change."

"Thanks." Bryan thought for a moment. "So, a minute ago you said there were a few circumstances in which I might be able to get emancipated without getting my parents involved. What are those?"

"That would only come into play if you could convince the judge that your parents aren't trying to find you to bring you back home, or if you would be in physical danger if you returned home."

"Well, they've probably called the police, so that's out."

"Besides, to become emancipated, you have to prove that you have a secure place to live – meaning you're not homeless or couch-surfing, a steady job where you earn enough money to cover all your living expenses, and you're going to school. So, it's not like you could do this tomorrow. It will take some time to get all these things in place."

"And I'd have to do all those things with my current name."

"Yep. And speaking of which, do you have a place to stay?"

"For now. My boss knows these two guys who have offered to let me stay with them for a week or two until I can find an apartment or something."

"If I may ask, how much money do you have?"

"About $3,000."

"That's about $3,000 more than most kids have when they arrive. Still, it won't last very long out here. What are you planning to do for work, especially considering that you have to go to school in September?"

"I was going to try to get a job in a grocery store or something like that. That's what I did back home."

"Well, I have more bad news for you. Apartment prices are a lot higher in LA than they are back in Kansas. I don't see how you could earn enough money with a grocery store job to live in an apartment and buy food and pay bills unless you found two or three other people to share it with. Besides, once you start school, you can't work as many hours. Renting a room somewhere might be a better option."

"I would do that. I just need a bed and a bathroom."

"So, you're seventeen. You'll be, what, a senior this year?"

"Yes."

"What are your longer-term plans?"

"I want to go to UCLA. That's one of the main reasons I decided to come to Los Angeles. I figured that after living here for a year, I would qualify for in-state tuition. I'm going to try to get a scholarship. I'm a straight-A student, and I figure that since I'll have no support from my parents that might help me qualify."

"I can tell you're pretty smart. What are you planning to major in?"

"Computer science or something like that. I want to be a software engineer or an application developer. I've been the webmaster for my father's church the past couple of years."

Hal paused for a moment as if he was contemplating what to do next. Then he said, "Okay, I might be able to help you. Let me tell you a little bit about me. I own a house a few blocks from UCLA. That's where I went to school. I have four rooms I rent to college students. It's a nice bunch of guys – all gay. It's kind of a safe space, if you know what I mean. Anyway, one of the guys who was going to move in next month just told me he lost his scholarship and he's not returning to school, so now I have a room open. I've never rented to a high school kid before, but I'm willing to make an exception in your case since you'll be 18 in three months and you seem pretty well grounded. The rent is $500 a month. How does it sound so far?"

"Awesome!" Up to this point, Bryan had been feeling increasingly pessimistic about his prospects for making it on his own in this big, expensive city. Suddenly, things were looking up again.

"Okay, well, you should come to see the place first. Want to check it out now?"

"Can we be back here at 5:30?"

"What happens at 5:30?"

"That's when one of the guys I'm going to be staying with will be here to pick me up."

Hal glanced at his watch. 3:20. "Yeah, probably. Do you have his number?"

"Yes."

"Okay, let's go. I can call him if we're going to be delayed."

Hal and Bryan walked up to the reception area. Bryan asked the receptionist, "Can you watch my stuff for the next couple of hours?"

"My shift ends soon, but somebody else will be here. It's okay to leave your stuff here."

Hal said, "Why don't you bring your stuff along? If you like the place, you can go ahead and move in. If not, you'll have it with you and you won't have to worry about someone else watching it."

Bryan thought for a second. "Well, okay."

Hal took Bryan's smaller suitcase and trumpet, and Bryan carried his larger suitcase and backpack. Hal led him to a shiny black BMW hardtop convertible. Hal popped the trunk and they managed to fit Bryan's possessions into the trunk with not much room to spare.

Bryan, at 6' 6", had to scrunch a bit to fit into the car. Hal said, "It's a nice summer day, and we'll be driving surface roads. How about if I put the top down?"

Hal drove a couple of blocks south, then turned west onto Sunset Boulevard. For the next nine miles, Bryan was treated to an eye-popping view of some of the better parts of Los Angeles. The first couple miles were regular city blocks, but as they continued into residential areas, the surroundings looked nicer and nicer.

Hal pointed out several landmarks, like The Comedy Store and the Beverly Hills Hotel. They entered a winding section of Sunset Boulevard, and Hal pointed to a bunch of trees on the right. "On the other side of those trees is Michael Jackson's mansion."

Finally, they approached UCLA, where Sunset Boulevard formed the winding northern boundary of the campus. A couple of blocks past the campus, Hal turned into an upscale residential neighborhood, made a couple more turns, then pulled into the driveway of a well-manicured, modern-looking home. He pressed the garage door remote and pulled the car into the garage. The garage was at street level, but the home sat on higher ground, requiring a trek up about twenty stair steps.

Bryan stood in awe as he surveyed the exterior of the house. It looked more upscale and fashionable than any house he had ever seen around Prairie Village.

Hal opened the door and escorted Bryan in. The interior was even more impressive than the exterior. Hal gave him a quick tour, including the available bedroom. It contained a queen-size bed with a colorful bedspread, a computer desk and chair, a dresser, and a small dorm fridge. The closet was about twice as large as the closet in his former bedroom. The view out the window was to the side of the house, so most of what he could see was a tall dense hedge that separated this house from the one next door.

Next Hal led him into the kitchen. It was spacious and modern, with a large stainless-steel refrigerator and a Jenn-air stove. There was a large kitchen island with a row of four stools, and a fancy multi-light fixture hanging above it from the ceiling.

Hal said, "You're on your own for buying food and cooking, although sometimes the guys team up for meals or share leftovers. You can use the fridge in your room for things like sodas or beer – well, not beer for you yet – and some of your food. You can put the rest in here. You can use this freezer, and there's a standalone freezer in the utility room. We use little colored dot stickers so we can tell whose food is whose. We share the condiments, so we don't have five sticks of butter and five bottles of ketchup.

"Sunday evening, I usually cook dinner for everyone. Nothing fancy, just pizza or chili or hamburgers, something like that. After that, we usually watch a movie or play a game or something. It's the one time each week when everyone's together, kind of like a family night.

"Everyone's in charge of keeping the kitchen and the common areas neat and clean. As long as you do a good job of putting things away and wiping up after yourself, you'll get along with everyone fine. If you see the dishwasher is full, run it. If you see that it's been run, empty it. If the trash can is full, empty it. Everyone's really good about doing their part, so we don't have any issues."

Bryan was already in total disbelief that he could be living here, but then Hal led him out to the backyard. It looked like a tropical oasis. There were tall oleander hedges with pink and white blossoms, a couple of palm trees, and a variety of other lush plants and shrubs. The pool sparkled, and there was a raised deck with a sheet waterfall at one end. There was a hot tub in one corner and an assortment of lounge chairs and outdoor tables with umbrellas. There was a pass-through window from the kitchen to an outdoor serving counter and a tiki bar with a thatch roof.

Bryan was completely awe-struck. "This is unbelievable! I've never seen anything like this!"

"Welcome to Southern California. Lots of houses have pools. As you can see, the backyard is totally private, so the pool and the hot tub are clothing-optional. You do what you feel comfortable with, but you'll find that the other guys just go naked. Except for when we have parties – although sometimes those end up being clothing-optional too. The backyard is like everything else – everybody does their part to keep it neat and clean. So, if you come out here and leaves are floating in the pool, grab the skimmer and scoop them out."

"This is amazing!"

"So, are you interested?"

Bryan did some quick calculations in his head. *Once school starts, I should be able to work 25 to 30 hours a week. If I can get $10 an hour, like I was making at Price Cutter back in Kansas, I should be able to clear $800 to $1,000 a month. After rent, that would leave $300 to $500 a month for food and whatever else I need to buy. So, it might be tight, but I can probably make it work. And I have $3,000 I could dip into occasionally if I have to.*

"Absolutely! This is incredible!"

"Alright, then. Welcome to our little gay family." They shook hands. "By the way, the other guys' names are Ricky, Ted, and Darnell. Darnell's gone for a few more weeks; he'll be back in September. Ricky and Ted come and go. Just say hi to them if you see them. If I see them first, I'll let them know about you."

"May I borrow your phone? I need to call the guy who's supposed to pick me up and tell him I won't need to stay with them after all."

Hal handed Bryan his phone, and they walked back inside. Bryan dug out Trevor's phone number and called him. Then Hal helped Bryan carry his suitcases into his new bedroom.

"Mr. Morris, I can't thank you enough. I'll do everything I can to keep the place clean and get along with everyone else. Thank you, thank you, thank you!!!"

"You're welcome. And call me Hal. None of that Mr. Morris stuff."

"Okay, Hal. And speaking of what to call each other, I've decided that my new name is going to be Ryan Robertson. Even though I can't change it until I turn 18, can I introduce myself to the other guys as Ryan now? That way, they won't have to re-learn my name in a couple of months."

"Yeah, sure. That makes sense. Whatever you want."

Girl Talk

Tuesday, July 24, 2007

After breakfast on Tuesday morning, Brenda gave Brad a photo of Bryan she had selected from one of their family photo albums. It was a couple of years old, but it would have to do. She asked him to scan it at the church and crop it so it showed only Bryan.

After Brad left for the church, Brenda called Rachel Babcock, Ron's wife. "Good morning, Rachel. This is Brenda Bauer. How are you this morning?"

"I'm fine. I am so sorry to hear about Bryan's disappearance. Is there any news?"

"No, none yet. A police officer and a detective visited yesterday morning to gather some information. So, we'll see what they turn up."

"How are you holding up? This must be awful for you."

"It is. But I guess I'm doing as well as I can, given the circumstances. Anyway, I'm calling to ask if you might be interested in getting together for coffee or maybe lunch sometime soon, just for a little chit-chat."

"Oh, I'd love that. Since we moved here a couple of months ago, I haven't had much chance to make friends."

"Good. Are you free tomorrow?"

"Well, that's part of the problem. I'm never really free. Since it's summertime and the girls aren't in school, I have to keep an eye on them all the time or else bring them with me wherever I go. It kind of limits my available time."

"Yeah, I know what you mean. When Bryan was here, he could keep an eye on Brandon so I could get out now and then. Sometimes I can send him over to a friend's house for a little while. But with three, that must be hard to manage."

"Exactly. Especially since we don't know very many people yet."

"Wait. I have an idea. We can take our kids to the community pool for swimming. We can chat while they're playing in the pool."

"That sounds like a wonderful idea! How about tomorrow at 1:00?"

"Sounds great. We'll see you then."

***

The next morning, Brandon asked, "Mom, when is Bryan coming home?"

Brenda sighed. "I don't know, dear. We talked to the police on Monday. I'm sure they're doing everything they can to find him."

"I miss him."

"I know, dear. I miss him too. This is very hard for all of us. Anyway, would you like to go swimming this afternoon?"

"Sure!"

"Okay, good. Today we'll be going with a few new people. The counselor Bryan was seeing and his wife just moved to town a couple of months ago. They have three girls. So, I've invited them along."

"*Girls???* You mean I have to play with *girls*?"

"Well, honey, you don't have to play with them the whole time. But you have to be nice to them, and I know you will. They're new in town and they haven't made many friends yet. Maybe you can introduce them to some of your friends. It's a good opportunity to do something nice for other people. If you see any of your friends at the pool, you can go play with them."

"Okay."

The prospect of spending an afternoon at the pool was less exciting to Brandon after hearing this news, but it was still better than being cooped up in the house alone.

***

At 1:00, Rachel pulled their mini-van into the Bauers' driveway. Brenda and Brandon left the house and climbed in. Rachel introduced them to twelve-year-old Sarah, nine-year-old Rebecca, and seven-year-old Hannah. Hannah and Rebecca, in the rear seat, seemed shy and somewhat uncomfortable. They hardly said anything during the entire trip to the pool. Brandon, always the talkative one, tried to engage them in conversation. Sarah, the eldest and his seatmate in the middle seat, provided most of the responses, as if she was the spokesperson for the three of them.

The two mothers, with four kids in tow, found an empty spot in the grass area and spread out their blankets. The mothers sprayed sunscreen all over the kids and then each other. Brandon appointed himself the tour guide and escorted the three girls on a tour of the property. He spotted Chris in one of the lifeguard chairs and exchanged waves with him as they passed. Fortunately, he saw a couple of girls he knew from school and introduced Sarah, Rebecca, and Hannah to them.

With the kids out of the way, the two mothers were free to engage in some unfiltered conversation, which was a welcome opportunity for both of them. They broke the ice by talking about Brad's church and the role Brenda played as the pastor's wife. They talked about what Rachel liked and didn't like about living in South Carolina, where they lived before moving to Overland Park. They talked about each of their kids – the four that were present. Then, inevitably, the topic of Bryan came up.

Rachel asked, "So, pardon me for asking, and I completely understand if you'd rather not talk about it. But… why do you suppose Bryan left home?"

Brenda replied, "I don't mind at all. I could really use someone to talk to. Anyway, as you probably remember from the dinner the four of us had after the Rescued Through Love conference, Bryan has been struggling with homosexuality. He had three counseling sessions with your husband, but then he announced that he refused to continue them. So, Brad decided that we should send him away to this camp where they practice more intensive therapy to correct these kids' thoughts and behaviors. Well, Bryan found out about it. I have no idea how. Brad accused me of telling him, but of course, I didn't. So, he ran away to avoid being taken to that place."

"Where do you think he might have gone? Did he take one of your cars?"

"No, that's just it. I had one car, because I was taking Brandon to Tulsa to visit my mother. You know, so he wouldn't be here when they took him away, in case there was a scene. Brad had the other car. He didn't take his bike. So, we have no idea where he went or how he got there."

"What if he left town?"

"I don't even want to think about my child out on his own in the world somewhere! Anyway, the police are going to check with the airlines, the trains, and the bus lines, but they have to get warrants, so it may take a while."

"Do you think he's hiding at one of his friends' houses?"

"It's possible. We don't know. Brad called the parents of his best friend, the one who was recruiting him, and they said they haven't seen him. But of course, if they're hiding him, they're not going to tell us."

"Do you really think they would do that?"

"I wouldn't put it past them. We had them over one evening after Bryan and their son were caught making out in a car. And when we told them what the boys were doing, they didn't have any problem with it! They said they already knew their son is a homosexual and it's perfectly fine with them! They're not religious people. The police asked for their address, so they probably checked there. But if he's not there he could be at any of his other friends' houses."

"Did you give the police the names of his other friends?"

Brenda sighed. "No, and that's another thing. We had taken his phone away from him when we grounded him, so we figured we could go through the contacts on his phone. But somehow he got into the safe and took his phone, his Social Security card, his birth certificate, and everything else we had in there.

"Anyway, Brad's all upset because we sent him to the public school starting in ninth grade. We sent him to a private Christian school before that. I thought he would do better in the public school. They have a better band program, and he loves playing his trumpet. He was on the track team and did very well with that. And they have advanced placement courses that will make it easier for him to get into a better college. But then he met this kid, and probably some others like him, and it seems they were bad influences on him.

"I guess I failed because I didn't get to know his other friends better. Honestly, I can't even name hardly any of them. He was always so responsible and so well behaved that we had no idea he was getting into any trouble. And Chris – that's the other kid – always seemed like he was so nice."

Rachel searched for something comforting to say. "I'm sure you did all you could. As they get older, we have to let them go out on their own more."

"Yes, I suppose. But anyway, back to last weekend. Now, in hindsight, I never should have agreed with sending him off to that camp. Something told me it would be a bad idea. It just seemed a bit too extreme, you know? Like what were they going to do to him there? But Brad never listens to me. He's always going to do what he decides is best, and I have to be obedient to him and support whatever he decides. The only time I ever got my way was when I insisted on sending him to the public school, and now it turns out he was right about that, too."

"Is it really that bad? Because we are sending the girls to the public school in the fall. The money Ron makes from Family-Focused Ministries and the conferences he speaks at is enough to pay the bills, but until he gets his counseling practice built up we can't afford to send three girls to a private school."

"Yeah, it can be pricey. We've only had to send one at a time. Bryan and Brandon are eight years apart, so the year Brandon started first grade was the same year Bryan switched to the public school. But Brad is sending him to the Christian high school in the fall – that is, assuming we find him."

"And assuming he's not off at that camp."

Brenda hadn't thought about that. If Bryan is still at that reparative therapy camp when school starts, how will that affect his education?

Rachel continued, "I'm applying to be a teacher in the fall. If I can get on at one of the Christian schools, that may include tuition benefits for the girls. But I may end up teaching at a public school."

"Well, I hope it works out."

It was 1:45. The lifeguards blew their whistles, which indicated the start of break time. The kids all made their way to the nearest ladders and got out of the pool. The girls returned to the blanket where Rachel and Brenda had been talking. Some of the grown-ups headed to the pool to enjoy fifteen minutes of kid-free swimming.

Rachel asked, "Are you having a good time?"

Sarah replied on behalf of her younger sisters. "Yes! Brandon introduced us to a few of the girls from his school, so we've been playing with them."

Brenda looked around but didn't see Brandon. He was probably using the restroom or off somewhere with his friends.

Rebecca asked, "May we have some money for the snack bar?"

Rachel reached into her purse and gave Sarah a $20 bill. "You may get one drink and one thing to eat, each. Don't get anything too junky. And don't eat too much, or you'll have to wait to get back in the water."

The girls all said, "thanks!" and scampered off to the snack bar.

***

Brandon made his way to the lifeguard chair where Chris was stationed. Once all the kids were out of the pool, Chris climbed down.

"Hi Chris!"

"Hey, little buddy!" Chris high-fived Brandon. "How are you holding up?"

"Not so good. I really miss Bryan. I can't believe he's gone."

"Me too. Is there any news?"

"No. The police came over on Monday and asked a bunch of questions. I had to stay in my room."

"Yeah, they came to our house too. We haven't heard anything. I sent texts to all our friends at school in case anyone sees him."

"Oh, I don't think anyone around here is going to see him."

"What do you mean?"

"He went somewhere far away. I don't know where, but he's not here."

"How do you know that?"

Brandon looked around. He looked at the blanket where Brenda and Rachel were talking. Brenda didn't see him, but he didn't want to take any chances.

"Can we go someplace else? Someplace where Mom can't see me talking to you?"

Chris seemed a little puzzled, but he led Brandon over to a picnic area on the other side of the clubhouse. They sat down at a picnic table, facing each other.

Brandon said, "First, you've got to promise me that you won't say anything to anyone, okay?"

"Okay."

"Bryan and I always did this thing where, whenever we had a secret that just he and I knew, we'd always do this." Brandon held out his hand with his pinky extended, with a slight curl. "Put your pinky out like this."

Chris did, and Brandon shook it. "This will be our little secret, okay?

It's really important."

"I promise, I won't tell a soul."

"He gave me his trumpet – his old one, not his newer one – so I can play it when I start taking trumpet lessons. He put it in my closet. When I found it and opened the case, there was a letter inside. He said he had to go away. He said he didn't want to, but he had to. He said that Mom and Dad couldn't deal with him being gay, so they were going to send him away to someplace very bad."

"What kind of place? Where?"

"He didn't say. But he said he was going to be gone for many years. He said that when I'm grown up, he'll find me and we can be brothers and best friends again. And he said he'll think about me every day. And he told me he loves me."

Chris was doing everything he could to hold back tears. "I know he will. And I know how much he loves you."

"He loves you too. He told me."

"He said that in the letter?"

"Not in the letter. A few weeks ago, after you guys got caught kissing in the car."

"You know about that?"

"Yeah. He explained what being gay means, and that you two are gay, and he said he loves you."

Chris could hold back his tears no longer. "Thanks, Brandon. You have no idea how much that means to me. I love him too."

"I know. I already figured it out. You and Bryan were always so happy whenever you were together."

Chris cried some more. Brandon said, "I hope that someday when we're all grown up, he'll find you and you two can spend the rest of your lives together."

"Thanks. I hope so too."

Chris took a moment to pull himself together, then they got up from the table.

"Okay, well, break's almost over, so I have to get back to my chair. But thanks for everything you just told me. It really helps. And don't worry, I won't tell anyone. And… may I have a hug?"

Brandon smiled and nodded. Chris dropped to one knee, and they gave each other a quick hug.

***

Meanwhile, back at the blanket, Brenda decided it was time to introduce another topic she wanted to discuss.

"Your husband gave an excellent presentation at that conference. We learned a lot from it."

"Thanks. He's very passionate about his work."

"So is Brad. Anyway, I was wondering about something. And like you said earlier, if you'd rather not talk about it, that's perfectly okay. About that part of his story when he talks about how he used to be part of the gay lifestyle… How do you deal with knowing that he used to… you know… be with another man?"

"Well, I try not to think about the actual things they did. But that's in the past. As he said, he gave his life over to God and turned from his sinful ways. And I know God has forgiven him. So, if God has forgiven him, then why shouldn't I? I mean, we have all sinned, but what's important is that he has repented and is now following God's path."

"Yeah, I suppose. But do you ever wonder whether he still thinks about guys? Or if he has ever relapsed?"

"Maybe from time to time he'll see a handsome man and admire him, but doubt that he's ever acted on it. He's a good husband. He treats me very well, and he's a great father to the girls. So, it doesn't bother me. In fact, it makes me feel good knowing that I'm helping to keep him on the right path. You must feel the same way."

"What do you mean?"

"Well… Ron and Brad were roommates for three years, so I figured that–"

"WHAT??? They were roommates for three years?"

"You didn't know that?"

"No! Brad has only said that he *knew* Ron in college. He's never mentioned that they were roommates. Let alone for three years."

"Oh. Well, I don't mean to imply that anything was going on, necessarily. I mean, even if Ron knew he was a homosexual, it doesn't mean that Brad was, or that they were, you know, involved. It's quite possible that they weren't. Probably a bad assumption on my part."

Brenda thought back to when she first met Brad. She was a freshman at Oral Roberts and he was a senior. He didn't ever talk about his roommate, or if he even had one. She only met Ron a few times at parties or school events, but she recalled how chummy Ron and Brad seemed. She never knew Ron was his roommate.

She thought back to when she and Brad took Bryan in to see Ron in his professional capacity. She recalled how warmly Ron and Brad had greeted each other, and how they seemed to have such a natural rapport during the dinner the four of them shared after the conference.

Then she thought about last Sunday. Finally, she said, "You know… I think your assumption may be correct."

Rachel decided she needed to be very careful about what she said going forward. She may have already said too much. Today had gone so well up to this point and she was happy to finally be making a friend in her new town. She didn't want to ruin it right off the bat.

"What do you mean?"

"You know how Ron said in his speech that every day he says a prayer, asking the Lord to help him make it through that day without having any impure thoughts or acting on them?"

"Yes…"

Suddenly Brenda regretted that she had even brought this up. But she had, and she couldn't just say 'never mind' now. Besides, if the roles were reversed, she would want the other woman to tell her.

The girls ran up to the blanket. Sarah gave Rachel the change from their snacks. Rachel asked, "What did you have?"

Sarah replied, "We each got a soda. Hannah and Rebecca got fudgesicles and I got an ice cream sandwich."

"Okay, that wasn't bad. You may get back in the pool when the break is over."

Brenda looked around, then asked, "Have any of you seen Brandon?"

Sarah said, "I saw him over in the picnic area. He was talking to one of the lifeguards. Then he hugged him."

Brenda looked around again. The lifeguards were walking back to their stations and climbing into their chairs. "Which one?"

Sarah pointed to the lifeguard closest to the diving area and said, "That one."

Brenda stood up and took a few steps forward to get a clearer view. It was Chris. She returned to the blanket. "Thank you."

The lifeguards blew their whistles, signaling that the break was over. Sarah, Rebecca, and Hannah joined the other kids who were all rushing back into the pool.

Rachel asked, "Do you know him?"

Brenda replied, "That's Chris. The one who has been recruiting Bryan."

"And now he's talking to Brandon. And hugging him."

"I know. Well, they already know each other. Chris used to come to the house and he and Bryan would practice their instruments together. And they'd let Brandon listen to them."

Suddenly it dawned on Brenda. Brandon had been in Bryan's bedroom with Chris and Bryan on numerous occasions.

Rachel said, "I'm shocked that this place would hire homosexuals and put them in a position where they have such easy access to children."

"Maybe they don't know about him."

"Maybe we should tell them."

Brenda was repulsed by the idea that homosexuals were coming for all the males in her family – first Bryan, then her husband, and now Brandon. The fact that Brandon was still a boy made her blood boil. "Wait here. I'll be right back."

She marched to the clubhouse and told the first employee she saw, "I'd like to speak with the manager, please."

The employee said, "Wait right here, please," and disappeared behind a door labeled 'Staff Only.'

A moment later, she emerged with a middle-aged man who said, "I'm Leon Wilfred. How may I help you?"

"I'm Brenda Bauer. My husband, Brad Bauer, is the pastor of the Eternal Savior Christian Church. Are you aware that one of your employees, Chris Robertson, is a homosexual?"

Leon appeared taken aback. "Well, no. We don't ask our employees about their sexual orientation when we hire them. Is there a problem?"

"I'll say there is! He recruited my older son into the gay lifestyle, and now my son has disappeared. He's been missing since Saturday and the police are searching for him. And just now, Chris was seen talking to *and hugging* my younger son, *who is only nine years old.*"

"With all due respect, ma'am, Chris Robertson is one of our best employees. He passed his lifesaving course with flying colors, and he's punctual and attentive while he's on duty. He gets along well with everybody. I've never had any complaints or seen any signs of inappropriate behavior."

"I thought he was a nice boy too until he seduced my son. In any case, I trust that you'll fire him immediately. I'm sure you'll agree that it's entirely inappropriate to allow homosexuals to work in a job where they can be so close to children."

"As I said earlier, I had no idea until now what his sexual orientation is, and frankly it's none of my business. It's irrelevant to the qualifications of the job, and I am not about to fire one of my best employees for doing nothing worse than hugging a kid he already knows."

Brenda spun around and stormed away.

When she returned to Rachel at their blanket, Rachel asked, "How did it go?"

"Terrible. They're not going to fire him. They are perfectly content to let homosexuals work here and have easy access to our children."

"Well, there might be laws that prevent them from firing homosexuals."

"Not in Kansas! Maybe in liberal places like California and Oregon, but not here!"

"Anyway, you were asking about the prayer that Ron says every morning, asking the Lord for strength and deliverance from temptation?"

Brenda was hoping the distraction of Chris talking to Brandon would lead them away from this topic, but Rachel hadn't forgotten. So here goes…

"Yes. I don't know how to say this, but it appears that Ron forgot to say his prayer on Sunday morning."

"What do you mean?"

"Well, when Brad called me in Tulsa to tell me that Bryan was missing, I immediately packed up our things and drove back here with Brandon. Apparently, he thought I would stay down there until Tuesday, as we had originally planned. I mean, *hello*! Our son is missing! So of course, I got back here as fast as I could.

"But when we got home at around 5:00, Brad wasn't there, but his car was. I figured maybe he went someplace for dinner, but why was his car still there?"

Rachel asked, "So what does this have to do with Ron and his prayer?"

"I'm getting to that. So, when I got up to our bedroom, I saw that the sheets and the bedspread were all messed up, and there were some…

um… tell-tale stains on the sheets. Then I went into the bathroom, and I could tell the shower had been recently used. There were still some water droplets on the glass, and it was humid, like it is after someone has taken a shower. And there were *two* wet towels on the rack.

"So, a little later, Brad and Ron walked in. They had been out to dinner, AND… they had been drinking! Brad even brought another bottle in with him."

"So, what you're saying is…?"

"I'm saying all indications are that our husbands, shall we say, rekindled their romance on Sunday afternoon – in MY bed."

"But you didn't actually catch them in the act."

"No, but the evidence is pretty incriminating."

Rachel pondered this information for a few minutes. "And to think, the original plan was for them to spend the night together at a hotel in Montgomery."

"Exactly."

"What do you think we should do?"

"Let's each ask them about it. Then we'll compare notes."

"I guess so. But then what? I can't really divorce him. I can't provide for three girls and myself on just a teacher's salary, even with child support payments."

"Yeah, me too. I dropped out of college when I was a sophomore to marry Brad. I haven't worked since I was pregnant with Bryan eighteen years ago. I don't have any marketable skills or experience. I couldn't get anything more than a minimum-wage job."

"At least we can get it out in the open, talk about it, and maybe prevent it from continuing. I'd rather know the truth and try to deal with that, painful as it might be, than go on living naively in a make-believe world."

"Yeah. But the thing that really galls me is that Brad has come down so hard on Bryan for his same-sex attraction, but now look what he's done! Now that I know this about him, it seems like the ultimate hypocrisy."

"Same with Ron and his counseling practice."

They sat in silence for a few minutes. Then Brenda said, "What is it with men? Are there any real straight men left?"

Rachel shook her head. "I wish I knew."

When the lifeguards blew their whistles to begin the next break, Brenda and Rachel gathered their kids and drove home.

***

After they returned home, Brenda asked Brandon, "Did you have a fun time at the pool today?"

"Yeah, it was okay."

"Good. But honey, there's one thing we need to talk about. I don't want you to have any further contact with Chris. Okay?"

"Why not?"

"Well, we've learned some things about him. And as it turns out, he's the kind of person you need to stay away from."

"Why? He's always nice to me, and he's Bryan's best friend."

"Yes, well, that's sort of the problem. Remember how I've always taught you to never talk to strangers and never accept candy from a stranger? You know, because they might be bad?"

"That doesn't make sense. Chris isn't a stranger and he wasn't offering me candy."

"I know. It's kind of hard to explain. It will make more sense when you're older. But in any case, you are not to talk to Chris or go near him anymore. Do you understand?"

"No, I don't understand."

"Well, it's complicated. But basically, it's Chris's fault that Bryan is gone. And I don't want anything to happen to you. So, stay away from him. It's not open to further discussion."

Brandon frowned and went up to his room. He understood, alright.

He understood why his mom was telling him to stay away from Chris. He understood why Bryan was gone, and it wasn't Chris's fault. And he understood that he had just been lied to.

The Detective Returns

Monday, July 30, 2007

When Officer Garlow checked his messages on Monday morning, he found a message from Detective Wagner. 'Come see me when you get a chance. Interesting updates on Bauer case.'

Garlow walked over to Wagner's desk and said, "Good morning! How was your weekend?"

"It was good. And you?"

"Yeah, it was fine."

"Hey, I got some information back from the KBI. First, about his bank account. He withdrew all his money and closed his account on Saturday afternoon at around 3:00."

"Did he get a cashier's check?"

"Nope – he took it in cash. Too bad – if he got a check we could have found out where it was cashed."

"Smart kid. Obviously, he didn't want to leave a trail."

"Yeah, well check this out. On Sunday afternoon, the day his father reported him missing, he had an airline reservation for a flight to Montgomery, Alabama, departing at 2:55 p.m."

"So, he's in Alabama."

"Nope. He was a no-show. But get this. There were also reservations on the same flight for Brad Bauer and Ronald Babcock, all part of the same itinerary, all made by Brad Bauer the previous day and paid for with his credit card. But here's the odd part. Brad and Ronald had reservations to return the next day, but Bryan's was a one-way ticket."

"Verrrry interesting… So, what do you make of it?"

"It looks to me like they were going to take Bryan somewhere and leave him there. Where, I don't know. Apparently, Bryan didn't want to go, and felt he had no other choice than to run away from home."

"It must have been someplace he thought would be terrible."

"Yes. Now remember, his parents found out he's gay and they were trying to convert him to be straight. And Babcock runs some sort of counseling practice that purports to do that. And the church Rev. Bauer leads recently hosted a conference geared toward parents and families of gay kids."

"So do you suppose there's some kind of facility in Montgomery they were going to take him to that would try to make him straight?"

"That's a reasonable guess, but we don't know."

"And why would Babcock be going too?"

"Another good question. I think maybe we should pay another visit to the Bauer household. What do you think?"

"Yeah. But regardless of what we find out, we still have a missing kid. It doesn't really matter what they were trying to do or what we think about it, he's still a minor and he's missing. Did they ever send in a picture?"

"Yes. I forwarded it to the KBI and the National Center for Missing and Exploited Children. Oh, and here's another bit of info. On Saturday night at around 10:30, Bryan bought an Explore America pass at the bus station in KC. That's a pass that gives you unlimited rides for two weeks. The next bus that departed from the station was westbound, terminating in Los Angeles. Apparently, he got on it. But we don't know where he might have gotten off. The bus passed through Denver and Las Vegas, as well as a bunch of small towns. And we don't know if he will take another bus to another place before the two weeks have passed. Maybe he already has."

"He thought this through pretty well."

"A little too well. His father bought the plane tickets at 1:00 on Saturday afternoon. Bryan closed his bank account at 3:00 that afternoon and bought the bus ticket at 10:30 that evening. We don't know when Bryan found out they were going to take him to

Montgomery, but it doesn't appear that this was planned very far in advance. He may be smart, but I think it's a stretch that a 17-year-old could plan this out so carefully in such a short time."

"So, you think he had help?"

"Probably."

"But from whom?"

"I have no idea. And no, there is no homosexual organization that kidnaps gay kids or facilitates them running away. The KBI has never heard of such a thing. Maybe we can get some answers during our visit."

Detective Wagner called the Bauer home. Brenda confirmed that both she and Brad were home and a visit at 11:00 would be fine.

***

Officer Garlow drove Detective Wagner to the Bauer home in his squad car. As they were walking up to the front door, Wagner said softly, "Let's not say anything about the bus ticket just yet. I want to see how this goes."

Garlow nodded and rang the doorbell. Brenda answered and ushered them inside. Brandon had already been asked to stay in his room.

Detective Wagner said, "Good morning. How are you doing today?"

Brenda replied, "Naturally, we're worried sick about Bryan, but we're trying to hang in there. Have you found out anything?"

"Yes, we have. Rev. Bauer, have you been monitoring the call log on his cell phone account?"

"Uh… I checked a couple of times last week. Nothing at all."

"Well, please keep checking every day or two. Let me know if you see any calls. Now for what we've found. The Kansas Bureau of Investigation was able to obtain a warrant to gain access to any travel he might have done. That investigation showed that he had a reservation for a flight to Montgomery, Alabama, on Sunday, July 22nd. What was the purpose of that trip?"

Brad hesitated, then replied, "Well… uh… he was going there for summer camp."

"I see. What kind of camp?"

"A church camp. For religious study."

"How long was he supposed to attend this camp?"

Brad's increasing discomfort was obvious. "At least two weeks, maybe longer. It was kind of open-ended."

"We noticed that the airline ticket was purchased the day before the trip. When–"

"Ah, well, I kind of procrastinated on that. I meant to do it earlier, but I kept getting caught up in other stuff going on at the church."

"When did you and Bryan decide that he was going to attend this camp?"

"Well, actually, this was going to be a surprise for him."

"Wait. Let me get this straight. You were going to send him to summer camp, for an undefined length of time, and he didn't even know about it?"

"That's right."

"What made you think he would want to do this?"

"Well, it was more my idea."

"So, if this whole business of flying to Montgomery, Alabama for a summer camp was something he didn't know about, why do you suppose he suddenly disappeared?"

"I have no idea. I haven't been able to figure that one out, myself."

"What is the name of that camp?"

"Um… the Youth Leadership Proj… er … Camp. I think that's it."

Detective Wagner glanced over to Brenda.

She said, "The Youth Restoration Project."

"Thank you."

Officer Garlow was taking copious notes. Detective Wagner turned back to Brad.

"Rev. Bauer, the reservation had a one-way ticket for Bryan. It also had round-trip tickets for you and Ronald Babcock, returning the next day. Now, I can understand why you would want to accompany your son on an airplane trip, but who is Ronald Babcock and why was he also making the trip?"

"With all due respect, Mrs. Wagner–"

"That's *Detective* Wagner."

"Uh, Detective Wagner, I don't see what that has to do with where my son might have disappeared to, or how it's going to help us find him and bring him home."

"It will be helpful to understand the circumstances surrounding his disappearance, as well as who might have known about this trip. Plus, I need to either confirm or rule out the possibility that homosexuals may have kidnapped him, as you suggested."

Officer Garlow tried his hardest not to smirk. He wished he could give Wagner a high-five.

She continued. "So now, why was Ronald Babcock also going to take this trip?"

"Since he holds a Ph.D. in Theology, he has a professional interest in meeting the people who run this camp and learning more about the programs they offer. It was a networking opportunity."

"I see. So, let's assume for a moment that sending Bryan to this camp wasn't going to be a surprise. Do you think going to this camp is something he would have wanted to do?"

"Well, I assume so. I would hope so."

"Since he wasn't told about going to this camp and it seems to have come up on short notice, it's possible that the timing was merely a coincidence. Perhaps his leaving home and you planning to send him to that camp are unrelated. They just happened to occur at the same time. Can either of you think of any other reasons why Bryan would want to leave home?"

Brad replied, "Well, as I told Officer Garlow last week, he was probably upset because he was grounded."

Garlow said, "For misbehaving, correct?"

"Yes."

Wagner asked, "Can you think of anything else?"

Brenda couldn't stay silent any longer. "Yes. I can. You see, about a month ago, we found out that he was becoming a homosexual. And obviously, we don't want that for our child. So first, we sent him to Dr. Babcock, who runs this so-called ministry where he claims he can turn people away from same-sex attraction and lead them back to being straight."

Brad cleared his throat. "Uh, Brenda…"

Brenda continued, "Anyway, after three weeks, Bryan came home and said the sessions weren't doing any good and he refused to go back. In fact, he said they were the creepiest thing ever – those were his words – and Dr. Babcock had suggested some rather unorthodox forms of therapy. And then he claimed that Dr. Babcock was showing some inappropriate interest–"

Brad interrupted. "Sweetheart, I don't think they need to know the details–"

"Oh, SHUT UP. I'm talking now. Don't interrupt me. It's disrespectful." Brenda glared at Brad. He knew she had dirt on him. Better not provoke her anymore.

"Anyway, on Sunday, two weeks ago, we had this big blowout argument where it all came to a head. Bryan said he was fed up with being grounded and being sent to Dr. Babcock, and he said he wasn't going to put up with any more abuse – again, his words – and he demanded that we accept that he's going to be this way. And that's when my husband and Dr. Babcock hatched this plan to send him off to that place in Alabama. And for the record, it's not really a church camp, at least not in the way you would imagine. It's a place where they try to convert gay kids into being straight."

She paused for a moment to catch her breath. Wagner and Garlow were still trying to absorb it all. Brad was afraid to say anything.

She continued. "So, I don't know whether he found out about it or whether he was mad at us for how he has been treated."

Brad said, "Oh, come on. You told him. I didn't tell him. Ron didn't tell him. Who else would have told him? How did he find out?"

Brenda replied, "How could I have told him? I was in the car on my way to Tulsa with Brandon. Besides, why would I want him to run away?"

She turned back toward Detective Wagner and Officer Garlow. "That was part of the plan. I was to take his younger brother Brandon to visit his grandmother so he wouldn't see all this going down. They had arranged for two other men to be here to help with forcing him to go to the airport. And you asked why Dr. Babcock was going. Well, supposedly it was to help keep Bryan in check for the whole trip. You know, two against one, in case he tried to get away or something. Never mind that Bryan is one of the fastest runners on his track team, so they wouldn't stand a chance. But whatever. So, there were probably other reasons why he went." Brenda glared at Brad.

She continued. "But no, I didn't tell him. And I don't know whether he found out about this or not. But after the confrontation we had a couple of Sundays ago, I can see why he would be angry with us. He seemed to be okay with being a homosexual and he said he loved Chris, that kid who was his… boyfriend, or whatever they call it."

"The one who recruited him," Brad said.

"Whatever. What it all boils down to is this. My baby's gone, and we don't know where he is. And I would give anything to have him back."

Detective Wagner said, "Rest assured, we're doing everything we can. We have uploaded the photo you sent to the KBI and the National Center for Missing and Exploited Children. The Center has a communication network that extends all across the country, so posters with his picture are going up all over. The KBI and I will continue to explore any leads that come up, so it's important to let me know if anything shows up on his call log or if anything else happens. If you think of any friends or relatives who might know where he went, please call them and let me know what you find out.

"Also, the Center has some resources for families of kids that are missing, so you might want to visit their website and check those out. I think there's a local support group. And, um… you might want to consider counseling to help you work through your grief and your… feelings. This is an extremely stressful time."

Detective Wagner and Officer Garlow got up to leave. Brenda walked them to the door. "Thank you for all that you're doing. And sorry about all that."

Wagner replied, "You're welcome. I can only imagine how stressful this must be."

***

Once they were in the squad car heading back to the police station, Officer Garlow turned to Detective Wagner and said, "Well, you were right about your suspicion that he wasn't telling you everything."

"Sadly, yes. Wasn't that enlightening?"

"So, now what?"

"I don't know. There's not much we can do unless we get a tip from someone who recognizes him from a missing child notice or unless the KBI turns up something else. It's clear that he's not local anymore, so he's out of our jurisdiction."

"Regardless of whether he found out about their plan to take him to that Youth Restoration Project place or he was just angry with them for how badly they were treating him for being gay, I can't blame him for wanting to get out of there."

"I know, right? At least they didn't kick him out as some parents do. He chose to leave. But same result, I guess. But here's the thing. If he turns up and gets returned home, then what do you think will happen to him?"

"I bet his dad will try to take him to that place again."

"Yeah, possibly. That, or something worse. If he is returned home, I'm going to refer the case to Child Protective Services. His mother said something about him not wanting to be abused any longer. That really caught my ear. In any case, he might be better off wherever he is now. He had $3,000 in his bank account. It's not all that much, but it's enough to keep him off the street for a while. He's probably in no danger. And he becomes an adult in three months."

"And did you catch that bit about the counseling sessions with that Dr. Babcock guy? How he told his mother they were creepy and he felt the guy was acting inappropriately?"

"I sure did. I'm going to open a file on him if there isn't one already. I'm going to investigate whether he has a license to practice counseling or operate a business and if he has any complaints filed against him. Did you catch how Mrs. Bauer referred to it as a 'so-called' ministry?"

"Yeah. I got a weird feeling about him when I took the report last Sunday. I felt like he was checking me out the whole time I was there. So, if he's running some kind of counseling practice to help people turn from gay to straight, he should start with himself."

"And that answer Rev. Bauer gave about why Dr. Babcock was coming along on the trip wasn't very believable. I think there may be more to that story. But that's not relevant."

"Yeah, I think he was giving us a lot of bullshit. After three visits with that guy, I've decided I can't believe anything he tells us."

"Right. And then his wife started telling us the truth and he tried to shut her down. It's almost like he doesn't want us to find their son."

***

As soon as the police were out the door, Brad said, "Great. Just great. Way to go, blabbermouth. You just spilled all our private family business out there for them and the world to see."

"I can't believe you were sitting there lying to them!"

"I wasn't lying. I was being judicious about what they needed to know."

"You were being evasive. You were obfuscating the truth. They need to know the truth to have any hope of finding Bryan."

"Yeah, well now all that is going to go in their files, and who knows what will show up in the news media."

"But we want Bryan's disappearance to show up in the news! The more people see it, the better chance we have of getting him back!"

"No, dummy. I mean all the stuff about him being a homosexual. Nobody needs to know that. How's that going to help them find him? How's that going to make us look as parents? How's that going to make the church look after we just held that conference?"

"Who cares what other people think? I want our son back. Nothing else matters."

"I want our son back, too, but that other stuff absolutely matters. Image matters! Image is everything! That's how I earn a living. That's how I put food on the table and provide this house for us to live in. That's how I'm going to sell books and expand my ministry. No, Rev. Brad Bauer cannot have a son who's a homosexual. That would make me look like a hypocrite."

"So, your image is more important than our son. Well, listen here, Rev. Big Shot. YOU did not carry him in your body for nine months. YOU have not spent the last eighteen years of your life caring for him and nurturing him and thinking about him every hour of every day. No, you left all that to me while you were off building your big impressive church and your slick, powerful image. Well, I don't give a damn about any of that if I don't have my son. What's more important to you?"

"It doesn't have to be a choice. It shouldn't have to be either-or."

"You didn't answer my question. What's more important to you – having your big church or your son?"

"Why are you asking me this? It's a false choice. I didn't want him to run away any more than you did."

"You can't say it! You simply cannot say it! You cannot say that your son is more important than your church. Unbelievable."

"Well, okay. Yes. If it came down to it, like if he was being held hostage and they said I have to give up my church to get him back, I would. There. Are you happy?"

"That's nice, but that's not what I meant and it's not what's at stake. He's not being held hostage and the ransom isn't your church. What's at stake here is you accepting your son for who he is. What's at stake is you loving him unconditionally. What's at stake is you caring more about his happiness and well-being than your image and what other people think."

"Of course, I care about his well-being. That's why I've been doing everything I can think of to stop him from being a homosexual. Christ, I paid $2,400 to that camp – and that's just for the first forty days! I'll probably never see *that* money again. Not to mention another two grand for three airplane flights, a rental car, and a hotel stay. So don't tell me I don't care about his well-being, you stupid bitch."

Brenda hauled off and smacked Brad across the face. Hard. He felt a filling come loose.

"We'll talk about the hotel stay another time. You were worried about looking like a hypocrite? That ship has sailed. And you will continue to sleep on the hide-a-bed until further notice."

"Fine. You never put out anymore anyway."

"Then you can sleep on that hide-a-bed for the rest of your fucking life!"

Brenda stormed up to the master bedroom and locked the door.

Brandon closed his door just in time. He ran to his bed and tried to cry softly enough that no one would hear him. Brandon wished, more than anything, that Bryan would have taken him along, no matter where he went.

Settling In

Monday, July 30, 2007

It had been one week since Bryan arrived in Los Angeles on the bus – tired, hungry, sweaty, and with no idea where he would end up living. Bryan recalled his initial impressions of LA – clogged freeways, smoggy gray sky, graffitied freeway walls and buildings, dirty unwelcoming streets, and homeless encampments. It was hard to believe that the bus station, enclosed in a barbed wire-topped fence with security guards, was a mere 15 miles away.

By the end of his first day in town, he had lucked into an affordable room in a modern, luxurious house with a private pool and four gay housemates, all within walking distance of UCLA.

The next day, he strolled into Westwood to discover what was there and found a job at the Pure Foods grocery store. By the end of the week, he had opened a bank account, bought a new phone, and enrolled in high school for his senior year.

Last night was his first Sunday evening family night with Hal and two of his three new housemates. They seemed like nice guys.

It was a beautiful day and he didn't have to be at work until 3:00, so he decided to relax in the pool for a while. He hadn't packed a swimsuit, but Hal said the other guys didn't wear them anyway. Bryan had never skinny-dipped before. In fact, to the best of his recollection, he had never been naked outdoors. No one else was around, so why not? His life these days was full of new experiences.

He wrapped a towel around his waist, grabbed a can of Dr Pepper from his fridge, and headed out to the pool. He selected one of the inflatable rafts stacked by the edge of the patio and jumped in. After he got acclimated to the water, he climbed onto the raft and relaxed. The gentle current of the pool jets propelled him slowly around the pool.

As the raft gradually rotated, Bryan gazed at this amazing house – his new home. He admired the oleanders, the palm trees, and the clear blue sky. He closed his eyes and savored the light breeze blowing across his face and body, and the feel of the cool water his feet were dangling in.

Over the past five weeks, he had dealt with a lot of shit. It was difficult to leave everything he had ever known – his family, his friends, his house, his school, his neighborhood – with just a couple of suitcases full of possessions. It hurt to realize that his father could be so dogmatic, stubborn, self-centered, and cruel that he would subject his son to such humiliating treatment and try to send him away to a gay conversion torture camp. It was disappointing that his mother would go along with it, even though he felt in his heart that she didn't want to.

Most of all, it was painful to leave behind his precious younger brother Brandon, whom he loved so much. He felt bad about not being able to say goodbye and leaving Brandon to deal with his parents – and life – on his own.

And then there was Chris, who had tried so hard to help him come to terms with being gay, and who he finally realized he loved. He regretted that he wasn't able to be the boyfriend Chris wanted and deserved, and that they had parted on bad terms. Maybe, someday, they could have a future together. Maybe.

But yet, he was filled with gratitude. Gratitude for Russ Simonton, who supported him through his crisis and helped him plan his escape, and who was his first role model as a happy, self-accepting, partnered gay man. Gratitude for the friendly, helpful people at the Los Angeles LGBT Youth Project, and that such a facility exists. Gratitude for Hal Morris, who had offered him a place in this wonderful home, and who would serve as his legal counsel. Gratitude for his new job, his new school, and his new city.

The past was the past. Bryan was filled with hope and optimism for all that lay ahead.

After floating in the pool for half an hour, Bryan returned to his room and put some clothes on. He remembered there was still one loose end he needed to tie up before he could close the previous chapter of his life.

He sat down at the computer desk and turned on his laptop. He logged into the web hosting account for the Eternal Savior Christian Church to complete his final task as webmaster for the church's website.

He opened the Resources page he had created just two weeks earlier, which had links to all the presentation notes and supporting documents from the Rescued Through Love conference the church held on July 14. He deleted all the content on the page and all the linked documents.

In its place, he added a link to the Kansas City chapter of the Parents Support Network – the group that provides support to parents and families of LGBT children. He found an informative article about what the Bible says and does not say about homosexuality and added a link to that. He created a list of gay-friendly churches in the Kansas City area, as well as the LGBT community center and the Pathways youth group.

Once he was satisfied that he had created a Resources page that provided positive, affirming support for people who were coming out as LGBT and their parents and families, he published it. Then he navigated to the Users section. He downgraded the privileges of his father's account and the accounts of the few other people who had access to the website, so that nobody else could add, edit, or delete webpages. Then he navigated to the Account Profile and changed the login password for the web hosting account. He logged out for the last time and shut off his laptop.

Afterword

Thank you for purchasing and reading this book. I hope you enjoyed it.

This is the first in a series of seven books that follow Ryan as he finishes high school, goes to college, launches his career, forms relationships, and comes to terms with his past.

I invite you to subscribe to my newsletter. I'll keep you informed about my upcoming books and offer them to you at a discount. I'll share background information about the stories and the writing process. From time to time, I may solicit your input which will help make the books even better! To join, visit my website: AuthorDaveHughes.com.

To thank you for joining, I will send my short story, *Cruise Virgins*. In it, Ryan (as a young adult) and Ted (whom you will meet in the next book) experience their first gay cruise – and confront their feelings for one another.

Now, I have a small favor to ask.

As a new, self-published author, it's incredibly difficult to get my books noticed in a world in which hundreds, if not thousands, of new books are released every day. It's challenging to build an audience for my work. If you enjoyed this book, please consider posting something about it on your social media platform of choice. All it takes is something simple, like 'I just finished reading *Maybe Next Year*, by Dave Hughes. It was great! Check it out.' Also, please consider leaving an honest review on Amazon or wherever you purchased this book.

Thanks! I truly appreciate it.

I would like to thank my beta readers who provided valuable feedback that helped me improve this book: Linda Magata, Jeff McKeehan, Kalp Parikh, Gary Parks, Russ Smith, and Michelle

Taquino Alcina.

Very special thanks to Mark McNease – friend, prolific author of LGBT-themed mysteries (check them out!), and promoter of all things positive about aging – for his generous and enthusiastic support of all my writing, from RetireFabulously.com and my three retirement lifestyle books to my current fiction projects.

Most importantly, I would like to thank my husband, Jeff McKeehan, who has supported and encouraged me every step of the way, provided great ideas and valuable feedback, and tolerated all those times when my mind was immersed in the world of my characters. Every spouse of an author knows exactly what I'm talking about.

About the Author

This is author Dave Hughes' first novel. It is the first of seven books in various stages of development.

Before writing fiction, Dave wrote three retirement lifestyle planning books, *Design Your Dream Retirement, Smooth Sailing Into Retirement,* and *The Quest for Retirement Utopia.* Dave created the website RetireFabulously.com, which enables readers to envision, plan for, and enjoy the best retirement possible. In addition to writing hundreds of articles for RetireFabulously.com, Dave's writing has appeared on US News & World Report, lgbtSr.com, Medium, Yahoo! Finance, CNN/Money, Next Avenue, Tiny Buddha, and others.

Aside from his writing, Dave is also a jazz musician. He plays trombone and steel pan in various bands in the Phoenix area. He owns an embarrassingly large collection of jazz, Brazilian, exotica, steel band, jazz/rock, and vocal ensemble CDs and videos.

Before retiring early at age 56, Dave was a software engineer for 34 years, working for companies such as Intel Corporation, Computer Sciences Corporation, McDonnell Douglas Space Systems, and NCR Corporation. Throughout his career, his assignments included software development, customer support, training, course development, and management.

Dave resides in Chandler, Arizona with his husband Jeff and their dog Maynard.

Dave is available for interviews, book readings/signings, speaking engagements, and panel discussions. You may contact Dave at AuthorDaveHughes@gmail.com.

Visit AuthorDaveHughes.com to learn more and subscribe to his newsletter.

www.ingramcontent.com/pod-product-compliance
Lightning Source LLC
Chambersburg PA
CBHW031936110726
47902CB00001B/202